A Yellow Raft in Blue Water

Michael Dorris

WARNER BOOKS

A Time Warner Company

This is a work of fiction, and any resemblance to persons living or dead is purely coincidental. All characters, events, and details of the setting are imaginary... except for Babe.

Grateful acknowledgment is made to: Warner Brothers Music for permission to reprint portions of "Love in the First Degree" by Tim Dubois and Jim Hurt, © 1980 House of Gold Music, Inc. All rights reserved. Used by permission of Warner Brothers Music.

Combine Music Corporation for permission to reprint portions of "Lookin' for Love," © 1979 Southern Nights Music, 35 Music Square East, Nashville, Tennessee 37203. All rights reserved.

Parts of this book appeared in slightly altered form in the following publications: The New Native American Novel, a book by the University of New Mexico Press, 1986; chapters 5 and 6 in Seventeen magazine; chapter 17 and part of chapter 18 in Southwest Review; chapter 1 in The American Voice; chapter 2 in the Minneapolis Star & Tribune Sunday magazine; chapter 9 in Cutbank magazine.

The author would like to thank the Rockefeller Foundation and Dartmouth College for their support during the time this book was completed.

This Warner Books edition is published by arrangement with
Henry Holt and Company, Inc., 521 Fifth Avenue, New York, New York 10175
Warner Books, Inc., 1271 Avenue of the Americas, New York, NY 10020

Visit our Web site at http://warnerbooks.com

 A Time Warner Company

Printed in the United States of America
First Warner Books Trade Paperback Printing: April 1988

30 29 28 27 26 25 24 23

Cover photo by Ken Robbins

Text design by Giorgetta Bell McRee

Library of Congress Cataloging-in-Publication Data

Dorris, Michael A.
    A yellow raft in blue water / Michael Dorris. — Warner Books ed.
      p.   cm.
    ISBN 0-446-38787-8 (pbk.)
    1. Indians of North America—Fiction.   I. Title.
[PS3554.0695Y4 1988b]
813'.54—dc19   87-27768
                                                                              CIP

FOR LOUISE

Companion through every page,
Through every day
Compeer

ACKNOWLEDGMENTS

My thanks go first and foremost to my mother, Mary Besy Dorris, and aunts, Marion Burkhardt and Virginia Burkhardt, who gave me good reason to listen and the words to speak; to my grandmother, Laura D. Hamilton, for her strength and stories; to my mother-in-law, Rita Gourneau Erdrich, who read till midnight; to the late Annie Medicine, for her eagle wing; to Nancy Nicholas, Charles Rembar, Blanche Brann, and Jeannette Seaver, for their encouragement and suggestions; and to Richard Seaver, our editor and publisher, for his act of faith.

Rayona

1

I sit on the bed at a crooked angle, one foot on the floor, my hip against the tent of Mom's legs, my elbows on the hospital table. My skirt is too short and keeps riding up my thighs. Mom has earlier spent twenty minutes pulling my long frizzy hair into a herringbone braid and has tried to give me beauty magazine tips to improve my appearance—cosmetics to highlight my cheekbones or soften my chin, a blusher that might even my skin tone. I check the clock on the wall. Five minutes till the end of visiting hours. I want to leave but Mom would hit the ceiling and tell me I'm not polite.

We play solitaire on the sliding desk pulled across the foot of the electric bed. With the back moved all the way up and a pillow wedged under her knees, everything Mom wants is within her reach. Her round face is screwed into a mask of concentration, like a stumped contestant on "Jeopardy" with time running out, and her eyes see nothing but the numbers on the cards. She wears her favorite rings, a narrow abalone, an inlaid turquoise-and-jet roadrunner, and a sandcast silver turtle. Dwarfed among them, the thin gold of her wedding band cuts into her third finger. She's on her throne, but her mind is with the game.

In the last two hours we have each drunk three plastic glasses full of warm ginger ale and Mom has sampled a second lunch, abandoned as the two other women in the room sleep through the afternoon visiting hours. We talk softly to keep our privacy.

Mom turns each trio of cards and slaps them down clean so

that only the top one shows. "This time I can feel it," she tells me.

I don't disagree but I could. The last pass through I have seen a two of clubs and a jack of spades hidden below an early ten of hearts. The cards will win this hand.

After squaring the deck Mom starts through again. This time she snaps the sets into her palm before she lays them out, and the first face to appear is the black two. She pegs it onto its ace without changing her expression, but does seem pleased to see the jack.

"Come to Mama," she whispers and matches it to her queen of diamonds. The ten follows suit. "What did I tell you? Nothing to it." Her eyes are large and brown, dull from her morning medication and from not enough sleep, but they flash with her victory.

I can't help it, her cheat bothers me, but I go along. It's not worth arguing about.

"You're on a roll," I tell her when all fifty-two are distributed, ace to king, in four matching rows. "Now try the other kind, the jump-over."

"I quit when I'm ahead." She pushes the pile in a jumble toward me, finds the button that adjusts her angle, and sinks to a reclining position.

I take the cards, shift my weight, and shuffle, riffle, and pat them even. Out of habit, I offer Mom an illegal cut, which she ignores, then I pick up the deck and peel off a four of clubs.

"Do you remember how?" Mom asks.

The object of the game is to reduce everything to a single pile. You set the whole deck down, one by one, then find a match with the card that comes before, either by suit or number: a six on a six, a spade on a spade. You can find its mate next door or by jumping back two, no more no less. I usually end with about twenty short stacks. This time it's eighteen.

"I never win this," I say, rising to leave.

"You fold too easy. Let me see those cards once . . ." But Mom doesn't move. Something's wrong. She seems suddenly smaller, as if she has shrunk in her bed. Her eyebrows relax and she stares to the ceiling. Her hands go limp at her side. It occurs to me for the first time that this hospital visit might be different, that she might really have a disease. I start to reach for the white cord with a button on the end, but Mom snatches it first and puts it under the sheet. She looks over my shoulder and makes like she's trying to smile but can't quite bring it off.

I turn and see my father in the doorway. For a big man he's quiet, and I'm always surprised when he appears. He's tall and heavy, with skin a shade browner than mine. He has let his Afro grow out and there's rainwater caught in his hair. His mailman uniform is damp too, the gray wool pants baggy around his knees. At his wrist, the bracelet of three metals, copper, iron, and brass, has a dull shine. I've never seem him without it. He looks uncomfortable and edgy in the brightly lit room, and wets his lips.

"Rayona, what's happening?" he asks me.

These are the first words I've heard from him since my fifteenth birthday five months ago, when he telephoned to say he'd be late to the party, so I'm not friendly.

I stand. I push five-ten, taller than any other girl in my school, but I still feel short in front of him.

"Don't you say hello to your father?" Dad asks me.

"Elgin," Mom says behind me. "I thought you only visited when I was asleep."

Visited? Mom must have called to tell him she was out of commission. There's no other way he could have known because her friends are not permitted to speak to him these days.

"You go on now, Ray," Mom says. "Elgin and I have to talk." She has been busy rearranging herself and the bed. The cards have disappeared and the table is pushed off to the side. She's now lying almost flat, with the sheet tucked under her chin. The pillow still supports her knees, though, so she has to lift her head to see us.

"Now don't rush off," Dad says to me. "Let me get a look at you."

He inspects me like a first-class package, looking for loose flaps. His eyes measure and weigh, take me apart and put me back together. I wait for him to compliment my height, to say, as he likes to do, that I take after him rather than Mom, who only comes up to my ear even in her highest heels. I expect he'll judge I'm too skinny. But he just shakes his head, half sad, half confirmed in some belief.

"I'll see you tomorrow, baby," Mom says like an order. She's impatient for me to go so she can have Dad to herself, and that makes me curious.

I don't know what she sees in him. She has other boyfriends who call when they promise, pay the check at restaurants, and want to live with us.

"Ray doesn't have to leave, Christine. She's no fool."

Dad's words run along my backbone and make my shoulders tighten. I'm interested in all opinions regarding me that don't have to do with my height or weight. I file away that I'm not a fool, according to my father who hardly knows me, and stay tuned for what he thinks I'll understand.

Dad reaches into his pants pocket, takes out Mom's beaded key chain, and jiggles it from his fingers. "I'm returning your car."

Mom shakes her head no. "Keep it till I'm ready to come home. Come collect me."

"That takes more than a dented Volaré."

"Is that what you say to a sick woman? It's got new plugs!" Mom says.

"It takes more than new plugs. And anyway, you don't look so sick."

He's right. She looks disappointed, mad. Her chin juts. She props herself on her elbows, bringing her chest close to her knees. Her eyes are narrow slits buried in the fullness of her flushed cheeks.

"Look at the chart. Ask the goddamn doctor. I'm sick enough for him."

Dad tucks the keys into my shirt pocket, together with a green parking lot stub. "Hold these for your mother. A-6. Don't forget."

Mom is ready to explode. Her lips press together in a tight seal and she tries to drag the pillow out from under her legs. She opens her mouth to say something but all that comes out is air. It is as if she has just run a long race and lost. She tries to sit up the rest of the way, to get out of bed, but she's tangled in the sheet, trapped on her back.

"Get the hell out of here." Mom's voice is rough, hard-edged. Her body twists on the mattress. I can tell she hates to be helpless when Dad's so indifferent.

He watches her as though she's some stranger. "It's not going to work this time. Just give it up."

"You give it up. You! I don't give nothing up."

Dad touches my arm. "Go on now. I have to talk to Christine."

Mom is furious, maddened by the snarled bedclothes. One of her rings hooks in a flaw of the sheet and she tries to rip it free, but the material is too tough.

"I'll call you," Dad says, and points a long finger at my chest.

"Go back to your little black girl, then," Mom shouts. "Forget us. Who needs you, anyway." She collapses into the pillows, throws her arms over her face, then stops all movement. She's listening, waiting. She expects Dad to apologize like he always does when things go this far. She's pulled her ace from the hole and bet her whole pot.

Dad watches for a second, then quietly backs out the door. His jaw is set, his wide curved lips are hard, his half-closed eyes look as if they're painted on his face.

The two other sick women in the room are awake, and as alert and interested as if they were watching TV. They are old ladies straight off the reservation, their eyes bright and full of gossip, although their bodies are fed with tubes. I can read their thoughts: *That little Indian woman, I don't know what tribe, with a big black man. And a child, a too-tall girl. She looks like him.* They are delighted. They have a story to tell if their children visit that's more interesting than rough white doctors and Indian nurses with boyfriend problems. They look from the door to me to Mom on the bed, and then back at each other.

Mom's breathing is rain in the night, beating on the windows and blowing the curtains. I don't want to be here when she peeks and discovers Dad's gone, so I leave too, heading for the stairs, away from the elevators where he might be waiting, wanting to explain himself on a slow ride to the first floor.

I open the exit and take the flight up instead of down. I'm not ready to go home. Without Mom the apartment is like a closet packed with our rented furniture. Without her there, I hear noises I never otherwise notice and smell food the neighbors are cooking. I listen to the broken TV, and eat standing at the table.

In the last year Mom has become a regular customer at Indian Health Service. Most of her ailments surface in the middle of the night. She wakes wheezing from too much party or from passing out on top of the covers and the next thing she's back in the ward for tests. The first day in, she calls for a priest, though she never goes to church. She says she's entitled to the Last Rites, that it's part of being in the hospital, that she's earned it by making the nine First Fridays when she was a kid. The doctors tell her if she doesn't slow down she's going to shoot her liver, but she won't take care of herself. "It's just the way I am," she says. She claims she is indestructible.

When she gets home, ready to celebrate the return of feeling good, she tells people she's been to Mexico, that she's a new woman. Not that she fools anybody. Most of them don't care one way or the other, except for Mom's best friend, Charlene, who works at the hospital pharmacy and lives in our building. Whenever she sees Mom dressed to go out on the town, she makes some joke about medicine.

"I hear they're giving prescriptions out cheap at the Silver Bullet," she said the last time. Mom just rolled her eyes at Charlene, reminding her to act as if I don't understand what they're talking about.

"Don't kid yourself, Christine. The human body can only take so much punishment."

"Punishment! I love it!" Mom sparkled her eyes and, with her fingers, formed a tight curl in the center of her forehead.

And now, here she is, back in the hospital again.

The corridors are quiet for the night. On the top floor a few people in green uniforms pass without noticing me. I could be invisible. For a place full of sick people it's too silent. You'd think the patients would let the world know their troubles, that they'd moan or sigh or yell out. But the ones I see through the open doors of their rooms just lie gazing into space, as though they're already dead. I take the down elevator. Dad will be long gone by now, to wherever he goes. Or whoever. Mom said a little black girl, but that's what she's accused him of, a hundred times before.

"We're the wrong color for each other," I heard Mom tell him a long time ago. "That's what your friends think."

"We may be different shades but look at the blend." Dad's voice had been low, almost singing. He probably wasn't talking about me, but he might have been, since my skin is a combination of theirs. Once, in a hardware store, I found each of our exact shades on a paint mix-tone chart. Mom was Almond Joy, Dad was Burnt Clay, and I was Maple Walnut.

The lobby is deserted, but I know my way around. I follow the yellow line that leads to the room filled with vending machines. Now that I understand what's going on, I don't blame Mom for using the car as bait. I have tried things on Dad too, before I became no fool: tears, good grades, writing letters, getting him presents. At first every one of them seemed to do the trick. He'd smile or send me a postcard or promise to call tomorrow and then weeks would pass.

One time I even hung around on the route he was delivering. I cut school and stood on the corner at ten o'clock in the morning, listening for the bark of dogs or the sound of banging porch mailboxes. I had it all pictured in my mind. He would be walking along, his head down sorting the letters, and wouldn't notice me until he looked up to cross the street. Then he'd do a double take, grin, and say he didn't believe it. He'd invite me to share his bologna and cheese under a shade tree, and people passing in cars would smile at us, a father and a daughter who looked so much alike, having their lunch too early in the morning just because they enjoyed being together.

But Dad was a temp and that meant his track was unpredictable. When the mailman finally came that day, it was a mean-looking woman with red hair and M A R Y tattooed on her knuckles.

The Snack Room is empty and I buy an ice cream sandwich for dinner. It's so cold that the wrapper is frozen to the cookie part, and I have to pick ragged scraps off the end of my tongue after each bite. I get a drink at the water fountain and wipe my mouth with a paper towel. I think of stopping in to see if Charlene is still in the pharmacy, but it's after five and she's on the eight-to-four shift.

I take a side door into the parking lot and head across to the bus stop. There are plenty of streetlights burning and not many cars. I pass A-6 and it doesn't take much to see the Volaré, missing one taillight, in the Employees Only zone, straddling two spaces. And there, big as life, is a fat candy striper from the hospital trying to jimmy the door.

The car isn't much but I can't stand by and watch some teen volunteer, smaller than me, rip it off. She's busy poking an unbent coat hanger through the crack in the window and doesn't hear me creep up. I hold my breath. When she sees me, tall and dark in the night, she'll freak. The-red-and-white-striped material is stretched to the breaking point across her hips. I give a karate yell, and, with all my strength, slap her on the butt with my open palm. She screams louder than me, and just then the door swings open, sending her backward, and me with her. She's punching with her elbows and hollering like that baby-sitter in *Halloween*. The car lamp comes on as she turns, her face scrunched into a thin-lipped growl, the coat hanger clutched in her hand like a murder weapon.

It's Mom.

I don't know which of us is more surprised. She has herself

squeezed into a red-and-white uniform but she still wears her slippers and the white ID bracelet with her name and blood type.

Mom recovers first, takes a deep breath, stands, and brushes off her knees. She tosses the coat hanger in the backseat. "You scared the shit out of me," she says, all irritated.

I'm still shaking. I can't get over that it's her and not some maniac.

"Go home, Ray. And, here. I won't be needing this." She hands me her green leather purse, then reaches back and takes out her driver's license.

"What are you doing?" I ask her, coming back to my senses. "Why are you dressed like this?"

"I've had it," Mom says, slamming her hand onto the roof of the car. "First he cheats on me. That's not news. Then he won't keep the car to ride me home. I can read between *those* lines. Then they stash my clothes somewhere so I can't leave the goddamn hospital of my own free will. Now *you* show."

I try to figure out what Mom is so upset about. She and Dad never live together for more than a week before they start picking on each other and talking divorce. But they never go through with it. Being married never stops either one of them from doing what they want. It doesn't interfere.

"What's different?" I ask her. "Did I miss something?"

"What's *different*? Goddamn him anyway! And after fifteen-going-on-sixteen years of marriage your father thinks he's in *love*"—she pronounces the word as if it was spoiled fish in her mouth—"with some twenty-two-year-old bubblehead doper named Arletta. *Arletta!*"

I don't react enough to suit Mom, so she sticks her face right under mine and yells up at me. "It's common knowledge. She's hanging off him in every bar in this town. He might as well take me out and shoot me and get it over with."

In the uniform, two or three sizes too small, Mom looks bursting with strength. Even in the dim light of the parking lot, her eyes shine, and I notice she has brushed her hair and put on makeup.

"Let's go home," I say.

"I'm not going home." She settles herself behind the wheel, points toward my pocket for the keys, and I hand them over. She grips the arm rest and slams the door. "Don't let him have *anything*. Keep it for yourself."

"Hold on," I say and run around the back of the car to the other side. She reaches over to push down the lock but it doesn't work. I get in. "What are you talking about."

"What I'm talking about," she starts loud, and then takes a breath, calms her voice. "What I'm talking about is this: we're broke. We owe two months back rent on that lousy apartment. My unemployment is expired and I'm tired of finding two-bit jobs. I'm past forty years old and my husband wants to ditch me and marry some Arletta. I figure I've wore out my welcome in this world and the only thing I've got that's worth anything is the insurance on this fucking car. So it's going to have a little accident and you're going to win the lottery. Kiss me good-bye."

She pushes her cheek at my face but I pull back. Her hand is so tight on the wheel that her rings stand at attention, reflecting the lights in the parking lot. Some of what she says is news to me and some of it isn't. I stay put.

"Don't tell me," I say. "You're going to Tacoma, to the park where Dad asked you to marry him, where I was conceived." This is the destination she threatens whenever she's depressed, but she never actually goes.

"Don't think you're so goddamn smart."

"That's it, though, right?"

"It's one place your father will understand," she says, with a gleam in her eye.

It's a good hour away, even how Mom drives.

"Well, I'm coming, too. I've always wanted to see this park since you talk about it so much."

She turns her head and glares at me. If she could move objects by the force of her mind, I'd be out.

"It's a long walk back." She unclenches her hands and hoists them like claws, then bangs them back onto the steering wheel so hard that the car shakes. She scares herself and that scares me. She glances in my direction again, dared into actually going through with her plan, but I don't give an inch. I'm tired of convincing her to be reasonable.

She backs out of the lot, and peels onto the street. All the way down the hill and across the bridge she takes curves on two wheels. I try to calm her by reading signs, making jokes, but there's no getting through. A few blocks later, she guns the engine, sending the car up the south ramp of Interstate 5. The fingers of her right hand fiddle with the radio dial until she finds a station with a country song that matches her mood, Kenny Rogers's "Coward of the County," but it's just ending and the next one they play is an old Patsy Cline song.

"To hell with that noise," she says and switches it off. We drive for a long while in silence. The highway is wet, and the white and red lights from the cars around us are as bright as rocks under water. The night air smells of wood pulp and rain, and from above comes the sound of jets flying low to land or take off at Sea-Tac. The flat buildings of the Boeing hangars are lit and most of the traffic turns off on the airport exit.

"You'll do all right, Ray," Mom says at last. Her voice is changed, dreamy, as if she's telling a story. "This car is good for a thousand. I'm just sorry I lapsed that policy they took on me at the last job."

We keep driving. I think of things to say and then don't say them. I can't very well tell her that everything is great, that our life is so hot, that she is imagining her troubles. Everything she says is true. But she's leaving too much out. Most of the time Mom's off to the races, excited at every chance. She fills out a dozen Publisher's Clearing House sweepstakes tickets and then watches the mail for the news she's won. The future never discourages her, since she doesn't think about it from a distance.

"Go to Aunt Ida on the reservation," Mom says. "She liked you. She brought you a doll."

Mom took me to her brother Lee's funeral in Montana when I was too little to remember much. Her mother, whom everybody—even Mom—calls Aunt Ida, visited us once in

Seattle when I was about eight. I remember her as big and forbidding, a woman who refused to speak English and loved TV. Mom sends her a present every Christmas and birthday and makes me sign the card, but they aren't close. Mom always tells me how lucky I am, since *her* mother drives her crazy.

"Aunt Ida wouldn't know me if she fell over me." I wouldn't know her either. I try and think of her face without much luck. I have a scene in my mind from the night she went back home. Mom and I stood by the side of the Trailways, trying to see through the bus windows to where Aunt Ida sat, and I had to keep waving and waving. I looked up at Mom to complain, to say I was tired, and she was biting her lip, as if she didn't want Aunt Ida to leave. But she stopped when she noticed me seeing, and we left before the bus did.

"We could both go there," I suggest, thinking maybe that's what Mom wants to hear. Then suddenly I'm terrified she'll agree. The last thing I need is to leave Seattle and be stuck on some reservation with people I don't know.

"Ha!" she says. "I'm not going back *there* alone."

I don't count. Mom means she has to have a husband or at least a boyfriend who's serious enough to endure the long drive and all her relatives. Mom hasn't been back since she came to Seattle at twenty-three, except for that one time.

"Well, if you won't go, why should I?"

She has no straight answer for that. "Look, Ray, don't ask me questions. Start figuring things out for yourself. If I had any answers I wouldn't be here right now."

Tacoma is the next six exits, the sign reads. Mom turns off the highway and takes a ramp that leads to downtown, then twists and turns her way along the shore to the park. It's late by now and the place is deserted. The trees are dark blots against the cloudy night sky and in their shade the land is pitch black. Signs appear out of the night, illuminated by our headlights, arrows pointing, falling rock.

After a mile or two, Mom pulls the car off onto the pine needles that line the road and idles the motor. "This is as far as you go."

"Forget it," I say. "You're bluffing."

"The hell I am."

"I'm not getting out."

"This is a solo." Mom is rough and knocks me with her elbow as she reaches across and flips the handle on my side. Her arm is hard as a stick. The door falls open. "And after all those damn State Farm payments it sure isn't going to be Elgin who collects as next of kin."

"You're just going to dump me here like this? In the middle of nowhere late at night?"

She sits there with her hands in her lap waiting for me to leave.

"This is the kind of thing that could scar me for life." I use a phrase I've heard on "All My Children." I'm over my limit with Mom. I can't keep pace with her. Ever since I can remember I've been caught in her ups and downs and all it leads to is this: me sitting in a dented car with a mother convinced she's about to drive herself off a cliff in a public park, just to spite my father, whom she's just told she never needed anyway.

"You win," I say. "Go for it. I just hope the policy is paid."

I slam out the door and stand by the car. The night air is chilly and smells of saltwater and fir trees. I look around for anything I can see, but it's too dark. I kick the side with my heavy boot, deepening the dent. I kick it again. Mom glares at me from the driver's seat, her mouth open in shock.

She sits there for a minute, not moving. I think she's changed her mind, but no, she turns the key. The engine catches, then dies. She tries again, pumping the gas pedal with her foot with such force that the car rocks forward. Still nothing. "It's flooded," she announces, and we both wait, pretending to ignore each other. In the distance, on the highway beyond the park, I see the headlights of cars move by, back and forth, out of reach. I count the seconds, slow like you read a pulse, one-and-two-and-three, and when I get to twenty-eight she turns the key again. Not a sound.

"Shit!" Mom says. "Shit, shit, shit, shit, *shit!*"

She gets out of the car on her side, and stamps the ground

with her bedroom slipper. She balls her hands into fists and beats them against her forehead.

"He brought me back the car without even gassing it up!" Mom shouts. My anger is nothing compared to hers. She's so mad she seems to light in the dark, but it's only a match flaring for her Kent. "It was full when he took it." She stomps across the road, stands there awhile, then comes back.

I wait for her to calm down. I open the car door to get her purse.

Finally she says, "How the hell are we supposed to get out of here?" She's on her second cigarette by now and is halfway back to normal.

"I saw an all-night Gulf station near the off ramp."

"That's miles from here! All I'm wearing is a pair of paper slippers."

"I'll go," I tell her. "You stay with the car."

"In the *dark? Alone?* No way, José. There's muggers out here. Anybody could come along. A girl could get hurt."

I wonder if she means her words to be as dumb as they sound. She does. In the glow of her cigarette ash her eyes are ready to laugh. "You wouldn't want anything to happen to your mother," she says. "You could get scarred for life."

I don't know whether I'm ready to make peace or not, but she gives me no choice. "Well, there's all that insurance money," I say.

"For the car, you stupid, not for me. For you to get rich, they have to trash the car."

"Somebody already did." We both look. The taillight dangles from the rear fender, spilling a red beam at a funny angle. The dent in the side door has grown from my kick, and the lying, broken gas gauge, illuminated on the dashboard, still points to F. Hunched onto the side of the road, the Volaré looks like a bum down on his luck.

Mom must be thinking the same thing. "This car could use a drink," she says, and finally laughs. It is the kind of noise you make at a bad joke, at a pun. The kind where the air busts from your mouth like a car backfiring far away or a jet breaking the sound barrier in the movies. It's a late-night laugh, a cross between surrender and letting go.

"Walk in the grass," I say. "Spare your feet."

"Just a minute." She reaches into the backseat and comes out with the coat hanger. "Just in case." She slaps it a few times into her palm.

So off we go. Me toting the banged-up gas can and Mom padding along next to me, complaining about the dampness of the ground, complaining she is catching a cold, complaining about my father being too cheap to fill the tank of a borrowed car, complaining that with his long legs I walk too fast for her. The red-and-white uniform shines whenever we cross under a streetlight. I return her purse and she runs the brush through her thick curly hair, but she never stops, never drops back, and by the time we reach the Gulf station she's the first one in, all smiles, ready to charm the sleepy man behind the desk into giving us a lift.

2

Three gallons of Gulf gas start the Volaré's motor going and we get back to Seattle from Tacoma about midnight. Once she decides we're going to Aunt Ida's, Mom sees no reason to delay. There aren't many things, or many people, she wants a last look at, and I think the hardest thing for her to abandon in Seattle is her lifetime membership at Village Video.

A week before she went into the hospital this last time, she saw the ad in the paper. I thought she was checking out the Classifieds like she did every morning, hoping to improve her prospects, but she had browsed too long in the Arts and Leisure.

"Look at this," she said, excited. "For only ninety-nine cents you can join this club for life, with all the privileges!"

"We don't have a VCR," I reminded her. "We don't even have a TV that works."

"Well, you never know. If we ever do get one we'd kick ourselves if we passed on this deal. Listen: you get movies for a dollar off on Tuesdays and Wednesdays. You can reserve ahead. You get a free subscription to their literature."

Mom put down the paper and went to the kitchen drawer for her scissors. She cut out the ad in a neat square and folded it twice before putting it into her purse. She was always one for a bargain.

The next time we were out in the Volaré, she drove to a shopping mall on the north side of the city. We worked our

18

way through Sears and K mart and into an immense building full of stores that sold shoes and cards and sports equipment and dresses with Japanese writing on them. Finally we came to Village Video, a small glass room with racks of cassettes lining the walls. Two people, a man and a woman, were ahead of us, and the manager was talking to them.

"Ninety-nine cents is what it says in black and white and that's what I'm sticking to," he said. "Village Video does not go back on its word."

"But I paid twenty-five dollars for the same thing four days ago," the woman complained. Mom gave me a look with her eyebrows raised, as if to say "See!"

"I know, I know," the manager said. He seemed truly sad, but helpless. He shrugged his heavy shoulders in despair. "I can't do anything about that. We have competition coming into this mall." He looked from right to left out the door as if expecting to see competition arriving any minute. "We have to build our membership."

"But . . ." the woman said.

"No retroactive," the manager cut in before she could go on. "I understand, I really do, but that's just the way it has to be."

Mom was delighted. The woman's loss was her gain. I could tell she felt proud that she had not come in here last week and plunked down twenty-five dollars. It would have done me no good to point out that the thought to do so would have never entered her head.

"How long does it last?" said the other customer, a man wearing a tan shirt with little straps that buttoned on top of his shoulders. He looked as if he was comparing all the pros and cons before shelling out ninety-nine cents. You could see he thought he was pretty shrewd.

"It lasts for as long as you live," the manager said slowly. There was a second of silence while we all thought about that. The man in the tan shirt drew his head back, tucking his chin into his neck. His mind was working like a house on fire.

"What about other people?" he asked. "The wife? The kids?"

"They can use your membership as long as *you're* alive," the manager said, making the distinction clear.

"Then what?" the man asked, louder. He was the type who said things like "You get what you pay for" and "There's one born every minute" and was considering every angle. He didn't want to get taken for a ride by his own death.

"That's it," the manager said, waving his hands, palms down, like a football referee ruling an extra point no good. "Then they'd have to join for themselves or forfeit the privileges."

"Well then, it makes sense." the man said, on top of the situation now, "for the youngest one to join. The one that's likely to live the longest."

"I can't argue with that," said the manager.

The man chewed his lip while he mentally reviewed his family. Who would go first. Who'd survive the longest. He cast his eyes around to all the cassettes as if he'd see one that would answer his question.

The woman had not gone away. She had brought along her signed agreement, the one that she paid twenty-five dollars for. "What is this accident waiver clause?" she asked the manager.

"Look," he said, now exhibiting his hands to show they were empty, nothing up his sleeve, "I live in the real world. I'm a small businessman, right? I have to protect my investment, don't I? What would happen if, and I'm not suggesting *you'd* do this, all right, but some people might, what would happen if you decided to watch one of my movies in the bathtub and a VCR you rented from me fell into the water?"

The woman retreated a step. This thought had clearly not occurred to her before.

"I don't want to be sued by your estate, do I? By your orphaned children?" The manager continued, now leaning his elbows on the counter and putting his weight on them. "I don't want to be held responsible for you if you electrocute yourself by mistake."

The woman put her expensive contract into her purse and drifted off. At first she pretended to browse through New Selections, but actually she was working her way toward the door and when she thought no one was watching, she cut out.

Mom stepped up to the counter in her place and pulled out a dollar bill.

"I'm joining this thing!" she announced brightly, "and I want you to know," she said to the manager, "that I intend to get my money's worth!"

"That's good, that's good," he said, handing her a blank contract card.

"What if I live for fifty years?" Mom asked.

"You're covered," he nodded.

"What if I put it in her name," Mom said, jerking her head in my direction, "and she lives for a hundred years. You know, medical science."

"You can both use it during her lifetime," the manager answered, giving me an appraising look. "As long as you continue to share the same domicile."

"She wouldn't evict me, would you, baby?" Mom said. "And this way, if the worst happens to me, you can still rent tapes at the members' rate. It's like something I'd leave you."

"This low offer may not be repeated," the manager agreed.

"Well, that's that," Mom decided. She wrote my name on the dotted line and had me sign on the bottom. "Till death," she said proudly.

I can't explain how I felt, but it was as though a part of my life was over. As far as video clubs went, this deal would last as long as I did, no matter what else ever happened to me. No surprises. Someday, if I was lucky, I would still be a name in the records of Village Video, an old lady whose charter membership had never expired.

"Remember," the manager said as we left the store, "I'm not responsible. What you do with your cassettes is your ball game."

"We are not idiots." Now that she was the mother of a

lifetime member Mom could afford to be more herself. "Some of your people may watch shows in their bathrooms, but not us."

"We don't watch them anywhere," I reminded her as we searched for our car in the huge parking lot. "We don't have anything to watch them on. Our TV barely has sound."

"Go ahead and be smart," she said. "But you'll be laughing out the other side of your mouth if we ever get one of those players and can watch all the movies we want at the special prices."

At the time I didn't say it was unlikely that we'd be getting a VCR soon, or that, even if we did, it was a sure bet we wouldn't come all the way out to the suburbs to rent films for it. I figured we'd never lay eyes on Village Video again. Then, the next week, Mom checked into the hospital and I forgot the whole thing.

Now, while it's still night, we clean out our closet and pack Mom's scrapbooks and the odds and ends that we want to keep from our apartment. The building manager is asleep with the TV on downstairs, so we tiptoe. After Mom's flirtation with suicide, she's in no mood to stay around arguing about the rent we owe or the security deposit we have borrowed against. She changes out of her candy striper uniform, and holds it in front of her.

"I'm just going to run this over to Charlene so she can return it," she says, and rushes from the apartment. I hear her knock on the door down the hall.

Finally Charlene answers.

"Do you know what time it is?" she shouts in a whisper you could hear on the next block, but then it hits her that Mom is standing there and not asleep in the hospital. "What are you doing? You're sick in bed."

"We're taking off," Mom says. "I'm going home."

"I don't believe they checked you out," Charlene hisses back.

"They didn't. I sprung myself wearing this."

I imagine her displaying the red-and-white-striped dress. I

wait for Charlene to scream her shocked disapproval. But there is just a pause and then Charlene almost sounds sad. "You're crazy, Christine. You're killing yourself."

"Not if you be my friend," Mom says. Something rattles. "Here's my address. You can get more medicine from the pharmacy. Send it to me here. But don't let *anybody* know where I've gone."

I recognize the sound I heard: pills loose in a plastic bottle.

"I could lose my job for that," Charlene says. "They check inventory once a week."

"Well, don't, then. I don't need the fucking stuff anyway."

I hear Mom coming back. Her steps are fast and close together, proud. Just as she reaches our door, Charlene's voice catches her.

"All right then. Some. But you go see a doctor out there. I can't keep ripping off Percocet without getting caught."

Mom's feet turn and she rebounds to Charlene.

We pack everything that matters in four jumbo green plastic garbage bags that we find in the kitchen cabinet. Each one gets labeled with masking tape: two with "Christine," one with "Ray," and one with "Junk." We have to squeeze them into the backseat of the Volaré, since the trunk is permanently wedged shut. It's five A.M. by the time we're done. I'm all set for the long drive, but not Mom.

"We can't go yet," she says. "We have to wait till the stores open."

"Stores?" We're low on cash, as always.

"Village Video. We can't blow into Aunt Ida's like deadbeats, alone and empty-handed. We'll rent a couple of movies at members' prices and take them along for a surprise."

"To Montana?" I say. "It's probably a federal offense to take stolen videotapes across state lines." I remember that the membership is in my name. I'll be the one the cops come after.

"They won't be stolen," Mom corrects me. "They'll be rented for life. It's completely legal. You just have to read the contract the right way."

• • •

The manager is rolling back a metal gate, opening his store, and Mom greets him like an old friend. "My daughter is still alive," she announces, pointing to me. "We're just going to exercise our privileges and borrow some tapes."

"Fine, fine," the manager says.

"What if we are a little late bringing them back?" Mom's voice is casual, cagey.

"Oh, not to worry. A little fine, reduced to almost nothing because of your charter membership. It happens all the time."

Mom presses her foot on my toe to show she has been right. After five minutes of browsing, she picks a movie about a jealous old car named Christine that murders people. She loved the ads when the film came to a theater in Seattle.

"Look at this," she said that day, shoving the Amusement section under my nose, and then reading the ad: "I am Christine. I am pure evil." She cut the slogan out and stuck it on the refrigerator with a magnet, and was thrilled to get the same thing printed on a bumper sticker the third time she saw the movie.

For the second tape, after a lot of considering, she picks *Little Big Man.*

"I dated a guy who played an Indian in that movie," she whispers at me.

She tells the manager an almost similar story when she has me sign for the tapes.

"This one is special to me," she brags. "I was once engaged to the star."

"Dustin Hoffman?"

Mom smiles as if she knows a secret, but doesn't say yes or no. "Did you see his face?" she asks when we're out of the store.

But I just think that now he'll remember who we are.

The gray sky has started to sprinkle. The two tapes, in a yellow plastic bag decorated with a red v.v., are on the seat between us, in for a long haul. I let the noise and steady motion of the windshield wipers hypnotize me, lull me into drowsiness. Mom is talking, telling me what to expect in

Montana, whom we're going to meet, what a rotten drive she had the last time we made this trip in winter when I was a baby. I nod whenever she pauses for breath. Her words rinse through my thoughts, clear as water, disconnected as rain.

Mom insists that we take a two-lane highway instead of the Interstate because, she says, she knows the way. The traffic is light and in between naps I watch the scenery roll by. Compared to western Washington the land on the other side of the mountains is at first dry and flat and then thick forest, but always empty of people. There are miles between towns so small that I can see their whole length as we approach. Late the first afternoon, a pair of black eagles circle above the road and Mom almost veers onto the shoulder with trailing them. I try to convince her to rest. All along the side in Montana you see little white metal crosses that mark the spots where people died in accidents, and I don't want our trip to end with two more, but she has energy to spare and drives all night, humming with the radio, learning new songs.

We grow accustomed to the car's tickings and clanks. Mom compensates for the steering wheel's tendency to pull to the right by bearing down on the left. We come to ignore the blinking emergency lights of oncoming cars. We *know* that one of our headlamps is out and there's nothing much we can do about it. When the service station attendants fill the tank and frown at our old credit card, its expiration date smoothed out with Mom's penknife, we ask them to check the tires. That changes the subject fast, since every one of them figures they can convince us that if we keep going on our smooth tubes the next mile might be our last. By the time they realize we aren't buying, we're already rolling.

The car is just one of the things Mom worries about. Her relations are her main concern.

"Do you remember Aunt Ida?" Mom wakes me in the middle of the night to inquire. Our speeding light illuminates a sign that says we're in the Kootenai National Forest. I think before I answer.

Aunt Ida is nobody's aunt, at least that I know of, but she wasn't married when Mom came along, so rather than have her only daughter remind her of this fact, she settled on being an aunt. By the time Mom's brother Lee was born it was natural that he'd call her that too. People get used to anything. I made the mistake of using "Grandma" when she came to Seattle. She was mixing flour for fry bread in a yellow basin, and her hands stopped in the wet dough. "Aunt Ida," she said, staring me down. "Aunt Ida."

Even after eight years, I flinch at the memory of her tone, and answer Mom's question with one of my own. "Are you anxious to see her?"

"Oh I'm looking forward to it," Mom says. "About as much as snow in March."

When Mom and I have conversations, they mostly involve subjects not personal to our lives. We discuss the cost of shoes, the marriages and divorces of TV stars, the plot of "Hill Street Blues." Mom tries not to ask me questions, and I'm not supposed to mind her business either. But sometimes she forgets, and chats with me as though I'm a girlfriend like Charlene. Very late, once in a while, she'll have a glass of wine and start complaining about her latest job, or how the guy she went out with was too rough, or how she's heard Dad has been seen with the same woman more than once.

I listen, eavesdropping into her life, while she lights Kent after Kent and the room fills with smoke while she kills the bottle. Those evenings always end with Mom's thoughts returning either to the day in Tacoma that Dad proposed to her, or to something about her brother, Lee, who was killed in Vietnam. She confuses who I am and asks me if I knew him, asks me if he had any last words for her. Those nights I help her to bed.

On this night, though, as we clatter over Route 2 and try to find good stations on the radio, Mom wants to hear about me.

"Are you going to miss anybody in Seattle?" she wonders, but before I can answer, she goes on. "No you won't. Bunch of punks. You wait. Out on the rez it'll be different."

She's right in a way, there isn't anybody to miss except the hope of Dad that I used to have. As we've moved around from one apartment to another I've changed schools so often that I never get past being the new girl. Too big, too smart, not Black, not Indian, not friendly. Kids keep their distance, and most teachers are surprised, then annoyed, that I know the answers on their tests. I'm not what they expect. About once a year I get discovered, get called a diamond in the rough. Some eager young counselor has big plans for me, but before they pan out, we're gone, living in another neighborhood, and the whole shooting match starts all over.

"Me neither," Mom goes on. "Charlene's been okay, but she's no mental giant. And screw the rest of them."

She means Dad.

"I shouldn't have stayed so long. When I was a kid, I thought Seattle was Hollywood. I was going to hit it big. I applied for relocation and before I turned around I had a husband and you. And then just you."

I don't ask Mom what she intends to do with herself back on the reservation. I know she doesn't know. She makes her plans from one day to the next, always sure that a happy ending is just out of sight. I try and imagine what it would be like if we settled in one of the places we drive through. Each of them was the end of the line for people who took off from their homes somewhere else and beat a path to Shelby or Pinnacle or Dunkirk. We could do that too, move anywhere, be anybody.

The Volaré almost makes it. All the next day, descending the Rockies through fields of wheat and lentils and mint, we parallel a black ribbon of railroad track, underlining scattered patches of short mountains to the north. Clouds seem low, within reach, larger than life. Distance is measured by hours instead of miles and sea gulls patrol the pavement like vultures. Once we reach the high plains where Mom grew up, the car seems to relax, and quiets down. The worst is over, it seems to realize, and it's a straight coast the rest of the way. After a

Conoco station east of Havre, Mom turns to me, shaking her head.

"Maybe we should have done us all a favor and let that hippie pump jockey unload some new tires on us. I don't want Aunt Ida to think I'm down on my luck."

Mom calls every man with a ponytail a hippie. "What were you planning to use for cash?" I ask.

She pats her green purse where it rests against her thigh on the seat. "If that old card will fill the tank for a thousand miles, I got to believe it will replace our tires too," she says. "Besides, that guy was so out of it he didn't even try to check the expiration date."

She seems about to turn back but reconsiders and keeps driving. "Four retreads would just make the rest of this car stand out old," she decides.

We whiz through the small towns, ignoring their offers of a real country breakfast, a fill-up, or a Dairy Queen, and come, about one o'clock, to the turn-off that leads to the reservation.

Mom is so relieved to be close to a place she can stop, she gets careless and forgets about potholes and flood washes that have been baking unrepaired in the spring heat. Less than a mile away from Aunt Ida's, she drives straight into a dip and the Volaré stalls, then dies. It sounds as if something falls off the bottom of the car and hits the gravel below, but Mom and I are not in a mood to check.

"Maybe it threw a rod," Mom says.

"What does that mean?"

"Who the hell knows? But it's beyond my powers of fixing and we're close enough to walk. I'll tell Dayton the car's out here and he can look."

Dayton is her friend from high school, a mixed-blood living on lease land close to Aunt Ida's. He's the person she says will be glad to see her after all these years, the person she talks about connecting with. "Dayton and Lee were real close," she says. "He was a pallbearer. Do you remember him?" She sets her mouth as if she's recalling something she would rather forget.

"I was only two," I say, but Mom is already standing by the road, stretching her arms, arching her stiff back.

We are almost directly next to a faint track that Mom says leads over a rise to Aunt Ida's house, so we start out. Mom carries the two "Christine" garbage bags, and her big carved-leather purse. Crammed inside it, keeping the flap from snapping, are the two videocassettes she has rented for life. I carry the two other plastic bags: the "Junk" and my own. Mom doesn't want to leave anything in the car.

"This is a poor place," she says.

It's hard for me to imagine that anything we have would tempt anybody.

As soon as we clear the top of the ridge, Aunt Ida comes into view. Her house, its boards warped and turned gray by too much weather, is the only structure you can see in any direction, and Aunt Ida is in front of it. She's not an unusually tall woman, but her arms and legs are long. A black bouffant wig is tacked to her head by bobby pins that shine in the sunlight, and beneath men's bib overalls, a dark blue bra dents deeply into her back and shoulders. Her skin is a darker brown than Mom's, though not as deep as Dad's or mine. Behind her sunglasses, her eyes are invisible.

Aunt Ida is pushing an old lawn mower back and forth across a plot of scrub grass. As we get closer I can see that it's not doing any cutting. Either the blades are dull or the grass is too tough: the stems flatten as the mower passes over, and then spring back. But she isn't aware of it, or of us. The speakers of the Walkman we sent her last Christmas are plugged into her ears. Her craggy, accented voice, surprisingly familiar to me, is off-key but loud as she accompanies the tape.

"*I've been looking for love in all the wrong places,*" she booms out, and then something makes her notice us. At first she pretends not to have seen anything out of the ordinary, and goes back to her pushing.

"*Looking for love in too many faces,*" she shouts, then stops again and drops her forearms on the handle of the mower. Finally she glances over her shoulder and sighs as she pulls off the headset.

"Well, what did the cat drag in," she says in Indian, in a voice as scratchy and knotted as a fir tree. "My favorite thing, a surprise visitor."

"I came home, Aunt Ida." Mom stands in the yellow field, her hair blowing across her face like dark string, the green garbage bags full of Seattle clothes at her feet. She's nervous. The wind rises, filling her blouse like a kite and outlining her short, square body. I have a sudden, sure sense that for Mom this is an important moment, a beginning or an end of something, and she's scared to find out which. I have the idea to walk over to her, punch her on the arm, and tell her to lighten up, but I stay put and watch as though I'm seeing this scene on an old movie and a commercial could come along any time.

The music leaking out of Aunt Ida's earphones is tinny and low, but it fills the air around us and we listen. I think it's the Oak Ridge Boys or a group like that, but it's a song I don't know. Hearing that tune gives us all something to do, though, while we wait for what Aunt Ida will say. She's taking her time, giving Mom a chance to put in another word more if she wants.

"Give me three good reasons why I should be glad to see you." Aunt Ida's forehead bends into a frown. She pulls a red kerchief from her hip pocket and wipes her mouth.

Mom doesn't move. She doesn't even relax her scared smile. She tenses as though she's thought of an answer but she's not sure it's right. Then she gives it a try anyway, as if this is a quiz show and she's out to stump the stars.

"One, Mother, I'm your daughter, your only living child."

Aunt Ida doesn't like to hear this. Her face twists as if Mom has punched her below the belt or whacked her from behind when she wasn't looking.

"Two, I need someplace to stay."

Aunt Ida's expression changes fast. She has hit upon some good comeback, something that will start with "Ha!" and not quit until "I told you so" is thrown in.

"Three . . ." Mom hesitates. She has been watching Aunt Ida too and knows that the minute she finishes her answer, no matter what it is, Aunt Ida's going to let go with something mean. As long as she doesn't say the third reason she's safe, Aunt Ida's hands are tied. Mom's eyes are bright. She looks from side to side, not seeing anything. Her fingers are shredding the top of one of the "Christine" bags, stretching and punching holes in the dark plastic. She seems to see something on the ground and stares at it, pries at it with the toe of her boot. Nobody breathes.

"Three," Mom says, looking up, straight at Aunt Ida. "Three, go fuck yourself anyway."

Mom picks up the bags in her fists and turns away, walking, and then, off balance, doing a jerky run down the hill toward the car. Her feet start landslides of pebbles, storms of dust. Aunt Ida's mouth is open now. She is shocked, she's amazed, she can't believe her ears. She's reacting like there's an audience ready to laugh or hoot, but there's only the noise of the whispering tape and of Mom's jagged steps, running, tripping, the bags slapping against her legs.

She's almost to the car before I remember that I'm really here, that this is really happening. I turn to Aunt Ida, expecting her to do something, to call Mom back, but her expression says she's just heard bad news or the worst joke in the world. She puts on the earphones, silencing the tiny speakers. I grab the other bags and start down the hill and build speed as I go.

"Wait a minute," I yell. "Hold on."

Mom doesn't look back, doesn't slow down, even when the sack with the videotapes spills from her purse. She hits the dirt road and doesn't pause as she passes the Volaré.

The land folds and slopes around me as I chase after her. I can see for miles. The "Junk" bag snags on the gray remains of a tree stump, ripping a gash in the bottom and spilling a trail of towels and postcards and half-read magazines. I stop to try and scoop them up, but the bag is useless and my arms won't contain them. Every time I collect one object, two others fall, and finally I let everything drop.

Mom has reached the main road, far below, and she's still moving. Her body is small and tight, crouched in a low jog. Nobody would guess that three days ago she had been flat on her back in the hospital. She can't keep going, I figure. I have time to catch her, to become part of her plan, but as I think this I see dust disturbed on the road further away. A blue pickup, jarring through the rain ruts, is heading in our direction. It stops next to Mom but she doesn't slack her pace, so it starts again, slowly lurching beside her. She's talking to the guy behind the wheel, talking and running, dragging her garbage bags, and finally the door opens and she hops in. The truck gathers speed, kicking gravel. It gets lost in its own dust.

My head is buzzing. I'm not used to running. I hear my heartbeat inside my ears. I look down. The earth is ugly. The way the grass grows out of the tan soil reminds me of a photograph I saw of a bald man who had a hair transplant. His scalp was a wide empty place with dark stalks poking out of little black holes. A Barbie doll scalp. The ground seems to me the most disgusting thing in the world. It makes my skin crawl. I drop to my knees, surrounded by our blowing junk, and pull weeds out by their roots, scratch them out with my fingernails. I must make the soil smooth, even, without bristles. No matter how much I pull there's more. I will never clean it all, and yet I can't stop. I pound at the earth with my flat hands, pushing it pure, scraping it loose. Nothing else matters to me. Nothing but fixing this dirt.

I know Aunt Ida is close by me but I pay no attention until her hands seize my wrists and hold them still. I won't look at her when she moves before me. I could never explain about the grass. My muscles strain against her arms, strain and pull until they cramp, and still my fingers arch into rakes.

I'm no match for her. I try to tell her to let go, but instead of saying words I am screaming, howling like a crazy person, and she hangs on. She hauls me in like a trapped salmon and imprisons me. I am kneeling into her, my face forced into the warm, damp skin about her bra, her breasts against my neck. I can't move, no matter how I struggle, and finally I surrender. The strength goes out of me, the hate I feel for the ground leaves as completely as a day-old dream. I press against her fine grass-smelling skin, sink into the basket of her arms.

She lets me stay that way for some space of time. It seems long because I keep dreading it will end, and at last it does. Her grip relaxes on my wrists and there's room between us as she steps back. I lift my face but the sun is behind her and shows me only the outline of her head, round and clean as a street lamp.

"Save your belongings before they blow away," she says, and turns for the house.

But I don't save them. I am afraid to look down, and so feel and step around them with my feet as I follow her up the hill, over the crest, out of sight of the road.

3

Aunt Ida and I don't know what to do with each other. We are unexpected surprises, spoiled plans, bad luck. We bump against each other in the three rooms of her house, four if you count the bathroom that doesn't work. Aunt Ida sleeps propped on a studio couch in the small bedroom, her head and back against a mountain of pillows crocheted and knitted into the lumpy shapes of dull-colored small animals. Against one wall of the living room, lined in a row facing the outer door, are the cookstove, washing machine, and television, and just beside the set of wooden stairs leading to the attic leans the refrigerator. Spotting its white surface are yellow magnets, each printed in the shape of a Happy Face with HAVE A NICE DAY written around the edges. I thought they might be arranged in some pattern I could figure out, but I finally gave up and asked Aunt Ida.

"They come in my cereal," she said. "Plastic crap to hold grocery lists. I save them for Bingo covers."

Water is a problem at Aunt Ida's house this summer. There isn't any most of the time, thanks to a dry spell that has depleted the runoff into the dug well. Twice a week—more often now that I'm here using it too, Aunt Ida reminds me—she walks to her neighbor's creek, fills a red twenty-five-gallon plastic jug and hauls it back to live off. Between uses, the jug is stored in the sink, ready for when a cup needs washing or your hands are dirty. The drain still works fine. There are

34

stacked boxes in the kitchen area and on the attic stairs, filled like shelves with dried and preserved food—commodity peanut butter and powdered eggs and canned lard. I ask her about that too, why she hoards so much, but even before the words are out of my mouth I see a box of kindling and remember what Mom always said about the winters in Montana and how they made her glad to be in Seattle no matter how rotten things got. During the long, dark blizzards Aunt Ida's house would be cut off for days from everywhere in the world. There's no way she'd want to depend on electricity, a BIA check, or the reservation store.

I have the room that was once Mom's, and when my jeans get too dirty, I wear any of her teenage clothes that I can squeeze into: green pedal pushers and patched white socks and a Bobby Rydell sweat shirt. Still tacked to her wall are pictures of Elvis Presley, Jacqueline Kennedy, and Connie Francis, and on the sagging shelf in the closet, piles of red and blue and yellow high-school notebooks. Each one is labeled on the cover— Religion or English or Civics—but inside there is no work, just a page or two of Mom's drawings of faces and horses and zigzaggy beadwork designs, and long lists of her name, written in purple ink with all the I's dotted with hearts: "Mrs. Christine Doney. Mrs. Christine Presley. Mrs. Christine LaValle. Mrs. Christine Garcia."

In a box under the bed is an album still wrapped in cellophane and piles of loose pictures of Mom, school portraits, snapshots with her friends, an eight-by-ten graduation photo in color. In that one, her head is turned back toward the camera. She is posed like a saint that I recognize from a painting in church. I forget who, some Lucy or Bernadette or somebody having a vision. Her eyes are lifted up and a light shines on her hair and forehead. Her lips have been carefully colored in with a red marker. She wears a white blouse that's pinned at the neck with a silver-and-turquoise circle that Mom still wears for special.

When I come across that picture I can barely look at it. I slam the lid of the box shut and push it under the bed. But five minutes later I take it out and study every detail. I try to see a resemblance, something in me that looks like her at my age. I even hold the picture to the mirror next to my face and go over it again—hair, eyes, nose, mouth, chin. But she still is Mom and I still am me. She is holy, one step from shooting off to heaven, and I look ready to fight.

Once I read a story in a magazine about how some man from the city came out to a farm and couldn't get to sleep at night because it was too quiet. He would have had no trouble at all at Aunt Ida's. There is always at least one radio going, and half the time a tape hums in the Walkman. Noise fills the house and squirts outside under all the windows that won't shut flush and through the TV antenna hole in the roof where rain gets in. I swim through commercials and on-the-air auctions and news updates and pick hits like a fish in a crowded dime-store aquarium. In every room my head buzzes with voices twining in Montana accents, and outside the wasps and mos- quitoes are so thick that I can't find a place to think. I spend my time reading stories in Mom's old *Seventeens* and pasting her pictures in the album.

Aunt Ida's real life is squeezed between the time of her programs on TV. She knows and is annoyed with all the characters on "As the World Turns" and never misses an episode. She loses her patience with their ignorance, their slowness to figure out what's happening around them, what plots are taking place. The first few times I heard her yell, "Wake up and see what's before your face!" or "He's just after your money," I thought someone was visiting, but quick enough her voice became part of the background I ignore. Sometimes when things in Oakdale drag, Aunt Ida leaps from her rocker and turns off the sound. She can't stand to hear her people be so dumb.

In the late afternoons she watches Judge Wapner and "The People's Court" and it's even worse. She doesn't trust the men and women who come in to tell their bitching stories. She mimics their words and snorts at their excuses. "Serves you right!" she shouts at the screen. She saves her worst contempt for the judge himself. She doubts his credentials, the existence of his brain. "How'd *you* like to be on the other side sometime?" she asks him when she disagrees with his verdict.

Except for that first afternoon when she held my arms behind my back she hasn't touched me at all, and we don't talk much. She points her fingers at things she wants me to see or do, rolls her eyes when I get it wrong, and shushes me if I interrupt during one of her shows. I am her duty, she says with her long sighs and banged-down plates, but she doesn't have to like it.

I tell myself that it's not me causing Aunt Ida's irritation. Mom's the one that's eating at her, and I'm just the unwelcome reminder, a bad news list stuck under a Happy Face on her refrigerator. Aunt Ida watches me for mistakes, begrudges me the space I take. She follows the same routine of TV and work every day as if her life depended on it, and I am a distraction, a strange-looking unknown relative who fell into her life like something dropped out of an airplane to lighten the load.

On Sundays she insists that I listen with her to a Mass that's broadcast from the Catholic cathedral in Denver.

"I was there once for the feast of Corpus Christi," she told me the day I arrived, when she was still feeling sympathetic and hadn't realized she was stuck with me. "I was a bead in the living rosary at the racetrack, between the first and second joyful mysteries."

Aunt Ida will talk to me only in Indian, though I suspect she knows English. It's a lucky thing Mom always spoke the old language, like a secret code, around the apartment and when she and I were alone together. This was to give me my identity, according to Mom, and thanks to her I can understand Aunt Ida, even if at first I'm too shy in answering.

I decide Aunt Ida made up her story about Denver to seem important, to seem as though she belongs to this big church in Colorado. I think she needs a reason to explain why she stays home and listens to the radio every week instead of going to the Mission church ten miles away. Late one afternoon of the first week I'm there, I hear the sound of a car and sneak a look from my window to see an elderly priest get out of an old pickup with HOLY MARTYRS MISSION stenciled on the side panel. I listen from the bedroom as Aunt Ida stands with him at the front door. He asks in Indian if she has time for a cup of tea.

"I have this girl here," she says, "that I have to watch."

"Is Christine back? Is she with you for long?"

I'm surprised he knows our language, surprised at how much else he seems to know, and I hang on what Aunt Ida will say next. These are questions I want answered.

"Her mother left her. Pauline heard she's over living with Dayton."

Living with Dayton? Here? I thought Mom had gone back to Seattle, or anywhere away from this reservation. How does Aunt Ida know this? Was it on some radio show I missed?

"And she left her little girl with you? Rayona must be almost grown by now."

Silence.

"Will she be completing her school year at the Mission?"

Before Aunt Ida can answer, if she's going to, I come into the front room. The priest is a short gray-haired man with blue eyes and a big stomach. His skin is weathered and tan against his wrinkled black suit. When he sees me he looks to Aunt Ida in amazement.

"This can't be Rayona."

Aunt Ida has her arms folded across her chest, her feet apart, her eyes directed at the clock on top of the washing machine. "As the World Turns" came on two minutes ago.

The priest turns to me. "My name is Father Hurlburt," he says in English. "I met you as a baby. And of course I remember your mother very well. . . ."

His words slip through my defenses and bring Mom's face to my mind. She appears as she was the morning we left Seattle, tired but satisfied with herself at Village Video. I flash to the bumper sticker on the back of Mom's Volaré.

"I AM CHRISTINE. I AM PURE EVIL," I quote aloud without thinking.

Father Hurlburt grabs his hand to his chest as if he's

shocked into a heart attack or else ready to withdraw a crucifix. He thinks I'm a space cadet, but Aunt Ida glances at me and bites on her lip. I've said something she likes, something she doesn't think is dumb. Then her face sets again.

Father Hurlburt lets out his breath and tries to act as if I've made a great joke. "You had me going," he says. "Oh yes, you really took me by surprise." He clears his throat and changes the subject. "This reservation must seem very different from Seattle."

" 'The land of the sky-blue waters,' " I say, taking a line from a commercial that plays all the time. Aunt Ida shoots her glance over at me. This time she actually smiles for a split second before she turns expressionless.

"What would she know? She sits in that room all day." Aunt Ida rolls her eyes in the direction of Mom's door. "She speaks Indian," she adds.

"You're so very tall"—Father Hurlburt switches languages and says to me—"but too thin. Have you made any friends yet around here?" He has not mentioned the color of my skin. I'm supposed to think he hasn't noticed.

I shake my head. I have no friends.

"And you are, what, about sixteen years old?"

"She's fifteen," Aunt Ida says before I can feel good that I look older. It takes me a second to realize she knows my age, that he knew where I was from. I can't imagine that Aunt Ida has ever thought of me or mentioned me before my arrival, but she must have.

"Perfect, perfect." Father Hurlburt rubs his hands together as though he is warming them before a fire. His fingers are stubby and thick. He nods at me while he talks. "We'll enroll you at the Mission high school, starting next week, but in the meantime I know exactly the way for you to get acquainted, provided you have been raised a Catholic?"

"Sort of." Mom pointed me in the direction of Mass most Sundays, sent me to the nuns whenever we were close enough to a Catholic school in Seattle, and trivia-quizzed me on the lives of all the saints, but she never set foot inside a church herself that I can remember.

"Excellent. The God Squad it is, then." He swings his mouth-open smile from Aunt Ida to me and back again. The skin of his face is creased and rolled. He's relieved to know what to do with me, but sees my doubt.

"Don't let the name fool you. It's a nice group of young people, and my new assistant pastor has taken a great interest in the organization. There are weekly meetings and teen dances. Only one retreat a year. St. Dominic Savio is the patron. It's not as bad as I make it sound."

I'm not convinced. I know all about Dominic Savio, the preteen saint. The nuns at my last school in Seattle were crazy about him and had his plaster statue on a pedestal by the door of the classroom. He stood watch above the holy water font, dressed in lemon-yellow pants and a lime sports jacket. In one hand, close to his heart, he clutched a book, a Daily Missal probably, and from the other hand he held up a single finger. The hair on his too-small head was an unnatural black and from his bright red lips he seemed ready to say "No, no" or "Better not." His motto was "Death Rather Than Sin," and he died at twelve. I wait for Aunt Ida to refuse, to tell the priest I can't make it.

"There's only one problem," Father Hurlburt goes on. He reaches inside his coat, pulls out a small pocket calendar, and licks his finger, turning pages until he finds the one he wants. Then he frowns. "I'm so swamped this week! And unfortunately my poor old truck does not have the bi-location!"

Father Hurlburt winks at me as if he has said something cute, and I remember Dominic Savio's trick of being in two places at the same time. Aunt Ida's eyes are focused so hard on the television that I wonder if she can follow her program through the blank screen. Finally she glances over at the priest as he continues to talk to her.

"Either I can have Father Novak stop for Rayona on Saturday and take her to the God Squad meeting, or we can skip that and I'll run by on Sunday morning and bring you *both* over to Holy Martyrs for eight o'clock Mass."

Two days later I'm sitting in the Mission pickup next to Father Tom Novak on my way to the God Squad. He talks nonstop, as though he's answering the question "Tell me everything about yourself," except I never asked it. He wants me to call him "Father Tom."

"Guess how long I've been here?" he says. He's wearing a big beaded medallion that rides low on his black cassock. He's the kind that wants to be everybody's buddy, the kind they bring in for guitar Masses.

When I don't guess, Father Tom jumps right in. "Two weeks! Imagine, just three weeks ago today I was walking down the street in Milwaukee. I had never been west of Wisconsin!"

I could see him. He'd have his arm bent with his Missal clutched in his hand. His black skirt would swing as he walked and his balding head would shine like it had just been buffed. He'd be looking for people to talk to, to tell how he was all set to come out to Montana and save the Indians.

"I hear you're new in these parts yourself, Rayona," Father Tom says.

I wonder what he's heard, if he knows about Mom or where she is. The ruts in the road are deeper, closer together, than they were with Mom. Green alfalfa grows behind wire fences in the leased land along the side, and as the car approaches, two large sea gulls lift slowly, circling overhead until we pass. They have been stabbing at the remains of another bird, struck and flattened by an earlier car. Its one undamaged wing rises straight from the asphalt and moves in the wind, as if to wave us down.

"You don't talk much, do you?" he says. "But that's okay, since I talk enough for an army!"

He is a real jerk, a dork, the kids in Seattle would call him. Somewhere Mom is off having a good time with her old boyfriend. Aunt Ida finally has her house to herself. I imagine that Mom and Dad are the gulls and that I'm driving. I surprise them by gunning the engine and come faster than they expect. They try to flap off sideways to avoid my grill. Their eyes glint, betrayed, scared shitless.

"Here we are." The God Squad meets in the basement of the Mission hall. Father Tom parks the truck and I follow him inside, but he stops to talk to a couple of old men who are sitting on the steps.

"Howdy, Mr. Stiffarm," he says, reaching for and pumping the hand of the nearest one. "I must have missed you at church last Sunday."

The old man's stare is milky as cat's-eye marbles, and when he smiles, I see he has no teeth. He's dressed in a tan-and-black-plaid wool shirt and gray pants. His hair is white and mussed, recently washed.

"This new priest, he's so dumb he thinks I'm Henry Stiffarm," the man says in Indian to his friend, raising his thin eyebrows and pursing his lips. He laughs and nods his head. They ignore me as if I don't exist. They have no idea I understand their words.

"Just lucky for you he doesn't think you are *Annabelle* Stiffarm," the other man answers, all stone-faced. "He might try to convert you then."

That starts the two of them giggling, and Father Tom joins right in, laughing at himself as if this was the funniest thing he'd ever heard. I close my eyes at his stupidity.

The old men are enjoying themselves, but they become quiet in noticing that I've caught their joke. Their vacuum-cleaner eyes scan and study, pulling out information and storing it away. And yet there's no sign of welcome, no softening. I think of a worm's esophagus, stained blue under my microscope in biology class.

"Here's the clubhouse," Father Tom says when we get to the basement. The walls are cement block, painted green, and the floor, littered with Pepsi and 7-Up cans, is concrete. Facing me is a black-and-white poster with Chief Joseph's picture on it and "Indian Pride" printed underneath. Fluorescent lights span the ceiling. A pool table, two broken-down couches, and a garbage can full of empty McDonald's boxes are the only furniture. From an invisible radio, Kool and the Gang sing "Cherish." And sitting on one of the sofas are two of the meanest-looking people I have ever seen. The fact that they are young, not much older than me, the fact that one of them is a girl, is not at all reassuring. I think again about those sea gulls on the road and mentally floor the gas.

The two on the couch look me up and down. I know what they see. Wrong color, outsider, skinny, friend of the priest, friend of the dork.

"Here is a new member," Father Tom says. His voice is loud and blasts into the dim room. "Her name is Rayona and she's here visiting all the way from Seattle, Washington."

The girl laughs into her hand, and pushes the boy's side with her elbow. Her long black hair is teased into a rat's nest and she wears tight jeans, a cowboy shirt, and too much eyeliner.

"This is Annabelle Stiffarm," Father Tom says. "She's one of the founders of the God Squad and a senior in the Honor Society at the Mission school."

Annabelle tries to look at me but I am too funny. She laughs harder, finally calming herself by taking a package of extra-long Salems out of her fringed and dirty brown leather purse and lighting up. She has a hard time.

"This is Kennedy Cree, but everybody calls him Foxy." Father Tom grins at the boy, who looks like a snake turned into a human being. Not that he isn't good-looking. His black hair falls over his forehead, and his coal eyes paralyze me. "I know who you are," he says.

There's something in the way he stares at me that makes me feel ugly, off-balance, and it shocks me. It's like sticking out your hand in the dark and touching something soft and damp. Your stomach sinks and you want to bear back on your neck, hunch up your shoulders. But I don't let on. I ignore him and pretend to read the caption under the Chief Joseph poster as though I had never seen it before.

"You're Christine's kid," he says. "The one whose father is a nigger."

People don't usually come right out and say it, so in a way his words are a relief. If that's the worst he can do, it's not so bad.

"We're cousins," he goes on. "My mom is Pauline, Aunt Ida's younger sister. They're real close. Of course my mom had a husband."

I've relaxed too soon. He's trying for a way to get to me, trying to impress this Annabelle, who's laughing so hard now I think she'll beat her head on the wall.

"Foxy!" Father Tom says.

He's coming to my rescue. He doesn't know enough to keep quiet, to let the words wash over without snagging.

"That's no way to talk, especially here. I persuaded Rayona to join us because she's alone and needs some friends her own age. I am highly disappointed in you."

Foxy reaches over to put his hand on the back of Annabelle's neck. I think he's gentle with her but then I see his muscles tense, his fingers squeeze and dig. Her laughter stops. She twists her head, ready to let him have it, but when she sees his eyes, cold and flat, she changes her mind. He releases her, and she rubs the base of her skull in resentment.

"Rayona doesn't care," Foxy says. "She's *glad* to meet her full-blood cousin."

They all look at me. What do I say? What do I do, not to be dumb? I do the safest thing. I pretend that everything's fine. I smile out of the corner of my mouth and nod my head at Foxy. I'm offering to side with him and Annabelle and cut loose of Father Tom. Us together. Everybody understands what's happening except the priest. He thinks his plan has worked. But we know different. They can take me or leave me. If they take me, I'll be the butt of jokes, the one they dump on. If they leave me, it means I'm not even good enough for that.

They leave me.

"We've got to be somewhere," Foxy says. He motions Annabelle to her feet and pushes at her back as he heads for the stairs.

They could ask me to come along. They don't. They could at least say good-bye, something mean, that would give me a place. They don't. They walk up the steps. Foxy's voice, a mumble I can't understand, drifts back, followed by wild laughter from Annabelle and the slam of the outside door. I am their fool, the thing to tell other people.

Father Tom and I sit on the couch and wait an hour for more members of the God Squad to arrive. Finally, he drives me back to Aunt Ida's. He's sorry. There is a lot going on today, probably. Next time will be different, I'll see. I shouldn't be discouraged. Foxy is really a nice young man and Annabelle and I will become great friends.

When I walk through the door, Aunt Ida is involved in "The People's Court." A woman claims that a man promised to groom her dog and then clipped it too short. She wants a hundred dollars for her anguish. Judge Wapner laughs in her face. He said the dog isn't even a purebreed. The man gets off free and the woman is mad but still glad to be on television. Aunt Ida is disgusted with all of them. She says they waste her time with their fighting. She doesn't ask about my meeting and I go back to Mom's room. Radio music seeps under my door. On the wall, Connie Francis and Elvis Presley flirt at each other. I open the album and look at Mom's smiling mouth.

It's clear that I'll wind up Father Tom's favorite. There's no avoiding it. Mom is gone and Aunt Ida barely pays attention to me. I'm on my own and it's just a matter of time until Father Tom decides I'm his special project. There's no one to stand in his way.

Only four weeks of school remain, but I have to go anyway. I'm in a class of twelve people, one of them Annabelle. They have heard about me before I enroll and don't take any chances by being friendly. I'm taller than any of them, and darker. I wear Mom's twenty-year-old clothes, which, no matter how much Aunt Ida springs the seams and rips the hems, are still too tight, too short. I look ridiculous, like someone who grew overnight, or I look like a boy. Aunt Ida's sister, Pauline, feels sorry for me and sends over hand-me-downs, things Foxy doesn't want. This gives him another thing to laugh at. I make my mind a blank, and the nuns have to call on me twice before I hear them.

My school in Seattle was better than the Mission, and I know more than anyone expects. The nuns call the principal where I used to go and find out that I have good grades, that I have potential. They announce this news to the class, and the other students look at me as if I come from Mars. I don't care. I do no work, but the nuns praise me anyway. They read my papers aloud to show how smart I am. They pin my tests to the bulletin board. This wins me no friends. Annabelle makes sure everybody sees and hears the things I do and that they realize I'm a jerk. I don't care. If anyone looks at me, I duck my head. If anyone talks to me, I frown.

Mom doesn't come by or send word, and there's nobody I can ask about her. I don't know Dayton's last name, and no Daytons exist in Mom's school yearbook.

One day Father Hurlburt brings a brown parcel addressed to Mom. I see it's from Charlene, and remember about the medicine she was going to send. I'm impatient with Aunt Ida, since she leaves the package sitting on the table by her front door and makes no effort that I can see to tell Mom it's here.

"Shouldn't we forward this on?" I say at last. "It might be important." Aunt Ida puffs her cheeks and blows out air.

"I think it's medicine," I say.

But she won't talk about Mom with me and doesn't touch the package. Sometimes I think of it as bait, a piece of ripe meat set in a trap for a hungry animal. Sometimes I think of it as Mom herself, hiding under wraps and watching everything that I do. Having that box in the room makes me feel better, like a promise that might be kept. Sooner or later it will lure Mom. I convince myself that Aunt Ida cannot help but let

Mom know. The package is too loud. I pretend to know what's going on and wait out each day, sleep out each night.

Foxy calls me "Buffalo Soldier," after the black men who were cavalry scouts and fought Indians a long time ago. He leaves a note stuck in the Africa section of my geography book. "When are you going home?" it says. Even Manuel Isaacs, who has the blond hair and green eyes of his white mother, takes a shot.

"Hey, Ray," he calls to me one day in earshot of everybody. "You sure you ain't looking for the *Blackfeet* reservation? You must of took a wrong turn."

For sure, there's no avoiding I am going to fall into Father Tom's clutch. I know he's finally taken a bead on me the day he comes to Aunt Ida's and asks me to be his special assistant at the Mission.

"I really need you, Rayona," he says with a big wet smile. He must count me for at least two of those three-hundred-day indulgences each Beatitude is worth. I recognize all the signs. People have taken me under their wings before.

"I don't know how," I tell him, but he says I can learn, he'll teach me.

I admit I give in without a fight. Father Tom is the last one on the reservation I want to know, but he's the only one who wants to know me. And he needs me more than he thinks.

"I hear you speak your native tongue, Rayona," he says one day after I've arranged the altar for his morning Mass.

Why do they always call it that, "native tongue"?

"My mom is from here." I state a fact he has to know already. "She talked it at home. I can understand it okay."

"I smell like dogshit!" Father Tom booms out at me in Indian. The church echoes with his voice.

I've heard him say this before. Foxy told Annabelle, who couldn't believe her ears that such a hilarious thing had happened, that when Vance Windyboy, on the Tribal Council, found out Father Tom wanted to learn the language, he gave him some private lessons.

"You shouldn't say that," I say. "Vance is pulling your leg."

Father Tom's face sags. He looks like some kid who just dropped his Popsicle in the dirt. "What does it mean?" he demands, but I shake my head.

"Just say *hello*," I tell him, giving him the ordinary word, "if you have to say something."

Hello doesn't sound halfway as interesting as *I smell like dogshit* to Father Tom's ear. He looks at me and doesn't trust me one bit.

"Ask Father Hurlburt," I suggest, but I can tell from Father Tom's expression that this is not the way he wants to go.

"I guess I'm just no good at languages," he says.

However, from then on, he checks most things with me before he leaps, and I get pretty well used to having him around. Sometimes he makes me so nervous I want to run from him. But there's no place to go. And sometimes he's all right, kind of familiar. He comes for me two or three times a week. He asks how I am. He talks to me as if I have sense. He reminds me of social workers back in Seattle, and with them I know the questions and the answers I'm supposed to give.

I become the one loyal member of the God Squad, and some meetings it's just him and me and too much Kool-Aid. Each get-together is supposed to have a theme, but no matter what's scheduled, Father Tom finds a way to talk about sex, which he calls "The Wonders of the Human Body." This is a subject about which I have great curiosity but little know-how. People I've known, kids my age, have gotten mixed up in it already and it seems to change them for the worse. Plus, Mom swears off of it for weeks at a time. But I can't help thinking that, if I had the opportunity and knew all the facts in advance, I could keep the situation under control.

It's clear that Father Tom is no expert himself, at least as far as girls are concerned, since all his examples have to do with boys.

"At the age of fourteen or fifteen," he tells me one day as we drive back up the hill to Aunt Ida's, "boys begin to have dreams."

This does not strike me as all that amazing.

"Do you ever have them?" he asks, blushing but trying to act as though it's the most innocent question in the world.

At first I think he means medicine dreams, which I have read about and which the old folks say are supposed to come at about my age, at least to boys. They're the kind of dreams that tell you about who you are and what you're supposed to be. Vision quests. I am interested that Father Tom believes in them too.

"Not yet," I say. "They never write about girls getting them. But I dreamed of a bear once two years ago. Do you think that means something?"

We've stopped at Aunt Ida's house, and the truck engine is idling. Father Tom gives me a cross-eyed look.

"No, *dreams*," he says. "About the Wonders of the Human Body."

He means sex. His skin turns splotchy red and he looks like one of those mooseheads that are stuffed with a grin on their face. "Have you had that kind of dream?"

I am so surprised by his question that I say yes, which is dumb to do because he wants to hear what they were about.

"I will understand," he says. "No matter what they are."

"It's bad luck to tell your dreams," I warn him, but he won't stop.

"I can help you, Rayona. You need the guidance of an older friend. You have reached the age of puberty and are turning into a young lady."

I get out of the truck and don't look back. His words lasso me.

"An attractive young lady."

It's the first time since the day Mom split that I think I'm really going to lose it. Something rises inside me so hard I think it will lift me off the ground and ram me into the side of the house. I start to turn and face the truck. But it's in reverse. I hear it back down the hill, whining and clanking over the rough ground. When it hits bottom, before it heads toward the Mission, there is a pause. I know without looking that it's out of sight, that Father Tom can't see me standing here, can't know I'm caught by his words. The horn sounds once, twice, more times in a kind of beat. The tires catch, the truck moves off, and for an instant there is a hole of quiet, a pocket of air without any noise, before the call of radios and televisions and bees and wind rushes in to fill my ears.

4

As the days get longer and hotter, Foxy starts in about my Coppertone tan. I've been looking forward to summer vacation as if that would be the end of a bad time and the beginning of something else, but one day I walk Aunt Ida's hill from the schoolbus and it's like a curtain is pulled and there's nothing behind it. I haven't become popular and I haven't turned invisible. I am Father Tom's good deed. The way things stand I have my choice of distracting Aunt Ida all day at her house or of staying out of Annabelle and Foxy's way off her property. Or of leaving altogether.

I'm ready to pack and take my chances. Maybe I can jump the Great Northern back to Seattle and locate some of the kids I used to know. I figure I'll take off school for a day or two to plan this out, but not two hours after classes at the Mission start, who taps at the door but Father Tom. Aunt Ida has gone off to visit her sister, so I come outside to talk to him.

"We missed you in Religion, Rayona," he says.

"I must have slept through the alarm."

"Is something troubling you?"

It has rained the night before and the gravel in front of the house sparkles in the sunlight. The air from the mountains is sharp and dry and the breeze has a bite in it. I don't say anything, just drill the toe of my boot in the ground and wait him out.

"You know you can talk to me, Rayona," he says. He's like

somebody who has just sat down to watch his favorite show on TV, who doesn't know what's going to happen next but knows he'll enjoy it. He has on his shiny black pants and a washed-thin T-shirt, with a black windbreaker that says SAINTS on the back in gold writing. He has nicked himself shaving, and the dried blood looks like a vampire has dropped on him in his sleep. His skin is as pale as peeled potatoes, and the little arteries show through under his eyes.

"There's nothing to say," I tell him. "I'm just considering how to get out of here, that's all."

He nods, pretending to take me seriously.

"And where are you off to, if I may ask?"

"Back to Seattle, maybe," I say, and then watch his reaction to this idea. He gives a poker face that says he holds a full house.

"When do you leave?" He's stringing me along good, setting to knock my house of cards out from under me. I can smell his "counseling strategy" a mile off.

"Forget it," I say. "I'll come to school. I'm not going anywhere."

Now he's disappointed. He can't take credit for putting me on the right path. I have caved in too quickly and dodged his influence.

"Tell you what." He acts as if I haven't said anything, as if he still has to turn me around. "Come this weekend I'm borrowing Father Hurlburt's pickup and taking you to Helena. To the Teens for Christ Jamboree. You'll represent our local chapter of the God Squad. There will be hootenannies and rap sessions and even movies in the evenings. What do you say to that?" He cracks the knuckles of his dry spaghetti fingers while he talks.

It's a time of day when nobody makes noise on the reservation. People who are usually loud are either gone visiting or sleeping it off or sitting in school, so the quiet kind of settles over us as we stand there, him waiting for me to say something and me trying to think what. At least it's somewhere away from here.

"I say all right."

"All *right!*" he repeats, but a lot louder. His TV program has turned out okay after all. I'll be his sitting duck for two days.

"We shall have a chance to *talk*," he says, and reaches out and pats me on the shoulder, then pulls his hand back. He's trying hard.

For the first time since I arrived on the reservation the time passes too quickly. On Friday afternoon Father Tom, dressed in a green Sears short-sleeved Western snap-front shirt and stiff new jeans, pulls beside me in the Mission truck as I walk on the road home from school, and gives the horn three quick taps.

"God Squad Express all set and ready to go, Rayona!" he shouts loud enough for all the other kids to hear. "I've taken care of everything. Hop in!"

I put my head down and step high onto the running board, then swing myself in through the door, but not fast enough. Behind me I hear Annabelle say, "How many sleeping bags you bringing there, Rayona? Two or one?"

Father Tom stops by Aunt Ida's, but the pump has broken again and she's at the creek for water. I go inside for a change of clothes and my heavy coat, and the first thing I see is what's not there. The package addressed to Mom, the package that sat untouched on the table for weeks, has disappeared. And there's only one way it could have left the house. I go into my room, her old room. Maybe she's left me a note.

And she has been there. I know because her senior high school yearbook, the one with no Daytons, is gone from the bureau where I had left it. She's seen my things scattered about. She knows I'm still here. But she didn't wait. Part of me doesn't want to give up, and makes excuses. "She'll be back," it says. "She just didn't want to run into Aunt Ida. Now that she knows you're here . . ." But she knew it. Where else would I be? I have to face it: I'm not as important as some package she needs from Seattle. My presence won't bring her back.

I meet the frozen eyes of Jackie Kennedy, staring from the opposite wall.

I don't have much but I pack everything that's mine and stuff it into the same plastic garbage bag I came with. I don't take Mom's old clothes and Mom's old pictures. But I do throw in the *Little Big Man* and *Christine* tapes Mom dropped during her escape, in case they have a VCR at this Catholic jamboree. Afterward I can sell them for bus fare, or maybe I'll return them to Village Video if I go back to Seattle.

The door's open, letting flies and hornets into the house, and I don't shut it as I come out. I hurry to get away before Aunt Ida comes, before anybody else sees Father Tom and me leave together. He's busy looking at a map he has folded backward. He gives off a tight, clean smell that even the rolled-down windows of the cab can't camouflage. It reminds me of the atmosphere in a dry-cleaning store, stuffy and overheated. His fingernails are bitten short and square.

The truck springs are old and the road is still rutted from the winter runoff, so we bounce our way back to the main state highway. A month ago I was on this same route with no idea what was in store. I don't talk much, just answer Father Tom's questions with a word or two and keep my face in the wind, counting telephone poles along the track. Finally, after about an hour, he snags me.

"What about your parents, Rayona? Your mother and father."

I try to imagine what he's heard.

"My mom's dead," I say right off. I wait for him to contradict me, to tell me where she is, what he knows. But he lets it pass. His eyes don't even stray from the road. Either he's in the dark or he's smarter than I give him credit. My words ring in my ears and it scares me that I've said them. I've never actually thought of Mom dead, not with all the times in the hospital or all the nights she's stayed out so late that I thought of calling the police or listening to the CB emergency frequency on the radio. I think of her laid out like I've seen people at funeral homes. She'd be pretty. I know just which dress she'd want: the royal blue. I get so into my idea of her gone that I'm light-headed, lost. Father Tom has said something I haven't quite heard. He repeats it.

"And your father?"

I think of Dad standing at the foot of Mom's casket, wringing his hands. I zero in to see what he's worn for the occasion, but it's only his mailman's uniform, like always.

"My dad's a pilot. He flies jumbos, all over the world. That's why I can't live with him. But he's planning to get a place, in L.A."

I never told that story before. I don't know where it comes from—the uniform I guess. But it's not bad.

"A pilot?" Father Tom frowns and steers with one hand. "*Where* does he fly?"

"All over. Japan. South America. Switzerland," I say, naming the first places I think of.

Father Tom takes off his sunglasses and gives me the eye so he can judge whether or not I'm telling the truth. I return him one of Dad's looks, my lashes half down, my stare flat steady. He doesn't know what to think.

"I never knew that, Rayona. I didn't know your father was living."

"Oh, he's living, all right," I say. "He's doing great."

That shuts up Father Tom for a good thirty miles. He can't very well ask me if I'm sure. We're climbing into the mountains now and it's getting dark and cold. Finally I have to close the window. The radio's busted, so we just sit there in the dim light of the instrument panel, waiting to get where we're going.

Father Tom can hold it in no longer.

"Is there anything you need to talk to me about?" he asks.

I don't say a word. The cab seems too small a place, his words too loud. I can hear him breathing while he waits for me to answer.

"It's not easy being a young person alone at your age," Father Tom says, "when you're different."

"I'm not different."

"I mean, your dual heritage," he says. "Not that you

shouldn't be proud of it." This is the first time he's admitted to my skin color, to the shape of my nose, to the stiff fullness of my hair.

"And . . . you spend a lot of time by yourself. I don't imagine your aunt is the kind of person you can come to with the questions you must have at this time in your life."

"Are we going to drive all night or what?"

"Are you tired? Do you want to stop?" His voice leaps at me like some pent-up dog who's rushed to the end of its chain.

Stopping, being still, seems even worse than to keep going, so I say no, I'm fine.

"You must notice the changes in your body, the coming of your womanhood," Father Tom continues. Against the night sky his head looks like a comic-book drawing, round and bald on a thin neck. "Has anyone talked to you about your puberty?"

"My dad," I say quickly to cut him off. "My dad told me all about it. He talks about it all the time."

Father Tom is stalled for a minute. "I was very much like you when I was a boy. I didn't have a father either. He was killed when I was just a baby and my mother raised me all alone. I lived with her until I went into the seminary in high school."

"That's real bad," I say, "but I have a father." Then, "Why did you go there, to that seminary?"

"I always knew I had a vocation." It's as though he's talking to himself. "So did Mother. There were moments I tried to fight it, but in the end I always felt God's call, and had to respond."

"So you joined? Just like that?"

He remembers that I'm here. "I went in for you, Rayona. I am God's helper."

Off the reservation, alone in the truck, Father Tom is different than he is back home. Here there's nobody to laugh at him. Here I'm the strange one. His voice is smooth, slipping through the darkness. I don't object. I don't know what to say.

"God loves you, Rayona. You are His perfect creation."

Father Tom puts his hand on top of mine where it rests on

the car seat. Our hands lie there together for a minute, then he squeezes my fingers and lets go. I tilt my head against the glass of the window and close my eyes, trying to sleep, trying to keep his words, his moist skin, out of my head as the springs bounce up and down and my teeth bang together in the empty night.

"Wake up, cowgirl!" Father Tom shakes my knee.

The car has stopped at a gasoline station across from the Bearpaw Lake State Park main entrance. From the colorless sky, it looks to be about seven A.M., and Father Tom has on his Saints jacket. He's drinking Coke from a can.

"This is the end of the trail for today," he says. "We're close enough to Helena and I've had it. I need rest. The jamboree doesn't start till tomorrow anyway."

He looks half crazy, even paler than usual, and his eyes are all bloodshot from driving through the night. His lips are red too, and there's a black stubble over his cheeks.

"Do you have to use the powder room?" he asks. "It's right over there." He says this as if it's a joke of some kind, as if it's really daring that he can ask me such a personal question.

The rest room is around to the side of the gas station. To get there I walk between two wrecks propped on blocks and past an overflowing trash bucket. The stale piss smell cuts through the morning air, and the toilet is clogged with wadded paper.

There's no mirror to look into but I can feel that my hair has flattened where I slept on it. The cold water tap is broken and runs continuously, so I cup my palms to splash my face and rinse my mouth. I'm surprised at Father Tom's announcement that the Teens for Christ meeting doesn't begin for another day. He was in a rush to leave the reservation and now we have time to kill. What am I supposed to do while he rests?

Back at the car Father Tom has explained to the bored, sleepy service station man that he is a priest, that I'm really a full-blooded Indian, and that we're here at the lake on our way to some weekend R & R in Helena. I can feel the man looking at me, searching for the Indian, and tuning out Father Tom's long string of words. I wonder if he recognizes me from four weeks ago. He's the one who tried to sell Mom four new retread tires and she almost let him. I wonder if her credit card charge has bounced yet, if he'll ask me about it. But he doesn't know me. And he doesn't like Father Tom enough to ask questions.

We follow the signs and come to the campsites. The park has just opened this week and so it's almost deserted, but Father Tom has to look at five or six spots before he finds the one he wants. It's some distance from the others, behind a stand of pine, and bordered by a stream. Without talking much we unroll the sleeping bags, then collect some wood scraps for a fire. Father Tom has thought to bring hot dogs and buns for lunch, and has bought pop at the gas station to drink.

"We'll have a picnic first."

The ground is spongy and damp, and he can't seem to settle down. The bugs are bad—small, stinging insects that whine close to your ear and then veer away before they can be crushed. He swats at his face and tries without success to start the grill. He goes back to the car twice but doesn't find what he's looking for.

"Tell you what. I'm so tired I can't sleep, and it's such a pretty day. Let's get out of these clothes and into our swimming suits. We'll take a dip before lunch and then have a good long talk while we eat. Then I'll take my rest."

Five minutes down the trail, there's a pier that extends for ten feet into Bearpaw Lake. The blue water is held in a bowl formed by mountains that rise gray above the timberline on every side, and it reflects the sunlight in bright planes, each dazzling as the winds stirs waves on the surface. It reminds me of the sound in Seattle, of the foghorns you could hear throughout the city some early mornings. Reeds and soggy grasses weave a border at the edge of dry land, and the moving air is damp and fresh.

Father Tom wears red swimming trunks with a white stripe down the side. His body is hairy and soft and a chain with a miraculous medal circles his neck. It embarrasses me to look at him. My cutoffs, passed on to Aunt Ida for me from Foxy's mother, are too big and are cinched by an elastic stretch belt with a *Star Wars* magnetic buckle. My Holy Martyrs T-shirt has a hole under the right sleeve. In the sunlight my skin is the color of pine sap.

Sitting on the end of the dock, Father Tom sticks his white feet into the water and kicks up a spray.

"Oh, Ray," he says, laughing loudly, "it's too cold to swim. Look, I'm getting goose bumps. We'd better head back to camp."

Out about fifty feet is a wooden raft, painted yellow. Squinting past it, I can see someone canoeing on the far side of the lake.

"People are out there. I'm going in."

Without testing the water I run off the end of the dock and suddenly am surrounded by icy pinpricks, contracting my skin and blasting the tiredness. All sound is blotted out. Even the bubbles from my mouth make no noise as they rise from my lips. It's like entering a room in an empty building, like going into space. My feet sink into plants and soft mud that squeezes out between my toes as I push off. I never knew before that there are smells underwater, but there are—greens and browns. I feel totally clean.

"Rayona." Father Tom is calling at me. His voice whines. He's standing with his feet apart at the end of the pier and is upset. "You'll get a cramp. Come out."

I don't hear him.

"The water's fine," I shout and start kicking and paddling away from the shore. I'm no swimmer but I can stay afloat, and slowly I make progress. My eyes are at sea level, washed by the lake like a windshield in a rainstorm. By the time I get to the low yellow raft, I'm out of breath and chilled. I pull myself over the side and lie on the sun-warmed dry boards, panting and soaking up the heat. The silence is wide as the sky, brushed only with the sound of splashes striking the beams under the platform.

After a while I hear the crash of a dive, and watch as

Father Tom sidestrokes his way out into the lake. He points his long toes with every kick, and slants his mouth to gulp air. He isn't six feet from where I rest when the noise suddenly stops and he looks at me in surprise.

"Holy Jesus," he says. "Rayona. It's too cold. I've got a cramp." Without closing his eyes his head dips into the water as he curls into a cannonball.

"Rayona," he calls when his face rolls again.

I jump, the water a freezing slap against my dry skin. He has not sunk far and lies calm and pleading when I reach his side.

"Rayona," he says a third time as I tilt his chin to the air. With my other arm grasped across his chest, I tow him toward the worn, splintery raft. His breath rasps in my ear, and he begins to sink whenever I let him go. He makes no struggle, speaks no more words. I hold on to him as I throw one of my legs, then the other, onto the flat lumber, then reaching under his arms, I drag his shoulders and chest over the edge until he cannot fall back. The rough boards scrape his skin but he won't protect himself. Finally I grab the red trunks and haul the rest of him out of the lake. He lies on his side, staring toward the shore. He starts to gasp.

I'm winded myself, but I wonder about giving him artificial respiration. I remember something about pushing on the back and pulling on the arms. I crawl to him and try to roll him onto his stomach, but at last he resists and instead turns to face me.

"You have saved me," he says, and, reaching his arm around me, he pulls me close. Our chests crowd together and I feel the pound of his heart as the medal he wears digs into me. He's colder than the lake, so frozen that it burns where our skin touches.

"We are alone," he says, and moves to line the length of his body against me. We are the same size, from toe to head. He presses, presses, presses, and the air leaves my lungs. I want to sleep, to drown, to bore deep within the boards of the raft.

Father Tom has ducked his head, has closed his eyes tight. His hips jerk against me.

In my dream I move with him, pin him to me with my strong arms, search for his face with my mouth.

His body freezes. It turns to stone. I release my hold and we fall apart. I breathe.

"What are you doing?" Father Tom whispers.

"I don't know," I say. "I was afraid. I don't swim that good."

He sits, swivels away from me.

I roll onto my back. It's still the same day and the sky is blue.

"I'd say you swim pretty well," he says.

The skin on his stomach is red and chafed from the boards. He hugs his knees to his chest. He shakes his head, as if he has water in his ears. He's busy thinking.

"Rayona, we have experienced an occasion of sin." He doesn't look at me as he speaks. "What would your parents think? I could be your father. I have taken vows."

I hear the blame in his voice and I tense to defend myself. It occurs to me to say my parents wouldn't be surprised, that nothing happened, that he was the one that started it.

"I made up all that about him being a pilot. He's a mailman."

Father Tom makes a sound like a crow. I can't tell if he is laughing or crying or clearing his throat of the last drops of swallowed lake.

"We must go back to the reservation," he says finally. "We should never have come."

"What about the jamboree?" I ask Father Tom, but he slides off the raft and into the water. This time he has no trouble swimming. In fact, he is already half dressed, pulling his black pants over his wet swimming suit, by the time I reach the pier. What little hair he has, above his ears and on the back of his head, stands out like some sort of halo from where the towel has rubbed it.

"Rayona," he says, "I should never have gone in when I was so tired. I had no rest. You understand that? When we get back, we should forget this trip ever happened. It was a bad idea, something I should have foreseen. You need friends your own age. Some people might misunderstand if they see us together all the time."

He's cracking his knuckles again. The sound they make is as loud and hollow as a woodpecker hammering against a dead tree.

"I'm not going back. I'm going to Seattle."

"Oh yes, Seattle. I'm sure you have somewhere to live in the city?"

"There are lots of places. I could look up my dad."

"That might be just the thing for you to do." He acts as if this is funny. He nods his head, making the halo wave like October grass in the wind.

I turn away from him and pull my too-big pants over my too-big wet cutoffs. I'm afraid of him, the way he's behaving.

"Rayona? Are you serious?"

"Yes," I say, trying to keep my voice tough.

"Do you have any money?"

I don't.

"Well, if you're truly set on going, maybe I can lend you some cash for the ticket and for cab fare from the train. To tide you over."

I don't answer him.

"Are you positive that this is what you want?"

He's getting interested in the idea of my departure. He skips flat rocks on the lake while I finish dressing.

"You know," Father Tom says, "it doesn't really make a lot of sense for you to come all the way back to the reservation with me if you're going to Seattle. It's the wrong direction. I noticed there's a depot right at the park entrance."

There's no stopping him now.

"A ticket would be cheaper from here. I can put you on the train and with what you save you can take your dad out to dinner. I can retrieve anything you need from your aunt's and send it on to you."

Yesterday he didn't believe in this Dad. Now he's buying him a meal.

"I should tell Aunt Ida." I should tell Mom too, I think. But he's ready for that.

"I'll make a special trip there the minute I return and explain the whole thing to her. Don't worry. I'll make sure she's all right."

I try to imagine him talking to Aunt Ida. I feel bad that she should find out from him, but I can't admit it. Whatever she thinks about my leaving, he'll never know.

I can't think of another reason that will get me back, so I walk the trail to the campsite with my head buzzing. We collect our things and load them in the truck without exchanging another word.

In the next town, Father Tom calls the Great Northern ticket office to find out about the train. They report it comes through at 10:17 tonight. Father Tom buys me a hamburger and a *Sports Illustrated* to read, and keeps going on about how interesting Seattle must be—a lot like Milwaukee, which is one of his favorite places—and what a bright young lady like me can do there.

"And you won't feel so alone, so out of place," he says, smiling that stupid grin of his. "There'll be others in a community of that size who share your dual heritage."

The hours of that endless afternoon pass, and at last we sit in the cab of the truck, waiting by the crossing for the engine's beam to slice into the night. When it does, Father Tom is supposed to blink the truck headlamps three times and the train will stop to let me board. We have fallen quiet, with nothing more to say to each other.

I feel the rumble from the earth before I see the light. First the tires, then the worn springs of the truck begin to quiver and shake. Father Tom blinks his brights once, twice, three times and the sound starts to cut down. The night beyond the tracks' illumination is very dark.

"Rayona, I want you to have this."

He pulls something over his head. I think it's the holy medal that cut into my chest at the lake and I reach to take it, but it's only the beaded medallion he wears on the reservation, big and gaudy. Tourist bait.

"Wear this. Then people will know you're an Indian." He gets out of the cab at the same time I do, as the train continues to slow, and stuffs some dollar bills into my jeans pocket. Through the cloth I feel his fingers.

"Don't worry about repayment. I know we'll meet again."

He grabs me to him, quick and hard, then pushes me away just as fast.

"I'm going to leave you now, Rayona. I'm bad at good-byes. You'll be in my prayers."

He climbs into the truck and backs it to the black tree line before hitting the lights. Then he revs the engine and turns onto the highway, heading east.

He doesn't look at me, so he doesn't see me wave the train on, or hear the engineer yell a fast-moving curse at goddamn Indians playing tricks. He doesn't see me toss his medallion onto the track to be ground into plastic dust.

When the earth has stopped trembling, when the sounds of wind and frogs and crickets have returned, I stand alone in the cold night. Clouds block the sky and all directions are the same. I can smell the lake. I've never felt further from sleep.

I search and cue memories of Dad that would allow me to believe he'd be glad if I appeared out of the blue, but there aren't enough. I try recalling what Mom says when she's sentimental and lonesome: how he was the best one, the only one, because he left her me. How I'm her sterling silver lining, the one who'll never leave her like he did.

Like she did me.

I hunch into a pocket of gravel between two ties and lean back against the track, still warm from the train's passing. I settle in, roll my head so I can see through the tree limbs as the clouds slide across the sky. I'm in a tight spot but it could be worse. I have the priest's money and the whole night to think before morning comes. I'm happy without reason.

5

I wake up lost. My back is stiff from sitting through a second night in a row and sore from where the railroad tie has pressed. When I dozed I put my hands under my hips to keep them warm, and now the palms are impressed with the patterns of gravel. They look like sandpaper, but then it comes to me that they remind me of the relief map of North America in my social studies book at Holy Martyrs. I have no memory of actually sleeping, but hours have passed and it's light. My thoughts are gone, humming along the track that supported my head.

I stand, brush off my jeans, and lift the plastic bag with my extra clothes. There's an edge like frost, but it's not that cold. I could be alone in the world. I could be some ancestor of mine, alive five hundred years ago.

I walk out of the weeds to the road with no plan. Even the highway is deserted. A wind moves the telephone wires above my head and on every side of this narrow valley mountains sweep into dawn mists. Nothing will be open. I walk across to the entrance of Bearpaw Lake State Park, and, to avoid the dew, lean against the metal chain that blocks the driveway. My feet are planted but the chain moves and creaks. The noise is loud in all that silence and it's as though I set off a bell that starts everything going: birds, truck traffic, even my own breath puffing in and out. In front of me is a large red sign that says ATTENTION HIKERS! IF LOST, STAY WHERE YOU ARE. DON'T PANIC.

YOU WILL BE FOUND. I take the advice. I stay, I don't, and, before long, I am.

The first person I see is the man from the gas station, the guy who just yesterday tried to puzzle out the Indian in my face. He's skinny and wears his hair, brown with some gray, in a long ponytail.

Someone has let him out of a car up the road, and he walks in my direction toward the dark red-and-white Conoco sign. He looks spaced out, but I can't tell if that's him or the time of day. When he sees me, he has no reaction. You'd think that every morning at five-thirty he runs into a strange, cold, hungry girl carrying nothing but a plastic garbage bag full of earthly possessions and a rolled-up *Sports Illustrated* stuck in her pocket. He nods at me as he passes, and I follow behind him, casually, as if I happen to be going the same way.

"So where's your Father Joe?" The man's brain is not as fried as I thought. His beaded, peyote-stitched keyring is hooked to a loop of his jeans, and he has to twist sideways to the door and shuffle the fat bundle of keys that dangle from the end to reach the lock.

"He went to heaven," I say.

He peers at me cockeyed, then starts fighting a smile on the right side of his mouth, finally loses it, and snorts. He rises on tiptoe, and eases the key out. The door springs open, as if the empty glass room within is filled to exploding.

"I've got to fix that hinge," he says.

I follow him into the oil-smelling, dead-aired office and sit on a chrome-and-vinyl chair when he points to it. I squeeze my sack between the metal legs.

"Did you hear the one about the priest, the rabbi, and the Hindu?" he asks, but doesn't wait for me to say yes. "They was all walking out in the woods at night and needed a place to sleep. So they go to this farm? And the farmer says, 'I only got room for two in the house and the other will have to sleep in the barn?'"

Selecting another key he opens the cash register, punches

No Sale, and checks the money drawer, even raising it to inspect underneath. It's empty.

"So the Hindu says, 'Hey, that's cool. You fellows go inside and I'll be perfectly comfortable out here in the barn.' They all say good night and are ready to hit the sack when a knock comes to the door. It's the Hindu." The man, who has SKY stitched in red above the pocket of his gray shirt, plugs in a beat-up hotplate and runs water in a dented kettle.

"'I can't sleep there,' the guy says. 'There's a cow in that barn and we ain't supposed to sleep next to them. It's against our ways.'"

Sky makes his eyes round to show that the oddness of beliefs is a mystery to him. I nod that he should go on. Satisfied I'm paying attention, he carefully licks his little finger and touches it to the metal ring, which has turned from hard gray to rust. There is a sizzle and he snaps the finger to his mouth and sucks. With the other hand he sets the kettle on to boil and turns back to face me.

"'Oh, hey,' says the rabbi, 'that's no problem. I'll be only too glad to trade you my place,' and out goes the Jew. So . . . they was all settling down"—he pauses to remove a pile of magazines and credit card slips from the chair on the other side of the cash register—"when again, a tap-tap-tap at the door. And it's the rabbi!"

Sky takes down two cups and measures a level teaspoon of instant Maxwell House into each one. He gestures with his eyes toward the creamer and sugar packets, stored in an empty tissue box on the shelf above the desk, but I shake my head no. He uses three of both, mixing the white powders with the instant brown coffee in the bottom of his cup until they are sifted together. He rests his hand on the kettle's handle and waits for the whistle.

"'I hate to say this,' says the rabbi, 'but there's a pig too, and *we* ain't supposed to lie down with them.' So then it's the priest's turn and he jumps in and says, 'You know I was wanting to be in the fresh air all along. You come here, Rabbi, and I'll head for the barn and sleep like a baby.'" Somehow Sky has made his body different when each of the people in his story has spoken. He's tall and thin for the Hindu, short for the Jew, and fat for the priest.

The water boils, rattling the lid of the kettle. Sky pours it into the mugs and stirs each one, testing to make sure that everything is dissolved. He is in no hurry. Finally he hands me the black, and drops heavily into the cleared chair, hanging one leg over its busted armrest. The sole of his scuffed boot needs stitching. He blows on his coffee, takes a loud sip, then, rinsing it from one unshaven cheek to the other before swallowing, he leans forward and around the cash register. His pupils are the size of tiny buckshot.

"They was almost asleep at last," he whispers, "when comes another knock." Sky sits stone still, letting the moment build. Then he shouts: "It was the *cow* and the *pig*!"

I have heard the joke, of course, so I only kind of twitch my mouth at the punch line. This is not enough.

"The *cow* and the *pig*," Sky repeats, planting both feet back on the ground. "Get it? They don't want to sleep with a priest."

"I don't blame them," I say, and take a drink of my coffee. The taste of it makes me look closer at the cup, to see if it's clean.

Sky pauses, gives a hoot, stops himself to make sure he's understood my meaning, decides he has, then hoots again. He tips his head like a chicken and studies me closely over the rim of his cup, pretending to take little sips while he gets an eyeful. He can't decide if I'm serious. Another question comes to him. It wants to escape but he doesn't know how to ask.

I read his mind. "There's Indian on my mother's side," I say. "Not my father's."

"Ha! I knew it." Sky slugs down the last of his coffee and shakes the cup above his mouth for final drops.

I get up to check the contents of a vending machine that leans at an angle against the wall. I have some change in my pocket.

"You're one of those fresh air funds, ain't you?" asks Sky as he counts dollar bills from his wallet into the cash register. "Where you from?"

If I answer the reservation he'll ask when I'm going back, and that's a question I'm not ready for.

"Seattle." I drop a quarter and a dime into the slot and pull one of the pale green knobs. An orange package of Reese's Peanut Butter Cups falls with a dull thud into the tray.

"Never been to there myself," says Sky. "I did a stint up in Regina a while back, and that was city enough for me."

"You Canadian?" I ask. I can tell he likes to answer questions about himself.

"Me?" he says, amazed, and points with his thumb to his chest. "No. No way! Things just got a little hot around here so I went north to the future. That's what they say up there: north to the future."

It's a thought. I might as well travel north as anywhere.

"What was it like?" The coffee is cold but it does wash the peanut butter from the roof of my mouth.

"Far out," he says. "Good people. They took me in. Found me a place to stay, a factory job. I had me a cool lady. A Ukie. Blond hair. Looked as straight as they come but she could be crazy."

"They took care of you? Just like that?" Saskatchewan sounds better and better. "Why'd you leave?"

"The war was over. You know, the amnesty. My old man left me this station, even though he never did speak to me after I split. But he didn't change his will like he told everybody either, so when he kicked off I came back. The scene had changed up there anyway."

I had guessed wrong about Sky. I had pegged him as a Vietnam vet. He had the burnt-out look of half the guys that hung around the VA in Seattle, men full of stories about places with funny names they'd roll off their tongues as if you knew where they were. Every so often one of them would come home with Mom. She'd feed them supper and listen to their ailments, out of sympathy she said. If she liked them, she usually asked if they had met her brother before he was killed. She talked about him so much I almost believed I knew him myself.

I was a baby when they shipped Lee's body back, but I heard Mom tell the story a hundred times—how she took me on a bus to Sea-Tac to meet the transport plane. The army was scheduled to bury him at Fort Lewis because Aunt Ida hadn't answered the letter they mailed her, but Mom insisted that they send him on out to the reservation. It was the middle of the worst winter she ever saw, but she drove to Montana alone, with only me for company, and got there for the wake. I have a kind of a memory about that time, but I don't know whether it's real or just the way I colored in Mom's story. It's a scene like a powwow, all singing and drumming, with people spinning around me, crying. I'm curious about it, since it's the thought that comes to me when I stretch my mind back as far as it will go, but I never had the nerve to ask Mom. Whenever she thinks about Lee, she gets weepy.

"My uncle died in 'Nam," I tell Sky.

He unlocks the vending machine, removes the change, and deposits it into the compartments of the cash drawer. He examines the date of each coin before dropping it into its slot, then speaks under his breath.

"Each one had to make their own decision."

If Mom gets to drinking and talks about Lee she eventually says she wished he had gone to Canada so he'd be alive today. I tell Sky that, and he looks almost grateful.

"You're a runaway too, ain't you?" he says, pushing the drawer shut. "Didn't they treat you good at that camp?"

I think fast.

"They were all right, but they tried to convert me. That's what I was doing with that priest. They thought he could make me see the light."

"It's always the way." He gets out papers and tobacco and starts to roll a tight cigarette. "So you're an outlaw, a regular Bonnie and Clyde."

"You going to turn me in?"

"Hell no. What do you take me for?"

I don't answer. Not being turned in leaves me nowhere to go.

Sky twists the ends of his smoke, lights up, and inhales. "So you going back to your folks now?"

"I can't," I say. "They took off on vacation till the end of August. My dad's a pilot on jumbos."

"No lie? So that leaves you up shit creek without a paddle, don't it?"

I hold my hands up to show I have no paddles. Streaming through the plate glass that fronts the office, the sun is hot and getting higher in the white overcast clouds.

Sky examines the room as if searching for customers or activity of any kind.

"I guess I don't need any help," he decides. As he talks he keeps sharpening to a point the ash at the end of his cigarette, turning it first one way, then the other, in the base of the tin Coors tray. When it burns down, he rummages in the drawer of the table until he finds a roach clip, and snaps it on the tip. He takes one last, long drag.

"Those things will kill you," I say automatically, and then am embarrassed. It's what I tell Mom, but she laughs it off and tells me to M.Y.O.B. She says that's the least of her problems.

"You're as bad as my wife. She smokes Merits and keeps after me to use a filter. But shit, this ain't the worse thing I ever smoked."

I'm relieved that he's taken no offense, but I don't know where to go from here. I put my hands on the armrests and push from the chair. I have doubled the wrapper from the Reese's into tiny tight points, one over the other. I hoop it into the full trash can, and move toward the door.

"Well, take it easy."

"Not so fast. Where's the fire? Just hang on a minute and let me think."

He thinks.

"You know," he says finally, "I'll call Evelyn. That's my wife that you remind me of. She's a cook over to the park. Maybe they're still hiring."

I stand in the doorway, watching trucks tool the highway, while he takes a dime from the cash register, puts it in the pay phone on the wall, and dials five numbers.

"Evelyn around?" he asks into the receiver, then waits, drumming his fingers on the wall. "Hon? How're you doing? . . . Nothing. . . . Well, it's just I've got a girl from Seattle here, is looking for work. Anything over there?"

While he listens he looks at me, rocking his head back and forth and moving his lips, mimicking somebody talking fast and furious.

"You got it all wrong," he says, staring hard at the telephone dial. "This here's a kid. The Catholics is after her and her folks have taken off for parts unknown. She was waiting at the station when you dropped me off."

More imitating. His wife has a lot to say.

"I *don't* even know her name. It's . . ." he looks at me with his eyebrows raised.

"Rayona," I say. "Rayona Taylor."

He repeats my name, imitating the way I said it, then asks me how old I am.

"Eighteen."

He gives me a doubtful glance, but doesn't argue.

"She says eighteen." He listens, and begins to nod in agreement. "Will do. Will do. She'll be over."

He replaces the phone and pauses for a minute, his hand still on the receiver, then he turns to me and winks. "You're in luck. All I had to say was the Catholics. Go to the door around back of the lodge and ask for Evelyn. She thinks she can set you up with something."

"Hey, thanks," I say.

He brushes it off. "Sky's the name," he says, pointing to the stitched writing on his shirt, and then into the air.

"Sky," I repeat.

"For Big Sky, like on the Montana license plates. That's what they called me in Saskatchewan."

He holds out his hand and we lock thumbs in the same kind of shake lots of Mom's boyfriends use.

"I can't let you leave without asking how you got a name like Rayona."

I've heard this question so many times. "My Mom couldn't think of a name when I was born since she had planned on me being a boy. When they brought me to her in the hospital, she looked around for an idea and the first thing she saw was a tag on her nightgown. Rayon. She thought that was pretty, so—Rayona."

"That's real unusual." Sky is impressed with Mom. He reaches into the cash drawer again and picks out some change. I think he's going to give it to me, and I'm ready to refuse, but instead he drops it into the vending machine and starts to shop for what he wants. He's still lost in concentration when I pull out my clothes bag, open the screen door, and leave.

The sun is full now, building toward a hot afternoon. I cross the black asphalt and pass the blue-and-white gas pumps. The skin of my long arms is brown and smooth, too dark not to notice. In the unreflected light, every color stands alone.

U.S. 2 is the main east-west highway, and it gets its share of traffic. You can hear the big semis before you see their dust. I stand between my most likely destinations, and it enters my mind to straddle the middle stripe, stick out my thumb, and go in the direction of the first ride that takes me. But when a path across clears, I make a beeline to the other side and head for the park entrance. The chain is gone from the road, and there's nothing to stop me.

I find the screen door to the park kitchen with no trouble. A woman stands against the counter with her back to me. Her white hair is cropped short and ends far enough above her collar to show an inch of creased brown neck. She's dressed in wide blue jeans and a green plaid wool shirt. Her shoulders are almost as broad as her hips, and on her feet she wears overrun work boots. When she turns from the kneading board at my knock, the first thing I see are her eyes, and they are bright and suspicious. She's younger than she looks, but still older than Sky.

"He didn't mention you was Black," she says.

It comes to me that Sky might not have noticed, but I just shrug and enter the room so she can have a closer look.

"What are you doing in Montana?"

I repeat my story, which is becoming familiar. I can almost feel the shiver of Dad's big transport landing and taking off. I think how surprised he'd be to find I've put him in the cockpit.

"And you're supposed to be eighteen," she says, sizing me up. "When donkeys fly!"

"I'm young for my age," I tell her, and arch to my full height. "I can work hard as anybody."

"Well, there ain't much left," she says. "Just some of those maintenance shifts. Goddamn college kids got everything. Some of them make more than me, more than the cook. Ain't that a kick?"

I return her frown. I'm on her side, whatever she says.

"Where are you fixing to live?" she asks. "You got a work permit? You got references?" She stands in front of me, her hands on her hips, her voice harsh from smoking. She wears a flour-stained dishtowel tucked like an apron into the waistband of her pants. She can see right through me.

"Forget it." I turn to go. There is too much I don't have.

"Now don't get your bowels in an uproar." Evenly wipes a hand through her hair, trailing little bits of dough. "You ain't the first one ever been down on her luck. You eat breakfast?"

"I had something at the gas station. Sky made some coffee."

"'Sky,'" she snorts. "You better pray coffee was all it was. Dump that garbage bag and go sit." She gestures to the big board where she's been pounding bread dough. Off to the side some pans are covered and others are oiled and dusted.

"Eighteen," she mutters. "Well, you're big enough to pass it with some, I guess." She reaches into a huge refrigerator for a grapefruit, which she halves with a butcher knife, then puts in a bowl. From the cabinet over the counter she removes an opened bottle of vin rosé.

"This is good for what ails you," she says, and splashes a

dose over the top. "Dig in while I fry some eggs. I could use a few myself."

The wine makes the grapefruit sweet and juicy. I put the seeds around the lip of the bowl.

"Whereabouts in Seattle?"

"The North End," I say.

"Jobs here don't pay beans."

"I don't need much. Just enough to last me till I go home in September when my folks get back from vacation. But I need someplace to sleep."

"They must be having a grand old time." She looks me up and down and sets a plate with half a dozen fried eggs before me. I can't read the expression on her face, so I study my breakfast. The eggs have spread to the shape of the cast-iron skillet and have been flipped in a perfect circle. The pale, hard-cooked yolks in the shiny white ring remind me of something. My roll of dice has come up a boxcar.

"You eat first," Evelyn says. "I like mine over easy." She turns back to the stove, breaks more eggs into sizzling lard, and reaches a decision. "You can bunk with us. There's room enough. I should ask Norman, but he don't care. I'll charge you a fair price."

Things are moving fast and beyond my control. But there is no reason to say no.

"Who's Norman?" I ask her.

"Sky to you," she says and sits down next to me. I'm hungry and go after my eggs, but I can't help watching Evelyn. First she uses her fork to trim all the white from around the yolks on her plate, then cuts the white into triangles and eats them, one at a time. Finally all that's left are six round yellow domes, shimmering like half-full water balloons. Carefully she slides the prongs of her fork beneath the first one and lifts it, then pops it into her mouth and swallows without chewing. In Seattle I've seen people eat oysters that way. She knows I've been looking.

"I hate yolks, but they're healthy." She refills my coffee cup and goes back to check her bread pans. Some of the dough has risen. She makes a fist and punches it, and then, like she's folding sheets, she flaps dishtowels back over the tops.

"When you're done I'll put you together with Mr. McCutcheon. He's the one that hires the maintenance. If he says okay, you're in."

I'm in. For my new career I am provided a long pole with a nail on the end, a full box of two-ply green Hefty lawn and leaf bags, and Section Seven of Bearpaw Lake campground and lakefront to patrol. Mr. McCutcheon is an overweight man with bad teeth and a belt with STANLEY spelled out in metal studs around the back. He takes his job as supervisor seriously, and I sit before his desk in the equipment cabin as he reads three pages about the laws of litter from the *Official Park and Campground Handbook and By-Rules.* The State of Montana does not look kindly on trash unless it is collected and stowed in designated closed containers.

As a park employee it is my duty to uphold that position, as well as the Constitutions of Montana and the United States, and to be firm but polite in confronting any tourist who thinks otherwise. I am not to interfere with normal recreational activities, but when the time comes to pack the Winnebago, the governor and I have every right to expect a clean site for the next camper.

"You must keep your equipment in good working order, Rayona," says Mr. McCutcheon. "It is your foremost responsibility."

He sights down the broom handle with the nail on the end, inspects it from top to bottom to make sure that it's A-OK upon delivery.

"Have you used one of these devices previously?" he wants to know when he hands it back.

I admit that I haven't.

"It's a handy thing to have at a picnic," Mr. McCutcheon observes, balancing the pole in his hand. "You can never predict when you will encounter rubbish, and it is much more sanitary to spear it"—he makes a jabbing motion to demonstrate—

"than to soil your hands." I notice his fingernails are perfectly clean. It has been a long time since he touched rubbish directly.

He passes me the pole and I treat it with respect as Mr. McCutcheon watches my every move. I know how he wants me to act. I imagine I'm assisting at Father Tom's Mass, and it's my turn to hold the paten under the chins of the faithful while he delivers Holy Communion.

"Mrs. Dial tells me that you are eighteen years of age." He folds a park trail map, with my patrol area marked in a red circle, back into its original shape. His fingers automatically pinch and smooth the creases and when he's done you'd never know it had been used.

"Yes, sir!" You can sense when people like to be called "sir" or "ma'am," and my words make him stop in his tracks and appreciate my manners. I almost hear Mom saying she told me so.

"You're going to do all right, Rayona," he says. "You know, we've never had anyone of your race to work here before, and we've never had a young lady employed in park maintenance. You are something of a ground breaker, and I expect you to do us proud."

"Yes, *sir*!" There's never too much of a good thing. He can no more prevent himself from smiling than he can fly, but he inflates one smooth-shaven cheek to disguise his pleasure.

"We must have a uniform that will fit you. You're very . . . like a fashion model. But slim. What size do you take? Large? Medium? Certainly not Small!"

It's his way of observing that I'm tall and skinny. I have no idea of my size. In the past few months I've grown so much that even the clean underwear that's twisted in a knot at the bottom of my plastic bag is too small.

Mr. McCutcheon finds a dark green park outfit for me and hands it over in a perfectly square bundle. The material makes me think of Dad's mailman suit, damp as he stood in Mom's hospital room and refused the Volaré.

I go to the Ladies', which has a cartoon picture of an

Indian squaw on the door, and change my clothes. The mirror above the sink is missing, so there's nothing I can do about my hair. I stash in my sack the clothes I have been wearing, and come back outside. The door to the Men's, decorated with a chief in a warbonnet, stands wide open. It's larger, a kind of locker room with a big mirror, and unoccupied—so I duck in to see myself.

As it turns out, I'm too tall and too small around the waist for Medium, but it's probably the closest fit. Topped off with a Smokey the Bear hat, I'm a cross between Dad and a scarecrow.

I jump away from the glass when I hear people come through the door. There are three guys, all older than me, all white, all friends with each other. I act as though it's the most natural thing in the world for me to be in the Men's room, as though I'm in a hurry to get some important place where I am expected, and I'm behind schedule. In the city there's an expression I assume that informs people to leave me alone, and I put on that face. But they don't get it.

"You got to be Ramona, the one they just hired," says a deep voice. When I check to see who's talking there is no doubt in my mind that he's a size Large, maybe even Extra Large.

"*Ray*, yeah," I mumble. How do I get out of here? They block the door, and this is the last place I want to meet boys.

"My name's Andy, and this is Dave, and this is John," the guy says, nodding at two other Larges. They give me the high sign and start fiddling with the combinations on their lockers.

"Excuse me," I say and head for the hall. They follow me.

"What cabin are you in?" John asks.

"I'm in a private home."

They all look at each other funny.

"Where do you go to school?" Andy wants to know.

"Nowhere. I'm just working here for a couple months." If I knew where I was supposed to be next, I'd go this minute.

"No, I mean which college?"

"I'm still in high school."

Their interest in me takes a fast nosedive.

"Well, if you don't know anything, just ask," says Andy. "The job's a bitch, but this isn't a bad place to hang out. Where'd they give you?"

I unfold my map and point to the red Magic Marker circle.

"Shit." Andy snatches it from my hand and turns to his friend. "They gave her Seven."

"Fuck," says John.

"So ends the mystery of why they hired a girl," says Dave.

"Is that bad?" I ask. "Seven?"

"She wants to know if it's bad." Andy is like somebody on TV, with thin lips, real wavy brown hair, and eyebrows that almost meet above his nose. He probably lifts weights or maybe plays football.

"Ooooeee," whistles John. He reminds me of the chubby guy on "Happy Days." Except mean.

"Yeah, it's a real combat assignment." Dave's the type you see on "It's Academic," who brags he belongs to the Science Club and wants to go to the U of W to become a veterinarian. He's even skinnier than I am.

"It's *only* the Panty Zone," groans Andy.

"Surf City," says John.

"The girls' water safety instructors' cabin," explains Dave. "You can smell the suntan lotion from here. It travels on the air like pheromones. A mating call."

"Anytime you want to trade off," says Andy. "If you need to take a break..."

"Call on me," interrupts John. "I can see it now: '*John, will you rub some suntan lotion on my back? A little lower. Oh, that's soooo good.*'"

"Dream on," says Dave. "That's as close as you'll come."

"DeMarco!" John calls out, screwing his eyes shut and grabbing at Andy's arm. "It's not fair! She is so fucking hot!"

"I'm late." I grab my pole and my trash bags, the ones for campers' litter and the one with all my clothes, and head for the door. I don't know where I'm going but it's better than where I am. As I pass Dave he surprises me by patting me on the back.

"Welcome to Bearpaw Lake," he says. "The state park that time forgot."

Usually it's a toss-up, which bothers me more, being the center of attention or being ignored, but this time I don't have to wonder because I'm both. I think how I look in the green uniform: the belt pulled tight, making gathers in the waist of the pants, my ankles and wrists sticking out, the stupid hat. Dave is all right, but Andy and John treat me as if I haven't got ears, as if I'm not a girl. I'm not their type. If it was Mom here instead of me, even Mom as she is now, a lot older than they are, it would be a different story. She'd have the two of them eating out of her shoe. I've watched her in action, but I could never get away with it. And, I console myself, being cute hasn't made her all that happy.

That first afternoon I learn all there is to know about my job. Since there are almost no tourists, Bearpaw Lake State Park has precious little trash to pick up. By four o'clock I have my zone clear, and my guess is that most of what I found has been there since last fall. The M&M's wrappers are soft and tissuey, as if they've spent months under snow and dried out fluffy in the chinooks. The two potato chip bags I spear have puddles of water inside, and the three flashlight batteries are cracked and pushed in.

Just when I'm about to quit and see what time Evelyn is leaving, I make my find of the day. Square in my path, snared by the root of a cedar pine, is a fresh piece of torn white paper. I stab it with my nail pole and notice that there's writing on one side. I unhook it carefully, like a fish that is too small and should be thrown back to live longer. Squatting on the ground I examine it more closely.

It's the bottom half of a letter written with bright green ink:

mowing the lawn right now. It finally stopped raining and the grass was overdue. I just want you to know how much we miss you already, but we both hope you have a great

time out there. It will be an adventure, and Dad and I will
be anxious to hear all about it. Rascal is scratching on the
door to get in, so I'm going to cut this short, but don't
forget to write. We love you.

Mother & Pops

I go over that letter I don't know how many times. It's
disturbing in a way I can't put my finger on. Dad sent me a
postcard one time. It had a picture of a place called the
Aspiring Motel on one side, and on the other he had written
"This is where I'm staying in Victoria. Don't do anything I
wouldn't do." It took me a day before I figured out who sent it.

I keep staring at the letter, and now it's Mom reading in
my head, like in the movies or on TV when the voice of the
person who wrote something comes out of nowhere so the
audience will know what it says and who it's from. I don't know
why I think of Mom—I never got a letter from her unless you
count when she left me notes taped to the refrigerator, and
then they were just short messages like "Sam came to town and
wanted to party! Don't wait up!" or "If you need me I'm at
Charlene's!"

This scrap of paper in my hand makes me feel poor in a
way like I just heard of rich. Jealous. What kind of a person
would throw it away? I tell myself that's a load of crap and
reach for the Hefty that lies open at my side. But I can't drop
that letter in to mix with the soggy plastic bags and year-old
candy wrappers.

I reach for the other bag I've been dragging around, the
one with my clothes, and fish out my hand-tooled wallet. I
smooth and fold the letter, and tuck it next to Father Tom's
money. Then I slip the wallet inside the back pocket of my
uniform and button the flap.

Nobody's around. The clearing where I stand is the only
place where the sky can reach the ground, and is as still as if
every surrounding tree and bush and blade of tall grass swallows
noise like the thick carpet of a funeral home. Without thinking
about it, I balance my pole way back and throw it like a javelin

toward the parking lot. It goes too high and falls short, sliding in the dirt and scaring up dust.

But the words of that letter won't leave my mind. They make me miss rain. When I awoke in our Seattle apartments, half the time I'd hear drops hammering against the window glass and feel warm and dry. Some days a shower would catch me on the way home from school, and I'd duck into a storefront and wait it out with a bunch of other people who like me had left home without an umbrella. For a few minutes we'd bunch together, washed by the cool wet breeze, squeezing out of the spray. It seems as though in Seattle it was always raining or about to rain or just had rained.

Mornings that she went to work, Mom carried a rainhat case in her purse. Inside was an accordioned plastic with two tie strings. She said she didn't spend half her life in rollers just to have her hair straighten out in some sudden storm. But when we were coming back from the hospital last fall, she couldn't find the hat, and before we could get under cover, her waves and curls hung around her face in long, black lines. Even the dark mascara she wore on her eyelids ran in streaks. "Never mind," she said to me that day. "It's too late anyway." Then she just stood in the open and held tight on to my hand, letting the water run off us in waterfalls and streams, filling our shoes and spilling off the sidewalk into the street.

6

"Wipe your feet," Evelyn tells me. "Don't leave tracks, though God knows it ain't nothing fancy."

It isn't, but when she switches on the light in her trailer and I step inside, it seems somehow familiar. In front of the big woodgrain TV is a lopsided green plaid couch, scarred with cigarette burns and decorated with a bed pillow in a yellow case. Above it hangs an eight-year-old 1978 calendar printed with "Sky's Park Service, Last Complete Lube Before the Rockies" and showing Sky, younger and with his hair cut, but still looking stoned, holding a wrench to the camera. Against the side wall, copies of *Grit*, *The National Enquirer*, and *The Star* are tossed in a pile on a table littered with half-filled blue enamel coffee mugs, an overflowing ashtray, and an opened bottle of Heinz ketchup. A patch-square afghan in browns and pinks is spread over the back of a red recliner.

Evelyn had stopped for Sky at the station and to do some shopping at the Jiffy Mart on the way home. I carry a grocery bag with six macaroni-and-cheese TV dinners, two for each of us. "I cook all day," Evelyn says when I observe what she bought. "I let somebody else do it at night." Now she unpacks a sixer of Rainier and a bag with two of her park-kitchen loaves. Sky follows us inside and shoots an Alabama tape into the cassette player on top of the TV.

"The set's busted," he explains, adjusting the volume of the music and then snagging a cold can of Evelyn's beer from the table. "It ain't worth the price of repair. We keep it for the cabinet." He still wears the Born To Rock T-shirt he had on underneath his uniform this morning.

"Make yourself to home," Evelyn tells me. "You'll be on that couch." She goes behind the counter, turns on the stove, tears open the boxes that hold our dinners, and puts the aluminum trays inside the oven. "I don't believe in preheat," she says, and leaves the room.

I put my bag of clothes next to the couch and sit. The cushion is soft and the upholstery bristles through my T-shirt against my back.

"You and Evelyn must of hit it off pretty good," Sky says. "And she don't take to everybody."

I shrug, embarrassed at his compliment. "I'm paying my way."

"There ain't no such thing as a free lunch," he agrees, then laughs and coughs and tries to catch his breath.

"That you hacking, darling?" Evelyn reenters wearing a sleeveless housecoat and fluffy slippers that remind me of Mom's in Seattle until I stop myself. Her arms are large and full. She pops a beer for herself and puts the rest into the refrigerator.

"No, it's the dog catcher," Sky says.

"More like the hound dog." Evelyn settles in the recliner with a sigh and flips up the footrest. She pushes the back of her chair to its full extension and lies almost flat, suspended in the room like the lady in a magic act. We're all silent, listening to the tape: "I once thought of love as a prison/A place I didn't want to be/So long ago I made a decision/To be footloose and fancy free."

There's a kind of peace in the room. I think of the trailer, how it must look from outer space. A lighted box in the dark night, with Alabama coming through the rolled-open windows. The music somehow makes things more quiet. I lean back on the couch and close my eyes. The energy drains out of me and I let myself focus on Aunt Ida for the first time in two days.

Off to the east somewhere she's in her house. It's Monday night, so she's watching "TV's Bloopers and Practical Jokes," laughing at the celebrities when they get caught with their pants down. She has her chair pulled close to the set and talks back to the show. "You old idiot," she fussed last week to Willie Nelson when he got fooled. "Watch out next time."

Aunt Ida is a mystery to me. She seems to take everything as it comes, but it's all a burden. I tell myself she won't miss me, she won't care that I left the way I did. She fed me and got me Foxy's old clothes from her sister, Pauline, and lately turned her cheek for me to kiss when I went out, but she'll be glad to have her house to herself again. I wonder what Father Tom told her. She wouldn't have asked any questions, just nodded and waited for him to finish so she could go back to her programs. I think of calling her long distance to tell her I'm okay, but she doesn't have a phone. If I want to get her a message, I'd have to call the Mission, and I don't want to talk to Father Tom. He probably hopes I'm in Switzerland by now.

"Ain't that so?" Sky asks. He's talking to me and catches me just before I lapse into sleep. I push myself erect and lean forward to put my elbows on my knees. The seat slants down in back.

"I said they wanted you for the heavenly host, but you couldn't take it."

"Is that right?" Evelyn asks me. "Is that what the Catholics planned for you?"

"You should have seen the priest she was with," says Sky. "Creep city. How'd you get rid of him, anyway?"

"You got it all wrong," I say. "He ditched me."

Evelyn floats before me, huge on her pedestal. "Just like my first husband. Them Catholics is all alike."

I realize I'm tired beyond my experience. When the timer bell dings and Sky and Evelyn rise and move toward the kitchen, I stay on the couch and let myself tilt sideways until I'm lying down, my feet still on the brown linoleum floor and the rest of me wedged into the crack between the cushions and the back. I'm so beat that I fall asleep with my eyes open. Evelyn and Sky are people in my dream, moving underwater. I close my lids so they'll go.

"She's wasted." Sky's voice is hollow, far away.

"Shut down and closed for the night," says Evelyn. "Put her dinners back in the oven."

I know they're standing by the couch looking down at me, but I don't care. I will them to leave so the last part of my brain can flick off.

"Cover her over with the spread," says Evelyn.

There's movement, a rhythm of footsteps rock the floor.

"You think she's who she says she is?" Evelyn says.

"Hell, probably some runaway. She's just a kid."

"She try to sell you that story about her folks on vacation?"

"What do you care? You think she's some escaped FBI?"

"Don't be smart," she says. "Go ahead and frisk her pockets. See if she's got any I.D."

I refuse to wake, even when I feel Sky's gentle fingers pat first my side pockets, then the rear ones. I'm made of flour, a sack too heavy to lift.

"Here's a wallet," I hear him say, then the crackle of paper unfolding. "It's from her mom. Says they hope she has a good time on her adventure."

"Don't that take the cake. I guess she was straight after all."

A layer of rough wool is laid on top of me. It smells of too much sitting and too many cigarettes, but I snuggle into its warmth. The last time I slept lying down was three nights ago in Mom's old bed at Aunt Ida's. It seems forever, a fantasy. My brain hums with half-told stories, with pieces that don't seem to fit anywhere, with things I should have said and didn't, and I can't tell the real from the could-be. It's as though I'm dreaming a lot of lives and I can mix and match the parts into something new each time. None pin me down. The last light in my head turns out, and I'm gone.

Just before dawn, Sky yanks on my foot. While I wash my face at the sink he uses a tablespoon to eat both my macaroni-and-cheese dinners from last night. Evelyn comes into the living room dressed in the clothes she had on the day before. Nobody says a word.

Sky and Evelyn could be two feathers from a single bird, they are that much alike. Their faces are both long and big-jawed. They have the same gray eyes, the same ball noses. And it is clear to me that neither one is what you'd call a morning person. They look as though sleep beats them down rather than picks them up.

I take after Mom. No matter what happens the night before she always wakes fresh and ready for action. In the early morning her eyes are clear and she scrubs her face and ties back her hair. Whoever's there, a date or some girlfriend sleeping over or even when Aunt Ida came to Seattle to visit the hospital, Mom and I always get up first.

Sometimes she squeezes real orange juice or even rolls out Bisquick and uses the rim of a water glass to cut rolls. Other times we eat waffles heated in the toaster or a leftover piece of pizza. We turn the radio real low and when one of her favorite songs comes on—"Country Bumpkin" or "Coat of Many Colors"— Mom closes her eyes, tips back her head, and mouths the words as if she's singing. She knows them all by heart. Her teeth are big and white and shine when she smiles, all happy with herself and me and everything else.

Sky and Evelyn have a vehicle that has seen better days. The door on the driver's side is permanently tied shut with a length of plastic clothesline and there's a shatter on the windshield like a fly in a spiderweb. The floor tumbles with cans—Miller Lite, motor oil, Mountain Dew—and the backseat is piled with old Sears catalogs whose weight, Sky explains, is meant to give the tires extra traction. I noticed last night that the wipers are dead.

Evelyn drops Sky at the Conoco and parks the car behind the lodge. In the kitchen she feeds me six more fried eggs and a cup of tea before taking off her coat. I eat standing at the table, then take my plate over to the sink and rinse it. She has already started to knead out the day's dough, and the shoulder muscles flex and move beneath her plaid shirt. She has her third Merit of the morning going in the corner of her mouth.

"Mr. McCutcheon says I'm paid three-forty an hour," I announce. "But no paycheck for two weeks. Can I owe you?"

"Ain't nothing owed as of yet," says Evelyn. "You didn't eat a bite last night, and I can't see as how your sleeping did my couch any harm."

"I'm going to pay you. Fair is fair."

"Okay, okay," she says, balling the dough tight, then slamming it onto the board and raising a storm of flour. "I'll start planning my trip to Paris, France, with my fortune. You won't have anything to pay if you're late on the job the first full day."

Sky was right: Evelyn does like me. And it isn't a Father Tom sort of liking either. She doesn't even want my paycheck.

"See you at five," I say. "Thanks."

"Be here at noon," she answers, intent on her work. "You eat lunch, don't you?"

I like Evelyn back. I think about that for a second, but I don't know how to say it.

"My mom . . . makes biscuits sometimes."

She turns to look at me over her shoulder but her hands never stop their work. "If that's a hint," she says, giving the dough a slap and flipping it over, "you just blew this afternoon's surprise." Her lips close over her cigarette, straightening it. The end glows beneath its long ash, and Evelyn sends smoke through her nostrils in slow streams. I take it for a smile.

It's still chilly but the sun's high. A heavy dew covers the ground and my sneakers are soaked before I reach the parking lot. Nobody else is at the equipment cabin yet, so I change into my uniform in private and am out the door with my nail-pole and trash bag before seven-thirty. The day stretches in front of me like a long hollow log and I find I'm hoping for trash. But that has to wait for tourists to arrive.

I walk down the path to the lake, drinking in the early

morning quiet and my aloneness. In our neighborhood in Seattle the street this time of day would be crowded with people walking, people standing and watching, people dodging between cars. There was too much to absorb and I never saw anything except straight ahead. Mom used to send me out to the twenty-four-hour market for a coffeecake or donuts, whatever she felt like. "Don't hurry," she'd say to me once in a while when she had a guest, and I'd wait in the phone booth on the corner until the coast was clear.

Through the trees I catch flashes of the lake. It throws back the sunlight in shining beams that curve through the leaves and branches, cutting strange patterns of shadow on the cushion of pine needles that spreads across the ground. It's a different place without Father Tom and I get the idea to drop my clothes and go in before anyone else is around. I can almost feel the cold water sliding along my body, slicking back my hair, washing away everything that isn't attached.

But when I reach the shore, there's already somebody swimming off the raft. I feel shy and out of place and step behind a tree, but from the sound of the splashes they're doing laps back and forth and back and forth at a steady pace. Just as I crane my neck to look, the noise stops and I see a girl, a little older and a lot more developed than me, in a white tank suit. She hoists herself onto the yellow boards in one smooth, strong motion. Her hair is black and long, and shines like a seal's fur in the sun. Her skin is tan and her suit clings to every curve and movement of her body.

She turns her face in my direction and I pull back, even though from where I stand I have to be invisible. I'm afraid to see anything more, to see something wrong, something out of place, something to ruin the picture. But when at last I raise my eyes, there's nothing but her, framed by the lake and the sky. In that moment she's everything I'm not but ought to be.

Below me at the water's edge, somewhere to my right and blocked from where I hide, another girl calls out.

"Hey, DeMarco! You're going to freeze your buns off."

"I wish!" says the girl on the raft. "The Bearpaw Lake diet! Come on in. It's all right."

"No way. I just washed my hair."

"Well, bring the canoe then. It's so awesome here this morning. I could stay forever."

"You're wasting your time, Ellen," says the voice. "None of the guys are even conscious."

"Fuck you!" Ellen stands, runs lightly, and dives, barely making a splash. My shoulders hunch. I feel the cold, the flat slap it makes against her stomach and thighs. I hold my breath, waiting for her to break the surface, but she swims with her head underwater, reaching her arms out in a straight line and moving like a dark torpedo through the little waves.

You get to know campers by what they throw away. The ones who play their music loud, the ones who ignore the rules of water safety, which are posted on trees throughout my zone, are my best clients. They leave a trail of wrappers and wipettes from their cars to the lake, and their children forget shoes and windbreakers and plastic buckets. Some of these items give me trouble. Do I throw them away or save them for the lost and found? It's a choice that doesn't sound important, but it can be. There's only so much space for storage and just as soon as you figure that a thing is worthless and toss it, some lady in purple sunglasses starts yelling about how her prize possession has been ripped off.

I don't steal, but when stuff doesn't get claimed after three weeks anybody can have it, so my wardrobe begins to grow. The clothes I choose at lost and found aren't the things I'd pick at a store, but they have the advantage of fitting. At nights I show Evelyn and Sky my new possessions, and they are always excited and enthusiastic, especially if I bring something for them too. Sky, for instance, is really happy when I produce a ripped and sun-bleached Grateful Dead T-shirt.

"This is an antique!" he shouts. "I'd say 1971, '72, no later." He refuses Evelyn's offer to fix the tear. "No way. You never know how this happened, what was going down. It might be wrong to just sew it up." So he wears it the way I found it, and I have an idea he wants people to ask him questions about The Dead and when he last saw them.

Evelyn is harder to shop for, since not many people with her shape or her taste in clothes hang around the lake beach. One day, though, I spot a discarded cotton blanket that I know she'd love. Printed in the center of the material is a huge brown buck, its eyes soft and blurred from many washings. He stands on a little tuft of grass with a red sunset behind him. All day I watch to see if someone will come back for the blanket. I even kind of bunch it together and stick it off to the side of the cleared area—so that it doesn't trip someone, I tell myself. Every time I make my rounds, stabbing and poking the ground for wastepaper, I check and see if it's still unclaimed, and at the end of the day I bring it into lost and found. Dave's there before me.

"Looks like you hit the jackpot," he says. "Let's see it opened out."

I think he'll laugh, being in college and smart as he is, but he surprises me.

"Oh, wow! Too much. One hundred percent. God, what I'd give to hang that in my dorm room."

"Are you kidding?"

"Kidding! That is classic American kitsch. The Lonely Stag. Bambi's lost father. I'd make a coat out of that blanket and never take it off."

I'm not exactly sure what he means, but Dave makes me laugh. Of all the ones I work with he's the only guy who pays attention to me, who asks me anything except what the girls in the Instructor's cabin are doing. Dave and I eat lunch together most days. He gets a burger from the stand and I unwrap the sandwich that Evelyn fixed for me, an exact copy of those she makes for Sky and herself. I have in mind that one of the reasons Dave sits with me is to see what Evelyn has devised, since her sandwiches are never ordinary: peanut butter and red onion, pickle and banana, and once, a Hershey bar with almonds between two pieces of white bread.

"She's the *cook?*" Dave asks. "Why doesn't she ever make something wild like that at the Lodge?"

"Evelyn gets tired of the same old stuff all the time," I tell him. "When she's home she likes to experiment." It's also true that Evelyn hates to shop. At the Jiffy Mart, she grabs the first things she sees and rarely walks down more than one aisle. For a week after a trip to the grocery, all the things we eat at her trailer have a sort of common theme. One time it will be fruits and vegetables, another time soup combos, another time frozen diet dinners.

She's been nice to me, though. When my paycheck finally comes, I have to stuff the bills into her shirt pocket and button it before she stops protesting, and then, as though she's irritated, she insists we all go out to the Hitchin' Post diner and celebrate.

"Get anything you want," she tells Sky and me. "I'm rich today and I'm buying." Sky orders a country-fried steak sandwich and whipped potatoes and I get the Bearpaw Burger Platter, which comes with a drink and lime Jell-O for dessert. Evelyn buys herself the Shrimp in a Basket and says she's never tasted anything so good. I know the meal cost almost as much as the money I gave her. She hates to take cash, she says, which is why I'm anxious to get this lost deer blanket for her.

"If you don't want it, if nobody claims it, let me know," Dave says as we leave the storage cabin. "I'd even buy it off you."

"Not for sale. I know a good thing when I find it."

Days go by and the blanket stays put, but not free-and-clear mine until the end of the first week of July. I worry that somebody will walk in off the street and pretend that they lost the blanket. I tell the others in the crew that it's tagged for me, and to make double sure before they hand it out. They think I'm crazy, except for Dave, but say okay. They figure if they're nice to me I'll put in a good word for them with the swimming teachers in my zone.

The maintenance boys are barking up the wrong tree with that plan, though, because the only way I know those girls is from a distance. My favorite remains Ellen DeMarco. I can't get out of my head the first view I had of her, diving off the raft. It seems to me she has everything, and I hate to say it but there are times I would trade places. I'd drop my uniform and underneath would be this girl right off a magazine cover with no excuses to make and no lies to tell. While I'm working, I pretend we're friends, and try to overhear as much about her as I can.

I don't meet Ellen in person until the tail end of the four weeks of June I work at Bearpaw Lake, but by then I've become an expert on her likes and dislikes. I piece together the odd bits that others know, and fill in the space between with links of my own imagining. When I ask Evelyn for information, I get an earful.

"She's some kind of vegetarian," Evelyn reports with distaste. "Except the only thing she won't eat is fish. Not tuna salad, not fish sticks, nothing. 'Don't serve me anything that ever had scales,' she tells me the first day. I thought she was nuts. 'What do you think this is, a snake farm?' I asked her, but it's fish she was talking about."

"What does she like?"

"For breakfast she drinks a glass of grapefruit juice is all I know," says Evelyn. "The first morning here she asks me 'Is it fresh?' and I tell her 'Right from the can,' but she just rolls her eyes. What do you care about her for anyway?"

Sky is more sympathetic.

"Oh, man," he says when I ask him. "That lady surfaces at my station in a red Toyota Celica, looked like it was right off the boat. She just sits there behind the wheel wearing reflector shades while I come out and walk around the car. 'Fill it with Premium,' she says and then pays with her daddy's credit card. Her license plate says ELLEN."

"What state is it from?" I ask him.

"New Jersey or New York. New something."

"Does she get her gas at the station all the time?" I want to know. It might be worth hanging around there sometimes.

"Never does," he says, shaking his head to make the point. "Could be her engine started to knock on her."

"Why would that be?"

"I don't stock Premium," Sky explains. "It don't pay. I don't even carry much no-lead. Around here I cater to trucks that take diesel or regular, and the tourists that pass through don't know the difference till they're miles gone. I adapted my nozzles and I just give them what they ask for."

"Well, what did you think of Ellen?" I say, trying to get us back to the point.

"Evelyn says she don't eat fish." Sky scratches his chin and thinks. "But I told her, 'Hell, as long as the kid don't hurt anybody she's got a right.'"

It's no good talking to Andy about Ellen. I only try it once, when I run into him outside the locker room one morning.

"Bazzooms!" he says.

I start to walk away. This isn't what I want to hear.

"Just place your bets, Ray," he says. "Before this summer is over you're going to see me with that chick. It's got to happen."

He makes me uncomfortable. He talks about Ellen the way I used to suspect men talked about Mom. I want to hit him.

"Did you ever even meet her?" I ask.

"Every night." He winks. "She's just finished her freshman year at UCSD, and John says that there's no such thing as a San Diego virgin. It's a contradiction in terms."

He finishes buttoning his shirt and begins to thread a new lace into his boot.

"Did you hear what John did?"

I haven't asked John about Ellen. I don't have to. He talks about her all the time, but he doesn't know anything. Once when all the water safety girls were teaching their classes he sneaked into their cabin and came out with what he claimed were Ellen's underpants. After showing them around to everybody, he hung them on the wall over his bed.

I'm dressed and impatient to start work, but Andy is determined to retell the story.

"He actually told her, actually *told* her," Andy says. "He said she could come and get them back any night between ten and two."

"What did she say?" I ask, as he expects me to.

"You're not going to believe it." Andy screws up his face and bangs the bench with the sole of his hiking boot. "She told him that they couldn't be hers because she didn't *wear* underpants. *God!*"

Dave's opinions are harder to block because he's intelligent. We sit together as usual during lunch break, watching campers scatter the rubbish we'll collect all afternoon. He eats a Devil Dog and I have a sandwich made from leftover canned stew.

"She's a bubblehead, Ray. Classic."

"You don't know that. And besides, she's beautiful."

"The woman has the IQ of an ant, a goldfish," he goes on. "I asked her what's her major? And she says arts and sciences! What does that mean?"

I don't know what it means, so I say, "Maybe she likes them both and can't make up her mind."

Dave closes his eyes at my answer. "There's no mind there to make up. All she wanted to know about me was whether or not I had joined a frat at OSU. When I said no, she switched off fast."

"Well, maybe . . ." I begin.

"No, really. I know the type. Did you see the car she drives? It means rich father, private schools, designer brain cells. What do you want with her anyway?" He gives me a closer, serious look. "Did she make some remark to you, or what?"

"I'm just interested in her, that's all. She seems like a real nice person. Maybe she could teach me to swim better."

"No chance, she'd have to get her hair wet. And anyway, John's already thought of that one," Dave says. "The second day out he hits the water and starts yelling for help. He figures DeMarco will give him mouth-to-mouth, but all she does is flip him the bird."

I think that's great. "She doesn't sound so dumb to me."

"Well, she has her specialties, I'm sure," says Dave. "She probably majors in guys."

"Are you saying you wouldn't like to go out with her?"

"No," he answers, "I'm human." He spears a paper towel that has blown into his range. "I'm saying it's a lost cause."

Ellen herself is my best source of information. One afternoon when I'm patrolling the picnic area, I observe her as she sits on her high lifeguard's stool, dressed in her white bathing suit, a whistle around her long neck, her nose smeared with sunscreen and her legs oiled and shining. She takes her job seriously and leaps to her feet when anyone violates the safety code by paddling a canoe too close to the beach or by taking food in the water. She keeps a sharp eye out for Frisbee throwers in crowded areas and for water fights that get out of hand. She twirls her whistle around her finger in one direction, then back in the other, never talking, just pointing and waving and rubbing lotion on her arms. She doesn't fool around on duty like some of them do.

Another morning I watch her ten o'clock swim class with the tadpoles, the under-seven's who are mostly afraid of the water and never want to go in. Unexpectedly she lifts her head and stares right at me. I'm standing there like a jerk, poking at the same newspaper without putting it in my bag.

"Take your snack bags over to the garbage can," she tells the little kids. "Don't make work for people who have to clean after you."

And she actually smiles at me.

I stuff the newspaper into my Hefty and stab my way to the road. When I finally glance back, she's turned away. It's nothing like a real conversation, but I can't forget it.

The only person to tell is Sky.

He gives the incident his full attention. As we talk he carefully marks an X through each day on the May page of the gas station's Budweiser calendar before he tears it off, then starts on June.

"Very interesting," he says, licking the end of his pencil.

"It probably didn't mean anything."

"Hey, man, everything *means* something. There ain't nothing that's an accident. Like what are you doing here?" he asks, cocking his head in thought. "Out of nowhere. Here you have this big house in Seattle, a mom and dad, a big yard and a dog, right?"

Ever since he and Evelyn read the letter they found in my pocket they keep trying to uncover more about my background.

"Right."

"And here you are, in the middle of Montana, sleeping on Evelyn's couch and your folks off to . . ."

He waits for me to fill in the blank.

"Switzerland," I say.

"Switzerland!" he exclaims. "Fucking Switzerland! How do you figure?"

I say I don't.

"But that don't mean it don't mean something," he says. "We just don't know *what* yet."

"Ellen," I say, to get him back on subject.

"Has she been to Switzerland too?" His eyes go wide with the wonder of things.

"No. I mean, what do you think about Ellen smiling at me? Don't you think she's nice?"

"Could be," he says. "Why don't you ask her?"

But I don't ask Ellen. I don't even ask myself Sky's questions, like what am I doing here, or what's happened to Mom or Aunt Ida or even Father Tom. It's as though I'm suspended in a time warp and nothing in the world matters but policing my area and helping out at the trailer and passing the days. I don't know where I'm going any more than when I left the reservation, any more than when I visited Mom in her hospital room in Seattle. It's as if I've taken on a new identity and sometimes I halfway believe that at the end of the summer these parents I've concocted will come back loaded down with souvenir cuckoo clocks and take me home to our house in Seattle with its overgrown lawn.

On weekends the other maintenance crew members rotate their schedules, but since Sky and Evelyn work seven days a week, I do too. That makes me popular with Andy and John, who always want me to sub for them, and it pleases Mr. McCutcheon no end.

"You are a credit to this park," he tells me. "You have surpassed the trust I placed in you." In fact, when the director of the Montana Department of Recreation is invited to the opening of Bearpaw's new parking lot, Mr. McCutcheon makes a point of introducing me and saying how I fill two separate Affirmative Action slots at the same time.

"Our Rayona is the daughter of a black airline pilot," he brags. "We are lucky to have her with us on the staff."

People at the park have become used to me. They wave when I go by and ask if my folks are having a good time overseas. Montana's not like Seattle where I moved around invisible, or where I always had to wonder if somebody seemed too friendly. When I help out at Sky's station, the regulars all say hello or joke as though they've known me for years. And Sky and Evelyn seem to forget that there's a stranger living with them. They fight and joke it off and listen to their music and clomp around in their underwear like zombies in the morning, and I no longer feel I'm in their way.

When I get paid at the end of June I count what I've saved and am amazed. With all my overtime and extra hours, my checks have gotten bigger each week. Evelyn won't take any more for my board, so I put what I've earned together with the money Father Tom gave me, and it comes to over five hundred dollars.

Everybody starts talking about the Fourth of July, when there's scheduled to be fireworks at the campgrounds and a big dance. Some of the staff's parents are coming out to visit from all around the country, and people ask if my folks will return in time.

"Still on vacation," I answer.

"Not much in the way of letter-writers, are they?" Evelyn comments one day, but I let it pass.

I see in the paper that there's going to be a big Indian rodeo in Havre, not far from the reservation. They're offering five thousand dollars in prize money and it says that there'll be participants from all over Montana. I wonder if Mom will come, and I think she will. It's the kind of place where she'd see a lot of those she went to school with, where she'd have a chance to party and forget her troubles. With all my money and the time I've got coming I could get a bus ticket and be there myself, surprise her. I'd be something to explain to people she hadn't seen for almost twenty years! But how would I account to Evelyn and Sky where I was going? And besides, Sky said the Fourth was the busiest day of the year at the station and had already asked me to work for him.

"It's when I make my Christmas money," he says. "People buy things that day they'd never get otherwise—used tires, inner tubes, maps, windshield wiper fluid, you name it." He rubs his hands together and is so happy I wonder what he wants to splurge on.

Just after dawn on the Fourth of July I'm sitting in the lodge kitchen with Evelyn, eating my regulation six over-hard, when in the door walks Ellen DeMarco with two people who have to be her father and mother. She's wearing a dark blue UCSD sweatshirt and red shorts, and even over the grease and coffee I can smell some kind of perfume. I quickly look down to my plate.

"Mrs. Dial . . ." she says in her low, clear voice.

"There's grapefruit juice in the fridge," barks Evelyn. "Fresh."

"These are my parents, Mr. and Mrs. DeMarco," Ellen says. "They would like some breakfast, if it's not too much trouble, and I was thinking I might have an egg."

I glance up. Ellen is watching me again, just like the day when I saw her with the tadpoles at the beach.

"Those sure look yummy." She nods at my plate.

I follow her gaze to the curling brown edges, the chalky yolks, and the soggy end of the piece of toast I have been using to scrape.

"I thought you was on a diet." Evelyn doesn't hide how she feels about Ellen, but it's water off a duck's back.

"Well, an egg won't kill me," Ellen answers. "And my mother and father are starved. Do you *mind*?"

"Your wish is my command," says Evelyn in a fake restaurant voice.

While she waits, Ellen slides onto the bench next to me. I try to think of something to say but nothing comes into my head. Mr. DeMarco is dressed as though he's on his way to church, with a light blue suit, a striped tie, and a white shirt. He wears sun filters clipped over his glasses and shiny brown shoes. Ellen's mother has on a green pantsuit and a shirt with streamers she has tied in a bow under her chin. They both look at me like they wonder who I am.

I cut a piece of egg and pierce it with my fork. It is full of yolk and I rush it into my mouth before any of it spills on my uniform. It shatters like a bomb the second it hits my tongue.

"Where are your manners, Ellen," says Mr. DeMarco. "Aren't you going to introduce us to your friend?"

To my surprise Ellen is full of facts.

"John told you about her," she says to her parents, "this is one of the maintenance *men*! Her name is even Ray."

"It's a pleasure, Ray." Mr. DeMarco smiles and holds out his hand. "I'm Burt DeMarco and this is my wife Dell."

I chew with my mouth shut, swallowing the egg in small bits.

"Where are you from, Ray?" Mrs. DeMarco asks me.

"She's from Seattle," Ellen answers. "John says her father's some kind of pilot."

"Oh yes, I remember him mentioning that last night at dinner," Mr. DeMarco said. "I believe he also thought you had been at a Roman Catholic camp before coming here? And there was some kind of trouble?"

I look at Evelyn. She and Sky are the only ones who know that part of my story and I'm shocked that they have talked about me to other people. Evelyn has stopped dead still at Mr. DeMarco's words, but she won't turn and face me.

My brain is overloaded. Why are Ellen's parents out to dinner with John? Doesn't Ellen know about her underpants hanging above his bed in the boys' cabin?

"It just didn't work out," I finally manage to say.

"Was it a missionary place?" Mr. DeMarco asks me. "Where you were?"

"Sort of." I think of Father Tom.

"Wonderful people," Mr. DeMarco says. "You'd be interested in this." He reaches for his wallet and flips it to a part full of photographs.

"Not *Rocky*," Ellen cries. "For Christ's sake, Daddy."

"Ellen, that's no way to talk," her mother says.

Mr. DeMarco shows me a color picture of a boy about ten years old wearing a white T-shirt and jeans. He could be a younger version of my cousin Foxy: light brown skin, straight black hair. He leans against a blue bicycle.

"Rocky Begay is Ellen's foster brother in Arizona," Mr. DeMarco says. "He lives on an Indian reservation there and we discovered him through Save the Children."

I say Rocky looks nice.

"He lives on a mission now," Mr. DeMarco goes on. "He is the product of a broken home and was with a foster family when we first contacted him. When he writes to us now he calls us Mother and Pops just like one of our own kids."

Twice I have stayed for a few days with foster families in Seattle, once when Mom was getting herself sick, and the other time when she was pulling herself back together. It's funny how little about those people I remember. At one place they fixed string beans and mushroom soup mixed together with those little crispy fake fried onions on top. I told Mom about it when I got home and she always cooked it for me on special occasions after that. At the other place there was a dog named Petey who didn't like strangers.

Staying with those fosters was like going to another country. The corners in their rooms seemed sharper, the smells were different. I missed our old towels when I took a shower. One family was white and the other was black, but I didn't get to know either one. We mostly just watched each other. They were relieved that I wasn't as much trouble as I could have been, and I was happy they weren't the hard cases I had heard about from other kids. They were uncomfortable in asking me questions because they didn't know how I felt about Mom's problems. I didn't know then, either. Those times she was gone I forgot everything bad she ever did. I listened for the telephone or looked out the window for the signal that it was time to go back, that she was ready to make a new start. Then, when she did come for me, things were great for a while.

"Burt, you're boring Ray," Mrs. DeMarco says and wakes me back to the here and now.

The three DeMarcos are eating their eggs, and I see that Evelyn has sprinkled them heavily with pepper.

"You must know Ellen's friend John?" Mr. DeMarco asks me. "Isn't he in the park maintenance area too?"

I nod.

"*Nice* young man," Mrs. DeMarco says. "So polite."

I realize I haven't been polite at all, something I've been trained to be no matter what, so I say, "Ellen is a very good lifeguard. The little kids love her."

"Little bastards," Ellen says. " 'Get me this, do that,' and always fighting with each other. I could drown them."

"Ellen has always been good with children and animals," Mrs. DeMarco says, ignoring her daughter.

"Speaking of animals, you never even asked about Rascal yet," Mr. DeMarco says. "The poor little fellow is so lonesome without you!"

I swing around to see if Evelyn has heard, and she is staring right at me.

"I've got to go," I say and push away from the table.

"You have a nice Fourth, now," Mrs. DeMarco calls. "Don't work too hard."

I'm out the screen door and down the path to the lake before I let myself think. Then I reach back for my wallet and take out my letter. The words dance in my mind. I hear the sound of the lawn mower. The dog. Rascal scratching to come in at the door. I crumple the paper in my hand and let it slip through my fingers. It falls to the ground like another piece of trash that has to be collected.

A tourist in a long square dance skirt crosses in front of me, stepping on the letter as she goes to see the lake. Her sandal leaves a dusty print on the paper and I can't take my eyes off it. I try to picture Mrs. DeMarco using a green felt-tip pen at the kitchen table in their house wherever it was. I look through her eyes out the door and try to see Mr. DeMarco in his blue suit and tie, cutting the grass.

And I can't. They don't fit the letter that I've heard again and again in Mom's voice. It's Mom I've imagined. She chews the end of her Flair before she writes each line. She has her hair pulled back with a porcupine quill clip. She wears her yellow sleeveless top that I gave her for her birthday last year. There are hot dogs cooking on the stove. The table wobbles where the one leg is too short. She's tapping her feet to the radio, but above the music I hear the lawn mower.

I cross to where the letter lies on the ground and pick it up. I smooth it against my thigh and unfold its creases. I read it and I read it and I read it and I see only my own picture again, clearer than ever.

7

I'm not that hard for Evelyn to find. I'm stopped, halfway down the trail, with my eyes fixed on the empty yellow raft floating in the blue waters of Bearpaw Lake. Somewhere in my mind I've decided that if I stare at it hard enough it will launch me out of my present troubles. If I squint a certain way, it appears to be a lighted trapdoor, flush against a black floor. With my eyes closed almost completely, it becomes a kind of bull's-eye, and I'm an arrow banging into it head-first.

Evelyn has a right to say anything, to call me a liar, to laugh, to demand an explanation, and when I sense her presence behind me, I'm ready for her. She has never seen me angry and I'll surprise her when I turn, lashing out and defiant, making fun of what suckers she and Sky have been. But Evelyn does the worst thing she can do. She doesn't say a word.

It's as if she sends off radiation that tickles the back of my neck and blows against my legs. I know exactly how far away she has positioned herself, right on the edge of my shadow, a smaller, heavier, older, unknown image of myself. I can wait her out. If silence is her plan, she'll have to forget it and go away if I keep quiet.

But she doesn't. We stand like two leafless trees that have grown on the path overnight, and she's the tougher.

"Now you know," I say. It's her move, but not a word. I feel the energy draining, flowing down my limbs and into the ground. If she touches me now I'll crumble. I can't take the suspense. "Say something."

"Oh, Ray," Evelyn says. "I'm so sorry." Her voice is new. Her lungs have cleared of their years of smoke and what comes out her throat is cool as cotton, young. I think it can't be Evelyn after all and twist around to see with my eyes. Evelyn still wears her white dishtowel apron and in her large, strong hands she shapes a ball of creamy dough. Her eyes are different though. Before I've always seen in them a suspicion of the world, a fine edge of disbelief, a glint that says "sure, you bet, uh-huh," and today that's gone. They look back at me like two bright jewels and I'm helpless.

"Now you know," I say again, and she shakes her head no.

"I don't know shit."

"I lied from the beginning." My voice is low, pulled from me.

"It doesn't matter. It's nothing."

I turn back to speak to the raft. "I'll tell you the truth."

"You don't have to," she says. "Sometimes it's better to leave things be. No one else has to know, and I can forget. I'm expert at that."

"Why are you being so nice?" I ask her. It's the tip of the iceberg of what I want to know. We both listen as my words float in the air and slowly break apart. "Why?"

"Don't ask me that," she finally says in her clean voice.

"What then?"

"Tell me if you want to."

So I tell her. We are stuck in a stable distance from each other, magnets connected by the stream of my words. I start my story in the middle and move in both directions. I tell her unimportant things, memories of little events that happened to me, clothes Mom wears and Dad's funny mailman adventures. I tell her Aunt Ida's favorite programs and I tell her about Father Tom and the yellow raft. I tell her yes, Seattle, but the reservation too, and Mom there somewhere with a man named Dayton and all her pills from Charlene. I tell her I wanted to trade places with Ellen. I tell her about my lifetime membership and I tell her about Mom just walking off and leaving. My story pours like water down the drain of a tub, and when the last drops cough out, I stop.

I don't hang for her answer anymore. There's a weight off me. I said it all out loud and the world didn't come to an end. I listened to my story, let loose, running around free in the morning air, and it wasn't as bad as I expected. It didn't even take that long to tell, once I got started.

From the parking lot comes the sound of the early-bird tourists arriving for the holiday, their ice chests full of food and litter. If Evelyn and I stay like this much longer, we'll take root.

"Now I know." Her voice is back to normal, full of gears that need oiling and rough edges. I wonder if I've imagined that it was ever different. "So what are you going to do about it?"

"I don't know."

"Well, figure it out. Nothing good's going to happen as long as you hide here. Your poor aunt is probably worried to death, that damn priest should have his ass kicked, and your mother is off sick somewhere."

I turn, and her words are a lightbulb switching on in my head. Of course Mom's sick. She was in the hospital. She has to take pills. That explains a lot.

"What do I do?" I say, more to myself than to Evelyn, but she answers first.

"Norman and me are driving you home."

"But you have to work," I say. "It's his busy day at the station."

"Don't make excuses. I haven't had a trip in a year and it's about time. It's a holiday. Anybody can cook the crap they'll eat today, and Norman can either close the damn Conoco or find somebody to run it."

"Why are you doing this?"

Evelyn pulls a leaf from the nearest tree and rotates it in her hand. She looks at it long and close enough to memorize the pattern of its veins. "Because somebody should have done it for me," she says. "All right?"

She turns and walks heavy but quick back toward the

lodge. She bends forward, adjusting for the slope of the path, and her hips push like pistons as she plants each foot firmly in front of the other. Fueled with her idea, Evelyn looks as though she could march through solid rock to get where she wants to go. I follow in her wake, littering the trail with my unused box of Heftys. While Evelyn gets her keys I run into the equipment cabin and take the one thing I don't want to forget.

Sky does a double take when Evelyn pulls the car in front of the station.

"Be ready to roll when we come back in fifteen minutes," she yells out the window. "We're hitting the road."

Sky gets an expression on his face like he seriously wonders if this is happening. He's interested in all departures from what he expects, and he's sparked at the surprise of Evelyn's announcement.

"Just like that? Just take off?"

Evelyn nods her head, her mouth narrowing to a wide grin.

"Far out," Sky says. "Let me just lock the pumps and I'll be waiting." Before we pull out, he makes a show of taking the sign that hangs on the glass door of the station and reversing it to show CLOSED.

"And you wondered if he wanted to play hooky," Evelyn says to me as we reverse, and then head for the trailer. "He's an overgrown kid." There's color in her cheeks as she lights a cigarette with her. Bic and blows out smoke. "Sky," she says to herself like he's beyond her understanding. "He didn't even ask why." She can't conceal her approval. "That's the kind to find yourself someday. You should have met my first husband. Scared of his own crap. The first thing he did when we got married was to open a savings account, but I didn't wait around for the interest to collect."

When we return for Sky and ease onto 2 going east, Evelyn treats him as though he must have known all the facts about me and just forgotten them.

"Ray was *always* leaving after a month," she tells him. "Where's your brain?"

"I don't get it," he says, confused. "Let me get this straight. Your folks have come back from Europe and are meeting you out *here*?" He draws his eyebrows together over his round, fleshy nose and turns to me for enlightenment.

Evelyn cuts in. "Come on. You knew she was pulling your leg. Don't let her see what a clunk I'm married to." She reaches across the gearshift to the other seat where Sky is sitting and slaps his thigh.

"Well, wait a couple or three minutes," Sky says, twisting so he can see me in the backseat. "You mean you *are* a full-blood Indian now?"

"You're the one that's full of it," Evelyn says. "Don't ask so many questions and they will all be answered." She drives us down the flat, straight highway. At the horizon line, miles ahead, the road seems to come to a point and at that place, in the glare of the sun, to merge with the sky.

"It looks like the edge of the world," I say, leaning forward. Next to me on the backseat is Evelyn's old suitcase, full of my things. When she saw me about to leave with my same plastic bag she rummaged in her closet until she found what she called her valise, a hinged box covered in worn, shiny pale green cloth with a strip of tan running like a strap around the middle. I offered to pay her for it but she laughed.

"I should pay you," she said. "I've kept that contraption for fourteen years without using it. It belonged to my mother, and I carried it when I left my first husband, and then again when I came to marry Norman. I'm not likely to be needing it a third time."

I transferred everything from my sack to the case, and on top put my money and the two VCR tapes from Village Video. In all this time they'd never been out of their boxes. I left my park uniform at Evelyn's for her to return, but I wore a B.L.S.P. T-shirt.

We stop for coffee and food at a cafe in Kremlin, fifteen miles west of Havre. The sign says it's the town where you're a stranger only once. Evelyn gives her Western sandwich an extra dose of pepper and asks, "Well, where to?"

I've thought about this. "There's a big Indian rodeo in Havre today," I say. "I think Mom'll come. Anyway it's as good a place as any to look."

After I say this it dawns on me that my return to the reservation isn't my idea but Evelyn's. I've been so caught in her determination that I left off thinking for myself, and now I'm about to be thrust back into the thick of what I escaped. I start hoping we'll have a flat, anything, to delay our arrival and give me a chance to get my bearings. We arrive at Havre, however, without a hitch. At the top of the hill, seeing all the people milling about, all the Indian trucks with "Fry Bread Power" bumper stickers and little moccasins hanging from the rearview mirrors, makes me want to throw the clutch in reverse, rewind back to this morning, and think things over. A clown with a dead flashlight waves us through a gate with a giant fiberglass wagon wheel suspended sideways over the top, and into the Hill County Fairgrounds. We pass the H. Earl Clark Museum, a train caboose, and a sign that warns against loose dogs. I tell myself I'm making too much of things, that I won't see anyone I know. People sometimes leave a rodeo early if things aren't going their way.

The parking lot has a SORRY FULL sign across the entrance. I take a long-shot chance. "Why don't we go up to Canada?" I suggest. "Saskatchewan is less than fifty miles. We can see your old friends."

Sky has an argument with himself about this idea and his face changes back and forth depending which side he's on, but Evelyn pays no attention. She swings the car around a dusty corner and noses into an empty space. The sounds of the crowd surround us as soon as the engine quits, the choppy rumble of conversation, the calls and clapping.

After we pay admission, Sky and Evelyn stick to me like pennies on a Bingo card. They stand close together, shifting their weight, looking in every direction, and making a point to talk loud to me. They act as though I'm their safe conduct, the reason they're allowed in. For just a flash I see them through Aunt Ida's eyes: a skinny middle-aged hippie and a heavyset woman in Bermuda shorts and a yellow nylon shirt with STAFF written in brown thread across her breast, her gray hair short as a man's, and her mouth blazing with bright lipstick for the occasion. Their skin is colorless and loose over their bones. They're nervous, not used to being strangers surrounded by Indians.

But they can relax. They aren't the ones who are about to be challenged.

I'm not five feet inside the gate when I come face to face with the last person I want to see. Foxy Cree is standing in the shade under the bleachers, and is in the process of violating the Absolutely No Alcoholic Beverages rule that is posted at every entrance. His half-closed eyes scan the crowd, pass me once, then zero in. He smiles to himself and moves in my direction.

"Find some good seats," I tell Sky and Evelyn. "You don't want to have to sit in the sun."

At my suggestion, Sky wanders off toward the stands, but not Evelyn. She waves him on when he looks back. "I'll be there, darling," she says, but she's looking at Foxy and knows trouble when she sees it.

"Do you know that one coming?" she asks, punching me in the side.

I have to admit that if you're not acquainted with Foxy he's handsome. He has a thin straight nose, deep-set black eyes, and long hair, divided today into two leather-wrapped braids. Beneath his weathered blue jeans jacket he wears an unbuttoned cowboy shirt. On his head is a black Navajo hat with a beadwork band. He's taller than me by a good three inches and so slim he can slip out of the window of a car without opening the door. But once you know him none of that counts.

"Rayona," he says, all sly. His voice has a lilt to it that usually shows on people about the same time their vision goes blurry and their drinks spill. It's the voice of a person who thinks he's a lot wilier than the one he's talking to. "I saw this dark patch against the wall and I thought, Foxy, either that's the biggest piece of horse shit you've ever seen or it's your fucking cousin Rayona."

Evelyn is on red alert. This scene has no part in her vision of family reunions.

"We thought you was dead," Foxy goes on. "Or gone back to Africa." He says that last word real slow.

"Fuck you," I say.

"Rayona, Rayona, *Rayona*," Foxy sings. It isn't three o'clock and he's loaded already. His dirty cowboy boots stay in one spot but his body revolves as if moved by a breeze. He sways toward Evelyn.

"You here for the show, white lady?" he asks her. "You like dark meat?" He looks her over and stops at her chest. He laughs real low.

"Is this the piece of trash you were telling me about?" Evelyn has forgotten about being a stranger. I see her muscles bunching beneath the thin yellow material.

"No," I tell her. "Don't. Go with Sky."

She doesn't want to leave. She's ready to wipe the floor with Foxy but my look stands in her way. "This is my cousin," I say. "He might know what we came to find out. Let me talk to him."

All this time she's staring Foxy down, telling him with her eyes everything she thinks, and I can see she has penetrated his muscatel. His mouth hangs open as though it has been slapped and his face is full of complaint. He's wounded by the injustice of Evelyn's power, but that will turn to spite once he has me alone.

Without blinking, Evelyn asks if I'm sure, and when I say yes she suddenly takes a step toward Foxy, which makes him jump back.

"Norman and me'll be waiting for you. Don't take any crap." With a last, narrow-eyed warning look at Foxy she turns her back and disappears into the crowd.

I don't wait for him to recover. "Who's here?" I ask.

Foxy's still watching the place where Evelyn was standing and it takes a second for him to swing in my direction. "Holy shit," he says. "Where'd you find her?"

"What are you doing here?" I ask it a different way. This time it gets through.

"I'm here to *ride*, Rayona," he says. My name is ugly in his mouth, just as he means it to be. "I got me entered in the bareback bronc on a hand-picked mount." He reaches into his pocket and draws out a piece of paper with 37 written on it in black Magic Marker.

"You'll never make it," I say and laugh at him before I consider what I'm doing.

His face clouds over. "You think?"

I don't know what to say. He's about to get madder no matter what.

He looks blank and rubs his registration paper between his fingers. I think he might pass out on the spot, but instead he's gathering an idea.

"Are you here with anybody?" I ask him. "You can't compete."

"If I forfeit I'm disqualified for all the fucking rodeos this summer."

"Come on, Foxy. They'll bump you anyway. You'd break your neck. You're drinking."

The bubble of Foxy's plan has popped in his brain and he's ready to deal. He reaches into his pocket for a piece of paper.

"But you're not. Oh no, not Rayona. How's your priest boyfriend?" He balances himself with a hand that weights my shoulder. His fingers dig into me.

I go cold. "Shut up." I push him away and he falls heavily onto the ground. He shakes his head as if to clear it, then climbs to his feet.

"You turd," he says. "You're going to ride for me."

"Don't be dumb. I've never even been to a rodeo before."

"Well, you're here now. All you have to do to keep my qualification is be sober enough to make it through the chute."

"No way."

"Do it for your mom. My horse belongs to the guy she's shacked up with."

Dayton, I think.

I want to hit Foxy, to kick the drunken leer off his face. I close my hands into fists and then I see a knife open in his palm. He holds it loose, ready. His legs seem steadier. His eyes are flat and red and I know he'd cut me without thinking twice.

I take the easiest way out: I surrender. I don't know whether it's that I'm scared or that I'm defeated by the mention of Mom. I don't really believe they'll let me ride in Foxy's place anyway. When they see I'm a girl they'll disqualify me. And, too, the idea is impossible. The only experience I've had with horses was one summer in Seattle when Mom had a boyfriend who took us to a park where they rented saddle rides and I took a few lessons. I liked it all right, but those ponies were tame, trotted along in a line on paths through the trees. I can't imagine myself on a wild bronc, so I agree.

"What time?"

"Now you're talking, cousin," Foxy laughs. He clicks the knife closed in one hand, and focuses his eyes on the form he still holds in the other.

"Three forty-five," he says. "Number thirty-seven. Horse named Babe."

He hands me the registration and then feels into the side of his boot for the long paper bag around the wine held tight against his thin leg. He tips it to his mouth, drinks, then wipes his dripping chin. "I'll be watching, just in case you forget."

He starts to walk bowlegged to the stands, when the drink in his brain splashes the other way and he turns back.

"If they think you're a girl," he says, figuring it out as he goes along, "they won't let you ride." He wrestles with this thought, then slips off his jean jacket and hands it to me. "Put this on and button the front."

It's large for me, but Foxy is pleased with the effect. He walks behind me and tugs on the thick black braid of my hair.

"Now this," he says, and sets the black Navajo on my

head. I can't believe Foxy and I have the same size brains, but we must because the hat fits.

"They'll just think I sat out in the sun too long." Foxy breaks down at his own joke. He laughs so hard he loses his breath in wheezes and coughs and finally spits on the ground. "You're a real Indian cowboy," he says.

It's less than a half hour until the event. I don't look for Sky and Evelyn since I have to figure this out for myself. The news that Mom is still on the reservation is sinking in. There's a part of me that's relieved. Ever since this morning, when Evelyn said Mom was sick, I've been worried in some nameless place, and now that relaxes. I wonder if in the weeks I've been gone, Mom has tried to find me, if she and Aunt Ida have made peace and worried together that I disappeared. No. She's still at this Dayton's and I still don't know how to find him. My one path to his door is through his horse. He's got to be around when she's ridden. Maybe Mom's here with him. Wouldn't she be surprised to see me contest? How would she feel if I got thrown on my head?

How will *I* feel? Fear rises in my neck at the thought of actually going through with Foxy's plan. I've seen bronc riding on "Wide World of Sports," and all I can remember is the sound of big men falling hard on the ground, the sight of crazed horses tossing their heads and kicking their hooves.

I've been walking toward the stock pens while I think, looking into the crowd for Mom's face, but instead I see Annabelle, and she's spied me first. She's dressed for the rodeo in tight jeans, a purple Bruce Springsteen T-shirt, long silver earrings, a bunch of turquoise bracelets on each arm, and blue Western boots. Her straight black hair hangs below her shoulders and her skin is tan and smooth. She has circled her eyes with dark liner and her fingernails are long and perfectly red. There's something about her that reminds me of Ellen, but then I realize that it's Ellen who's reminded me of Annabelle. Ellen is dim in comparison.

Annabelle comes up to me and demands, "Why are you

wearing Foxy's hat." If she's surprised to see me, she doesn't let on.

"He gave it to me."

"Is he drinking?"

"He's drunk."

"Shit," she says. "He's up in a few minutes. He'll get bumped."

"He wants me to ride for him." I'm unbelieving all over again at the idea.

Annabelle cannot trust her ears. She doesn't know whether to laugh or get mad. She decides to get mad. "That asshole," she says. "I told him to stay straight, at least until after his event. I've had it with him."

No matter how many jeans jackets and hats you put on Annabelle, nobody would ever mistake her for a boy. She opens her purse, shakes out a Virginia Slim, and taps it against her lighter. She seems to notice me for the first time.

"Where have you been?" She's impatient and pissed off, but all the same this is the friendliest she's ever acted. It's the first time she's talked to me directly and not just to make an impression on whoever else is listening.

"Working at Bearpaw Lake State Park." I speak quickly, steeling myself for a mean reply.

"Really?" she says. Her imagination is caught. "God, I should get a job and get out of this place."

Now I know who Annabelle reminds me of. She's like the pictures I found in Aunt Ida's trailer. This is how Mom must have been, young and pretty, when she left, when she met Dad and they got married.

"Well, are you going to?" Annabelle asks.

"To what?"

"To ride for Foxy?"

Annabelle will be impressed if I say yes. I'll be different in her eyes, dumb maybe, but worth knowing. I take her question seriously. I consider what Evelyn would do if this was happening to her.

"Yes," I say.

■ ■ ■

Dayton could be any one of the men clustered around the corral when I come in answer to the announcer's call and hand over my credentials. The starter pins 37 to the back of Foxy's jacket, and like a robot I mount the fence and stand above the trapped brown horse. Lots of cowboys grow their hair long, and a braid is nothing strange. No one looks at me. Maybe they're embarrassed to see the fear in a rider's eyes.

From the instant I lower myself into the stall and onto the mare's broad and sheening back, I buzz with nerves. She inclines her head and regards me with one rolled eye, and I feel her quiver through the inside of my thighs as I grip her high around the shoulders. It's the kind of vibration that comes when you touch a low-voltage electric fence, enough to scare back cows and sheep. Tensing with not even a blanket or saddle between us, her skin seems tight-stretched. With one hand I take the rope that runs from the bit in her mouth and with the other I reach forward to pat her back.

"Hey Babe, hey girl," I say.

It's a game, I want her to know. We're just playing. We don't mean it for real.

She paws her feet, snorts. A cowboy hanging on the fence touches my hat and motions for me to hold it with my free hand. I take it off and am sure that now, at last, they'll get a clear view, realize I'm a girl, see that I don't know how to sit, and call it off. But they still don't see me.

I nod to the gate. I'll never be ready, but now is as good a time as any. There are dangers to staying in the chute too long. If the horse panics she'll heave herself against the sides, crushing my legs. Or worse, one buck in that packed space would throw me to the ground with nowhere to roll away from a kick. It's happened more than once on "Wide World." The announcers talk about the metal plates in riders' skulls.

The sounds of the rodeo around me fade in my concentration. There's a drone in my ears that blocks out everything else, pasts and futures and long-range worries. The horse and I are held in a vise, a wind-up toy that has been turned one twist too many, a spring coiled beyond its limit.

"Now!" I cry, aloud or to myself I don't know. Everything has boiled down to this instant. There's nothing in the world except the hand of the gate judge, lowering in slow motion to the catch that contains us. I see each of his fingers clearly, separately, as they fold around the lever, I see the muscles in his forearm harden as he begins to push down.

I never expected the music.

Wheeling and spinning, tilting and beating, my breath the song, the horse the dance. Time is gone. All the ordinary ways of things, the gettings from here to there, the one and twos, forgot. The crowd is color, the whirl of a spun top. The noises blend into a waving band that flies around us like a ribbon on a string. Beneath me four feet dance, pounding and leaping and turning and stomping. My legs flap like wings. I sail above, first to one side, then the other, remembering more than feeling the slaps of our bodies together. Things happen faster than understanding, faster than ideas. I'm a bird coasting, shot free into the music, spiraling into a place without bones or weight.

I'm on the ground. Unmoving. The heels of my hands sunk in the dust of the arena. My knees sore. Dizzy. Back in time. I shake sense into my head, listen as the loudspeaker brays.

"Twenty-four seconds for the young cowboy from eastern Montana. Nice try, son. Hoka-hay."

A few claps from the crowd. I know I should move. I've seen riders today limp off when they fall, their heads hung, their mounts kicking two hind legs at the end of the ring until the clowns herd them out.

But Babe is calm. She stands next to me, blowing air through her nostrils, looking cross-eyed and triumphant. She wins the hand. Her sides ripple. It could be laughter, it could be disgust for having been touched. Dayton's horse.

So I don't leave with a wave to the stands. The first toss is warm-up, practice. I grab the rope, throw my arms around her neck and swing aboard. She stiffens, fuses her joints. The broad muscles of her shoulders turn steel under my gripping legs.

And bang! We're off again. This time instead of up and down she bolts straight ahead. The wind whips my braid, blows dust into my eyes till I have to squint them shut. She runs one fast circle around the pen, her body in a low crouch. She's thinking.

When you don't know what to expect, you hang on in every way you can. I clasp the rope in one hand, her mane in the other. I dig my heels into the hollows behind the place where her forelegs join her ribs. I lean into her neck, and watch the ground rush by on either side of her ears.

Without warning she slows, moves close to the rough plank fence where the Brahmas are milling, and shifts her weight. She stops on a dime and, still clutching her with every part of me, I roll to the left. I'm pinned between Babe and the boards, with my back against the wall. My breath is squeezed out and there's no way I can protect my head, lolling above the pen. Then, without once lightening on the weight she presses against me, Babe walks forward as if to clean herself of me, as if I'm mud on the bottom of a boot.

It works. The next thing I know I'm on the ground again, Foxy's jean jacket ripped and torn across the shoulder seam, the air rushing back into my lungs, tears smeared on my cheeks. My ribs hurt, and behind me the bulls knock on the fence with their horns.

And before me is Babe, her lips drawn over her yellow teeth, her head low and swinging back and forth, her legs planted far apart. She looks astonished, at herself or me I can't tell.

As I stand she begins to retreat, one foot at a time. For an instant, I hear the crowd again, but I can't bother with them. I have Babe in my bead, our eyes in a blinding fix. Our brains lock, and she stops while I grab her mane and hook a leg over her back. Before I'm balanced, she rears. Her front legs climb the air, and I dangle along her back, suspended. When at last she drops, I'm low on her flank, our hips one on top of the other, my body fitted into her length. She rears again, and again there is air between us, yet I hang on. I smell her sweat, feel the warmth of her skin beneath my face and hands. There is nothing in the world but her and I think I can stay up forever.

When she kicks out with her hind legs, though, I slide over her neck, down her long head, and slam into the ground. I concede for the second time today. I'm so winded I can't move, stupid as I must look, my face in the dirt, my ass in the air, and my legs folded beneath me. When my ears stop ringing I hear the loudspeaker again.

". . . give this kid a hand, folks. He may not be much of a rider but he ain't no quitter! Looks like he damn well wore out that wild mare too, even if he didn't bust her."

There's real clapping this time, a few whistles, but I get strength more from my curiosity about the last thing he said. I open one eye and the world is upside down, but that isn't the strangest thing. Not ten feet from me, sitting like a big dog and nodding her head, slumps Babe. She looks as bad as I feel, and as it turns out, we both need a hand from the clowns in getting out of the ring.

Some of Mom's navy boyfriends in Seattle used to talk about their sea legs and I never knew what they meant. They tried to explain how once you became used to the roll of waves, walking on dry land was never the same again. It felt lifeless.

Now I catch on. I'm back from throwing up behind the pens. I've rinsed the dirt from my face and dusted off my pants and jacket and the black hat someone handed to me as I limped out of the corral. Wild horse riding is the next-to-last event in the rodeo. As I lean back against the announcer's stand, I keep shifting my legs and waiting for something to happen under my feet. My muscles haven't yet set into the hard, stiff ache that lies ahead, but all through me I feel a ticking that hasn't run down.

There's a part of me that wants to submerge and disappear. Everybody that passes has to say something they think is funny about my ride, and I have to laugh at myself with them or be a bad sport. But there's another part of me that would climb back on Babe in a flash, no waiting, if that horse would appear in front of me. People tell me how lucky I am that I didn't break my neck or my back, or at least bust a shoulder, I fell so hard, but when I was riding I was mindless and beyond hurt. I was connected to a power I never knew existed, and without it I'm unplugged. On Babe, I would have burned out my circuits rather than choose safety. Up there, my only worry was gravity.

But on earth, my troubles haven't gone away. I stand, puzzling out what to do next, while the MC reads out the list of winners: Best bull ride. Longest saddle bronc. Fastest hogtie. I can't return to Bearpaw Lake with Sky and Evelyn. At the end of the season, when I would have no choice but to move along, I wouldn't be any closer to knowing what to do than I am now. Already Ellen and Andy and John, even Dave, are as removed and strange, as ancient history, as kids at my schools in Seattle. The ride on Babe is a boundary I can't recross, and I'm stuck on this side for better or worse.

Evelyn and Sky are different because they're here, because they brought me, because even though she doesn't know it, Evelyn got me on that horse and kept putting me back, because Sky closed the Conoco and gave up his Christmas money without asking any questions. But I can't live in the trailer with them any longer. My parents have returned from Switzerland.

Brahma riding. Bareback bronc. The fear comes back.

Annabelle pushes through the crowd and walks to face me. She carries two red paper Coke cups and hands one over. Her dark-rimmed eyes are excited.

"I wouldn't have believed it. I don't believe it," she says. "You're out of your mind. You're a maniac."

This is a compliment from Annabelle. I take a long pull on my Coke and discover it's beer.

"Do they know you're a girl?" Annabelle whispers. "You're insane."

The MC is about to announce the All-Around, the award for the cowboy who has done the best at the most events. It's what everybody waits to hear, and the crowd noise simmers down.

"Before the last prize," he says, "the judges have voted an unscheduled citation, one that's only given on rare occasions."

He holds up something shiny and silver that gathers light from the late afternoon sun and reflects it back in a bright beam.

"It's engraved special," he goes on. "I wish you folks could see it. This buckle shows a bronc and a rider throwed in the air, with genuine coral and jet inlay. One hundred percent nickel silver plate."

I see Evelyn and Sky in the bleachers, straining to hear. Their hands shade their eyes against the afternoon glare, but I'm standing under the judges' box and have my borrowed hat pulled low in front of my face.

"So come on, folks, and give a real Havre hand for the roughest, toughest, *clumsiest* cowboy we've seen around here in many a moon. It gives me genuine pleasure to award the hard-luck buckle, for the amazing feat of being bucked off the same horse three times in less than a minute, to a home-grown Indian boy, number thirty-seven, Kennedy 'Foxy' Cree!"

Some people let out yells and war whoops, and everybody starts pounding me on the back and shoving me forward. Kennedy Cree is Foxy's real name, and this minute it's mine too. Annabelle gives a sharp piercing whistle through her fingers and stomps her blue boot in the sawdust. I fill my lungs with stockyard air. There's no escape.

So I run the steps and reach to shake the MC's hand. He looks close at me this time, then closer. He realizes I'm no cowboy. I pry the buckle from him anyway and hold it to my right and left for the stands to see. Behind me there are surprised voices talking to each other and when I look down at the other winners assembled nearest to the grandstand I see their eyes are wide too. It's no use pretending. I knock off my hat, undo the rubber band, comb with my fingers, and shake out my braid. With my free hand I unsnap the ruined jacket and shrug it from my shoulders. I thrust out my chest.

At first there's silence. Everyone gapes at me and then at each other and then at me again. The quiet hangs like a Seattle fog as we stand there, facing off in the long afternoon light. And finally from far away, clear and proud, Evelyn shouts: "Rayona!" Annabelle whistles again, loud as a siren. And when I raise the silver buckle high above my head, the rest of the crowd joins in.

8

On the "Late Show," the good guy escapes. His faithful sidekick comes along to shoot the noose rope in two just as the trapdoor springs, and arrives on a fast horse to catch him when he drops free. There's a secret, forgotten exit to the mine, unknown to the gunslinging gang ready to throw a smoking torch into the entrance. Somebody hitches a rope to the bars in the jail window from the back of a wagon and pulls a hole in the wall. The cavalry is there when you need it.

I step off the platform with a silver-inlay hard-luck buckle and onto the path of nowhere I want to go. From the shaded seats of the bleachers, Evelyn is waving at me and tugging on Sky's shirt. From the other side I see Foxy propped against one of the columns that supports the stands. He's madder than an overheated engine and scowls at me with the mean, glazed eyes of a half-gone bully whose name has just been publicly taken in vain. And to top it off, who's walking toward me, the toes of his black shoes pointing outward with each step, his red mouth grim and a frown on his sunburned face, but Father Tom.

He's all decked out for the rodeo. A red bandanna has replaced the Roman collar on his neck, a too-small Stetson perches on top of his head, not quite hiding the baldness beneath, and I can spot, even from a distance, that he's found himself a turquoise ring the size of an egg. It makes his hand look thin and small.

I take a step backward. I am like a contestant on "Let's

Make a Deal," except that there's no vacation trip to Acapulco behind any of the three mystery doors. When I feel a hand on my shoulder, I spin to see a heavyset, mixed-blood cowboy, not very old, with a plug under his lower lip and patchy two-day whiskers on his cheeks.

"Foxy, you've changed," he says, giving me the once-over. "And for the better."

I twist from under his hand, but he doesn't move away.

"Who are you then?"

"I'm Ray," I say. "Rayona Taylor." Annabelle has inched her way in my direction and the sight of her, all glittery and dangerous, makes me braver.

"Rayona?" he says, knitting his bushy eyebrows. "Christine's girl, Ray?"

"You're Dayton," I guess, but I know before he answers that it has to be him. I'm one step away from Mom. "What's your last name?"

"Nickles."

I have no time for small talk. Father Tom is within hailing distance. I expect him to be staring holes through me, but he can't seem to take his eyes off Dayton. I've lost track of Sky and Evelyn, which means they're on their way. At least Foxy hasn't budged. He's holding up the grandstand and hasn't remembered yet how to move.

"Is my mom with you?" I ask Dayton, under my breath. "Is she all right?"

He hesitates, runs his hand through the long dark curly hair that has been plastered by sweat in the shape of a hatband. "Goddamn" is all he says. "Ida said you had taken off back to Seattle."

"When did you see her?"

But it's too late for him to answer. Father Tom prances up, favoring his new ring and acting as if my appearing in Havre is nothing out of the ordinary.

"Rayona!" he says as though we're old friends, "I thought you were in Seattle having the time of your life. Hello there, Dayton." Father Tom sticks out his hand but Dayton just gazes at it. He treats Father Tom the same way many of the younger men on the reservation do—that is, he pretends Father Tom doesn't exist.

Father Tom is used to this but it still makes him nervous, and he centers his attention on me. "You could have blown me down when I saw you on that horse, Rayona!" He puts his unshook hand in his pocket as if that was where it wanted to go all along. "I didn't even realize you knew how to ride." His eyes go to the buckle, so I display it on my flat palm.

"I don't. That's why they gave me this."

And there's Sky. He's bought himself a souvenir program and holds it in his grease-stained fingers. "Will you autograph this," he jokes, all his earlier shyness gone. "Did you see there was a TV camera trained on you?"

From his superior expression, it's obvious that Father Tom sees Sky as an outsider, some unknown white man who's come to the wrong rodeo, and that ticks me off.

"This is Sky Dial," I say to everybody. "I've been working with him and his wife over at Bearpaw Lake State Park. I've been living in their trailer."

Sky's serious about me signing his program, so finally I take it and then the pen he locates in his pocket. I feel stupid, but it's for Sky, so I scribble "Your friend, Rayona" on the red-and-black cover and hand it back. He reads what I wrote and grins. There's no doubt in my mind he'll hang it on the wall of the Conoco.

Evelyn's here too, sweating patches on her nylon blouse and full of private glances in my direction as she inspects each person in the group.

Father Tom is unglued. He purses his lips as though he has a peach pit he wants to spit out but doesn't know where. At the mention of Bearpaw Lake, his eyes light like a video game once you drop in the quarter.

Dayton nods at Sky.

Evelyn can't stand it anymore. "Did you find her?" she demands, ignoring everyone.

"I found *her*," Annabelle says. "Who are you?"

Evelyn looks eagerly in Annabelle's direction, then whips her eyes back to mine, all confused.

"This is Annabelle," I tell her. "She's..." I pause a second. What *is* Annabelle? "...she's a friend." And, incredibly, I'm right. Not only does Annabelle not object to what I've said, she flashes her white teeth in a smile. Evelyn edges closer to Sky and tucks her hand in the back pocket of his jeans.

"This is Evelyn," I say.

Evelyn will not be diverted. "So?" she asks me.

"My mom is at Dayton's." I point him out with my eyes and Evelyn is almost satisfied. "Yes," I tell her.

"And this one is?" Evelyn asks, raising her brows.

"Father Tom."

He has been about to say something, but his words dry up fast when he sees Evelyn's face. He knows she knows, and she knows he does. They're like two computers talking to each other without sound, the information flying back and forth. He glances to me for help, for me to tell him he's wrong, but I won't. Evelyn beats him down with her gleaming look, reads him his rights, and gives him no more chances.

Father Tom shrinks into himself, tight as a stuck zipper. "I just stopped by to say hello," he explains in a high voice. "It's been, yes, well, I'll, I'm..." Evelyn's concentration doesn't flicker for a second. He's revolving that ring so hard I think his finger will unscrew. "I thought you might need a lift to your aunt's, but of course if you'd rather..."

"I've got a ride." I speak with a sureness I don't feel, but Dayton's head moves almost invisibly in agreement.

"Well, if you think your aunt would approve." There's something Father Tom isn't saying, but nobody throws him a line. There's nothing for him to do but fade into the crowd.

"We'll go now," Evelyn tells Sky, who looks at me. "She's staying here. With her mom."

"Oh." He thinks he understands. "Sure. Well, I hope they had a good time over there."

"My stuff's in the car." I look at Dayton. "Don't leave. I'll be right back."

I follow Sky and Evelyn. He has his arm across her broad shoulders and his ponytail hangs limp and scraggly down the center of his back. She's searching in the pockets of her shorts for the keys. They don't belong together, but there they are.

When we reach the car, Sky bends into the backseat through the window of the tied-shut door and pulls out the suitcase. It rests on the ground like a fence between us.

"Well, good luck to you," Evelyn says at last.

"There's one thing." I kneel on the ground and flip the snaps of her valise. Folded beneath the videotapes, ironed flat from being pressed into the tight space, is the lost and found blanket. "For the trailer," I say. "It's not much, but everything happened . . ." While I'm talking I pinch the corners and flap it open so that they can see the buck posing on the grassy hill.

"Oh, my Lord," Evelyn says from the other side of its curtain. "If that isn't the . . ." Her voices stops and Sky chimes in. "It sure is," he says. "I'll say."

Evelyn gathers it from me and cradles it in a bundle against her body. She's blushing, the red spreading from her neck along her jawbone and down beneath her yellow blouse.

"You should save your money." She walks to the passenger side, gets in, and jerks her body across the blistering hot seat until she's behind the wheel. Sky gives me the peace handshake. "Don't be a stranger now," he says, and follows his wife.

Evelyn edges out of her space, pulls into a driveway, and points the car in the opposite direction. She stops as she draws even to where I wait and leans her arm out the window. "I take it back. Don't save a penny. Spend it on yourself."

"Maybe you'll come back again and see me on the reservation."

"That's a thought," she agrees. "Could be." The car is idling and we've run out of words, so Evelyn just says, "Okay . . ." and pulls out. I hear the beginning of muffler trouble, see that a rear tire is low on air. Halfway down the road, Sky raises his hand above the roof and makes a V with his fingers.

• • •

When I get back inside the gate, Annabelle has disappeared.

"I want to see my mom," I tell Dayton. Behind him, I catch that Foxy's shoulder has finally disconnected from the post he has been leaning against. He's sure to be disqualified now, and will blame me. But Annabelle materializes and intercepts him as he starts toward me. I can't hear what they're saying, but she's doing most of the talking and is not happy. It takes him a while to drop his eyes from me but finally he has to listen to Annabelle. She won't let up.

We ride back to Dayton's ranch in a clean new pickup with fence sections bolted to the sides to keep Babe from jumping out. Babe is good with Dayton, but when she sees me she snorts and pulls against the ropes that restrain her. When we turn off the highway onto the reservation road, the dust rises and trails behind like the smoke of a rocket launch. In the rear window of the cab, all I can see are Babe's eyes, blazing on either side of her long brown head, and a gold sky.

Dayton's an experienced driver, relaxed and easy. Whenever I ask him a question about Mom he says that it's for her to tell, and changes the subject. He holds an empty Mello Yello can between his thighs, and every once in a while he switches the plug to one side of his lip, and brings the lip of the can to his mouth.

"You and Mom used to go together." I say this as a statement, then ask, "In high school?"

"Christine was a couple of years ahead of me at the Mission. It was her brother, Lee, I knew better."

I breathe easier. I've had enough of Mom's old boyfriends to last me a lifetime. "I was at his funeral."

"I recall."

"I can hardly remember it." I polish the buckle on my pants leg. "I must have been two, three years old."

"That's why you don't remember." He raises the can again, looks over at me. "Christine talk much about Lee and me?"

I don't know what he wants to hear. "Sometimes she does. They were real close."

"Yeah." There's a tone in his voice that makes me wonder

what he thinks of Mom. He isn't like the men she usually goes with. I can't imagine him dressed for the Silver Bullet in Seattle, walking out of our apartment between Mom and Charlene, an arm around each one.

"Lee was quite a guy," Dayton continues. "Could have been the best bronc rider that ever came out of eastern Montana."

I don't say anything. Here was another relative who I'm not anything like.

"You could learn to ride," Dayton reads my mind.

"Sure thing." I give the buckle a final buff and slip it into my pocket.

"Today doesn't mean anything. Anybody can learn to stay on. What you can't learn, and what you've got, is desire. I saw your face."

The feeling comes back to me, just remembering it. The power. I think of Babe bouncing along behind us.

"Today was my first."

Dayton nods like he's impressed but not surprised, and I understand why Mom remembered him all these years.

The sun's almost down by the time we get to Dayton's. Copper light breaks over the tops of the ragged hills to the west and we have the visors down to spare our eyes. I'm slumped with my knees wedged against the glove compartment, and when we park I take my time unwinding. Mom's standing in the door of the house, dressed in a red robe, her brown hair short and still damp from a shower. The sunset's in her eyes and she can't see me, just my dark outline in the seat. I look at her through the one-way mirror of the windshield and let her wonder.

I get out of the truck, and I think Mom will bolt again. She's startled, blocks the light with her hand. She looks until she's sure, then she blazes daggers at Dayton.

"Now don't be that way," he says. "She was at the rodeo and wanted to come. What was I supposed to say?"

"Don't you want to see me?" I dare Mom to say no. I didn't know what I hoped she would do when I found her, until she doesn't do it. Now I mentally tick off a list of all the rotten things she's done to me, not just lately, but for my whole life. I could knock her over with the strength of my rightness.

"Aunt Ida said you walked out with not even a note good-bye," Mom has the nerve to say. "She was a crazy woman for two days until that priest came to tell her you went back home. I called Charlene, everybody, even Elgin, but nobody knew a damn thing about you. You're no goddamn good."

I'm shocked at the idea that in Mom's version of the story, I'm the guilty one. The things that come into your head when you're in the middle of things: I see the two of us, Mom and me, march up before Judge Wapner on "The People's Court" and tell our tales. He sits high behind his bench, bored and disgusted. Neither of us is worth two cents in his eyes. He hears us out and asks a few questions, then bangs his gavel. Whichever way he decides, Aunt Ida will turn him off, pressing the metal button on her TV to change us all into a million specks of snow.

I'm so used to being Mom's daughter, I defend myself.

"I meant to get in touch," I say.

"You meant to, you meant to!" Mom pulls the sash of her robe tight and ties it in a knot. "That's just great. Here I am, sick as a dog, and you're off..."

"I was working at Bearpaw Lake State Park."

"Having *fun!*" Mom shouts. "At some park."

"But you left first."

"That's right, blame me." Mom turns to Dayton. "It's my fault she walked out on her grandmother. Of course."

"Now don't get yourself all upset," he says. "When you calm down, you're going to be glad to see Ray."

"I thought something happened to you!" Mom screams at me. It's the worst thing yet she's said.

"A lot you cared." I've got my second wind. "You could come for your box of pills from Charlene, but not for me."

That stops her. "How did you know it was pills?"

"And all that time, here you are, not ten miles away. Don't tell me about leaving."

"She has no heart!" Mom appeals to Dayton. "She wants to hurt me, sick as I am."

"You tried that one on Dad and it didn't work." I'm mad beyond the bounds of what's fair. "You're not sick."

But of course she is. I see it the minute the words are out of my mouth. In some part of my brain it has been registering ever since the car stopped. She's ragged, pale. There are new wrinkles in the skin of her forehead, thin lines that stretch like threads above her eyebrows. Her cheeks are hollow but her waist has thickened.

"You're just like him," she says to me in a voice tied to a rock. "In every way."

We're out of control, fighting with no rules, hitting below the belt.

"Let's go inside," Dayton says.

He lives in a tiny ranch house, white siding and green trim. His walls are lined with wood paneling and there's an orange-and-brown braid rug on the floor. Mom leans on a green couch and covers her eyes with her arm, the sleeve falling back to expose her skin. Dayton sets my suitcase by the door, and flops into a recliner. I pull a kitchen chair away from the table and sit. We're all exhausted, a group of statues, the sound from the TV our only thing in common.

The ten o'clock news is on the Havre station, the familiar face of the anchorman who's Aunt Ida's nightly companion. As we watch, hypnotized, the stories change from weather to national to local to a feature on the rodeo and there I am, flashing my buckle and grinning. I shrink into my chair and lower my eyes.

"Look at that, Christine." Dayton leans forward to turn up the volume, and Mom peeks under her arm. She keeps watching.

"Your kid's a star."

I'm pulled back to the TV. The picture burns into my brain. The short men who stand behind me with their mouths hanging open are the ones who look dumb. The anchorman is not sure about me one bit. He calls me a brave young woman, but he wonders if I'm aiming to break the tradition of male dominance in the rodeo circuit, out to prove a female is as capable as a man. He forgets I got dumped, just that I rode and got a prize. The camera shows the crowd, hollering and cheering, some even waving their hats, and then it zooms in on my face. I fill the screen, dark and brown. My hair is wild as a star on MTV. To see me, you'd think I could do anything I want.

My head rocks with the pounding of my heart.

The next story is about baseball.

"They should have your horse's picture instead of mine," I say. "She won."

"Forget it," Dayton says, then speaks to Mom. "Babe threw her three times, but Rayona walked out." He's smiling from across the room.

Mom takes her arm down and looks at me. "You rode?" She can't believe it. "You don't know how to ride."

"She's got guts," Dayton goes on. "Pretended to be a boy. Foxy Cree! It's going to take him a while to live this one down, if he ever sobers up."

"Why in hell?" Mom asks me. Then, "Are you all right? Did you break anything?"

"She gets it from Lee, Christine, a natural. You should have seen."

"I can't take this in," Mom says. "I'm going to bed. We'll figure this out tomorrow."

She's not steady on her feet, and Dayton goes over to help. He guides her, holding her arm as she retreats to another room. Before she's out the door she looks back at me. Her face is a puzzle. She has her tongue against her teeth and takes a breath as though she's ready to say something more, but she doesn't, she just turns away and lets Dayton put her to bed.

The news ends, and the "Reverend Bob Treadle Bible Show" comes on. Reverend Bob believes the end of the world is at hand, and once a week he shows another proof. Greece has joined the Common Market, making just the right number of allies for Israel. Some credit company uses "666" as part of its code, and that's Satan's number. A former Miss America has seen the light and is ready for the Second Coming.

"Hey, rodeo queen, sit down before you fall down," Dayton says. He looks beat too. "She's just tired, she'll be fine tomorrow." He turns off the TV. "The couch opens out. Sheets already on it. You make yourself at home. I'm just going to turn Babe loose. She had a pretty rough day herself, thanks to you." He waits to see that I'm okay, waits until I say something.

"Good night."

And I'm alone in the brown light of the living room. It's as quiet as early morning. One green-shaded lamp constructed to look like a lantern is the only illumination, and on all the walls the shadows climb the long planks of stained wood.

The sun streams through the windows, and when I try to turn away, I can't lift any part of my body without pain. It's the kind of hurting that warns you. My arms and legs and neck all advise me I can move them an inch, maybe, but beyond that they'll break off. Somebody has poured glue on me in my sleep, and I have hardened into a solid block.

I glance around the stuffy room without turning my head. I can't see much of anything. I squint my eyes and the light gets filtered by tiny lines of floating dust that move if I try to focus on them. The ceiling is white and divided by a long structure crack in the shape of a lightning bolt. The walls could've been polished with Lemon Pledge.

The quilt weights my legs but there's no easy way to remove it. I'm in steady pain and I can't change the subject of my thoughts. I want to free myself, to be covered with nothing, to pour my heaviness into my feet. I pretend I have a bullet in my teeth and bite it, making only a constant hum, low in my throat, as I slide first one foot, then its leg, then the other leg, then my ass to the side of the fold-out bed. The couch hides a soft mattress, which has dipped into a funnel, and I slip down it until my toes sense the coiled rug. With an act of pure will I stand without bending at the waist. I'm like the Tin Man, in need of an oil can for my rusted joints. I march stiff-legged to the window but can't raise it since that means bending my elbows and pushing. But I can at least see straight ahead outside to a fenced yard, and grazing in that space is Babe, watching me.

I find the strength to dress, but give up on my boots and don't snap closed the front of Foxy's torn jacket. Even that pressure would be too much across the bands of strained muscle that hold my back together. Sideways, because it's easier, I pass through the screen door and inch across the grass toward the fence.

Babe lets me put my face next to her muzzle, smell her scent of hay and manure and body heat. She's calm as I unhook the fence and enter the yard, then close it again behind me.

Last night in the truck, Dayton told me two points about horse busting. First, you have to get right back on after you're thrown so there's no time to think about the fear. He said I handled that part like a pro. The second thing to remember is that once broke, a horse knows its rider. It's like making a friend after a clean fight, you shake and that's it. I became Babe's master fair and square, and I have the hard-luck buckle and the burning body to prove it.

It's time to cash in on my victory. While Babe stands quiet I nudge a block of wood over to her side, and she lowers her head to nibble at some feed as I slowly use it as a ladder. She merely twitches her ears when, creaking and tense, I rest my full weight upon her broad brown back.

But Babe has heard a different story about the morning after. With one buck, she tosses me like a bag of clothespins into the air and over the fence.

This time I stay where I land. I can move if I have to, but there's no place I need to be. In a little while I hear the door bang and feel footsteps approaching. It's Mom. I can smell her coffee, and I'm surprised how natural it feels to be with her now, especially after last night. Maybe it's because early mornings have always been our time together. She doesn't ask what I'm doing here, just sits on the grass beside me and starts in as though we've never been apart.

"I've thought about going back to the Church. Can you imagine?"

I don't know what's the right answer to that question.

"I helped out at the Mission," I tell her.

This information doesn't seem to excite her much. She's interested in her own revelations. "You know, I lost my faith when I wasn't much older than you."

There's a difference in the way Mom's talking to me, as if we've become closer in age during our separation and now I'm a girlfriend she can confide in, even in the daylight.

"Well," she says. "Don't you want to know how?"

I nod my head. Mom's taking an intermission, a news break, before dealing with the grief between us. And I understand. She's me staring at that yellow raft this time yesterday.

"I'm over forty years old," Mom continues, "and I lost my faith for more than twenty-five of those years. All because of the letter."

"What letter?" I think of Evelyn and feel my hot embarrassment once again.

"The letter the Blessed Virgin gave to Lucy at Fatima." Mom watches for some reaction, but I draw a blank.

"I heard of Fatima. In Spain."

"Portugal."

I wait for her to go on.

"They won't talk about it now." She starts to weave the long weeds that border the corral into a slim green chain. Link after link, it grows in her hands and trails over her legs. The air is rich with the smell of alfalfa.

"What did it say?"

"That's the sixty-four-thousand-dollar question." Mom angles in my direction to underline her words, and I see how worn out she is. She looks no better this morning than she did when she went to bed. "The whole time I was growing up, all I heard was The Letter, The Letter, The Letter. The Pope was supposed to unseal it in 1960. Either Communist Russia was going to be converted or the world would come to an end, one or the other. In school at the Mission, we prayed constantly about that letter, and sometimes we heard rumors. One day somebody would claim the Pope had read it early and fainted dead away.

Another time they'd say Lucy had cried when she snuck a peek inside the envelope."

Mom is pulling her chain apart now, rolling the little bits of grass between her thumb and fingers until the juice spots her skin.

"I regretted it, I really did. Russia wasn't getting converted, it was only getting worse, so there was no choice but for the world to end—and before I even got my driver's license. Do you know what it's like to be a teenager out here without wheels? You can't go anywhere."

I try to look serious. Mom seems to have forgotten my situation. I'm piled in a heap in front of her, and here she is, laying out her history.

"I read the Bible, the Apocalypse at the end, when they talk about the four horsemen and everything. Two things I'll never forget: one, when the world comes to an end you're in big trouble if you're pregnant, and two, for some reason you're supposed to get onto the roof. And I was prepared. I didn't even have a boyfriend, so the first part was no problem, and as for the second, I had rehearsed climbing out Aunt Ida's attic window and could be on top of that house in no time flat. I made a perfect confession on New Year's Eve, and refused the first party I was ever invited to."

"What happened?" I ask. I'm caught by her story. I know the world's still here but I want to hear her tell it.

"Not a goddamn thing." She slams her hand to the ground. "I listened to Guy Lombardo and his orchestra. They had New Year's 1960 in New York. Then an hour later they had it in Chicago. I heard the party in Denver on my clock radio. Nothing. I figured the last chance was if God was on Pacific Time, so I hung on till it passed midnight in L.A. I sat there by my window watching the sky, ready to take the stairs two at a time, rip out the screen, and be waiting on the porch roof for whatever came next. Finally I dozed off."

"You must have been relieved."

"That wasn't the word for it! First thing in the morning I tune in the news. Maybe Russia had converted, but not a word.

The next day I confront Sister Alvina. 'What about the letter?' I ask her. 'We're still here.' And do you know what she says to me, that woman who had scared the shit out of me for years about the end of the world, that woman who was responsible for me giving all my Christmas present money to the South American missions so that I could score some last-minute points before the Day of Judgment, that woman who convinced me to make the nine First Fridays six times and wear a scratchy scapular medal night and day, do you know what she says to me?"

I shake my head. Mom has risen to her knees, her hands balled into fists.

" 'It's a *mystery*,' she tells me. A *mystery*. The old three-in-one answer. I never went to church again."

"Maybe Lucy faked the letter," I say. "To get herself off the hook."

Mom considers this.

"But why did the Pope faint, then?" she asks. "How do you explain that?"

Christine

9

Mysteries were the least of my problems.

When the world didn't end, I got another chance. I became the most popular high school girl on the reservation and never missed another party. You might hear stories about me, how wild I was, how I got what I asked for. But I don't take back a thing. If I blamed myself for being dumb, I wouldn't know where to quit. I had to find my own way and I started out in the hole, the bastard daughter of a woman who wouldn't even admit she was my mother and the fat sister of the prettiest boy that ever lived.

Everywhere else in the world things were happening—wars, psychedelic drugs, love-ins—and there we were at Holy Martyrs Mission, still writing themes about whether if God could do anything, could He make a rock He couldn't lift. That kind of shit. No wonder I was screwed up. You try to make a real world out of what you see on one television channel and what you hear on the radio. You try to put together cute outfits from the secondhand trash from the charity store. You try to have fun when there's nowhere to go and you might be related to every other boy in town.

People on TV talked about the Sixties as if those were the best times of their lives. They brag on old pictures of themselves with dirty hair and strings of beads looped around their necks, and make victory signs with their fingers. But if they had ever shown themselves on my reservation looking like that, they would have been locked up or worse.

After supper, when there was nothing better to do, my girlfriends and I smoked Salems and Pall Malls and watched Walter Cronkite. He was the best the set at the Teen Snack Bar at the Mission could pull, and still his sound and picture didn't always match. One time we saw some hippies in Washington, D.C., stick flowers down the barrels of soldiers' rifles. We leaned forward with our mouths hanging open, trying to hear through the static and waiting for the fun to start, but nothing happened. Those GI's just looked straight ahead and held tight. You could imagine what was going on inside their helmets, but their hands were tied. There was a young guy who looked Indian and I watched him the closest. Maybe he was Mexican, I don't know. Either in real life or because of our reception, the muscles in his cheeks seemed to clench in and out, in and out. The boy with a ponytail, facing him, had a shirt made out of an American flag, and that had to drive the Indian soldier crazy.

You don't live on a reservation without learning respect for the red, white, and blue. Every powwow, every graduation, every grade-school basketball game in the school gym, out come the Honor Guard dressed in their fancy-dance costumes, with the man in the middle carrying the flag. When they appear, everybody gets quiet so that the only sound is the cowbells and jingles on the bearers' outfits. They do a circuit around the place and then park in the front while one of them offers a prayer in Indian, then they parade off slow and solemn. You stand at attention with your hand over your heart. It isn't till they leave, out of the light or the room or the gym, that you hear a kind of sigh pass through the crowd. Cards get dealt on plastic-covered tables, referees blow their whistles, baskets full of Bingo numbers spin, old ladies hitch their shawls and shuffle out for the first round dance.

My brother, Lee, was the best-looking thing on the reservation and he knew it. He could be sweet too, do what people wanted and get on their good side. He spoke the old language with the grandmothers and had clean English for his teachers in school. When he was no more than seven years old, he hoop-danced at powwows, and before long he was soloing with five hoops. Without ever missing a beat he threaded them over his twisting, bending body and spread them like wings across his back. He was magic, slippery as floor wax. My mouth would go dry watching him, afraid he'd drop a feather or trip himself. I didn't move, but when it was over and I stood, my muscles were as sore as if I'd performed myself.

When he got to be a teenager Lee bought a special tweezers to pluck any beard that grew on his cheeks or chin, and we fought over the mirror in the bathroom whenever I went out on a date. You try to get your makeup straight with a tall boy stooping in front of you, turning his jaw back and forth, looking for the sprout of a new hair. The color of his eyes got blacker the closer he got to the glass. They hypnotized me so bad I forgot myself in their reflection, and half the time went out the door without lipstick or with my hair a mess. If I complained, Lee would yell that I had the bedroom, so the bathroom was his.

It doesn't matter what a boy looks like, but there was Lee, long and loose-jointed, while I was short and had to watch my weight. His eyebrows, full where they began on either side of his nose and then tapering off to nothing, could have been drawn onto his forehead with a sharpened pencil. Even when his face was relaxed, he looked as though he had just heard something he couldn't imagine was true. Me, I had to spend hours with my two-sided magnifying mirror, shaping my brows into thin, straight lines, not near as nice. You could see the foundation of bones beneath Lee's cheeks, but no matter how much I angled my chin and clenched my jaws, I had the face of a squirrel hoarding nuts for the winter.

We were so different I wondered if we had the same father, and if we did, why it was the daughter got the short end of the stick. I studied middle-aged men on the reservation for a clue in their faces. Without my cosmetics, I could have sprung from anybody with a big nose and a gap between their front teeth, but looks like my brother's didn't appear from nowhere. Aunt Ida never gave a hint, except once to say she had been a fool twice and there wouldn't be a third time. She wouldn't let us call her Mom, since she hadn't been married, but she claimed we both favored her side. That was a joke. She was ugly the way some people get, each part of her too big or off-center, like a woman slapped together out of branches and mud. Her back was broad, her neck was as thick as her head, and on her left cheek was a burn scar the size of a plum. She always seemed old to me, though she couldn't have been much more than thirty on the New Year's Eve when the world didn't end. I thought it was the last chance I had to study my mother as a human being, so I paid her close attention. When all the living and the dead appeared at midnight, as the Apocalypse foretold, I didn't want to confuse her with someone else.

I memorized her too well. To this day I can't get that picture out of my mind, and every time I think about her as she is now, hard and mean, her image gets dressed in the damn blue flowery cotton shift she wore that night. She had it mail-ordered for $4.99 from an ad in the *Rocky Mountain News*, found anklets at the reservation store to match, and rolled them down over bleached tennis shoes. For Christmas, Lee gave her a navy blue muffler made out of washable yarn, and I bought her a pendant necklace with a little picture of the Sacred Heart on a gold chain. I thought it would be a safe thing for her to wear at the Last Judgment, when she had to atone for having Lee and me without a legal husband.

I was committed to her appearance. While Aunt Ida sat, stiff as a brick, I gave her a Lilt home permanent. Her hair had no white in those days, of course, and hung in a thick, coarse curtain to her waist. Following the directions on the box, I rolled it in clips and strips of soaked tissue paper that swelled above her ears like hot dogs. Her skull looked too small, the way a cat's does when it gets wet, but even that sight didn't slow me down. I carefully mixed the setting lotion and squeezed it from its pointy tube onto the top of each knob. Then I neutralized her whole head.

"Just wait till it gets brushed out," I told her. "You'll be beautiful."

Aunt Ida endured it all like a doomed martyr, like a woman in the electric chair, and humored me because of the Sacred Heart. Because she had given me no present, she was in my power.

Just before five o'clock, I took out the pins and her hair unwrapped in long ropy coils, matted and stuck together. A brush wouldn't separate it and I broke my comb's teeth trying to drag it through. Finally I pulled it apart and shaped it with my fingers as the fat muscles of Aunt Ida's neck flexed and strained against my hands. She looked like a wild woman, like someone who had just ridden a jeep through a tornado.

She walked to the bathroom mirror. Her hair stuck out in odd places and was straight on all the ends where I had not wound it tight enough. I frowned at Lee to keep his mouth shut, and followed.

"You could be a beauty operator," she said, pushing at a lump of wave the way you see them do on TV. "I resemble Jane Russell." The strangeness of hearing Aunt Ida pronounce a movie star's name among all that Indian, which is the only thing she ever spoke at home, made me find her eyes in the mirror and, for the first time in my life, they met mine, woman to woman.

The crags and crevices of Aunt Ida's face weren't as deep then, but they sealed into hard lines at the first sound of Lee's laugh. She backed out of the bathroom like a truck in reverse. I told Lee to shut up, but the damage was done. Aunt Ida banged the cast-iron skillet on the stove and dumped in a can of corn-beef hash. She tied Lee's Christmas scarf around her head, and ate alone in front of the television. When I woke the next morning to find the world still there, she had braided her hair so tight that it arched and forked like a sidewinder down her back.

But there was no way anybody, especially Aunt Ida, could stay mad at Lee for long. Even as a little kid, he was a boy people noticed, he was a winner. There were times I saw Aunt Ida wonder at him as though she couldn't believe he was hers.

Sure I was jealous. Everything was Lee this and Lee that from when he was a baby. But I've got to say he didn't let his looks go to his head as much as some would. There were times he forgot all about himself.

Lee never mixed much with kids his own age. He had no patience and didn't like to depend on others in a game, so all during my grade school he lived his life through me. I let him have his way, go with me wherever I went. Maybe I hung around with him because he was nosey and wanted to know my business. He said "What's the matter?" before I knew anything was wrong. He told me how to dress and listened to all my stories. He took my side against anybody. He could talk me out of a bad mood by telling me why he was worse off. I never did get over feeling good to hear him call me Tina, a name nobody else used.

Besides, I liked having an audience when I shamed the boys in my class by being tougher. They knew from experience that there wasn't one of them I couldn't take in a fight, so they tossed dares to test how far I would go, how crazy I could be. I stared down a rattler no further away from me than a creek's width. I stole a quarter from the collection basket at Mass and never confessed. I stripped off my clothes outdoors just after sunset one All Souls' night and ran to the bottom of our hill with the cool air playing on my skin and my hands over my head. And every time, my brother was there, ready to laugh at those boys when I came out on top.

Lee was everywhere with me, until the spring afternoon he saved my life.

That day the ground was still soggy with melted snow, but the light lasted longer, and when school was dismissed I wasn't ready to go home. Not far from our house there was a high block of yellow stone hollowed over the years by the finger of a fast stream. It stuck out of that flat land like a castle, its two sides sharp and spokey as towers. It was a ghostly place, whispering and lonesome and flaking chips. Some people claimed to believe it was where the spirit went when you died, but they said that about any place unusual, so I never paid attention. All I knew was that even on hot days, it stayed cool.

Some seventh grader bet me I wouldn't cross the natural bridge that stretched twenty feet above the creek bed. I laughed at him and thought it was an easy thing, but once I climbed I saw that the yellow rock was so thin and cracked it could break in a fast wind. The group of boys was gathered far below me, and short among them, his neck bent back and his thumbs looped in his belt, was Lee. He expected me to walk across as easy as I had done everything else. I was paralyzed by his excitement, and hated him for his lack of pity.

I straddled that bridge, scooted my butt out a few inches at a time, and looked straight ahead. The remains of a big nest hung from the other tower. There were holes in its twigs big enough for a baby to slip through. I went toward it, little by little, with the rough stone scraping the inside of my legs and my underwear pulling tight.

The idea of where I was never once left me. Wind moved my skirt and my hair, and I gripped tighter. My feet felt like weights in my shoes as I tried to keep them equally balanced. I kept sensing the beginnings of a fall, kept having that feeling that comes just before you lose control, and finally I stopped. My hands became a part of the rock. I wet my pants and didn't care.

The nest was the one thing tying me to the bridge, and I studied it, racing my eyes along the tracks of the bleached vines and grasses that held it together. I heard shouts below me, but I didn't look down. Maybe the hawks that built the nest would come back, maybe they'd rescue me with their clawed feet and fly me to the other side. My breath came short, my eyes swelled in their sockets. Then I saw something I did not believe. Lee's head, peaceful and natural, appeared behind the nest, like a bird spying over the side. Some hair blew into his eyes, and he pushed it back. His calmness flowed to me like rope. It ran the length of my arms and pried loose my fingers. It relaxed the muscles of my thighs and it supported my back.

"Come on, Tina," Lee said.

I slid smooth as oil as he pulled me in, stronger than the tug of earth. I scrambled through the nest, dislodging it to drop behind me. Even when I was standing on the ledge next to Lee, I didn't turn my eyes, I didn't look at anything but him. I grabbed his skinny arms with all my strength and felt his sun-warmed skin tense beneath my fingers. I smelled the yellow dust in his hair and the Juicy Fruit in his mouth.

"It's dangerous here," I shouted. "Don't stand so close to the edge. Are you loony?" I wanted him to know what he had made me do.

Lee got frightened, ready to cry. His lips trembled, his chin rose as he turned his head away.

"Don't be a baby," I told him, dragging him low to sit beside me. "They'll see." But I was the one. My legs were wet from my own cold piss. I had crossed the bridge, but not on my own, and we both realized it. I don't know what my brother thought about in those long minutes we spent flicking pebbles into the thin air and waiting for the kids below to go home, but me, my mind was making lists of all the things I should never do, could never try. And by the time we came down, step by step, Lee went first to test the path.

Midway through next year, when Lee was thirteen and I was a sophomore, a half-breed kid with curly black hair and green eyes moved to the reservation with his mother and took an old house on an allotment not far from ours. Right away, he leeched onto us. Though Dayton Nickles was a year older, an eighth grader, he followed Lee around like a shadow on a sunny day. You'd think the only thing in his life was being Lee's friend, and it didn't take people long to tease about it.

"Where's Dayton?" they asked Lee whenever he appeared someplace alone. "Did he get off his leash?" But my brother was in his own world and never joked back.

I thought it was funny too, at first, comical the way Dayton hero-worshiped Lee, but you can only laugh at something so often. Every time I blinked, there he was, even at

Aunt Ida's, dressed in jeans and a white T-shirt, hanging his head, a wad of snuff tucked under his lower lip and a tin can for spit in his hand. But no matter what I said, how I said it, Lee wouldn't tell Dayton to get lost. He just smiled and shook his head. "We're buddies," he said. "We get along pretty good." And that was it for the whole summer, for the next four years.

After I got popular, it mattered less to me who Lee ran around with. I had new things on my mind and a new body to go with them. I washed my clothes in hot water so they'd shrink, and I could harmonize the words to every good song on the radio. At night I set my hair, and in the morning, when it was ratted as high as it would go, I laced it with stiff Ray-Nette until even an Alberta blow wouldn't muss it. What I lacked in looks I made up in other ways, and a boy had a good time on a date with me. Some of the girls talked behind my back, as they always had, but they came to me with their questions about making out. I was the expert.

Most afternoons I lay on my bed listening to "The Teen Beat" on the radio and comparing popularity tips from my magazines. One day when I left my door open a crack for air, I caught Dayton snatch a glimpse at me from the other room. The color of his eyes was so bright it shocked me. There I was, memorizing the choruses of "Poor Little Fool" and "A Thousand Stars" and suddenly the Green Lantern was bearing down. I crossed my ankles and stuck out my tongue, but as soon as I noticed him, Dayton looked away, pretending he was just exercising his neck.

That started me thinking, and then everything made sense. Lee was just Dayton's route of getting close to me, which is what a lot of boys his age wanted more than they knew. When I thought of Dayton that way, as a boy, he still wasn't much, but it tickled me that he was so shy. I tried substituting Dayton's face for the older boys I usually pictured when I sang some of my songs, like "Lipstick on Your Collar." If innocent little ninth-grader Dayton was caught with my tangerine shade on his T-shirt, people's eyes would bug out. Some songs I listened to, like "Teen Angel," had the girl getting hit by a train or run over by a car, and I could see Dayton grieving for me, swearing he'd never go with anybody else as long as he lived, maybe becoming a priest. The more I thought about him, the more he looked a little like an Indian Frankie Avalon, which would make me Annette, one of my idols.

I had this game with her hit song. Every day I waited for the DJ to play "First Name Initial," and when it came on, I dropped what I was doing and experimented with my name and a different husband. My notebook was filled with decorated monograms, all starting with my C and each one ending with a different boy's last name. After I had curved and shaded it with my Magic Marker, C.N. was one of my favorites.

Locating Dayton without Lee was even harder than finding Lee without him, but that only made me think about Dayton the more. He was a challenge. If he and Lee watched TV on the couch, I squeezed in between them. I dropped back to visit my old teacher just to stand in the front of Dayton's classroom and show myself off. But nothing I did drew Dayton out. He'd lose his nerve and hide behind Lee until I thought I'd go crazy.

And then, one April night, I ran into him late, near the outskirts of a nighttime powwow. The woman's shawl contest was on, but I wasn't entered. I was dressed in pedal pushers and an off-the-shoulder blouse like Molly Dee wore, and my hair was curled and perfect. I was at my best. My fingernails were shaped into sharp ovals and I wore My Sin.

I was glad for every minute I had taken with my appearance when there, all alone under the lights, leaning against a post, was Dayton. He didn't look like any little boy to me. His eyes were open too wide and had that shiny, dreamy expression that comes from drinking wine too fast. The hair beneath his cowboy hat gleamed with Vitalis and he had rolled the cuffs of Lee's faded red western shirt halfway up his arms to disguise the fact that it was too short for him.

The powwow noise faded, as if the volume was lowered, when I approached him. We were just the two of us in a place with no walls. I slumped to make him taller and simmered from under my eyebrows like Annette.

"Lee's not here." Dayton's voice was mad, as if they'd had a fight, but I couldn't be bothered with that now.

I pulled my shoulders so my blouse pressed against my strapless bra. I was close enough for him to smell me. I ran my fingers, light as music, on the metal buckle of his belt.

Dayton's eyes wouldn't quite focus. He turned his head to the side and watched my dancing hand. That seemed to wake him up a little.

There's a certain way you act when you go courting at powwow, and the first step is to move away from the lights and into the dark air that surrounds the circle of contestants and spectators. I hooked a finger into the top of his waist-band and gave a little tug. "You want to go find him?" I said.

Dayton was three years younger than me and not yet used to drinking, but he wasn't dumb. There was no way he could say no. His dreams had come true. I stepped closer to him and let my knee brush against his leg. Then I moved away, out toward the open field. I went slow until I heard his steps following, and then I walked faster. There was a place, a hollow where the pasture dipped and formed a foxhole, where we could stretch out and be alone, if nobody had claimed it before us.

We didn't talk as I led the way. There was no moon but the spring night was clear and rose around me wide as blowing curtains. That land was so level that the only way you didn't see stars was if you looked at your feet, and the sky smelled of deep water. I could have jumped off into it and swum wherever I wanted. I stomped through the flattened long grass that had lain preserved under months of snow and felt on my ankles the scratch of new growth pushing through. Lee was going to be surprised about me and Dayton. I couldn't wait to see the amazement on his face when I told.

It was so dark that Dayton bumped into me when I stopped in the spot I had picked out. We stood in the center of a bowl in the earth, the sides sloping around us high as our shoulders, and I didn't move away.

"I guess we can't find him," I said. Every part of my body

was alert and ready. I could never predict what a boy would want the first time.

I heard Dayton breathing. He was a shape blacker than the night and suddenly a stranger to me. I found one of his hands and brought it to my stomach. Before I had a baby, that was a part, hard and round, that boys couldn't get enough of. Through the thin material of my cotton pants I felt the heat of Dayton's long fingers as I pushed them against me.

Finally he moved. He put his other arm around my shoulders and I leaned into him. He rubbed his mouth on my lips and I straightened my arms and laced my fingers behind his neck. I was ready to fall on the ground, ready for anything. He kept pushing on my mouth. His lips were drawn tight. I knew without any doubt he had his eyes shut too, blocking me out. As I bent my elbows, let my hands slide lower, Dayton tensed and shivered the way an animal does when it hates to be touched. I stepped back and he made no effort to stop me. Usually by this time things were beyond my control for a while, so I was at a loss.

"Well, what do you want to do?" I asked at last. I wished there was some way to turn on the lights and read his face.

"Maybe we should keep looking for Lee," Dayton mumbled too quickly. He was embarrassed, trying to pretend that he didn't know what just hadn't happened. He cleared his throat and made everything worse.

"It's just that you're a big sister to me, Christine."

Boys dreamed of having what Dayton was passing up. Most boys. If anybody was supposed to say no, it was the girl.

"Or a sister-in-law," I shot back, kneeing him with my words. I'm not a person who stops herself at the time and wishes later she hadn't. Dayton understood what I meant, though I bet nobody had ever thrown it in his face before.

"You've got it wrong," Dayton said, but I didn't wait to listen. I marched back to the powwow and left him to explain to the night what his problem was. I hated my outfit, hated the feel of the flimsy material of my pants as it strained against my hips and thighs, hated the greasy taste of the lipstick Dayton's kiss had smeared onto my teeth. Everything about me was all wrong, and it took me years to forget that it was Dayton who showed me.

After that powwow it wasn't the same with the three of us, though I'm not sure if Lee ever figured out why.

It wasn't that Dayton and I actually argued about anything, but our shame soured us on each other. We began to pull Lee in two directions, to force him to choose between us. I'd suggest we go joyriding in a borrowed pickup and Dayton would nag Lee to practice his lariat; I'd have my heart set on *Rome Adventure* at the drive-in and Dayton would tune in "Bonanza." Somewhere along the line, what Lee wanted got lost, and he had to divide his time pleasing Dayton and me. And that made nobody happy.

The one thing that was pure Lee's was rodeo. All over eastern Montana he was getting known, even when he was no more than a teenager. He climbed on any horse and rode it till it was kicked out and gentle. I had a life of my own, so when Lee went off to compete I wished him luck, but Dayton traveled along to carry Lee's saddle, and Dayton told the stories of Lee's victories when they came home. He boasted that Lee made jackasses of the older white cowboys who took bets on the side against him. He painted Lee as on the way to All-Around. And Lee would listen with the rest of us, shaking his head and laughing as though he was hearing it for the first time, as though it had happened to somebody else. When people wanted more details, they would ask Dayton instead of Lee because Dayton always made things sound exciting.

But when the talk started that Lee was poised to enter the big ones at Cheyenne and Calgary, Aunt Ida was dead against it.

"Look at those fools in ten years," she said. "Broken and stooped-over, pains in every joint, old before thirty. Good for nothing but shoveling the corral dirt." Actually what she said was sharper than that since she said it in Indian. English is mild in comparison, full of soft sounds that take the punch out of your thoughts. When she did speak English, Aunt Ida pronounced each of her words separately, as if surprised to find her own voice using a language she only heard in church. Her sentences crackled like electricity, tapping the air in code. Her face said she doubted these noises meant anything a person could decipher and so she broadcast at an angle, a question in her eyes, ready to confront confusion. Around us she didn't bother with English at all, and in Indian her words poured like thick whiskey that had never seen water, like hootch straight from the barrel.

I don't know what exactly Aunt Ida harbored in her mind for Lee, but she had an idea of him, no doubt of that. Every once in a while when she watched him she nodded her head, strong and sure, as though she just decided something. She ordered his clothes from Sears and kept them nice. She made his favorite corn soup whenever she could get the ingredients together. She wouldn't go to see Lee ride, but you could tell she listened to Dayton's stories while she was off in another part of the room, washing the dishes or pretending to search for her sewing.

When Lee danced at our powwow she decked herself out in her mother's beaded moccasins and wore porcupine quill earrings. The time he came in second in the Men's Fancy she sat long into the evening on her folding chair at the edge of the grounds as they had one dance-off after another, and when Lee finally lost she made him escort her in the closing Circle instead of letting him sulk. I never saw her dance before, and it amazed me. You forgot her weight, and her feet tapped quiet as deer hooves as she worked her way around the drum. She didn't have the prettiest shawl, just an old purple blanket she had crocheted herself, but with her head bent and her eyes lowered, her body floated steady while her legs stepped and crossed. Lee was just as taken aback as I was, and though he caught on eventually and bowed and wove beside her, the hand mirrors and cut-glass beads of his feathered outfit reflecting in the lights, Aunt Ida was the one you couldn't take your eyes off.

■ ■ ■

When John F. Kennedy was killed a few months after my falling out with Dayton, Aunt Ida sat like a doorstop in front of the TV in our house with Lee right beside her and Dayton next to him. They filled the couch. People had said Lee was going to be the Indian JFK because he was so handsome and smart, and I know that's why they were so fascinated. They saw Oswald get shot, they saw John Junior salute, they saw Jackie's eyes behind her black veil, they saw it all.

The sound came through the thin walls into my room, and Lee kept shouting to tell me what was happening. He wouldn't let me play records, and nothing but Kennedy was on the radio. Even "Teen Beat" was off. It's not that I didn't feel bad. I thought Jackie was a beautiful woman and I was sorry that she lost her husband so young and then had two kids to raise on her own, but I didn't take it personal like Lee and Dayton did. People got shot on our reservation all the time and nobody turned the world upside down about it.

Lee moped for weeks after, his mouth grim and solemn like he couldn't shake serious thoughts from his head. I never knew if Dayton was upset himself or just went along for the ride, but he was with Lee every minute, talking about how if it wasn't for JFK we'd have been bombed by Cuban missiles because we were a number-one target, being so close to where the ICBM's were buried.

Over the next couple years Lee and Dayton were like kids who wouldn't grow up, like Siamese twins who couldn't be cut apart. Even when they took out girls, they double-dated, and almost never went with the same ones twice. People had gotten so used to seeing Lee and Dayton together that they even stopped talking about it. But not me. Dayton had herded me out of my own brother's life and then as much as told me I wasn't good enough for him. I didn't forget, I just saved and waited.

After I graduated, I went to work part-time in the Tribal Council office and had a paycheck. Not a weekend went by when I didn't go to dances in town. I saw every double feature that came to the drive-in. I had my pick of boys. That

Christmas I got a 10-karat gold-plated ID bracelet from one guy and a Mexican leather wallet from another.

"You're turning into a slut," Aunt Ida spat at me on a Friday night as I was getting ready to meet a date. "Nobody will marry you."

"You should know," I said, and continued to line my eyes as if she wasn't there. You'd think she might have a little understanding, but she was a woman I could never make out because she kept her distance and acted as though she had never been my age, never had wanted to have fun. In her premature old-ladyhood, Aunt Ida had become respectable and we were supposed to go along.

Thank God for Lee because I could still tell him everything when we had some time alone. He listened and gave me advice about all my boyfriends, and wanted to see my new clothes and hear about the places I went. He wasn't just my best friend, he was the only one I trusted, the only one who never let me down.

When I was twenty, I took off to Minot for the first time and didn't even bring a toothbrush. I thought I was just going to the movies in Malta when I left Aunt Ida's house, but the guy I was with breezed through that cowtown without even slowing down at the four-way, and headed east.

"What's going on?" I said. "Where are we going?" But he just pinched my leg and answered we were taking a little trip to see his cousin and did I mind that much? I debated with myself for all of thirty seconds and decided I didn't. "I'll call in sick," I said. I was wild and ready to see the world, and I liked myself that way.

They call Minot "The Magic City" and you could see why. When we drove down Broadway for the first time at night, all those lights shining and people hurrying along, I felt like I was inside a movie. Every block I rode I saw more people than lived on the whole reservation, and not a one of them knew my business. When I went into a bar with my date and his cousin and his cousin's friends, everybody would look up from their drinks and take me in, and I could see they admired what they saw. With all those military from the air force base around, I never had to sit out a dance.

I returned from that first trip after only two weeks, but in some ways I never came back at all. I worried all the way down the road to the reservation, every step to our house, what kind of reception I'd get. Aunt Ida must have thought I was lost when she never heard from me in all that time. I wouldn't blame her for being mad, but when I described what happened maybe she'd be glad for my good time.

She didn't even glance from "The Guiding Light."

"I was in Minot with a boy," I said to shock her. If I started with the worst, it could only get better.

"Diamond Johnson," she said in a flat voice.

That stopped me.

"Married. With two kids."

"They're not living together," I told her. "His wife's gone back to South Dakota."

Aunt Ida kept me waiting until a commercial came on. "His mother came to see me. She claims it's because of you she lost her grandchildren."

I tried to explain. Being with Diamond was nothing. That wasn't what counted about my trip. It was me, all the new things I saw, how people treated me, but Aunt Ida didn't hear. All that mattered is that some woman had shamed her over me. I exploded. I was nobody she could treat this way.

"You want me to move away?"

She just set her big jaw and watched her program. I spun around and walked out the door. Once in the open air, I looked around for an idea of what to do next. I didn't have a thing of my own with me and I was too proud to go in and pack. I was breathless with my anger and the sound of the slammed door echoed in my head.

You get a good view from that hill, but no matter which way I turned there were no surprises. I knew the people in every house on this end of the reservation, and there weren't many that would want me for more than a day or two. I didn't even consider Diamond, though he might have said yes. If you take up with a man that way, you never get free again, and besides he was too old.

So family was my only choice, and I moved in with Aunt Ida's younger sister, Pauline, her husband, Dale Cree, and their first baby. I never got along with her, but I knew it would gall Aunt Ida for me to be there.

Sometimes when I came in at five in the morning, the music still in my ears, Pauline would be awake for a morning feeding.

"You're wearing yourself out, Christine," she warned, giving me her best Christian look. "This is no life for a young girl." But she always made me start my night from the minute I left the house and relate every detail. She liked it best if I told her things that made her clap her hand over her mouth, things for her to whisper, things that had the ladies at her church shaking their heads. That paid my rent as far as she was concerned.

I had accumulated enough interest in having fun to last me a long time. I had a reputation with men, you could see it in their eyes. I was the first one they called when the neon lights took over, and that was fine with me. There were girls my age already married with two babies, and others who went to daily Mass and were nuns in everything but their habits. When I saw them at the store, carrying full shopping baskets, I was glad for the cards I held.

My motto was "you're only young once," and I had the sense to make my youth count double. I was on the road nonstop, to Great Falls or Rapid or Billings, but I still saw Lee sometimes, whenever I could. He was the only person whose opinion mattered a damn to me.

He and Dayton finished their high school as Red Power Indians. They wore wrapped bandannas around their heads to hold their long hair out of their eyes. They took brand-new blue jeans jackets and bleached them until they looked second-hand. They sewed bright patches on their pants to cover holes that weren't there. They carried around Indian newspapers from California and New York that had headlines that wiped off on your fingers. They called the priests at the Mission "honkies" behind their backs, said our reservation was a "nation" and that we were Native Americans instead of Indians.

Between the two of them, Lee and Dayton, they wore more buttons with messages than you could ever read. When you met them on the road, they filled their chests so you saw "Custer Died for Your Sins" or "Indians Discovered Columbus." They got interested in Vietnam and every other damn place that made the evening news, and they hushed me when I told them that stuff had nothing to do with us.

"Shit, Christine, will you can it," Dayton finally said when a group of us were sitting in the snack bar watching bombs going off on the TV. Lee wasn't there, home that night with a rodeo-sprained knee, and I had just suggested a hand of Indian pinochle. "Those Vietnamese ain't so different from us," Dayton went on. "Same skin, same hair. Why don't you shut up, and learn something?"

I turned to him slow and let him wonder for a little bit which one of the things I *could* say, I would. He had spoken before he thought, before he remembered who he was talking to, and now he hunched in the broken-down chair, at my mercy.

"Those communists might look like *you*," I told him, "but not me. I'm American all the way. Why don't you just get out. You never belonged on this reservation anyhow."

Dayton kept his eyes on the screen, hoping that was as far as I'd go. He was no match for me without Lee to back him.

For his senior project, Lee went to the old folks at the retirement center and asked for stories about the way things used to be, and they were so glad for someone to pay attention to them, someone who could speak their language, that they told him anything he wanted to hear. The elders, he called those people, as though he hadn't known their names all his life. He started talking about Mother Earth and Father Sky, and had an answer for anything. To hear him talk, Indians were the center of the world.

One day I ran into Lee in the store, and he was wearing a long white feather, all fluffy on the ends, dangling from his left ear.

"Are you a hippie now?" I asked, joking around, but he acted like a stranger with my brother's face. He paid for his bottle of pop and turned to leave without even speaking to me.

"Hey, Crazy Horse, it's me talking. Tina." My voice was high like I was holding in laughter, but I knew none of the people standing around, listening, were fooled.

Lee paused at the door. His eyes were dangerous.

"I heard what you said to Dayton," he said, low and steady.

"Are you going to protect him from me? Did he go crying to you?" I had forgotten all about my fight with Dayton and didn't know what Lee was so mad about.

"*He* didn't tell me." Lee looked at me and chose the words he would say next. "Maybe if you stopped running around with all your redneck white boyfriends you'd care about what was happening in this world."

I stayed there, pretending to shop, walking down the aisle between the cereals and the paper products, and tried to compose myself. I knew my face was flushed and I hated to let anyone see.

When I finally got out I went straight to Aunt Ida, though we hadn't spoken in six months. She was alone, sorting scraps of material for a quilt.

"What are you going to do about Lee?" I asked her. She stood in front of me, with her hands on her hips. She had plenty to say but none of it about Lee.

"He's fine."

"He's turning into a criminal," I said. "Thanks to Dayton. They want to burn down the government."

Aunt Ida sniffed. Lee was still the Indian JFK. She could no more condemn him than she could fly to the moon.

"Lee knows what he's doing," she told me, sure and pleased with herself. "Him and Dayton."

A look passed between us, and in her eyes I saw her

victory, and in her victory I understood the battle we had fought for who Lee was going to be, my brother or her child. He couldn't belong to both. All along I thought it was Dayton I had to worry about, but I had been wrong.

"He won't stay with you," I said.

But pictures of Lee hung on every wall of the room: Lee with his hoops. Lee's tinted eight-by-ten grade school graduation portrait. Lee and Dayton ready to take the bus on their junior-senior year trip to Helena. Lee in his Fancy Dance outfit, his hair braided with strips of red cloth and falling past his shoulders. Lee's cowboy shirts, starched and pressed, hung on a clothesline stretched behind a curtain, and his boots, newly polished, were lined at the foot of the bed where he slept.

My eyes searched every corner before I turned to leave.

With the door to my old room closed, there was no sign I had ever lived there.

10

"What's your classification?" I asked Dayton.

He didn't understand. His wavy hair was bound with a handkerchief, and an Indian on a horse was painted with Day-Glo on the back of his jacket.

"The draft," I said. "What's your number?"

"4-A. So what?"

"What's 4-A?" That was a new one to me.

"Sole surviving son. My dad was killed in the navy."

I never heard him mention any Dad before.

"So that means you get off the hook?"

Dayton was uneasy. He didn't like to talk about this with me. "They can't draft me. But I wouldn't go in anyway."

I could tell he had been dreading this question and so had his answer all set. I kept talking while my thoughts raced ahead to how I could use this information.

"You'd go to jail?"

"Or Canada."

Easy for him to say. My ideas were taking shape.

"I never figured you for a draft dodger," I said, and left him to watch me walk away.

"I'm an enrolled member of this Indian nation," he called after me. "A sovereign citizen. My tribe has not declared war."

I moved, not looking back, not letting my face show what I was feeling. A solution to everything had been dropped into my lap.

Lee was my next stop. I borrowed Diamond's car and found my brother on the road north from Aunt Ida's.

"Hop in," I said as I pulled beside him. He thought I'd come to apologize and didn't offer an argument, but as soon as he was in the seat with his hat pulled down for shade, I went into action.

"What happens after you graduate?"

He tilted his brim and looked over at me, but I watched the highway ahead.

"I don't know." He thought a minute. "Get work, I guess."

"I mean after the two years."

"What two years? You mean rodeo?"

"Uncle Sam. You're eighteen."

Lee exhaled a long stream of air and rolled his head to stare out his side window. "Shit," he said.

I drove slow, kept quiet, gave him time to say more.

"You won't understand, Christine."

I didn't ask what.

"I'm not going in. I don't have to."

"Says Dayton," I sneered. "He's trading off of his dead father. Too bad you don't have one too."

"I'm not going to fight a white man's war." Lee spoke as if he was repeating something he had heard in church.

" '*White man*'!?" I said. "When did you start talking like that?"

"I mean it, Christine. Lay off."

I couldn't help thinking what my friends would say if Lee really did dodge. A lot of the guys I went with, the older ones, had done a stint in Korea or Okinawa, and all the younger boys were already enlisted or raring to. They had names for people who tried to worm out of the service.

"You'll change your mind when the time comes."

"No."

"Well, then you're done on this reservation. The U.S. army is good enough for everybody else."

Under his hat, Lee's face turned gray.

"That's enough," he said through his teeth.

"If you go through with this you're not my brother."

"Stop the fucking car."

Lee twisted like he wanted to hit me, but I kept my foot on the gas, daring him. It would be worth a punch to bring him back to his senses, and I knew if he saw me bruised by his own hand, he'd get a good look at what he was doing. I deserved to be hit, and he deserved to have to hit me.

"I won't fight you," Lee said, holding back.

"You won't fight anybody." I took charge. I jammed my boot on the brake and the tires skidded in the gravel of the road as we pitched forward. Before Lee could regain his balance, I brought up my arm and slapped him hard across his cheek. I couldn't look at his eyes and still talk, so I stared past him.

"You're hot shit to Aunt Ida . . . and Dayton." I spit Dayton's name as if he was so low he wasn't worth talking about. "But what it comes down to is, you're just a yellow kid who's ascared to defend his country."

Lee gawked at me. My hand had made a spot on his cheek red as Aunt Ida's burn scar. I had played all my cards, gone for a skunk, and now it was his turn to show. He left the car door open and walked back in the direction we had come, his hands dug in the pockets of his jeans, his head bowed over looking at the ground. I didn't start the car again until he got a ride going the opposite way.

For weeks Lee kept to himself, holing up at Aunt Ida's or Dayton's, and whenever I did see him, usually from a distance, I couldn't help remembering the sound of my slap, sharp as the snap of dry wood. I never felt so alone. I even skipped his graduation. Other people acted as though our family troubles were catching and never asked me to visit after work. All my regular boyfriends were either getting married or, like Diamond, back making a second try with their wives, or off somewhere raising hell without me. My fight with Lee poisoned the water, but the battle wasn't done and I didn't surrender. I had other weapons.

I ignored Lee and Dayton if they passed me as I walked on the dusty road to the tribal office. Sometimes I nodded just to

Dayton, and that was clear as a billboard sign. I stood for everybody Lee had to answer to, all those who would be disappointed in him. I told Aunt Pauline the whole story and she spread it around like Christmas presents in July. People started talking about what Lee would do, arguing over it, with the ones who didn't like him saying he wouldn't enlist, and his friends saying he would. When they asked me what it would be, I just shook my head and let them see how worried I was, how it pained me. Their bet was as good as mine.

Aunt Ida heard the details, of course, probably from Dayton, who I now realized told her everything. She ambushed me one day as I was hiking to my girlfriend's for a game of crazy eights, and spoke from the corner of her mouth, loud enough for me to hear but not face to face. Nobody could accuse her of out-and-out talking to me again. The edge that ran between us had sprouted broken glass and barbed wire. We would look over the top of it at each other when we had to, but neither of us was ready to cross.

"If you're so anxious for war," she hissed, not breaking her pace and using the old-time word for blood-fighting, "go become one of those women soldiers."

She meant a WAC, and the idea had already occurred to me, lonely as I was. It was an all-expenses-paid trip off the reservation. I imagined myself stationed near a beach, surrounded by men who thought I was beautiful and different. I had a shirttail cousin named Susie, a couple years older than me, who took her nurse's training into the service and came home on her first leave. I didn't run into her right away, but everyone was struck by Susie's tales of military life. She dated twice on weekends, they said, and went to dances in Seattle and at the Fort Lewis officers' club. She had plenty of money and was supposed to be sent to some hospital in New Jersey, near New York City.

Susie had never been much to look at. She had a long, horsey face the way some do, all teeth and oblong eyeglasses, with broad, flat hips and feet that were small for her heavy body. If the army could turn her into Miss Indian America, then it was worth considering.

But when I finally saw Susie, she hadn't changed much. She sat, half-gone, on a vinyl-backed folding chair in the tribal office, wearing an ugly green uniform and black laced shoes, trying to fill out some government form. She didn't even have the sense to hide her bad skin with foundation.

I could have all the soldiers I wanted without being one myself.

Lee, though, was another story. I imagined him all spit-polished shoes and creases in his pants, standing at attention, dark eyes bright under the visor of his hat. I'd get him to bring his friends along when he came home for leave, or maybe I'd go visit him where he was stationed and he could introduce me around. I planned what I'd pack to wear. I'd have to get a new dress, some spike heels. I could go back to being known as Lee's sister, the way I was when he was a rodeo ace.

My only wonder was how to get from here to there, how to get my brother away from Aunt Ida's house and Dayton's bad advice, and into the army. It had been almost a month since I had slapped Lee's face, but I saw no sign that he had come to his senses. It was time to escalate my attack and try something new.

The answer landed on my desk one day, in the form of a sign announcing tribal elections. The photographs showed the usual slate of old men in cowboy hats and horn-rimmed bifocals, all BIA types, full of hot air and their own importance, all running for the Council, but that isn't what I saw. I looked at that poster and in my mind I saw Lee's face, ten years from now, on the top of it. The Indian JFK. Handsome as a movie star. Serious, with a silver bola tie and a pen sticking out of the breast pocket of his sports coat. That was where he was headed, and whether he realized it yet or not, the one and only way he'd ever take his place at the head of the tribe was if it read "Lee George, Veteran," under his picture.

This time I bypassed Lee and went straight to Dayton. I caught him coming out of the store with a full brown bag under each arm.

"Are you trying to ruin Lee's life?" I asked him.

He shifted the groceries he carried and made himself comfortable. He had been anticipating some attack from me, and a smile started around his mouth.

I didn't give him a chance to answer, just hit him with my next question.

"Who are you for?" I pointed to the election flyer nailed to the outside wall by the door.

Dayton glanced at the slate and then back to me. "What's the difference," he said. "They're all the same."

"But who are you for?" I repeated. I wanted him to hang himself.

He looked at me suspicious, but he couldn't resist the chance to shoot off his mouth.

"Nobody running has the guts to do anything. Just a lot of old farts who line their pockets while this reservation goes to hell. No jobs, no money."

"Well, what's going to make things better then?"

"None of those," he said, nodding to the poster.

"So why don't you run if you're so smart and know all the answers?"

"Nobody'd vote for me. But someday Lee will..."

He stopped, detecting where I was headed. He didn't have to finish his sentence about how he wasn't born here, how he didn't speak the language, how he was half-white. He could see from my face I had guessed what he and Lee had been planning. I let it sink in a second before I spoke.

"The only way people around here are going to have an ounce of respect for Lee is if he serves his country."

I had slipped through a crack and got into Dayton's brain, and my words stuck like the barb on a fishhook. He couldn't shake loose from my logic.

"People have short memories," he tried. "It'll be years before Lee's ready."

I let him talk. Dayton might not have thought it all out before, but now he couldn't escape it.

I closed in on him like I was going for rummy and held the cards for a shutout.

"People remember certain things. They'd never listen to a draft evader."

Dayton chewed on the inside of his lip. I noticed he had to shave his mustache, that a long box of macaroni protruded from the top of the bag in one of his arms.

"You can't sell your principles," Dayton said, almost to himself. He was mad because he didn't believe his own words. His dream of Lee as an Indian chief was vanishing in smoke, and I let him work out what he had to do about it. Dayton could persuade Lee where I couldn't.

"Lee could do a lot if he got the chance," I said to jog him on.

Dayton shifted his load again. If only Lee sacrificed one little principle.

I knew when to leave—that's something that's almost always been true about me—and now was the time. I didn't want Dayton setting down his grocery sacks and freeing his arms. I didn't want him to figure me out.

Now whenever I saw Lee and Dayton together, Dayton was doing most of the talking. The first couple times I spied on them, Lee had a sour turn to his mouth, as if he had just had a drink of vinegar. Another time, late in the afternoon, Lee just looked off into the distance while Dayton preached on and on. They sat, shirtless in the August heat, on the steps of the Teen Club opposite my office window, finding little stones in the dirt and aiming them to fall close to a crack in the sidewalk. The low sun tinted their skin almost orange and for just an instant I thought it was too bad they had to turn into grown men, they were such a familiar sight to me. I couldn't hear a word but I didn't have to. Dayton was reading Lee his future, if he only wanted to snatch it.

Lee and Dayton disappeared without a word to anybody. Possibly they had gone to Seattle to be in that fishing rights protest.

Possibly they had headed for Canada. Possibly they went out to join the Indians-of-All-Tribes in Minneapolis or California. I didn't even think out loud my own possibly, in case it wasn't true.

People were still talking about the mystery on the night of the Mission Labor Day Bazaar. The cafeteria was arranged with the long tables lined in rows, and at each one, four to a bench, families bent over their baked bean suppers. For most of them it was like being students again, sitting on those painted wood seats and being served by women who spent the winter mashing potatoes and grilling cheese sandwiches for school lunches. It was a night to see who had made it through the summer and to exchange news, and nobody missed it, not even Aunt Ida.

Not even Lee.

When he and Dayton opened the outer doors and stepped into the room just before the cupcakes were passed around, the conversations dropped from the front of the room to the back like a wind over grass. A table of eaters looked to see why the one before it had grown quiet, then grew quiet themselves. The next one strained to see, then the next. Only those at the last tables still chatted, then suddenly heard their own voices loud in the room and broke off in the middle of sentences, held in midair the bowls being passed.

And there was something to see. Lee had cut his hair.

He let them take him in. He stood in a way I remembered and recognized, a graduated senior come back to where he had gone to school, a person on the other side of his past. He looked around the room, then he found the table where Aunt Ida sat with Pauline and her husband, and walked over. Dayton, I noticed, stayed by the door.

Without a word, Lee fished a stuffed brown envelope out of the inside of his shirt and laid it before Aunt Ida. She didn't make a move to touch it, but the whole room was curious. Lee reached down and nudged it toward her and finally she took it, slit the flap with the edge of her finger.

I was two tables away, watching with my boss and another girl from the tribal office, but I could see. It was Lee's braid, heavy and shiny, bound at either end by red rubber bands.

Aunt Ida grabbed it to her face and breathed through it slow and hard. It was black and ragged as a horse's mane. She stuffed it out of sight into the open pocket of her dress but it was too big and trailed down her leg. She let Pauline put an arm around her, turned her face away from Lee, but then she was lost to me in the crowd, lost in the sound of benches scraping back, of hands clapping Lee on the back, of talk starting, building, spilling over from one table to the next. I heard the word "enlisted." I heard it twice.

I stayed in my seat longer than most, long enough to see Dayton go out the door he was standing by, long enough to finish the coffee gone sweet in my cup.

The next day I sat at my desk, turning the pages in a file, when Emmet LaVallee, chairman of the Tribal Council, called Lee into the office and gave him a special eagle feather to take along to the army. It had got him through Sicily, he said, and now it was Lee's turn to serve in the great warrior tradition of our Indian people. All the councilmen had stories they wanted Lee to hear.

Lee looked at me above their heads. I tried not to smile, held my mouth in a tight line, waiting for him to make the first move. He shook his head like "I give up," and I nodded like "I told you." Then I raised my hand to my forehead and saluted. That cracked him up.

I never knew exactly where Lee and Dayton went for that week they were gone, or what happened when they got there, but things were never the same between them when they came back. Lee changed once he got used to the idea that he had turned out like everybody wanted, and he started running with a different crowd while he waited for his orders. When he and Dayton did get together, they talked "remember when" instead of times to come. It was like they were strangers attending a twenty-five-year class reunion.

It wasn't a week before Dayton got his hair cut too, and quit wearing a bandanna around his head and talking about Red Power as well, but he kept his 4-A, just as I thought he would. He convinced himself his mother needed him at home, but he was the only one who believed that. Even Aunt Ida turned her back when he tried to explain. She lost all interest in him.

My life seemed to improve overnight. Invitations came, and I spent my weekends on the road between the reservation and anyplace else. I was wild, but under my own control. And every time I met a new guy, I made sure to work it in that my brother was in the army, going to 'Nam. I described him as tough and rough, crazy brave, and sometimes the whole table would raise their beers to toast Lee. Everybody had brothers or cousins who were over there.

I was twenty-two and old to have never been married or had any kids, but I had my boyfriends use precautions. I knew I was bound for something special, and I was in no hurry for family responsibilities. It did occur to me, though, that I might be hard for destiny to locate. You didn't hear about a lot of wonderful things happening on the reservation. People there never even made the local papers, at least not on the front pages. So I decided to put myself in a more likely spotlight.

I visited Minot at least once a month, but by then I knew all of its surprises. It was my teenage town, and I liked it for that, but I didn't want to locate there. A big city was the next step, and when I heard about an employment program that would provide me with an apartment and a steady job in Seattle, I jumped.

As it happened, I left the reservation before Lee, which was right in a way since I was older. I went to say good-bye to Aunt Ida and she gritted her teeth and kissed my cheek. She was glad to see me go, glad to have Lee's last days to herself. She didn't want to do anything to make me stay just to spite her, so for once she was the way she used to be with me, packing me a lunch for the bus, giving me advice about city living even though she'd never been anywhere except Denver more than overnight herself. She got all her views of the world out of her television and so it's not surprising they didn't fall together in any kind of sense. She told me not to mix with private eyes and gangsters, not to smoke drugs, and to always pay my rent on time.

We acted out my departure on a tightrope that barely didn't break.

Lee was the only one hard for me to leave or sorry to see me go, and he prolonged our farewell. First he walked me to the store where I'd catch my ride, then he waited with me, then he helped me carry my suitcase onto the bus. We made big plans for him to visit me in Seattle after he finished his basic. By that time I'd have a place decorated and know all the good clubs to visit, and I'd be anxious to show him off. It wasn't like true good-bye we were saying at all, I told him, just see you later. He smiled and nodded his head, then surprised me by shaking my hand instead of kissing me before he turned and walked down the aisle. He stood outside my stuck window.

It's strange to talk when you can't hear the other person and when you don't have anything more to say. The motor was running, but the driver was in no hurry, so I made Lee laugh by pointing at other passengers who weren't looking and then doing imitations of them: an old lady asleep already, a drunk trying to pretend he was sober, a white guy nervous to be surrounded by so many Indians. Lee loved it. He laughed so hard there were tears in his eyes. He tipped his face to me, begging for one more, and I looked at him as if I was seeing him for the first time. Everything was new. His short hair bristled like a soft brush. His teeth were straight and close together and the muscles in his neck strained tight and strong out of his shirt. His eyes were excited and scared, holding me, drawing me in. I took a picture of him just like that with my brain and stored it away to be developed later. Lee was all I cared for in the world, and I was so proud to be his sister, so relieved to be friends again, I wanted to wake all the passengers and tell them.

The driver finally dropped into his seat and closed the bus door. The brake released and we paused for that split second before we rolled. Lee still looked at me, still wanted another imitation for the road. I couldn't pry my eyes from him, so I had no other inspiration: I did Lee. I turned my face to the sky, widened my mouth into a silent laugh and made myself look dopey, like some kid who's just seen a movie star. As the bus moved, I held my pose but glanced down to see Lee's reaction. He recognized who I was and didn't know how he felt about it. He was embarrassed that anybody could see him that way, but he was froze into his farewell and couldn't relax it. My window slid past him, standing like a statue in front of the store, and soon there was nothing outside but the wash of rangeland, the distant pearl hills, the sky that spread, ceilinged with shaved clouds, on every side.

Seattle was a big Minot with water everywhere. You couldn't walk in any direction without hitting the Sound or Lake Washington, and from above rain pelted down night and day, but never when you were prepared for it. It was hard for my hair to hold a perm in the first place, so I kept it short.

The job they gave me was all right, if you didn't mind doing the same thing hour after hour, over and over. I was part of an assembly line that turned out the black boxes they hide on big jets. Even if the plane blows up, this little machine holds together and keeps a record of the last words of the pilot and crew. I never knew how it worked since all I did was screw in the same bolt on each box, but I persuaded myself that I was important, that I was doing something that could survive a crash.

A couple months later, though, when I got bored with where I was living, it dawned on me that anybody could do my job, and I quit.

For months I bounced around western Washington from Everett to Olympia. I made a good appearance and had convincing excuses for why I left all my former employs. I was easy to hire. Personnel officers told me they could see I was smart and only needed a real chance. The problem was, I found myself screwing that same damn bolt, no matter what it was called, into one machine or another, and in the long run, none of them struck my fancy the way that black box had. Work just paid the rent, and I came to think of myself as the song "Tumbling Tumbleweed." One of these days I was going to blow against something good and hang on, and there was no rushing it.

In 1968 I was in Tacoma, dumping lettuce into little plastic bowls for airline salads. All the companies used us, but of course Northwest was our big customer. I imagined my mixed greens heading off to Alaska or Hong Kong and that kept me content for longer than usual. I had a nice little apartment, two rooms, right near downtown where the pulp smell wasn't too strong and where I could walk to all my hangouts in the evening. I had friends to burn, even some from home, and I never looked better in my life. Clothes off the rack fit as if they were made for me, a perfect size eight, and every week I would try out a sample of a new shampoo, a new lipstick shade, a new nail polish. I was a woman who changed her appearance the way cops on TV use clues to construct a picture of an unknown criminal, switching one part after another until they get it right. If I took my time, sampled every possibility, eventually I'd hit on the perfect combination and come into my own.

Lee sent me a postcard from boot camp saying that he was making out okay and that he would call me when he was coming to Seattle. I don't know whether or not he tried because I was out a lot then, always on the go, and after a while I moved so often it got easier for me to use a neighbor's phone than to have my own installed. But I always left a forwarding address, just in case he wrote. If he had arrived at my door, surprised me, I would have been happy to see him, but I didn't hold my breath. If I missed him this time through we'd just have more to say on the next visit. To tell the truth, I wasn't all that anxious to show off the places where I lived. A "Career Gal Efficiency" always looked better advertised in the paper than it did in real life.

Lee wasn't much of a letter writer but he must have been homesick because he sent me a Polaroid snapshot from Hawaii. He was standing on Waikiki beach with two other boys and they had dates with Hawaiian girls in grass skirts and flower necklaces. Lee was thin but looked as if he was having a ball. The card had been forwarded twice, and when it reached me, he was long gone to his next stop, but I liked to think of him still there. On the back of the photograph he had written, "Hey Sis, Aloha!" and signed his name. I wondered if Lee had sent Dayton the same picture and what Dayton thought of his 4-A now.

A couple weeks later I got a real letter. The return address

on the plain white envelope was APO San Francisco, California, but I knew Lee's handwriting. For stationery, he used a
piece of pale green paper torn from a stenographer's notebook.
He wrote in pencil, double-spacing each line.

Dear Christine,

*You would not believe the size of the bugs in this
place! I have made some new friends and two of
them are Indians too! One is from New York and the other
is from Arizona. Nothing much has happened yet, just
a lot of sitting around on our butts (pardon my
French!).*

*Have you heard from Aunt Ida lately? Say hello from
me if you write her, and Dayton too. Those sure were
great times, huh?*

*I'm sorry I never called you when I was in Seattle, but
the days went by so fast. Have you ever gone to the Roxy
Club? Don't mention my name there! Don't be mad,
promise? I'll see you when I come home!*

*Well, I better get busy! Write to the address on the
envelope. Promise? Don't do anything I wouldn't do!
Wish you were here! (Ha, Ha)*

> *Love,*
> *Your Brother,*
> *Lee*

I didn't know what Lee was doing in California, but when
I told my girlfriend at work she said APO meant Lee was
already in Vietnam and they sent on his mail. I read his letter
over a few more times, but I couldn't imagine him as a soldier
in a foreign country.

In the months that passed, I put it out of my mind, turned
the war off when it came on TV. There were enough stations
that you could always find a game show or a rerun. The one
thing I did was be nice to servicemen. Tacoma was full of
soldiers and I danced with half of them, treated them just the

way I hoped some woman would treat Lee, made them feel appreciated and forget being strangers.

One morning I was on my way to work, ready to spend the day pulling lettuce heads apart, dividing each one equally between ten little tan bowls on their way overseas, when an envelope came with my former addresses scribbled on the back. I felt important, as though no place could hold me for long and that it took the U.S. post office to track me down. It was typed. The first line confused me. "Dear Christine, I have to tell you that Lee is listed as MIA." Those initials were airlines shorthand for Miami—I sent salads there every day—and it flashed through my mind that Lee was in Florida now. I wanted to stop right there, wanted to fool myself.

My shoulder blades started to tense, and when I turned the letter over and saw it was from Dayton they practically touched each other across my back. My hand shook before I knew why it was happening, before I made myself read more. Lee had been on a mission. He had gone out and not returned. They had looked for him for days and finally decided he was captured or hurt. MIA meant missing in action, it didn't mean worse, I should remember that, Dayton said. Lee could be fine. He needed our prayers. I didn't have to come home. Dayton was keeping an eye on Aunt Ida. She was taking the news okay but she wouldn't talk about Lee, wouldn't even mention his name.

I took my eyes from the page.

That was the old way. When fighting men left you didn't use their names or anything that belonged to them because it might attract the attention of ghosts who'd want to snatch them. Ghosts were more lonesome than anything else. They watched the living through a thick plate of glass, a one-way mirror. Aunt Ida was protecting Lee, so she gambled he was alive.

Dayton asked for my current address and phone number. Nobody, not even Information, knew where I was. He would let me know when he heard anything.

◆ ◆ ◆

I didn't answer Dayton. I dreaded letters. I didn't want him to get in touch with me fast, I didn't want him in charge of Lee's trouble, I didn't want him to know he'd ever found me. I treated the news as though it had happened to somebody else, to somebody in a movie. I took the bus to work and flirted with the driver. I put on my blue smock and the showercap to protect the food from my hair. I stood at my station, filled my trays steady as a machine, and skipped lunch. I put my concentration into my hands. I shredded my lettuce the way I wanted to tear Dayton's letter, and I sent it off air-tight to nowhere.

Sometimes they begged you to work overtime and tonight for once I would have said yes, but they didn't ask. I didn't want to go home and have to think. It was Thursday and nobody on the line would party. "Tomorrow night," they said, but I couldn't wait. When my shift was over I headed downtown on my own, not even bothering to change my dress or put on my nice shoes. The bus passed a movie but by the time I thought to pull the cord it was two stops back. We went by a twenty-four-hour discount drug store, a furniture store going out of business, a post office.

I followed the woman in front of me down the steps, through the folding door, into the street. Directly across was a tavern named Barclay's. There was a blue neon Rainier sign and cafe curtains pulled together in the window so I couldn't see what kind of a place it was, but I didn't care. It was just for one drink, and rain had started to fall. I ducked through the door. The room was long and dark, with puffs of smoke blurring the light like patterns on a plastic shower curtain. It was too early to be crowded, but there was music playing from a juke, and a sweet smell, the combined aftershaves and colognes of all the people there, drew me in. I stood before the bar to order myself a stinger before I realized that everybody but me in the place was black.

I was disappointed because I wanted my drink, I wanted to stay there. It was bad enough being in a strange bar, much less being the wrong color. I knew blacks from my jobs and we usually got along okay, but then I listened to the news too and didn't want to find myself mugged.

The bartender materialized in front of me, a towel white in

his large hand. Above his long cheeks, his eyes were amused to find me there, but it was a free country and he would take my order.

To go or to stay. The rain. My rotten job. Alone tonight. No other Indians. Everything. I could barely see my reflection in the dark mirror behind the bar. My face rose above the rows of bottles, each a different brand. My hair was limp with the dampness. Without makeup, I looked older than I ever saw myself, even on mornings after no sleep. I put my hands on the counter to steady myself and they shone in blue light.

"Hey, pretty lady," a rich voice said in my ear. "First time here, you get a free drink, compliments of Corporal Elgin A. Taylor. What'll it be?"

I turned my head and stared into the face of a tall, very black soldier. His hair was clipped close and above his curved lip he had a neat mustache. His eyes were soft and sorry, with long lashes, ready to smile. His uniform was fresh and starched and in the dimness his skin looked polished. His cologne was sharp and lemon.

When I didn't answer him, when I just stood there like a fool taking him in, his eyebrows wrinkled and a look of pure concern came over his face.

"You okay?" Elgin Taylor asked me. "You in some kind of trouble?"

I found my voice. "I have a brother," I said. "Lee. I just heard that he's a MIA." I watched him. From his reaction I would know what soldiers knew about MIA's, know how bad it was.

Elgin pressed his lips together and slipped his arm around my shoulders, drawing me against him. My body held stiff at first, but he felt so good, so clean and warm, that I let my muscles relax for the first time that day, so fast and so completely that I almost fell. The material of his tan shirt was smooth against my cheek and I let him hold me while I listened to his heart. His hand smoothed my hair, found my neck.

"It's all right," Elgin said. "I know. I know."

"I'm okay." I spoke into his chest.

"I know."

■   ■   ■

He guided me to a table, held my chair when I sat.

"You hungry?"

I shook my head, but he ordered anyway—a steak sandwich and fries. I showed him Dayton's letter and he read it carefully, folded it, handed it to me. His fingers were warm to the touch.

After three drinks, we couldn't stay in the bar.

"Come on," he said. "I've got a place."

We walked down the rainy street, me leaning into him, holding on to his arm, afraid to let go. In his nervousness, he couldn't stop talking.

"I get out of the service in two weeks," Elgin said. "When you first came in I thought you were Chinese. The bars over in 'Nam are full of Chinese women. But then I looked closer. You've got meat on you, you're solid."

I didn't care what he said.

"What are you then?" he asked finally.

"Indian."

"No!" He was impressed. "You're really an Indian? I never talked to one before."

"You hit the jackpot," I said.

"You know, I'm part Indian too. My great-grandmother from Georgia was supposed to be some kind of full-blood Cherokee princess. I've seen pictures of her. She really looked Indian."

"I guess she would," I said. I wished he'd stop. He was going to make me come back down to earth, make me remember. He heard my thought in the tone of my voice.

"He'll be fine, your brother. They get lost all the time, then they get found. You wait. You're going to get a telegram delivered under your door saying he's okay."

It was what I wanted to hear. I clung harder to his arm, and when we got to his hotel, I followed him and waited while he opened the door to his room. He was just what I needed.

Elgin flipped on the light. The bed was made, and on the dresser there was a photograph of a man and a woman.

"Mom and Dad," he said, embarrassed, when he saw me looking. "They live in Oakland."

"Is that where you go when you get out?" I asked.

"I like it here," Elgin said. "Better and better."

He didn't rush, he didn't expect anything. I thought he was probably younger than me, about Dayton's age.

"Do you want to talk some more?" he asked. "About your brother?"

That was what I didn't want to do. I remembered the feel of Elgin, the citrus smell of his skin. I shook my head as I walked to him and kept shaking it, my eyes shut, until his lips made me still. His mouth was large and gentle, and when he held me I put my arms around his waist, pulled him close. He was a man who liked to kiss, who talked without words. And I answered the best I knew how.

In some ways I never had a man before Elgin. Through that night with him I forgot all about myself, all about time and who he was and what I wanted from him. No thought rested in my mind for more than an instant and then it was replaced. I studied each finger of his hand, each curve of his ear. I held nothing back from him, I threw away the Christine everybody thought they knew. We made love all night, all over that room, but when I think back on it, I can't separate it into parts. There were no seams, no limits, no beginnings and endings, just the strong rush of an unchoked river sweeping everything in its way.

I woke before dawn, dazed and stiff, my body flowing as if he were still touching it. My tips of my breasts stung and my mouth tingled. My hair had straightened and hung loose and heavy. Our clothes scattered on the floor and furniture in drifted piles, mixed and tangled. Next to me, lit by the gleam of the pulled-down window shade, Elgin sprawled on his stomach. I had seen plenty of men but he blotted them out. His legs and feet were long and slim, his back was deep with muscle. He gave off heat, and I moved to feel it against me. He raised his head, his eyes half-closed, his mouth warm honey. I said to him what I had never said to anyone before. I said I needed him. I asked him not to leave me. And when he said "Never," I crossed his heart.

11

I had walked into the wrong bar on the right night, and the experience left me temporarily insane.

In the days that followed I barely recognized myself—I acted like women I had never understood or believed. Living for February 18, the day Elgin was to be discharged, I went to work and came home and waited for his nightly call from the base. Neither of us was good with phones, but our three minutes passed like no time at all. Sometimes I simply listened to Elgin breathe while I squeezed my eyes closed and went over him, one part at a time, in my mind. Afterward, when the operator came on and we hung up, I became a high school girl again, made designs out of our initials with my purple felt-tip pen, covering the borders of the slick pages of *Cosmopolitan* and *Bride*. I told myself Elgin was my change of luck, and believed every promise he made. I even believed his guarantee could bring my brother back in one piece.

I was so sure, I thought of writing home that Lee was okay, but Dayton wouldn't trust my intuition, and Aunt Ida would claim I was just wishful thinking. She took inklings and feelings seriously only when they spelled trouble. I decided to wait until Lee returned, safe and sound, then break the news I had known all along.

After the first surprise at finding myself involved with a black man, I took it for granted. I bought myself new underwear and a pair of high white boots. Three times a week I filed my nails into perfect ovals, pushed every sign of cuticle out of sight, and laid on two coats of Revlon's finest. I lost eleven pounds in three weeks. I went to the Indian Health Service hospital in Seattle and had my sore tooth filled, and I got friendlier than I ever had been before with the black women on line with me at the airline caterers.

Yet I kept a secret edge of doubt like a card up my sleeve. I trusted Elgin more than any boyfriend I had before, but I didn't want to be a fool, to be another sad story. I told myself I could take any man or leave him. But Elgin wasn't just any man.

I took the eighteenth off to clean my apartment, to go to the market. I fixed Indian pinto bean chili like you never tasted. I was ready at four o'clock, though Elgin wasn't due till five-thirty. I was ready at six, but still not worried. I was ready at seven-thirty when I called to make sure the bus from Fort Lewis had arrived on time. And I was ready at nine when Elgin, beer-breathed and smiles and carrying a bouquet of live flowers in one hand and his suitcase in the other, blew through my open door.

The chili burned to the pan and then got cold, and the flowers wilted for lack of water. Our first days together had just been practice, Elgin said, and he was right. We were out of our minds. The lovemaking between us was so different from anything I knew before that I found myself wondering if we were under some kind of a spell, or making one. There was nothing we didn't try, and nothing that didn't work.

Tacoma in those days was not yet urban renewed, but we never noticed. Elgin had enough money saved for me to quit my dead-end job and stay home to study him full time, and every new feature about him gave me pleasure: his long sighs as he fell into sleep, the tease of his breath in my ear, the blunt shape of his cock, and the sensitivity of his nipples. He loved to be touched under his arms, and he stretched like a sleeping cat when I kissed the back of his neck. Some mornings he'd pull the shades down, then beg me not to dress at all. He had this game where he inked his index finger with his tongue, and then wrote on the bare skin of my breasts and stomach. He made me guess the words. The prize if I was right, and the penalty if I was wrong, were the same.

Elgin could make perfect hashed brown potatoes and could carry a tune when he sang. He read our horoscopes in the newspaper before he checked the want ads for work. He complained he had no skills, but I just laughed until he laughed too, low and sly and proud of himself.

Nobody can predict the future, but some things you can take into your own hands. For the first time in my life, I didn't take precautions. Every grown woman I knew had a child, and I wanted mine to be Elgin's. I imagined what he'd be like, a boy who took after his father. It never occurred to me that I wouldn't get pregnant.

Some women say they know just the moment their baby is made, and I'm among them. One spring morning too nice to stay inside, we got the idea for a picnic. We stopped at Mr. Chicken down the street and bought two box dinners, then took the Number 11 bus to Point Defiance Park, overlooking Puget Sound. I don't know where everybody was, at their jobs I guess, but the place was deserted. We hitched short rides and climbed the road, carrying our lunch and hanging on every word the other said. Elgin laughed at the sign on one lookout about how in 1841 some navy captain had said that with guns placed there and on the opposite shore he could control the world. I was so happy I could almost hear background music, and I took my steps to the beat.

Elgin wore a green T-shirt and rust-colored cotton pants. I had bought him a present from some hippies on the street corner, a bracelet made of three different kinds of metals—iron, copper, and brass—twisted together. A girl I used to work with had one, and she told me that in Africa it was supposed to bring good luck. Elgin wore it all the time, and that day it glinted in the sun where it hung low on his wrist. He was a strong man, tall. I rushed to keep pace with his long legs, but every so often I'd hang back for a full-length view.

He watched me too. I had my hair gathered in back with a beaded clip, my legs were bare below my cutoffs, and the flip-flops kept slipping off my feet. Elgin had gotten me a sweatshirt at the PX that said PROPERTY OF U.S. ARMY and I wore it without a bra, even though my breasts were large.

When we came to a private place with a good view of the Sound, we spread the horse blanket I had brought from the bed and opened our Mr. Chicken. Everything tasted better than it was. The sun was so bright on the water I had to squint my eyes to look across, and the heat soaked into my skin. I lay back on the warm, springy wool and pulled my shirt over my head. Then I unbuttoned my cutoffs and pushed them down. I took a deep breath and looked at Elgin. He faced me, his elbows on his knees, his arms in a steeple, his chin resting on his hands, his eyes quiet and dark as the night sky. Time passed while we stayed like that, only touching with our minds, then he lay beside me without a word and there, in a public park on a workday, in plain view of the ships that moved north and south in the waves far below us, we loved each other.

Later, while we caught our breath, as he trailed his thin brown fingers over my thighs and I cupped him gently in my palm, I told him we had made a baby.

"You're pregnant?" He stopped his hand, propped up on his elbow. His face became alert and tense. "How long?"

"Five minutes."

He didn't believe it, drew back as if to see me from a greater distance. "You can't be sure."

I made my mouth into one of those mystery smiles you see women on the soaps give when they know what only a woman knows. He could question it if he wanted to, but a month from now there'd be no doubt in his mind.

"You didn't use anything, really?" Elgin still hadn't moved his hand, and it grew heavy on my body.

"It's *okay*." I wanted him to be quiet, not to spoil how I

felt. "I don't expect anything extra from you. You don't need to be married to have a baby."

Elgin thought about that awhile, and then his hand began to move again. His fingers traced a word on the smooth, low curve of my stomach. He leaned over me to place his cheek against it. Finally he sat and looked at me.

"Yes?" I guessed.

"Yes, you do."

"Yes, I do what?"

"Yes, you do have to be married to have *my* child. You have to be married to me."

If you had told me, three years before, that at twenty-five I'd be living in Tacoma, engaged to a black veteran, carrying his child of my own free will, ready to settle down—I'd have laughed in your face. And if you told me that nine months later in the Seattle IHS hospital I'd give birth, married, halfway deserted, and near broke, to a slim, dark girl, as unlike me as a baby could be, I wouldn't have believed it.

In the beginning, my pregnancy seemed to make no difference in our lives. Being with Elgin, and morning sickness, blocked out all my bad habits, so I stopped smoking, quit drinking cold turkey, and we went to bed early most nights. Some days we never got up.

When Elgin's money ran low, we moved to Seattle to look for new jobs. Elgin had seen in the *Post-Intelligencer* that there was a call out for mail carriers, and he thought that would be decent temporary work while we figured out what to do next. But the first day he came home dressed in his uniform he looked so good I told him he had to quit. The pale blue-gray gabardine strained over the swells of his body, rough against the dark cream of his skin. I made him promise no C.O.D.'s.

With Elgin on the street every day, I was bored and lonesome. I never had been good company for myself. I didn't want to get trained again, so I went back to my first job in the city, making black boxes. The final design was a secret—I didn't even know what they looked like when they came off the line—but I had a picture all worked out in my mind: the surface was polished to a shine and there was no visible way to open it. It made no sound, no tickings or buzzing. Attached beneath a plane's instrument panel, so simple and plain that the crew would forget it was there, it was a silent witness to everything that took place. Day in, day out, the bolt I screwed would hold the spool that wound the tape that recorded every sound, every joke, from Seattle to Japan, from Japan to Hong Kong. If something went wrong anywhere in the rest of the plane, the box would know. Even after an explosion, it sent out silent beeps that could be traced to the deepest part of the ocean or the emptiest stretch of land.

There were times that I thought of my stomach as a black box. I wondered what the baby heard, what sounds took hold in its brain. It was my memory, so I let myself sleep as the honeymoon with Elgin slowed down. I got through the nights that no excuses of special delivery letters or working late could explain. Sitting home, huge and alone, I pretended that mail got sorted on Sunday afternoons. My baby, not me, recorded the jokes Elgin's new friends made about his Indian squaw and how he had got himself scalped before he made his last stand. My baby, not me, was the eyes that saw the biting, jealous stares of skinny black women, following us when Elgin and I went out in public. Like the pilot of an airplane with a slow fuel leak or low oil pressure, I sailed above the clouds, planning for tomorrow, never fearing that something important had broken and thrown the trip off course.

We were living in a hotel over on Ninth Street, the Excelsior, which suited me fine. The place had an elevator that worked, and our room had a sink and a tiny unit that contained a refrigerator and stove combination. It was handy for cooking, since the burners were built in on top of the small freezer, but whenever I fried anything for more than ten minutes, all the ice cubes melted. We slept in two soft narrow beds. At first we pushed them together so we could curl against each other, but often before morning one of us, usually me, would slip through the crack and get wedged in. I'd lie there like baloney in a sandwich, making little movements to wake Elgin without startling him. I learned early on that he would jump in panic if I shook him or called his name when he was asleep, and I was afraid his thrashing arms would hit me when I couldn't defend myself. I blamed his nerves on the army, since I'd known more than one vet who woke scared.

As my baby grew inside me, though, I left the beds apart. That way, when I had to get up during the night or when Elgin came back after the light was out, as he did more and more, we wouldn't bother each other. I liked to rise early and eat a good breakfast, but if he didn't have a route, Elgin would sleep until eleven o'clock. After he got used to my habits, he could tune out any sound I made on a regular basis.

One day, getting ready to go to the market, I couldn't button my raincoat across my stomach. I stopped trying and sat on the side of my bed, wondering what to wear. It was a Saturday, the end of the best week between us in some time. Elgin was delivering a neighborhood he enjoyed, not too hilly and no loose dogs, and I had finally settled on a name for our child: Raymond, after the actor who played Perry Mason and never lost a case. I felt one hundred percent, and when I caught my reflection in the mirror over my bureau, I liked what I saw. My skin was clear, my hair shone black after a brushing, and my shoulders were broad and strong. I even appreciated the sight of my high round stomach, big enough to support a TV dinner tray.

Elgin and I had filed for a marriage license in Tacoma, but my life had become so cluttered with trappings—a man, maternity clothes, a steady job—that I neglected to arrange the actual wedding. There were too many things to think of every day to plan for invitations or clothes or a big dinner. Now my raincoat made me remember.

"So when does the knot get tied?" I asked Elgin. I planted my arms behind me for support.

He was on the floor in his old army undershirt, shining his work shoes, and at first he looked at the laces as though I was talking about them. Then he gave it up, raised his head.

"You worried I'm going back on my word?" His voice was tight.

I hadn't, before that minute. I figured Elgin and I had to plow through some rough times before we got used to each other, but that was only normal. I spent my teenage years glued to "The Newlywed Game" and heard Bob Eubanks laugh off everything from husbands who dressed in their bride's panties to couples who got the measles on their wedding night. Compared to a lot of them, we weren't so bad. But it sounded as if the idea of not marrying me had occurred to *Elgin*, it sounded as if he had to fight that idea hard.

"Fuck your word," I said, struggling to push myself upright. "Fuck you."

Elgin dropped his shoe and jumped to kneel over me on the bed. All I really wanted to do was hold him close, but that wasn't how the game worked. He had to pin my arms and make me surrender. I was nearly a foot shorter, but he was afraid of my pregnant body and that evened the odds.

I spoke into his face, only inches above mine. "I want to wear...a long white...dress and...have a three-foot...wedding cake and...go to Hawaii...on my honeymoon...with Paul Newman." My words were forced out in bunches, as I strained my muscles against his strength.

"You're a crazy woman," Elgin said when, breathless, he rested his forehead on mine. He smelled like wintergreen Lifesavers. "Crazy." He dropped his body next to mine, folded me to him.

A long time ago I had stopped saying aloud how good our lovemaking was. I didn't want Elgin too sure of himself. But that time, that morning, I saw in his eyes that same look that hooked me at Barclay's, the same desperate stare that eclipsed the public park in Tacoma. It was an expression that had never been in anybody's eyes but his, and I'd kill to keep it there.

We married at the federal courthouse, with no witnesses that we ever saw again except each other. I chose a beige dress because it was on sale and it made me look darker, as though Elgin and I were closer to the same shade. Elgin dug out his dress army uniform, even though we thought that might be illegal. It was either that or the blue satin cowboy shirt I got him with my last black box paycheck. The woman judge wore a tweed pantsuit and pearl earrings. She smiled at us and wished us good luck.

Once we were outside again, Elgin put his hand under my elbow to help me negotiate the stone steps, then we stood on the sidewalk, letting the crowd flow around us while we decided what to do. Finally, we ate an early dinner of salmon steaks and rice, huckleberry pie for dessert, at a seafood restaurant, and went next to a C&W club everybody said was the place to go. We sat at a table, suddenly shy with each other, until the band started playing "Sweet Dreams." That song made me want to cry, and I reached for Elgin's hand. We moved out and danced close and clumsy, the baby inside me wedged between us, our arms around each other's backs, and we stayed that way, barely moving our feet, after the music stopped and the other couples sat down. When I opened my eyes and saw a middle-aged Indian woman spying on us with a question in her mind, I broke free.

"Today's my wedding day," I announced to that roomful of strangers, "and we're celebrating."

The woman was mortified that I had seen what she was thinking, and joined in when everybody gave us a hand. Those people acted like they had never heard of married before, they made such a to-do. All the men wanted to stand Elgin a drink and the women asked me when the baby was expected. The manager of the place wouldn't take our money, and when we scraped back our chairs to go home, the whole crowd whistled and pounded on the tables.

The chill of the damp night air outside that club was a shock. After hours of noise and music, the late silence made us whisper and then fall quiet as we crisscrossed the abandoned streets toward the Excelsior. We started with our hands clamped tight on each other in excitement, but by the time we had gone a few blocks we let go, tired from being the center of attention and I, at least, amazed to find myself a married woman. Elgin was wrapped in himself, a closed door to me.

You'd expect tonight we could coast through another hour, but it was clear we were heading for a fight. Elgin walked too fast for my new white heels, and I hung back even more to make him take a husband's responsibility. The gap between us widened. Under a streetlamp almost a block ahead of me, he halted and looked from side to side. When I wasn't there, he whirled around, then waited while I took my time catching up to him.

"I lost track," he said, and put his heavy arm around my shoulder.

I forgot about our fight. What mattered right then was the feel and smell and sight of him, and the fact that I knew I'd better not pass something when it was handed to me on a silver platter. I smiled and snaked my arms around his waist.

"Slow down, Mr. Taylor. Save some energy to carry me over the threshold."

Elgin's laugh, all warm and thick and bubbling from inside, colored the night. "I'll show you a threshold," he said.

He lifted me into his arms, supporting my back and under my knees, and held me to him like a sleepy child—with a beachball in her stomach.

"You're out of your mind," I cried, but he walked with me that way the last two blocks to our hotel, through the dimmed lobby, and onto the creaking, gilded elevator. I pulled at my skirt and hid my face in his chest so I wouldn't see the night clerk's face. When we got to our floor, Elgin carried me down the hall, shifted my weight while I searched in his pocket for the key, then he kicked the door shut behind us.

Aunt Ida didn't have a phone so I sent her a postcard with the Seattle skyline by night on the back. "I have a husband who's not an Indian," I wrote. "His name is Elgin Taylor and now I'm Christine Taylor. We didn't have to get married but I'm going to have a baby. I hope you're fine. Did you hear anything new about Lee? I'll write a long letter soon. Love from your *daughter*, Mrs. Christine Taylor." If I could be somebody's wife I could be Aunt Ida's child. I wrote the address of the Excelsior Hotel in the corner, zone and all, and sent it off to Montana.

Days and weeks passed without any word from her. I didn't know whether to be worried or mad, so I was both. My weight confined me by that time, and I had to leave my job. The mail was all there was to look forward to, but what I got were flyers and advertisements, mostly addressed to another Mrs. Taylor, who must have lived in the hotel before me.

Elgin was off before dawn every morning, and some nights he didn't come back until I was in bed asleep. Maybe I should have asked more questions, but I preferred not to suspect him. Men cheated on wives who gave them no peace or understanding, never wanted to have fun, and probably fooled around themselves. In my mind those wives merged into a fat, mean, money-mad woman. I had never blamed those husbands when they left her for a date with me.

One wet Friday afternoon the manager had been at the door twice wanting our rent, and I couldn't go out in public because I didn't have a raincoat that would fit. Hour after hour, I looked for Elgin. He could get us a pizza so I didn't make myself any dinner. Finally I went to bed, a ticking bomb.

Elgin waltzed in at eleven o'clock, no excuses, no how was your day. Beer marked him like aftershave.

I gave him a chance for the first word, but when he didn't take it, I spoke from the dark.

"Where the hell have you been?"

"I had to work late." His voice had a hurt tone to it, as if I had accused him of something he was ready to deny. He flicked a light and slowly hung his uniform pants on the metal hanger with two clips for the creases. Finally he turned toward me.

"I didn't know they had a tap in the sorting room," I said. "You run out of Lifesavers?"

Elgin's full lips firmed to a line, and he stared hard into the surface of the bureau against the wall, letting his reaction build.

"So what if I stopped off," he yelled at last. "What's there to come here for anyway? You sit around making lists of things to bitch about."

Now I was the one unjustly convicted. "It's not my fault," I said. "You think I like that fish-eyed desk clerk hounding me for what we owe? Did you cash your check?"

Elgin was drunker than I had realized. He moved, knocking a chair over backward, reached into his suspended uniform pants and emptied the pockets onto the kitchen table. Loose change, dollar bills, Kleenex pressed into tight clumps by his hands spilled across the surface.

"Does that satisfy you?"

I saw myself through his eyes. I was that fat, mean woman. He was one of those husbands.

"Who is she?" I asked in a quiet voice.

He didn't answer. He snatched his pants off the clips and put them on, then banged the door so hard behind him that it ricocheted ajar. I heard his steps hammering down the fire stairs, not even bothering to wait for the elevator. I heard the door open on the ground floor, and then nothing, just a hollowness, empty as a deep tunnel.

I got my unemployment. I got my Indian Health. I got by. Elgin didn't return for three days, the whole weekend, and when he did come back, something was missing. There was no time to fight before the baby was due, and I didn't want to scare Elgin away, so I didn't ask where he'd been. He paid our hotel bill, in the evenings told me stories of his day, stayed around more. Sometimes he watched me, and I knew what he was thinking because I thought it myself: what have I got myself into? I was too far along for our bodies to work their full magic, and it got harder and harder to trust that they'd ever be able to again. My stomach seemed to grow and stretch with every lying word and regret.

The baby poked and simmered night and day. Its hiccups made my body bounce. It stuck out a foot or a hand and held it firm until I rubbed it back into place. Sometimes I thought the heartbeat was loud enough for anyone to hear, and when the baby dropped and its round, heavy head rested low, I couldn't take a step without remembering it. It took me over and held me in its time, and I was a prisoner of my own body.

My due date was December 3, and I was a week past on the morning the desk clerk delivered a letter addressed to me in Dayton's handwriting.

It was eleven o'clock and I was still in my gown, still in bed, waiting for my water to break. My wedding ring cut into my swollen finger. I had felt the first fluttery contractions before dawn, nothing I couldn't handle, and I didn't mention them to Elgin as he dressed to go to work. On my last visit to the hospital, the doctor said this stage, when it started, would last for six to eight hours. Elgin would be long back from his route before anything was ready to happen, and if he wasn't, I'd leave him a note to meet me at IHS. The baby was only inches above the path it would follow into this world, and birth seemed easy and hopeless at the same time. I had a bag packed for the hospital, and the doctor's telephone numbers were written on a card in my purse. Alone this morning, I had French braided my grown-out hair tight against my scalp.

I studied the envelope a long time, as if I had X-ray vision. It was the kind you buy at the post office with the stamp printed on, and Dayton's script was large enough to fill the whole space. He used my new name, so I knew Aunt Ida had received the postcard I sent. I had never written her the long letter I promised.

Finally, I slit the flap with a nail file and unfolded the lined white stationery inside.

"Lee is dead . . ." seared my brain before I knew what I was reading. I crushed the paper, holding it with both hands against my chest, but it was no use. I panted, my breathing shallow and useless, my eyes closed. I turned to glass, I turned to shale. My mouth moved in automatic prayers until my tongue began to flap Lee's name, again and again, soundless, clacking in time with my breath. Pictures raced through my mind like snapshots, a newsreel of Lee's face, talking, sleeping, angry, joking, young, hair cut short, all ending with the flashing of Dayton's words. I raised the letter again, held it in front of me, opened my eyes. It poured like rain into a cave, striking here and there, forming puddles, running down the walls: ". . . fell behind enemy lines . . . all along . . . reported on a list of casualties . . . They won't give back his body until . . . No reason for you to come . . . Ida is taking it . . . Yours truly."

I threw my arm over my eyes, arched my back. I couldn't form a thought, couldn't cry. I gasped the air around me, swallowed it, drew more in. My body was a turtle shell and nothing could touch me. I pushed it all down from my head, down my arms, down my chest. My legs shivered, but I pushed harder. A warm flood washed from me, soaking my gown and the mattress. I looked, expecting blood, but I couldn't see beyond the mountain of my stomach. Everything below had disappeared. And as I watched a dent formed beneath my gown, changing my shape as if an invisible fist had driven into me.

When the cramping pain released, I rolled to my side and reached for my purse. I fumbled for the card with the numbers, grabbed the phone and dialed the hotel operator.

"This is Mrs. Taylor," I said. "Get a cab."

The ache overtook me again, and I gripped the receiver and watched my fingers turn thin. I dug my nails into the skin of my palm as if that could take the place of all other feeling. I drew back my lips, bit on nothing, and waited it out. Finally I could notice the female voice speaking from the phone, asking, over and over, was I all right?

"It's the baby," I said, and read her the doctor's number to call. I dropped the receiver onto its cradle and looked around the room to locate my clothes. I wanted to be ready to move after the next contraction. My purse lay open on the floor, and as I sensed, far away but coming fast, the pinching drag of my muscles, I took Dayton's letter and stuffed it deep inside.

◆ ◆ ◆

As soon as I reached the hospital, the labor slowed. I sat in a wheelchair in the hall for hours, answered the questions of a woman seated behind a glass window who typed them onto a printed form and checked me in. Three times that endless afternoon I called the hotel to leave messages for Elgin, but he never showed to receive them. I was pushing by the time they finally brought me to my first examination in the delivery room.

In maternity I had an idiot for a nurse, a woman who nagged, "Don't bear down until the doctor comes," and then, when he finally arrived, she stood at the side of my electric bed, fed me crushed ice, and wouldn't shut her mouth.

"Be a brave girl," she said as I seized her hand. "Don't be in a hurry."

I lost any sense of time, the limits of the world the space between my pain, my only guides "push" and "rest," until I heard someone say, "She's ready."

I paused for a turquoise instant, preparing to squeeze the baby from my body, but the nurse broke in.

"Do you ever watch 'The Price Is Right' on TV?" she demanded. I was dumb from exhaustion, my hair damp with sweat, my face streaked in tears, and I knew no better than to nod that I had.

"Well, come on *down*," she said. "Make this a real push!"

Before I could tell her to go to hell, to shut her face, I lost myself in the force of the contraction. I dug my chin into my chest, held my breath, and pressed so hard my eyes felt as though they'd burst from my skull. Alarm bells went off in my brain. The baby was too big for me, something was wrong. If I bore down again, even a little, my body would rip apart.

The doctor was a white mask, a pair of gloved hands. "Now," he told me, but what did he know? I gritted my teeth and to satisfy him, pretended, but I protected myself.

"It's worse if you won't help," he said, impatient and far away. "I don't want to use forceps."

"Just get *mad* at the baby," said the stupid nurse. "Just say 'Bad baby, bad baby,' and shove it out."

I could have killed her at that moment. The force of my

hate almost wrenched me off the table, and it gave me strength. When the next contraction came I put common sense away, tightened and loosened everything I could feel. I held my eyes on the nurse's face. "Good baby," I managed. "Good baby, good baby, good baby."

"Hold it. Hold it," the doctor said.

There was nothing but my pain. I gave myself to it, drowned in it. My thoughts were a white screen in a black room.

"That's the head. One more. Yes."

My muscles obeyed their own will. I fell back in relief, my body collapsing against empty space as the baby slipped from me. My mind left with it, losing the memory of every hurt, needing only to know the child was safe. I stared at the light above the bed, waiting to hear a cry, and when it came, reedy and high as a Cheyenne war dance song, I answered back, echoed the exact sound.

"Raymond," I demanded, holding out my arms to the doctor and nurse busy at my feet. My neck strained for a look. "Give me Raymond."

"That's a funny name for her," the doctor said, and lifted my daughter for me to see. I felt the heft of her in my hands and brought her to my breast.

She was a long dark shape, smeared with white cream. Thin black hair rose in straight, slick lines from her head as if she were a cartoon baby and had just been frightened. She had stopped crying but still moved her mouth, flexing and flexing her deep bowed lips. Her nose was large for her face, so broad. I took one of her hands, uncurled the fingers against my own. Her palms were a lighter shade than the rest of her, golden against rich brown. The clamped cord, which had joined us, stuck from her stomach, and below that, her legs were thin, curved in below the knee as if made out of rubber. Her toes bunched in a knotty line, each nail flawless, smooth, clean.

I guided her mouth to the hard nipple of my left breast, and she knew what to do, drew me into her, took what she needed. As I watched, she opened one eye, piercing, squinting in even the shaded light of the room, to search for me. The iris was muddy green, camouflage, the tint of a shallow lake. We stared at each other, strangers. I inhaled her damp, salty smell, my breath elevating and lowering her weight, as the heat of our bodies flowed together and once again became the same.

I hated the hospital. The nurses wouldn't leave me alone. They wanted to wash my baby, measure her, put drops in her eyes. They wanted to put my baby in the nursery and keep me in the ward, but I yelled when they tried to take her, and scared them with my willpower. They thought I was insane, whispered about me among themselves, but gave me my way, put us together in a private room they said I had no right to use. I forgot them the minute they were out the door.

Elgin came to see me later. Nobody gave him word, he said, nobody at the hotel knew where I had gone. It was lucky he had found me at all. He stood at the far end of the bed, his hands turning his hat, his eyes darting to the hallway. He was full of things he couldn't tell me, full of his secrets, but I had lost interest in them.

"They say it's a girl."

"They're right." I turned back the yellow blanket to reveal her face, and, as though she heard us talking, she opened those strange angry eyes and studied Elgin.

"She could stare down a train," he said.

I had a flash of my feeling for Elgin, a surge of wanting him to hold me in his big hands, a picture of the three of us, mother, father and daughter, smiling on a Christmas card. He sensed my softening and moved in, sat on the bed, touched the baby with silk fingers.

"She's got my mother's mouth," he said. "Little Diane."

"Diane?"

"My mama."

Elgin's parents and a couple of sisters lived in California, but he didn't talk about them. When he called them on the phone he never mentioned me at all. I wasn't going to have my

baby named after some mystery woman, much less looking like
her.

"I already picked out the name," I reminded him.

He raised his eyebrows. "Raymond." He said it flat, like it
was a joke.

"Didn't you ever hear of Ray for a girl?"

"Ray short for what?"

I thought fast. Rayburn. Rayton. "Rayon," I said. "Rayona."

He couldn't believe he had heard right. "Like nylon?"

"Like nothing." I wasn't going to argue with him.

Elgin shook his head. "Well, her middle name's Diane."

I didn't care. Nobody used their middle names, and I'd
never tell her.

"Did you call anybody?" he asked.

"There's nobody to call." I reached for my purse, dug out
Dayton's letter, and handed it to him without another word. I
hadn't looked at it again, but I hadn't forgotten. It was on the
back burner, keeping warm, ready to boil. Elgin unfolded the
paper and read under the light. His eyebrows drew together in a
frown.

"Damn."

He had been my last hope. Deep inside, I had been
waiting for him to tell me not to worry, that it was a screwup. I
wanted him to say the army made lot of mistakes and Lee was
alive, like he had promised. But he let Lee die right in front of
me.

I snatched the letter from Elgin's hands and balled it back
into my purse. I glared at him while he told me he was sorry, he
understood how I felt. I wanted him to get out, to leave me
alone with my baby, but he wouldn't quit.

"This Dayton says they're not going to turn back the
remains yet," he said. "It could be a while before they work it
out."

"I can read."

"That's shit," he went on. "What do they want with his
body?"

I thought of Lee's body, lean and loose on a rodeo horse,

his left hand thrown high in the air, his right hand on the belt, his long hair flying with every buck.

"Liar," I said.

The night nurse came into the room and Elgin was embarrassed that she might have heard. He spoke quietly, like he was talking to the baby, as he rose to leave.

"It's all going to change. Starting today, all new. Give me a chance." But when he fumbled for my hand, I pulled it away.

As my shock wore down, I let myself turn to Elgin for kindness—when I didn't need it too badly. I let him father the baby through her first months, let him walk with her through the halls of the Excelsior when she couldn't sleep. Some nights I let him push our beds together and blanked my mind to everything but his touch. But I never let down my guard, never believed him the way I used to, and when once again his days at work got longer, when his nights got later, I wasn't surprised and I wasn't too unhappy. I got a sitter for the baby, and met new people myself. I was still young and I had good times. Finally, when Rayona was nine months and I was back at work at a new job, I packed a bag and moved to a place of my own.

Even then, Elgin was gum on the sole of my shoe. Every once in a while he phoned late at night, lonesome and sad, to say we should start over. Sometimes I opened my door to his knock, sometimes not. And sometimes I was the one who called.

12

I cut without belief through that snowy land. Almost fourteen months had passed since Dayton's letter, and the government had finally released Lee's corpse. My brother's death was a place I had to go, a thing I had to do. Next to me on the front seat of my first Volaré Rayona slept propped against the door, her hands clasped together between her knees, as we crossed the mountains that separated home from Seattle.

I drove like a truck driver who has to punch a clock. Every three hundred miles I gassed up and filled my steel thermos with black coffee. Night and day meant nothing, and I rolled through the passing of light as if it were patches of water on the road. I concentrated on the space between the white line and the shoulder. I talked to myself out loud. "You're doing fine, Christine. Hang on."

My baby woke and looked at me, but I didn't answer her glance. My back hunched as though I was in a hurry and late. I steered for the space in front of my headlights and held my foot steady at sixty-five. My leg ached. My mind drew lines along the muscles that held me tense, but I didn't shift my gears. I drove a mile at a time, and I passed any car that got in my way. My teeth were set against each other, and I didn't think. I was a fish reeled on a steady line.

At dawn we hit the high plains of central Montana, the only car to break through the night. I took the short cut, the road nobody used, and it was empty. There were no signs, no

200

trees, no telephone poles to prove that people had come this way before. The sky was white as the swirl on either side of the highway, and threads of snow, even as bars, blew in constant streams across my path. It reminded me of something I couldn't place at first, and then it came to me: at the Indian Center in Tacoma a Navajo woman had set up her loom to weave a rug. A thousand rows of spun wool reached from ceiling to floor and between them, at high speed, she threw her shuttle with one hand and caught it on the opposite end with the other. An unfamiliar pattern developed before my eyes, inch by inch.

I turned the dial of the car radio looking for the weather. I was in a cave without colors, and in the rearview mirror I saw on my face a new line that reached like a gaff from my left eyebrow into the center of my forehead. If I stopped squinting it became fainter but didn't disappear, and then creased back when I concentrated to find direction. Glare ice, black ice they call it, polished the road and reflected first my headlights and then the rising sun. There were times I could see our own image, a closed car with fixed wheels, bearing down. I prayed not to skid. "Remember, O most gracious Virgin Mary, that never was it known that anyone who fled to thy protection, implored thy help, or sought thy intercession was left unaided..."

The land stretched flat and frozen on either side, slicked with hoarfrost and gleaming like washed china. There was nothing to turn our path or slow us down.

I had driven this stretch of highway a hundred times, but then I was always looking ahead or behind and it had been just the way from one place to another. Today was different. The land drained the life from me, pulled me apart in all directions. Any sound I made was soaked into those trackless miles like a drop of water on a dry sponge. Even the radio was no help. It brought in waves of unreasonable static that didn't hold long enough to make sense. News from Omaha or Saskatoon drifted by before I pinned it down. The voices scratched the whiteness like fingernails on a blackboard, so I shut them off.

There was one block of time where I was afraid to even look at my girl. I started to see if she was wet and needed changing, but, before I moved, the thought hit me that she was frozen pale gray, turned to stone. In my heart I believed this was true, so I denied it by not checking. My legs were stuffed with sawdust and my eyes blinked dry and the road would never end.

I didn't dare stop. I was afraid to hear the vacuum that sucked through the wind. The snow sparkled like sandpaper, like tarred and dusted roofing, and as far as I could see, the ground was hollowed by stiff pools filled with dark blue shadows. The only thing that kept me going was the sound of the engine drinking gas, burning it, sending us east like a rocket. Every now and then I'd feel the tires lock and float, blown off course and beyond my control.

I closed out Lee's face, the picture of him in his uniform. I shut off the stream of my own words that followed me, the Saturday night talk about how he had to enlist, how he couldn't be chickenshit, how I'd stop being his sister out of pure shame. I put Lee on ice to be examined later for his cause of death. In my head I sang every song I knew and held the wheel with hands formed into hooks as the snow rose like smoke before my windshield. My eyes strained through the blurred glass, and followed those dotted lines. I was alone in the world, except for my child, and she didn't even know it. I had to do the right thing and drive us through.

In school I had been warned about snow blindness. I remember learning the Eskimos wore goggles made out of a seal's stomach. They stretched swatches of it across a frame and used a bone needle to punch pinholes to look through. Without protection people saw strange things, saw too much, too wide. That's what happened to me. It wasn't that I dozed off, because I kept driving, kept tilting the steering wheel when the road curved, and kept remembering to coast without braking through the icy stretches. I kept alert to every sign.

Then out of the corner of my eye I saw a flight of golden stairsteps, and halfway up Lee was waiting, holding out his hand for me to take. He was dressed in new clothes, pointy tooled boots, and his braids were wrapped in otter pelt and hanging thick to his waist. He wore his solid brass buckle, and in every way he looked as fresh and new as a snake just shed of its old skin.

If I turned toward that sight, simply weighted down on the wheel with my right arm, tipped the balance of my hands where they rested on either side of the horn, I'd drive to meet him. I'd pull to the bottom of those steps and throw open my door. I'd leave the motor racing and run to Lee and together, the two of us, we'd go right to the top. I felt tears on my cheeks, and above the engine I heard the sound of my own voice, crying out in sounds I never made before. This must be scaring the shit out of Ray, I thought, but I didn't stop. The wind blew a mist of snow all around the car, enclosing every window in a fine white powder, and the world disappeared. I let it go with no regrets.

I floored the gas pedal and pitched my body across my baby to keep her from flying through the windshield. The Volaré lifted and skated, fast and smooth as a winter star.

When we finally stopped I didn't move or open my eyes. The car had spun so often, with such wrenching turns, that my nerves had unraveled and I had lost all sense. I clung to the side of the seat and held my breath. My daughter's knees dug sharply into my chest. The engine was dead, and red lights shone from the dashboard.

I looked at Rayona, and her expression was bright with excitement as she waited for my signal to smile or laugh. I steeped myself in the darkness of her skin, the black lights of her eyes, the sour warm smell of her wet diaper. Above me she craned her neck to see out the window, and her body twisted to find a more comfortable position beneath my weight. She wore a cheap dimestore parka of some material made to look like brown fur, and it brushed and bristled against my cheek as she moved. The breath from her mouth melted the air and rose in a steam that collected on the inside of the windows.

"Let's change you," I said, straightening myself, and Rayona scooted down on her back and stuck her legs in the air. I lowered her jeans and rubber pants and stripped off her diaper.

Her body was slim and perfect, warm as I spread powder into its folds and valleys. I put on her fresh pants. I turned the ignition, and the engine caught. The heater blew against my feet, and I drew my daughter onto my lap. She was more than a year and could manage for herself. She lifted my sweater, tugged down my bra and pressed her hot mouth against me. As the milk began to flow, she sighed and, lazy and slow, reached her hand to my face and traced the outline of my nose, my eye, my ear, every part of me for which she had a word.

Lee's body had come by train and beat us home. The box that contained him was set on the cot before the front window of the main room and covered with Aunt Ida's good tablecloth. The sight of that material, white with a border of blue windmills, was so familiar that, when I walked through the doorway, I didn't recognize the long narrow shape for what it was. Aunt Ida looked at me with an irritated expression, prepared to think my dress was too short or my makeup was applied too thick. She never behaved like a mother, even in her grief. She hadn't seen me for four years, but she was ready to take up where we left off, as though nothing had happened.

"You're supposed to cover it with an American flag," I said. "He died in the service."

She didn't answer, so I offered Rayona for her to hold. "This is the baby."

Aunt Ida didn't blink as she inspected my daughter. She saw everything: the curly hair, the dark skin, the full lips. If she was surprised Rayona's father was black, she didn't let on. Her gaze moved like a prison searchlight, but suddenly it stopped, halted by something she hadn't expected. I bent my head to see Rayona staring back, her face grim and suspicious as Aunt Ida's, as she added up the woman who stood before us. They had a resemblance I'd never noticed, but which both of them recognized immediately and with no pleasure. For a split second I felt betrayed by my own child, and put her down to stand on the linoleum floor.

"Well?" I said, and they both turned toward me. I was

squeezed out between their sameness, but still Rayona's mother. "Give Aunt Ida a kiss," I told her.

"They'll all soon be here," Aunt Ida said, turning to the stove in the corner, where four pots boiled on the burners. The smell of stewed meat filled the house.

I crossed the floor and opened the door to my old room. It was unheated, and a draft of cold air surrounded me. Nothing was altered, as if no one had entered since I left. My rock and roll pictures were still on the walls, my stuffed animals covered the bedspread. I dropped my suitcase, and shut my eyes. My hands were fists and my mouth was stale.

"There's coffee," Aunt Ida called from the other room.

All through that long night I held Rayona on my lap like a shield. Nobody asked me questions, and I kept my story to myself. The room was filled with people, some playing a quiet, nonstop game of pinochle at the kitchen table, a cluster of teenage girls on the couch looking at old comic books and magazines, my Aunt Pauline and the other church ladies bunched around the stove keeping busy. Aunt Ida sat opposite me in a chair at the head of the casket. She had placed a glass of wax yellow flowers on the flat surface, and Father Hurlburt, when he came and went earlier, had left a tall fat candle burning at the foot.

Aunt Ida had changed her dress and wore a rose-colored calico with short sleeves and a hem that hung long below her knees. On her feet were fresh white anklets and black shoes with high heels and a strap across the instep. They must have come from the Mission store, secondhand from a Catholic white woman who got them for a party and donated them before they had completely worn out. As the hours passed, Aunt Ida was always holding something, a baby, a cup of tea, a string of rosary beads Pauline put into her hands, the unopened leather box that contained Lee's Purple Heart. She looked straight ahead and her thoughts were sealed away. She did the least she had to do.

Children slept in their clothes in corners, in the attic and the closet. Six of them stretched unconscious across my old bed. A woman who was somehow related to us wailed softly from her chair and used a man's handkerchief to wipe constantly at eyes obscured by clouded glasses. Men stood smoking outside the front door, stamping their feet in the snow like horses to keep warm. One of them was probably Lee's father, my father, but that was an old question that would never be answered.

By the time we reached our teens, neither Lee nor I wanted to know. It was better as a mystery, better to switch off to whomever we preferred from one day to the next. Besides, Aunt Ida was more than enough for us to handle. And once Lee went on the rodeo circuit, every man in the tribe wanted to claim him. He had more fathers than he knew what to do with, and tonight they took his loss hard. Through the thin walls of the house I heard the rumble of their muffled conversations, the clink of their bottles, the pounding of their gloved hands on car hoods.

The person I thought I'd see who wasn't there was Dayton. I had spent long stretches of my drive wondering how he'd greet me, what we would say to each other. We both had our stakes in Lee, our rights to tonight's sympathy, and for once I was ready to credit that. Dayton must double damn himself for his draft-dodging excuse. If he had joined the army anyway, he might have protected his best friend or even took the bad luck himself. It was Lee who was going places, and Dayton the one who could be spared. Yet I was all ready to forgive Dayton, to let him cry on my shoulder. Between the two of us the memories of Lee had to be so strong we would almost bring him back to life.

Finally around midnight I leaned toward Aunt Ida and whispered, "Where's Dayton?"

"He knew you'd come."

I wasn't sure I heard right. It had been so long since I had spoken anything but English, except to Rayona, that Indian was strange in my speech and in my ears. Half the time I had to translate to myself the soft words and stories that filled the room. Then her meaning hit me, and my arms tightened around my sleeping baby.

It was me they blamed. No one looked my way but my mind raced back over the evening, tagging each visitor's face as they saw me for the first time. Aunt Pauline's lips had been pursed when she presented her cheek for my kiss. Willard Pretty Dog had walked by me with nothing more than a nod of his head. Esther Red Hawk, two years behind me in school, had made over Rayona but simply raised her eyebrows at me. Even Father Hurlburt had been distant and preoccupied. The whole crowd would switch me for Lee in a minute, say it was fair since I made him choose, me or Canada. I don't know which one told, Aunt Ida or Dayton, but now nobody could forgive that I was alive and Lee was laid out under that fucking tablecloth.

My fury woke me like hot coffee. Goddamn Dayton anyway. And goddamn Aunt Ida, too proud to use a flag or show she gave a shit about anything.

"Do you have a place for your granddaughter to sleep?" I asked across the coffin. "There's a draft from that door and I don't want her getting a cold."

Aunt Ida's eyes widened and her nostrils arched out. I knew she wanted to look around to see if anyone had heard, but that would break her act, reveal her as flesh and bones. A thin pearl rosary was lost in the grip of her square hands, folded in her lap. Her cracked yellowed nails climbed from bead to bead, pinching and swallowing the chain into her fist. She refused to give me the satisfaction of her anger.

"*Mother*," I said, loud and in English, "I'm talking to you."

This time her eyes did dart about the room before coming back to me. "Who asked you here?" she whispered, the old language hissing through her teeth, the beads disappearing faster. "Who wanted you?"

"Lee was my brother," I answered, strong as she was, stronger. "I came for Lee."

She narrowed her lids. We both knew she could say it, say it was my fault, say I had killed him the same as if I held the gun to his head. She could say it, and it would break my heart, but she'd lose from this minute the only child she had left, the only grandchild she'd ever have. It was her bid and I was ready to call.

One of the men stomped inside, looking for coffee. The night air blew a gust that folded a corner of the tablecloth and danced the flame of the candle. Aunt Ida drew her bare arms against her sides as the cold hit her. She seemed to shrink in front of me, to lose ground. I couldn't help it, I let myself know what she felt about grieving Lee and in that flash all I had been running from caught up and threw me down. The muscles of my face began to loosen and my mouth opened. I touched my tongue on dry lips. My eyes reeled to every corner for help, but finally the only thing I saw was Aunt Ida, and it was like looking into a mirror. We stared at each other over time, over Lee.

Off to the side someone won a hand of cards, the oven door slammed, a car stopped in front of the house. Aunt Ida unbent her arms, smooth and tan, and half rose from her chair. "Give her here for a while, then," she said.

Rayona barely stirred in her sleep as I lifted her across. She raised her hand to brush a wisp of hair from her face, but stayed asleep. She was a big girl, and my muscles ached with the release of her weight.

"Just for a minute," I said. "Just to spell me."

The next morning at nine o'clock Father Hurlburt came back, dressed this time in his cassock and purple vestments. His nose, swollen and marked with the scars of too much drink, was red from the cold and his eyes were rimmed and glassy beneath his bushy brows. He went to Aunt Ida and touched her shoulder. The skin of his hand was spotted and beginning to wrinkle.

"It's time, Ida," he said to her.

She stood quick and straight, giving no sign of stiffness, and went to take her coat from where it hung on a hook by the door. She shrugged off those who tried to guide her elbows, and pushed past people who waited for her to stumble. Everyone watched, and she was determined to disappoint them. She buttoned her coat and turned to me.

"Go wash your face," she said. "I'll get the baby ready."

Now everyone went into action. Car engines were started so they'd idle to warm before we headed out. Women tied scarves around their heads and brushed the hair of their sleepy children. Pauline put away the final washed dish and turned off the heat below the coffeepot. I folded the windmill tablecloth, pinching two corners and dropping and pressing it in perfect halves before me until it was small enough to fit back into a drawer. I splashed water on my face and left the house, the last to go.

Two men pushed the coffin into the back of Father Hurlburt's new pickup and closed the gate. The wind whipped their coats and blew their pants like sheets against their legs. In the cab next to the priest, Aunt Ida sat holding Rayona. She made room for me and I climbed beside her. We led the procession of cars and trucks down the hill to the church, our bodies bouncing high on the springs of the seat as we crossed the ruts and rocks that no reservation grader could ever keep smooth.

The smell of the tiny church—all stale flowers and incense—brought back every memory of my childhood devotions. It was as though I entered a past I hadn't visited since my end-of-the-world confession, and I cleared my mind against the shock. I didn't need to hear some middle-aged priest tell me about Lee and the mysterious ways of God's will. I stood in the rear, my hair uncovered, refusing to kneel even during the Consecration, and searched until I found the back of Dayton's head. He disguised his mixed-blood waves with a close-cropped burr, and his body had filled out. Alone in the second pew, he never once looked away from his missal, not even to glance at the polished wood box that lay before the altar. But when he walked from Communion, I placed myself square at the end of the middle aisle, direct in his line of vision. I unzipped my powder-blue parka and displayed my left hand so the wedding ring would reflect the light. I saw him see.

After the Requiem Mass, the mourners filed in a long line

past the coffin, each man and woman pausing at the left end to say his or her farewell. When it was my turn, second to last since I was the sister, Pauline took Rayona from my arms and I went to the exact same spot. I thought how embarrassing it was to be lying down when everyone else was standing. I closed my eyes and pictured Lee lifelike and done-up, just on the other side of those boards. He smiled like he did when he saw me off on the bus to Seattle, sad to see me go but no way he was going to show it. Afraid. Then he stood on those golden stairs, extending his hand.

Aunt Ida was breathing down my neck, so I moved along, and in less than a minute we were standing side by side at the center of a group in the cemetery behind church. A lot of people had cried, last night and this morning, but they weren't the ones who knew Lee best. Rayona was with Pauline and her little brat of a kid, Kennedy. I still hadn't connected with Dayton but he had to be a pallbearer. He'd have to walk in front of me.

The sky had cleared to a thin blue, and the far horizon blurred to a line between earth and air. The scene before me was flat as a child's drawing, the few scattered houses and trees close against the land behind them, everything white and still. It was an island, it was the roof of the tallest building. In jungles, like where Lee was sent, they say you have to cut paths with long knives through plants that grow right back, through vines and palm trees and razor-sharp grasses. Sunlight doesn't reach the ground because the trees are too thick. You can't see five feet in front of you. Everywhere it smells of rot.

The men walked by with the box and slid it on the school cafeteria table placed above where the grave would be dug. This late in February the ground was frozen too hard for even a pickax, and all the winter dead had to wait in the root cellar attached to the church basement until the first deep thaw. But we pretended. One of the altar boys brought around a plastic bag of potting soil, the kind they sell at every supermarket, and each mourner scooped out a handful. It wasn't real dirt at all, just black and dry tailings, dust that I squeezed in my fist while

Father Hurlburt read from his book. It oozed through my fingers as I pressed it tighter and tighter, etching onto its core the print of my hand.

Finally it was time. The words stopped, and above our heads the bell from Holy Martyrs began to clang as a nun pulled the rope to turn it back and forth against the clapper. Now was when the box should be lowered into a pocket of ground, but it fell to us. In the noon light we formed a circle as if for a dance, a ring within the ring of the world, and raised our hands.

"*Requiescat in pace.*" Father Hurlburt spoke, and threw his clump of soil against the casket.

Others followed, some calling "Lee!" others simply yelling, screaming, howling animal sounds that pounded together in my ears with the thuds of dirt on wood. My arm was cocked, ready, but unmoving as the bough of a tree.

When the thunder stopped, when only the crying remained, Aunt Ida, singing in a voice so high that I couldn't make out its meaning, stripped the red scarf from her head and used it to sweep and clean every trace of dirt from the coffin. She shook cedar on the lid in a six-point pattern, blessing each direction, then rummaged in the pocket of her long black coat and placed Lee's champion buckle in the center. Only then, when she was done, did she let Father Hurlburt lead her away with the rest of the crowd.

And still I stood there, poised and stuck, the center of nobody's interest. I searched my memory for Lee's face, but it was gone. I inhaled deeply and slowly, resolving not to breathe again until I had some image to take with me.

A hand closed on my wrist, broke the spell by bending my arm back an inch further.

"Bury him, Christine," Dayton said, and when he opened his grip, my arm sprang free.

Tomorrow in a flag ceremony the living veterans of the tribe planned to pay tribute to their newest hero. Tonight Pauline would host a feast, a potluck with hot dishes from all the neighbors. While eating through their exhaustion from the wake, people would begin to recite their funny tales of Lee, the wild things he had done, the silly mistakes he had made, the shy embarrassments he had shared with them. Everything would remind them of something they had to tell. They buried Lee, but now they'd bring him back, turn him into stories for children born too late to know him.

Yesterday, with Lee clear and alive in my mind, I would have had the best tales and made them funnier than real life. Everyone would have hung on my memories and forget I'd ever left.

But today I was different and Dayton must have been the same, because, when he gave me a ride home from the cemetery, he asked me to skip Pauline's and go into town with him instead. I agreed, and Aunt Ida was glad to babysit Rayona. Without me there, she could make up any explanation she wanted for a baby.

We went to a new bar in Ely—so dead on a Tuesday night they were even glad to see Indians—took a booth, and ordered two drafts. Dayton and I had said almost no words to each other, and we didn't know where to begin, so we just sipped our drinks and listened to the song on the jukebox. It was called "The Western End of Mountain Time," and went on about how the singer's girlfriend, Marie, lived in the next state, just across the time zone, and they could never get their hours straight to get together.

"So you got married," Dayton finally said.

"Not that you'd notice, lately."

"Your little girl's tall."

The song went on. Daylight Savings was just as bad as Standard, but even after they broke up the guy always thought of Marie when he watched the sun set.

"Are you ever going to move back around here?" Dayton tried again.

"No way. We'll leave as soon as the flag ceremony's over."

The mention of the flag brought back all my words about fighting for your country. I kept my eyes trained on the menu propped behind the napkin dispenser. I could have cut my tongue out.

"It's not your fault." The kindness in Dayton's voice threw me off, and I interrupted.

"That's what I was going to tell you. You had your chance to stay home and you took it, like anybody would." I reached into my purse for a cigarette to avoid his reply. There were only three in the pack.

The waitress arrived to take our order, and I paid her my full attention. She must have been sixty-five, but all the same she gave Dayton the once-over while she waited for us to decide. Dayton had a Montanaburger with fries, and I had the meatloaf plate with a tossed salad on the side.

"What kind of dressing you want with that, hon?" She peered at me from above her black and rhinestone glasses frames.

"What do you have?"

"French, Thousand Island, Green Goddess, and Creamy Italian," she recited.

"Italian," I said, like a city girl who knew her way around.

"I need a à la carte Italian," she called across the serving counter into the kitchen, and tacked the page with our orders on a metal wheel, though we were the only ones eating. The cook spun it to see what to fix.

Red and green holiday tinsel still lined the doors and a string of colored lights framed the mirror behind the bar. The waitress moved from table to empty table, sashaying her hips as she straightened the ketchup bottles. She had a high bouffant the color of washed-out lace, exactly like the angel hair that swirled beneath the artificial tree with gold ornaments that was balanced on a table at the end of the room. She was decorated too. Over her beige turtleneck she wore a black felt bolero with MERRY and CHRISTMAS written in green glitter on either side, and around her neck hung a pendant made from a Bic lighter in a gold lamé case. It swung like a charm between her low breasts.

Dayton got up to go to the can, and I watched him from behind. He must have been the only man in town who wore shoes instead of boots, and he had kept on his funeral suit. I couldn't see him without thinking of Lee. I stubbed out my Kent.

The food was already on the table when Dayton came back, and eating gave us something to do. I had nothing to say, no thoughts in my head.

"What did you name her, then?" He dragged the last of his potatoes through a pool of ketchup, cleaning his plate.

"Ray. Short for Rayona."

"That's real unusual."

"Well, that's me. Nothing the easy way."

"Christine . . ." Dayton's tone said he wanted to be serious, wanted to spill what he'd been building to tell me all night.

"Her middle name's Diane, but she doesn't know it." Talking about Ray made my breasts ache with milk, and I was worried I'd leak onto my green blouse. I zipped my parka to my chin and finished my salad.

"It doesn't have to be like this," Dayton said.

"What 'this'?" I made my eyes wide with not understanding.

"Goddamn," he whispered under his breath.

"Don't shed a tear for me, thank you. I've got everything I want. A good job in Seattle. A baby. A husband who would die for me."

Dayton pushed back in the booth. I could meet his gaze now, and showed no mercy.

Rayona stood on her long skinny legs in the Mission gym and swayed to the drum. "Dance!" she said. I stooped to quiet her.

"She's all right." Aunt Ida motioned me away. She sat on a folding chair at half court on the hardwood basketball floor, with Pauline's Chief Joseph Pendleton blanket draped around her shoulders.

"You look like a real Indian today," I told her, but rather than answering, she watched the three World War II veterans come out of the boys' locker room and pause on the sideline. They were dressed in their powwow costumes, polka-dotted colored-ribbon shirts, ruffs, cowbells on their high moccasins.

They waited for the drum to start the honor song, then began. The one in the middle, Willard Pretty Dog, was sour and scar-faced as he supported a fringed American flag, its pole fitted into a special belt around his waist. On either side of him, Vernon LaVallee and Sam Garcia, Sr., did a slow toe-heel progression as they made a circuit in front of the fold-out bleachers.

At the Home basket, Willard stuck the flag in its permanent holder, and made a prayer for Lee. He talked about him as a modern-day warrior, gone to his reward in the service of his country. He said how proud we all were to be related to Lee or to have known him, even though we'd miss seeing him around.

Rayona was anxious for the music to start again. She tugged at the arm Aunt Ida held firmly, and looked to me for help. But I had to hear every word Willard spoke. I needed for his speech to kick me over.

The large drum took the song, the five men sitting around the jump-ball circle each crouching forward, cupping an ear with one hand while beating a rhythm on the stretched leather with their sticks. Their voices rose in sharp, piercing falsettos.

Willard approached Aunt Ida to be her partner and lead the dance. She shook her head, turned away, but he wouldn't leave. There was something going on between them that I couldn't make out, some silent argument, and it shocked me to see Aunt Ida lose. All at once she handed Ray to Pauline and launched herself from her seat. She joined hands with Willard in two-step fashion, and shuffled onto the floor. A corner of the blanket trailed in her wake.

Dayton was heading my way, so I caught old Vernon's elbow instead and followed after Aunt Ida and Willard. But Dayton wouldn't give up. He bent and lifted Rayona into his arms, and began the circle on his own. Ray's face was thrilled, and she tapped her palm in time against the side of Dayton's head as he carried her among us, round and round like a screw in soft pine.

I lowered my eyes and followed the sound of the drum as it

escaped through the walls of the gym, as it floated through the air to pound softly against the outbuildings and the church, as it penetrated in a dull throbbing down the dark stairs to the root cellar where it sank, lost, in solid ground.

13

I thought maybe Aunt Ida had reformed when she packed Rayona some graham crackers for our drive back to Seattle, but when I went inside her house to get our suitcase, something in the garbage can caught my eye. It was the leather box with Lee's Purple Heart. I don't know if I was meant to see it or not, but I rescued it and brought it along.

Rayona hated to say good-bye, but not me. I left the reservation as easy as if I was coming back next week, as if I lived just over the highline. A chinook had turned the roads black and left water standing in the ditches. I rolled down my window and let the wind blow my hair out of its permanent while I breathed in the loamy smell.

For once I took my time, and made rest stops at motels in Kalispell and Wilbur. Ray was a good traveler for a baby and stared out the window as if she knew what she was seeing. The land hypnotized her, or maybe it was the motion of the car, climbing and descending, stopping and starting, mile upon mile.

You might know I'd get to the city on a Saturday night. I switched on the lights in my apartment and looked beneath the furniture. A note slipped under the door might have blown anyplace. Elgin would have heard about my trip, and should have come around to be by my side. But if he had, he left no evidence.

I turned on the radio and dressed Rayona in her sleeper. I

looked out my front window at the traffic, and knocked without answer on the door of the neighbors I'd met. I telephoned everyone I could think of, first my friends from work and then people I hardly knew, rehearsing what I would say while I dialed, but all I got was nobody home. I lay on the couch and read the ads in magazines. I was desperate as a bird in a box.

"Wake now," I told Rayona. I snapped her into her brown parka, and put on her snow pants against the chill, then lay her back in her crib while I rooted out my black bell-bottoms and a red top. I applied new makeup and styled my hair with a blow dryer. I put cologne behind my ears and under my chin, with a few drops extra on the crown of my head in case anyone rested his nose there while we were dancing. My winter coat was dirty, so I wore my pink nylon windbreaker, even though the zipper was busted. With my long red-and-white-beaded earrings swinging and my baby hard asleep on my shoulder, I locked the door behind me and didn't stop to think until I found a corner booth at the Silver Bullet.

I was a regular, and they knew enough not to ask questions. I made a bed for Ray on the seat with her coat for a cover and my jacket for a pillow, and by the time the man came to ask for my order I had lit a Kent and sent two perfect smoke circles floating like widening lassos above the crowd around the long bar. I checked out familiar faces, not lingering long enough at anyone to extend an invitation until I saw the full selection. It wasn't so much that I was choosy, as that I wanted to find the man who would stay the longest. I was almost to the end of the row, narrowing my list to one-two-three as I went along, when I saw Elgin's hand resting on some fat woman's back. There was no question. I followed the line of his arm over his shoulder and then jumped my look across to the mirror to see his face. He recognized me at the same time and blinked as though he thought I'd disappear.

He didn't have to come to a place I might be. I turned away so fast I tipped my beer, sloshing it across the table in Rayona's direction. I snatched my coaster and used it to block the flow. The waiter appeared with extra napkins, and I took a handful and sopped the small pools collecting in the carved initials and designs scratched in the wood. Without looking up I held out my hand for more paper but all I got was Elgin, standing by the table with his legs apart, his eyes going back and forth from Rayona to me, his hands on his hips. His mustache was longer.

"I was going to call you" was the first thing he said, but before that was out of his mouth he was accusing me: "Why the hell are you bringing her to a bar?"

"She's fine," I said. "Thunder won't wake her and I didn't have a sitter. What am I supposed to do?" I found my cigarette in the ashtray. It had burned down to the filter and gone out.

"How was it?" He meant Montana, and his voice became quieter.

"The roads were pretty bad on the way out, but it was all right coming back."

"That's not what I was asking."

"If you . . ." I said.

Elgin slid into the seat across from me. His legs were so long his knees rubbed against mine, and that contact made the muscles in my back tense. Rayona kicked in her sleep and one heel banged against the tabletop. Elgin's eyes rested on her pajama foot as it propped against the back of the booth.

"What did your mama say?"

I didn't need his sympathy.

"Who's your date?" I gestured with my glance. "You don't want to make her jealous."

"Don't be like that. I didn't think you were home."

"Even if I wasn't, this place is full of little birds to tell me you had been around."

"Look, she's nobody. I just dropped in, right, and we got to talking."

"I know your bar talk." I put my elbows on the table and rested my head on my praying hands.

"Get you another beer or what?"

The sounds of the bar nailed me to my seat. All I wanted was to lay down next to Rayona, fit her to me like a soft pillow, and drift away. I was out of gas, coasting in neutral, too beat to hold my end of a grudge.

"Let's go home," I said.

Elgin was cautious, suspicious I was setting him up. He looked to see who was watching, to see what the fat girl was doing. Without changing my expression, I tried to make my gaze shine pure, speak to him. They say the eyes are the windows of your soul, and right then my soul was all his, open all night with a red carpet running to the door. I wished so hard it seemed as though he should hear me.

"Just like that?" he asked.

With the last of my energy I bent over Rayona, threaded her limp arms into the sleeves of her parka. She was loose as a doll made from socks. I backed out of the booth, and reached down to lift her.

Elgin's hand was on my neck, between my shoulders. I straightened and turned to him, asleep on my feet.

"You go on," he said. "I'll bring the baby."

That time he stayed for almost two weeks.

By the time you realize that your life isn't headed the way you expected you're too busy to look over your shoulder to see what went wrong. That's what happened to me. I was going downhill with my brakes out, always barely avoiding a crash.

My energies went back and forth between Elgin and Rayona, first one then the other, sometimes both at the same time. My husband dropped in on me like the monthly bills he delivered on his mail routes, regular and when I was broke. Just as I was recovering from his last disappearance, the doorbell or the telephone rang and before I moved, before I turned my head to see, I knew it was him. He had radar that sensed my breaking point. One more day alone and I could shrug him off, but he never gave me that chance.

You wonder why I didn't let him ring, why I didn't pretend to be gone, or move, or at least change my number. You wonder why I ran my life by an alarm clock out of my control, why I didn't have the sense to answer his call with good-bye. You wonder why five minutes into his excuses I forgot what the fuss was about, why I stopped his mouth with the tips of my fingers, why I always checked the mirror before I went to the door, why I washed my hair and dressed on Saturday mornings instead of relaxing in my robe. Well, it's no secret: I was a fool for that man.

Once I understood that we couldn't live in the same house for long but couldn't stay apart forever either, I did what it took to get by. I went out. I met people. Some of them I brought home. Some of them stayed for breakfast.

I don't believe in divorce, but I don't agree with letting the grass grow either. I was still young. I was a famous expert on men. I was still the one they called for a good time.

Elgin, friends, cousins, neighbors, jobs, and social workers came and went, some faster, some better than others. I never knew what next, never got used to any of them long enough to forget my likes and dislikes or to expect they'd be around next week. Rayona was the one thing in my life I took for granted. Doing for her was not so different from doing for myself. We had the same tastes, more like sisters once she learned to speak for herself, though it bothered me that we didn't look more alike. Riding on a bus side by side we could be two strangers, who might get off at separate stops. Sometimes she seemed older than me, the way she cleaned after I had company or put the milk back in the refrigerator before it spoiled. She rarely needed me for more than my size and strength. There were things she was too short to reach, too weak to lift, too green to know for herself. It took me to pass her into movies or to bring her to the park, but once we got somewhere, I was on my own.

She was interested in her father when he was around, and more interested when he wasn't. I thought at first it was because she had his coloring and because he was bigger and stronger than me and so could do more of her chores, but really I think she liked the surprise of him. the same as I did. She never asked anything of me beyond what she knew she could get, so she always had her way, but with Elgin it was feast or famine. On good days, he was a storybook father who could make her wishes come true. And then when he took off with no warning, she dreamed him up and forgave him everything.

Rayona was a constant confusion to her father as well. Sometimes Elgin walked in the door and she threw herself at him like a mongrel puppy, and other times she pushed past him as though he wasn't there. He couldn't predict her, and mostly he made the wrong move: laughed when he should have smiled, got mad when he should have laughed, come when he should have stayed away, left before she had time to warm to him. In her frustration she blamed me, but I didn't take it personally. We were the only ones handy for each other, the only ones who couldn't walk away if we let off steam, the only ones guaranteed to forget every unfair charge between fights.

Rayona gave me something to be, made me like other women with children. I was nobody's regular daughter, nobody's sister, usually nobody's wife, but I was her mother full time. That was the one day we celebrated, Mother's Day. Every year I made her give me a frilly card, even if I had to pick it out and buy it myself. Before she was old enough to write, I signed her name at the bottom "Love, Rayona," and underlined all the sentimental words, then I taped it to the refrigerator door and left it there for months.

I was so impressed with my own motherhood that I spent a peaceful week with Aunt Ida in Seattle the spring before Rayona was seven. She came to see some relative of hers, Clara, whom she never mentioned by name before, and who was sick at IHS. Aunt Ida called me from the bus depot, said she was in town and how could she find our place. I hadn't had so much as a postcard from her since Lee's funeral, no presents for Rayona at Christmas, no thank-you's for the gifts I sent from time to time, nothing, and then she's on the phone with a local call.

"I'll come get you," I said. "I have my car."

But no, Aunt Ida had to take the bus. She might find herself obligated to me, might have to admit I could be of some use to her. She said she wouldn't wait, she'd ask directions of a stranger if I didn't tell her what to do.

"Take the Number Twelve and transfer to the AA," I said. "Don't forget you need exact change."

She hung up without saying good-bye and I imagined her busting through the doors of the depot out to the street, another middle-aged Indian woman with a scarf on her head and her clothes in a shiny suitcase. She would have exact change ready, she would be the first one on and off the buses. I didn't have much time to clean the place, change the sheets, bathe Rayona, and do my hair. It was lucky it was a weekend, but of course it wasn't luck. Aunt Ida made precise plans. It never crossed her mind I might be out of town, might have an unlisted number, might be busy.

Rayona didn't remember Aunt Ida at all, so I tried to describe her.

"She's a lot bigger than me, and very strong." My daughter's eyes were approving. These were things she took seriously.

"Has she ever seen me?" she asked, though she knew the answer.

"We spent time at her house when your uncle Lee was buried," I told her. "She took care of you and you learned to say her name."

"Did she like me?"

"She has a hard time showing what she likes. She doesn't talk much. She'll speak to you in nothing but Indian."

"Doesn't she know English?"

"Not unless she wants to."

I couldn't guess what Ray had in mind for a grandmother. Probably somebody from TV, Grandma Walton or even Granny from "The Beverly Hillbillies," but they were a far cry from Aunt Ida.

Aunt Ida stood at the door when I opened it and looked past me at the apartment. She let me know by the way she held her mouth that there was plenty she could say.

"You must be tired," I offered when it was clear there

wasn't going to be any kiss, any smile of hello. She entered, wary as a cat, placed her suitcase carefully behind the couch and took off her coat. She held it, waiting for me to bring a hanger, and didn't budge when Rayona came running into the room from the kitchenette. Aunt Ida affected my girl in a way nobody else ever had: Ray acted shy. She slunk her body along the walls and against the sides of furniture, hanging her head but keeping her gaze on Aunt Ida. When I told her to say hello, she hid her face.

All that afternoon and evening I waited for Aunt Ida to melt, to ask me questions, to remark about my place, but nothing brought a rise from her. She ate the food I cooked and washed her own dish. She said it didn't matter what program we watched on TV, and from time to time her eyes flicked in the direction of the door. Finally, at nine-thirty, Rayona was dressed for bed and ready to say good-night. I had braided her hair tight when it was still damp from her bath and now, dry and brushed out, it surrounded her face in a crinkling circle. She looked as pretty as she got, her dark skin startling against her green circus pajamas, her teeth clean and white. Aunt Ida stared in fascination, but instead of making over Ray, she finally said what was on her mind.

"I thought you were supposed to be married."

"I am, almost eight years."

Her eyes swept the room again, as if she could see through the doors of the closet empty of men's clothes, the bathroom with no razor, my bedroom I had insisted she use while she visited. They came back to rest on me.

"We happen to be separated at the moment."

My words amused Aunt Ida. She was itching to catch me out.

"What tribe is he, then? Where are his people?"

I wouldn't let her trip me in front of Ray.

"You know he's not Indian. He comes from California. His parents live there. And he has a name: Elgin."

"El-gin," Aunt Ida pronounced to Ray, the only audience she had.

"You're in there." I pointed to the open door of my room. "Ray has to go to bed now, for school, and she can't, as long as we stay talking. She's on the couch."

Aunt Ida hauled her suitcase into the tiny, windowless bedroom. I heard the locks spring, heard a rustling, and then she appeared back at the entrance.

"I brought her this," she said and held out a Kewpie doll in a purple and white crocheted dress, cape, hat, and slippers. "One of Pauline's ladies made it."

Rayona lit up with desire. The doll's skin was bright pink, and molded onto the top of its head was a single orange-painted curl of hair. Its eyes were sky blue and stared off to the side. Its outfit could have been cut from pot holders.

"That's cute," I said.

Aunt Ida stood the doll on the table and Ray ran to claim it. For half a second, as if Aunt Ida couldn't help herself, her hand grazed the top of Ray's electric hair. Then she went back into my room and locked the door.

That week Aunt Ida spent so much time at the hospital, and was so closemouthed about her visits, that I began to suspect that she was the one sick, but the next Saturday morning she announced that Ray and I had to come to IHS with her.

"Clara wants to see you," she said.

"I don't even know Clara." I hated to waste my day off with a trip downtown to that depressing place.

Aunt Ida sat heavily in a chair, folded her arms, and gazed at the wall. She could be patient, and the force of her will was irresistible.

I fitted Ray in her Little Red Riding Hood cape, and I put on a sweater that went with my jeans.

"Is that what you're going to wear?"

"What's the matter with it?"

Her lips tightened. I was giving her pain. It wasn't worth it.

"How do you want me to dress?"

"Like a grown woman."

"How?" I repeated.

"You could wear a skirt."

I parked Rayona at the kitchen table with a glass of milk, and stomped back to the closet. I found a yellow wraparound and flowered top.

"Aren't you going to run a brush through your hair?"

I could have explained to her about my special cut, that a brush would ruin its casual effect, but time was wasting and she would win in the end.

She was standing by the door with her coat on when I came back from the bathroom. "You look younger now," she said.

That was the closest thing to a compliment Aunt Ida had given me in years and it calmed me.

"Is Ray dressed right enough for you?" I asked.

"Rayona always looks good," Aunt Ida said, surprising me again.

On the bus through downtown, Aunt Ida sat next to the window and studied the rain-slicked streets. I was beside her, avoiding the curious glances of the other passengers who acted as though they'd never seen an Indian before, and Ray balanced in the aisle, tilting with every stop and start, hanging on to the seat back with one hand, her eyes bright with adventure.

"Tell me about Clara." If she remembered me I should have something to say to her.

"She's my mother's sister," Aunt Ida said. It took me a minute to figure out the Indian word she used. It means something like "little mother," but in English it would be "aunt." "She left a long time ago."

"Then she's my great-aunt," I said. "I don't remember anybody ever mentioning her." My grandmother had been sick for years and died a couple of years after I was born. My grandfather followed her before Lee was born. I remembered him as a large, heavy man with stone-gray hair parted in the middle and falling below his shoulders. Aunt Ida had his nose and his weight.

She watched the traffic light turn green, braced herself for the acceleration, and clutched her purse.

The Indian Health Service Hospital brought flashbacks of Ray's birth, the day I heard about Lee, the day Elgin was late. I had been back for Ray's baby shots, and once, after Elgin had been gone too long and I had partied too much, I was brought in an ambulance for five days of tests and dry-out.

The automatic door to the lobby opened, releasing the sharp smell of Lysol. Indians from all over, from Alaska and Idaho, Montana and the Peninsula, hunched in green-and-chrome chairs, not talking, absorbed in their troubles, home-sick, scared, prepared to die. Orderlies and visitors rushed by them as if they weren't there. Those sick people sat low, like moss on a rock, waiting for a strange doctor to give them bad news. They wore blue hospital bathrobes and thin seersucker gowns, tied in bows behind their necks. That room was a swampy place you had to cross to get to the elevators, and I poised to make it through as fast as I could.

But Aunt Ida had visited the hospital every day for a week and took her time. We stopped here and there, fidgeting until the old man or woman noticed us, worried, then relieved we weren't a doctor. Aunt Ida asked about their grandchildren, about their operations. With those who didn't speak our language, she talked English or gestured with her hands and mouth, and they understood.

"This is Rayona I told you about," she began again and again. "This is her mother, Christine." They had heard of us, but I wonder what. They squinted at Ray and commented on the length and narrowness of her hands. With fingers withered and flat-nailed, they touched her braided, flyaway hair and felt the material of her cape. They made small bows with their heads when I was introduced, embarrassed by their lack of teeth, their naked legs, but with Aunt Ida and Rayona they were quick with complaints and gossip.

I tuned out. Everyone was the same, and so it didn't register with me at first when we stayed with one woman longer than the others, and when she paid more attention to me than to my daughter. One of her eyes was white with glaucoma, the iris almost blue. Then I recognized her—she had been at Lee's funeral. In my memory I heard her low wailing cry, saw again the handkerchief wipe her cheeks. She had sat alone, like me.

Clara was not as old as she first appeared, no more than five years more than Aunt Ida, but small and bent and deflated like a ball that had lost air. Her dyed-black hair was thin and patchy, and with all its curl and arrangement, there was no mistaking that it was falling out. She had cancer of some kind, and was getting chemotherapy. There was a decayed smell about her, but I couldn't refuse when she turned her cheek for me to kiss, snatched for my hand. Her grip was tighter than I would have thought possible, alarming and pinching as an animal trap you trigger by mistake, yet there was no polite way I could shake loose.

Tears came to her sighted eye. She said something low to Aunt Ida, who nodded in reply. Clara drew Rayona to her side, patting her shoulder. I couldn't stand there like a deaf-mute forever.

"How are you feeling?" I asked.

The pressure on my hand increased even more. Her nose ran but she would not release us to tend to it, so Aunt Ida leaned across with a Kleenex. Clara whispered in Indian with a thick accent, barely opening her lips. This time Aunt Ida shook her head no.

"She says you favor your grandmother," Aunt Ida told me.

Nobody ever said I looked like anybody before and this interested me, but I recognized in myself no resemblance to pictures of Aunt Ida's mother. Before her illness she had been big and lean.

"I'm too short," I said to Clara, but she shook her head in denial.

"She's tired now," Aunt Ida said. She placed her large hand like a cap on Clara's balding head, petted her, then pulled back. Clara's eyes pleaded, but Ida lifted Ray and turned to me.

"Say good-bye."

"We just got here. We spent an hour on the bus. We can stay another few minutes."

But Aunt Ida was already leading Ray away, back through the lobby, weaving among the dozing patients, heading for the glass doors. I had to follow. I crouched down so I would be at eye level with Clara. With my free hand I reached for her wrist and gently pulled her fingers away from mine. She did not resist.

"I'll come back soon, little mother," I said, using Aunt Ida's old-fashioned word to please her. "Next time we won't be so rushed."

But as it turned out, Clara died before I thought of her again.

That night Aunt Ida said she wanted to go back to the reservation, and I called the bus station for the schedule. The last express to Spokane was at nine, with a connection to Billings, and even though it meant sitting up two nights, she was bound and determined to catch it.

"At least have supper," I told her. "I've got beef chunks." That was her favorite, and she agreed, but of course insisted on fixing everything herself so I wouldn't ruin it. She was in a bad mood, either because she was depressed by Clara's condition or because she dreaded the long ride, so I didn't argue. She put the meat on to boil with some potatoes, and heated lard in a skillet for fry bread. She scooped handfuls of flour into a blue plastic basin I kept under the sink, then added pinches of baking powder, salt, and sugar. She sifted and mixed with her fingers, adding water little by little, until she had a cream-colored lump of dough to knead. She worked automatically, her mind a million miles away.

"Can I do it, Grandma?" Rayona asked, nice as anything.

Aunt Ida stiffened. Without removing her hands from the basin, without even looking at Ray, she said, *"Aunt Ida."*

There was no softening in her, no changing.

Ray shrunk back. I know how she felt. I moved to comfort her, but before I got there she turned and ran for the bathroom.

The sound of the hooking lock echoed in the silent apartment. I turned to Aunt Ida with my stored-up anger, ready to tell her a thing or two, but she leaned into her work, forming the dough into a ball, mashing it together, tearing it into equal bits. She flattened them between her palms, patted them into squares, punctured them with her thumb and floated them like rafts in the boiling fat.

Elgin appeared the next day and I was so lonesome I welcomed him without an argument.

"You just missed my mom," I told him. "She was here for a week."

"I don't believe you have a mother." We were in bed together, warm in the touch of each other's skin, our legs tangled and shifting. I talked to hide how good he felt.

"She doesn't believe in you either. She wanted to know your tribe."

"Did you tell her I was a Mahogany?" I had introduced him that way one time at the Center when I got too tired of people always having some remark to make about who I married.

"I said she was right, I didn't have a husband," I lied. I intended it as a joke but it didn't come out that way. Elgin's muscles tensed all along his body.

Our silence covered us like a lead quilt, pinning us into our positions while we struggled for words.

"I didn't," I said softly. "I said we were separated."

"Maybe you were right the first time."

It wasn't fair that he was the one with his feelings hurt, that I was the one apologizing. I never agreed to the rules we lived by. I never approved a marriage where I was expected to take him back no matter how long he was gone, where I couldn't even laugh about the craziness of it.

"I'm sorry." I touched Elgin's chest and under his arm the way he liked. I trailed my hair down his side. He tried to lie still but we both knew he had no control and would give in.

His body gave a small jerk as he felt my breath. He smelled of my perfume.

"If I won't complain," I whispered, "what will you do?"

He strained to meet me now, arching his spine, flexing his feet, throwing an arm over his eyes. He was sleek as pressed satin, warm as June sun.

"I'll be there for you, baby," he said. "Oh yes. You need me, I'm there."

During those years since Ray was born, that was the way Elgin and I lasted, barely enough for our needs, always on the border. We stopped asking each other questions because the answers, truths or lies, didn't matter. It was as though we split our lives between different planets: just the two of us on one of them, and on the others, each of us dwelled separate with everybody else. But we had to come back to the first one every so often to breathe, to survive.

Rayona adjusted as well as you could expect. Before she started school I scrambled to find baby-sitters for her while I worked. Sometimes it was with neighbors, sometimes, if I had the money, a day-care center, and when she was about four, I even took a job as a preschool aide so she and I wouldn't be apart. But Ray was the only child there I liked. The others dragged at me, gave me their germs, fussed at every suggestion I made. I came home at nights tense and ragged, no good to anybody. I quit after two months.

I've got to say Ray was an easy baby, healthy and calm, thoughtful. She took care of herself if she possibly could. She even tried to change her own diaper until she realized it was easier to get trained. Oh, don't get me wrong, we argued like people do, but it never lasted. Whenever I saw Aunt Ida in myself, in my stubbornness to admit my faults or to get my own way, I did the opposite. I answered Ray's questions. I taught her to speak Indian as good as English so she'd know who she was. I bought her lessons in horseback riding and French horn and typing. I told her my business. When we moved to new apartments and she had to change schools, I went with her to register and told her teachers all her habits and pleasures. And she returned the favor by getting good marks, by fitting in wherever she landed.

It was her feelings for Elgin that brought out the worst in me. He'd call her on the phone and make grand promises to take her to the zoo or to a movie or to bring her a surprise on her birthday, and then he'd forget. She'd wait by the door, sitting carefully so she wouldn't muss her clothes, watching the time pass. Go on by yourself, I'd tell her, or, Let's go together, but she'd just shake her head, turn back to the clock, hold on to excuses longer than she could believe them. I'd put words in her mouth those times, say how angry I'd be if he treated me that way, but who could take me seriously? Elgin did treat me that way, and I endured it too.

Three or four days he took her out, just the two of them. I could never get Rayona to tell me much about what they did, but I wondered all sorts of things. I wondered was she still an Indian for those hours, did she wish I was out of the picture so she could be what he wanted. I wondered did she meet any of his family and did they talk about me. When Ray came home from those visits, it took effort to get her normal again.

I was jealous for her to go with him, but it wasn't all bad. Elgin was an improvement over the father I never knew, and Rayona was the link that made us a family. Our marriage license was lost someplace, left behind in an apartment I had to leave quickly, but she was more proof, more evidence of what had passed between Elgin and me than any piece of paper. She was our connection to the past and the future.

You might wonder, since Rayona was so important to me, why I never had another child. Elgin never used anything, and none of the rest of them after him did either, but in all the fifteen years we lived in Seattle after she was born, I never once forgot. I knew what another child meant. If I had a boy I'd have to name him Lee, and if he was pretty, if I was like Aunt Ida, Rayona would be out in the cold. I couldn't take the chance.

And there was another thing too. I never felt a second time the way I did on that sunny afternoon at Point Defiance. I never loved a man that much, even Elgin, and never felt that strong in my own powers. I was born that day too, just as sure as Rayona, and as time went on, I got older but I didn't get happier. I learned more than I wanted to know and never could completely let go of anything. What I had to give a child, Rayona got, and what I needed, she gave.

You hear of people who want to live their lives over through their children, who dream their kids can avoid every mistake. I didn't expect that much, or maybe what I wanted was more. I wanted to go back and do Aunt Ida's part better, and mostly I did. I set aside special times for Ray and me early in the mornings and fixed her healthy breakfasts. I wasn't ashamed to let her see me cry or to let her know I cared about her. I never lost my interest in her life. I never expected her to be perfect. I never wished she was anybody else but who she was.

14

When that doctor came into my room with his long face and the news I had burned myself out and probably wouldn't live another six months, I waved away his details and closed my eyes. I had lived for forty-one years without knowing much about my liver or my pancreas, and according to him it was too late to start now anyway.

All my life I spent my time like I spent my money, with no thought to tomorrow. There was always another first of the month, always another paycheck, always something. I measured by highlights, not years, and the space between the events worth remembering, I forgot. When I thought back, which I never did, I saw my greatest hits, the K-Tel Christine Taylor album, offered on a late show commercial: two or three bittersweet C&W cuts of Lee, a rhythm-and-blues section starring Elgin, a war dance song for Aunt Ida, and some rock and roll for my teenage adventures. Rayona was all ballads. That was what I amounted to, my big days revolving on the TV screen like Four Seasons titles.

I opened my eyes and the doctor, bad skin, eyes the color of cheese mold, nobody I'd even consider going out with, was still there. He was the foreman of a unanimous jury, a judge who had pronounced the maximum sentence. I was ready to plead my case, to beg him to change his verdict and let me try again, one more time, one last time. I was ready to confess my sins and blame myself, if that would satisfy him. I was ready to throw myself on his mercy. Anything to make him take it back.

But my dignity was saved by the sure feeling that I was in a movie, a tough woman with only a few months to live. A bad diagnosis. I'd seen it a hundred times. I knew how to act. I took myself on the other side of the TV screen, turned down the sound to mute the eerie music, switched channels. I fought for the controls until I shut off the set.

All this was invisible to the doctor. He still waited for my reaction, waited for me to say I'd thrown my chances away on fast living, waited for me to prove him right, but by the time I spoke, I just asked him for a deck of cards.

"I don't think you understand me properly, Mrs. Taylor," he said.

"What do you want me to do, croak on the spot?" I spoke my lines and pressed the button to raise my hospital bed to a more commanding position.

He ducked his chin into his neck and fingered his stethoscope. He wore a wedding ring and I wondered who would marry him, what he was like at home. I bet nothing suited him and his wife was a wreck.

"Well," he said, "if you have any questions, anything you want to know, how to spot the diabetes if it comes, you can ask me. . . ."

I shook my head.

"Or, on the other hand, there are counselors and clergymen who regularly visit the hospital. Perhaps you would feel more comfortable talking to them."

I went on shaking it.

"But I understand you have a young daughter," he said. "You'll have to make some provision for her. Nothing immediate, of course, but . . ."

He had me buried with a stone cross on my grave. I didn't care what he understood.

"Can't a person even get a deck of cards in this hospital?" I repeated, louder than I planned. I drummed my nails on the mattress. Each finger was decorated with a ring too tight to remove: a slender abalone, a cocky roadrunner of inlaid turquoise, my Sears wedding ring, my genuine Hopi turtle.

The doctor stared down at me, his skinny head tipped to one side.

"I'll send in the nurse," he said, and wrote something short down on his clipboard. I couldn't imagine what it was. "Cards?" As he left, his starched white coat flapped like a cape behind him.

"How come they don't make you wear black," I called after him, but he was gone.

When the doctor talked to me he had pulled the drapes around my bed and practically whispered, so I was curious to see if the two women who shared my room shot me any funny looks when he opened the curtains. I had given them plenty to gossip about this visit, arriving late at night, drunk out of my mind and full of fight. I wrestled over each piece of clothing they stripped from my body until finally the orderlies hid my things out of sight. I screamed as though I was being murdered when they drew my blood and I ripped the IV from my arm three times. The nurses had to strap me down and knock me out. When I came to the next morning, calmed and dizzy with drugs, I looked over at my roommates and tried to laugh at my performance, but they were prudish, too good to share a joke with me. They reminded me of my Aunt Pauline, straight-off-the-reservation types, scandalized at a city Indian, but curious as hell.

I almost felt sorry for them now when I realized that they had slept through my whole conversation with the doctor and missed the best part of the story, the part where I got my just deserts.

It was nearly visiting hours, and Rayona would arrive on the button and stay the whole time. More than anything I wanted to be alone to think things over and make a plan in advance, for once in my life. Thoughts whirled in my head like newspapers on a windy street, and Rayona was the last person who could help me, because what to do with her, as the doctor pointed out, was one of my two big problems. I didn't want to talk to anybody who might think my diagnosis was worse for them than it was for me.

My mind works fast when it has to, and that's how I thought of the cards. With them dealt between us, Ray wouldn't notice any hints I might accidentally drop, and besides, they say the order of the face cards will tell your future. Maybe I'd be lucky and beat the game.

Rayona's appearance gave me a shock. She might have had no mother already. Her hair was wild, her clothes were too small for her, and not a speck of makeup was on her face. At fifteen you'd think she might care how she looked to the world. When I was her age I was already popular, already knew my way around, but I honestly don't think Rayona had figured out what boys were for. Or maybe she'd seen too many bad examples of men under the weather at our apartment. There was so much she needed to know.

"Turn around to me," I said. "I'll braid you."

She sighed her big shoulders and stared at the clock. Two hours to go. While my arms moved in and out creating a herringbone effect that my girlfriend Charlene taught me, I noticed Ray had at least stopped biting her nails. They were pink, and curved against her dark skin.

"Did you ever think of highlighting?" I asked her. "Just a dash of color under the cheekbones would bring you out."

"I'm out enough already."

I twisted her hair tighter, my fingers working automatically, catching, blending, creating traps for the loose strand. A wave like the dry heaves passed over me and I wanted to hide my face against her back, smell the Tide I used last week on her blouse, make her react to me.

I changed the subject of my thoughts.

"Have you heard from your father since I've been here?"

Rayona was surprised at my question, and said no as if she was mad I even mentioned Elgin. He had disappointed her too many times, and she had grown unforgiving. As my hand continued to move, I put him on my list of things to talk to her about. When I was gone the only place I'd be remembered is where the two of them were. Elgin would have to arrange for Rayona to live with him.

The first morning in the hospital, I had called Elgin at the post office and told him to stop by on his way home from work and use the Volaré while I was sick. The nurse gave me a sedative with my dinner that night, and when I woke, the keys were gone from my purse—so I knew he had come. Elgin and I had been on the outs lately, hardly speaking and, me especially, running around with other people, but I depended on him when I was in trouble. There was a line he wouldn't go below, and if I ever needed him it was now.

With her hair done, Ray looked better. My roommates would have to admit she was presentable, if they woke. I didn't want to give them more to raise their eyebrows about than I had to. It was hard enough for them to absorb that this dark girl was my blood daughter.

With my hands free, I was at a loss how to pass the time, and Rayona would wonder if I sent her home early.

"You want me to buzz for some ginger ale?" I offered. She shrugged. She had told me the last time I was here that it was my own fault, and now she blamed me double. In school they had taught her all this crap about drinking and how bad it was for you, smoking too, and she was convinced that I used more than I did, that I was an alcoholic. Sometimes I found myself sneaking around my own apartment like some kid, hiding a bottle of V.O. in a shoebox and dreaming up excuses to satisfy her.

When the operator finally answered, I cleared my throat and asked for ginger ale, please.

"One glass or two?" the voice from the speaker demanded in a less than friendly tone.

"Hell, bring the bottle." I winked at Rayona, but she rolled her eyes.

When the nurse arrived, she also had the playing cards,

and I tried to teach Rayona a game. I knew six different kinds of solitaire, one more impossible than the next.

Halfway through the simplest version, I realized I would lose. The cards I needed to continue were buried with no escape. Ray saw too, confirming her worst suspicions, but today especially I wasn't going to let a poor shuffle defeat me.

"This time I can feel it," I said, ignoring her doubtful look.

And I did feel it, deep in my palm, as I flipped each set of cards an extra turn before I laid them out. Sure enough, the two of clubs, the one I wanted, popped up big as life.

"Come to Mama!" I acted enthusiastic, to lure Ray into the spirit, but her face was bored and she was just humoring a sick person. I knew she yearned to tell me I cheated.

"I quit when I'm ahead," I said, and pushed the deck over to her. Let her lose if she was so honest.

At first the cards seemed to appease her. I took it as a good sign when she tried to snooker me, inviting me to cut and give her a free shot, but then the fun left her and she made no effort to win. When the deck ran out there were nearly twenty small sloppy stacks lined on the table slid across my knees. It took work to play that bad. I thought I'd show her how again, give her an example to follow, when there in the door was Elgin, straight from his route, shining with rain.

Something was wrong, held back, about him. His shoulders were bunched high, and he wouldn't meet my eyes. I thought the doctor must have talked to him, that he knew my story and couldn't face me. All my fight drained out, changed to pity. I wanted to tell Elgin it would be all right. I wanted to go back into that world where it was just him and me, where I would get well if only to see him smile.

"Rayona," he said. "What's happening?"

"I'm surprised you recognized me."

I felt stupid in my thoughts. I might as well not have been in the room for all he cared. I decided to remind him who was sick, whom he had come to see, whose car he had driven to get there.

"I'm amazed you visited again," I said.

He knew what I meant, that all he wanted was the fucking car, and he rubbed his thumbs against the knuckles of his clenched fingers. At least I had his attention.

We always had to fight before we could get back together, and I was impatient to start. I shifted my body on the bed, a signal for Rayona to leave, but she didn't take the hint. Elgin turned to her.

"Your mama's in her usual good mood," he said.

"She's sick."

Elgin was looking for something in his pocket.

"I believe these are yours." He dragged out my keys and dangled them before me.

I shook my head, told him to keep the car. I put a special note in my voice.

"I'll call you when I'm discharged. You can give me a lift." It was our shorthand language, my way of saying I wanted him home with me awhile. He understood.

"This time it takes more than a beat-up Volaré," Elgin said, and I understood *him*. He tossed the keys to Rayona. I watched them arc through the air until she caught them with one hand.

The energy of anger shot through me, but I tried to be reasonable. I said I was sick, *sick*, but he wouldn't hear. I couldn't say more because of Rayona, and the frustration maddened me. I struggled to get out of bed. I wanted to throw myself on him and make him feel all the force of my body, to show him my desperation, but my legs were penned by hospital-tucked sheets.

"Just get the hell out of here," I told him. "Go back to your fat girl." I covered my face with a pillow and my own hot breath washed over my skin. I hated every rotten thing I had remembered when the doctor sentenced me. I hated Aunt Ida for what she didn't do, I hated Lee for what I did to him, hated him for waiting for me on those golden stairs, for the sound that that potting soil made against his coffin. I hated Elgin for his disappointments I got used to, hated him for his grudging jealousy, and hated him for the line he had just sunk under. I even hated Rayona, who was going to live without me. I hated the mess I made of myself.

And when I stopped, when I was hated out, I lifted the pillow and opened my eyes to a closed door. On either side of me my roommates watched, satisfied that I had been brought down, frightened and excited by the fight, talking with each other over my head without using words.

There was no way I could stay there, no reason. A hospital did me no good, if that doctor was right, and so I ran into the hall and opened the first door I saw, a closet filled with coats and uniforms. I found a red-and-white dress, poked around the floor for slippers, and ran back to my room. The two women were silent and on alert while I pulled off my gown, buttoned the dress tight across my body, and located the lipstick in my purse. I walked down the corridor, fussy and important as a nurse, nodding to patients in their rooms, carrying the uniform's coat hanger under my arm. I rode the elevator to the ground floor, and exited to the parking lot, to the section where Elgin told Rayona he had parked. I regretted now not taking the keys from him, but I knew how to hot-wire the engine.

The Volaré was illuminated by a blue streetlamp. I untwisted the hanger into a long wire, snaked it through the rubber seal at the top of the closed window of the door on the driver's side, and hooked at the latch.

Suddenly, I sensed someone big behind me and tensed to hurl myself backward to throw him off balance. Before I could move, though, he hollered out and grabbed me by the ass. I struck out with my arms and legs, growled in my throat. The car door popped open and we fell to the ground. I gripped the coat hanger in my fist and whirled around, ready to let loose, but it was only Rayona, wide-eyed and scared shitless. I needed a minute to take a breath myself.

Lately she was around when I didn't want her to be, and now she sprawled, gaping like a wino on Sunday morning. We both stood and brushed ourselves off.

"What are you staring at?" I demanded. "I thought you ran out with your father. Go home."

Ray made no move to leave. Where I was going she couldn't come, and she might as well get used to it. I gave her my purse.

"What are you doing?" she asked me, all confused. I didn't know how to answer. In that hospital room I had lost two big things I depended on: my better tomorrow, as they say on the commercials, and Elgin.

"I'm getting out of here, that's all."

She gave me a blank look.

"They discharged you?"

"Elgin. He's the one that discharged." She was too used to the way we lived, fighting and coming back together, so I gave her something new. I made up a story on the spot, mixing the gossip I had heard with all my fears come to life. I made it so real, I got to blame him for everything, and ended by announcing, "He's divorcing me. *Us*. He's been cheating with some black chick named Arletta."

"Oh, Arletta," she said, unsurprised. It made me crazy that my daughter knew at least as much about Elgin as I did.

"He killed me!" I yelled into Rayona's stunned face, but of course she still didn't get it. She thought I was unbalanced, off the deep end. I tried to see it from her side, but I couldn't. I had hit bottom and found myself alone. You had to have lived my life to understand it.

I realized there was a place I had to go. Tacoma was where the thing that was ending had started, and Tacoma was where I'd complete my own circle.

I slid behind the wheel, and pointed at Ray's pocket. She handed me the keys.

"Don't let the bastard have a thing," I said.

Before I could stop her, Ray ran around the car and climbed in too, then sat with my purse on her lap. She fastened the seat belt she had insisted I have installed, arranged her strap. She had decided I shouldn't be by myself, and was a lead weight too big for me to toss overboard.

"What are you talking about?" she asked me, so I answered her, plain and simple. I sang the blues about money and Elgin. I confessed that the most valuable thing about me was my State Farm insurance. I told her to kiss me good-bye.

And she made a joke, claimed to know where I was going. It pissed me off that she guessed right, as if I had confided about Tacoma being my special place so many times it had lost its meaning. She said she wanted to come too, and nothing I could do in my weakened condition was likely to change her mind.

If I hung around another minute I'd lose my nerve, so I didn't even try. I took the curves down the hill, past the Chinese restaurants and Korean markets, toward the Kingdome. I sped past the Goodwill, past the yellow billboard with the steaming cup of Millstone coffee. Rayona read the black letters of our favorite sign aloud: "If you must cry over spilled milk, condense it." But I didn't laugh. At the freeway entrance on River Avenue, out of habit I looked to see the view of Mount Rainier, but of course it was too dark.

The trip to Tacoma was like a dream for me, my mind racing faster than the engine. I don't know which of my thoughts I said out loud and which I kept to myself. In a trance, I drove without once losing my direction, every unfamiliar path I took, the right way to go. Traffic lights turned green when I approached, Smokeys stopped the cars in front of me for speeding and let us race by. Rayona braced her feet against the floor as if she was standing on the brakes, twisting to grasp the door handle with both hands. She was prepared for a crash, and her eyes reflected the streetlights whenever I glanced toward her.

Every one of my senses was open, wide as the gates on the Grand Coulee, pulling sensations into my brain so fast I couldn't tell where they entered from, or hold on to them once they were there: the sounds of the radio and our voices, the smell of the misty night air, the feel of the wheel tight against my hands, the ache in my stomach—which the doctor told me is my pancreas—the taste of ginger ale on the roof of my mouth, the sight of the bulky blurs of cars and trucks flowing with us and toward us like twigs on the fast waters of the Interstate. I'd been high this way, too busy absorbing impressions to think, too connected to the world to make logic of it. I was riding an arrow to the bull's-eye of a target, to the spot overlooking the Sound when I loved Elgin and he loved me. I was a threaded needle poking on the underside of the place I had pierced. If I could go back through the same hole I would leave no mark.

Minutes passed like the miles, without my notice. Tacoma had changed and the neighborhood was developed and cluttered. We came through the lights of Pearl Street, through the entrance of Point Defiance Park, and after a mile, I pulled the car to the curb.

"Get out," I said. I didn't want Rayona with me when I found that cleared ground, and I wouldn't take no for an answer. She was Elgin's problem now, or Aunt Ida's. I reached over and pushed her door open, unhooked her safety belt, pushed her to the far corner of my mind.

But she wouldn't leave in peace. She said I was bluffing, fought my hands, and when she was outside, she rocked the fender with her foot for all she was worth. The Volaré bucked under me like bumper cars at a fair. She screamed I was a lousy mother, that I had scarred her for life. She was mad and hurt and scared of how I was acting, of what I might do.

Her words flew by me, rattling through the calling sounds of night insects, distant traffic. The air smelled of evergreens and pulp mills, sour enough to taste. In the dark, the road didn't even look familiar.

There was nothing for me to do but answer her anger with my own, to give her something to regret when she mulled over this experience.

"I'm not going to forget this," I yelled out the window, and meant that now she couldn't forget it either. But just when I was about to make my getaway, the engine made a sound like Drano in a clogged pipe, and stalled. I fed it gas, stamped my foot so hard my sole stung, so hard it flooded.

I gave it a rest, then turned the key again. Not a sound.

The truth sank in: out of gas. Elgin returned empty a car I gave him full.

I clawed my way outside. I wanted to smash the Volaré against my forehead like I sometimes did with my used-up beer cans, to crush it beyond repair. It couldn't make the extra mile, it couldn't get me back to Go. I wanted to whirl, to fly like an unknotted balloon, to jackhammer the road. I wanted to run into trees with my eyes closed, to set myself on fire.

But all I did, once my breath came back, once I felt the ground under my feet, was reach back onto the dashboard, get a smoke, and light it.

Rayona stood on the far side of the car, watching my show, silently condemning me for my cigarette, so I turned and walked to the privacy of dark bushes. I grabbed a low branch and leaned my head against my arm. I looked up the road as far as the Volaré's burning headlamps would let me see, but the path disappeared in twenty feet, lost in the blackness, beyond my reach. I had the despair of the worst hangover of my life, that feeling you get when nothing seems possible, when it's better to drown than swim.

Then Rayona opened her door and the overhead light came on. Her face was illuminated, the yellow flame on the end of a tall, skinny candle. The braid I had formed still held her hair in place. Her nose was carved from soft wood, and her lips were as arched and sloped as ocean waves. She was a total miracle: the fact she breathed, the fact she wouldn't leave me, the fact she was here where she started and impatient to be on her way. There was no undoing her; she was in her own world. She was the best so far, the new improved model, and whatever else I had to do, it had to do with her.

"How the hell are we supposed to get out of here?" I said to feel her out, to return us to normal.

She said she had seen a gas station, that I should wait for her to come back with help. Her voice was tight with the shock of my strange behavior, with the stretch of acting older than she was. If I told her I was sick she'd feel sorry for me, but instead I kidded her, pretended to be scared to stay alone. "You wouldn't want anything to happen to your lousy mother," I told her. "You could get scarred for life."

Rayona took the bait, joked back about my beat-up old car. We walked side by side down the road that led out of the park. She was the first one all day to give me what I wanted, so I hid my true self in the dark. I had surprised her enough.

There were no two ways about it, I had to take Rayona to Aunt Ida's and make Aunt Ida agree to keep her. It was that or some foster home like the ones Ray had been sent by the Child Court the times I lost control. She never talked about those places, but I knew what she didn't say. It was no picnic to be the odd man out, the one the state paid for. She had three years till she was on her own and Aunt Ida was better than nothing.

The ache in my stomach that the doctor said would come and go was getting harder to ignore. I had a full bottle of pain pills, some Percocet, stashed in the apartment, and, when we got there, I swallowed two to keep moving. There wasn't much to pack, just some clothes and a few scrapbooks and knick-knacks I had collected over the years. In the bottom of my bureau drawer I came across Lee's army medal, still in its case, and I took that along too. I stuffed things in green three-ply garbage bags, grabbing whatever was in the range of my hand. Lots of junk I left behind, telling myself the landlord could apply it toward the rent I owed, but all together it couldn't have been worth five dollars. When we got done packing I saw two of the sacks had my name on them and only one had Ray's, and I asked myself all over again what kind of a mother I was.

I dumped practically the whole bottle of pain pills into a Ziploc bag, walked down the hall with what remained, and tapped on my girlfriend Charlene's apartment. She owed me for all the times I let her cry on my shoulder about men who did her dirt, about how homesick she was for her reservation in Arizona, about how bad the doctors treated the staff at the IHS hospital pharmacy where she worked. Charlene wasn't all that bright, and with her bad teeth she wouldn't win any beauty contests, but she was loyal. She'd stick by me and get me the dope I needed to stay on my feet as long as I had to. She knew everybody's sickness from typing the labels on their medicine, so she more than anyone else knew how bad off I was. She couldn't say no.

At first I thought she had a date with her, it took her so long to open the door. But when she stretched the lock chain to its limit and peeped through the crack, I knew she was alone. You don't wear curlers and a nun's nightgown for a party. It took her a minute to recognize me, and then she couldn't believe her eyes.

"You're sick in bed!" she said.

I told her I signed myself out, that I was going home. Ray was probably listening at our apartment door, so I couldn't go into any long explanations. Charlene was going to have to take me or leave me on faith.

"You're killing yourself," she whispered, loud as an auctioneer.

"Not if you help me," I answered and shook the almost empty Percocet bottle, with Aunt Ida's address written under the prescription number. Charlene had some evidence, I never knew what, on the head pharmacist, and so she could put her fingers on any drug she wanted. Unlike a lot of people I could name, I had never before asked her to deal me. There was a question in her eyes and I tried to answer it.

"Don't tell *anybody* where I've gone." She never liked Elgin anyway.

But that was not what was bothering Charlene. "I could lose my job," she said. "When they do the inventory."

I was tired of asking favors, tired of phony objections. I told her to forget it and left her standing there, her excuses still ringing in the air. She knew what I was up against and I wasn't going to beg.

"All right then." She called me back. She made me promise to see a doctor in Montana, warned me that she wouldn't be able to get me more than one refill. I gave her no arguments. I didn't need a year's supply, didn't need for her to use up her favors, and she knew it. I could tell from the way she hugged me.

Rayona and I wedged the bags into the backseat of the Volaré, and it struck me how little space they occupied. I wanted Rayona to have something to remember me by, something nice and expensive that didn't wear out, but I only had an expired Conoco Oil card, the rings that wouldn't come off my fingers, and about forty dollars cash left over from my last check. I wanted her to make an impression on that reservation, to turn people jealous with her city belongings, but there was nothing of mine I could give her. Even my good clothes were too small.

Then it came to me. Not two weeks before I had scored an unbelievable bargain, a lifetime membership in a videocassette club for only ninety-nine cents cash. What's more, I had put it in Ray's name, since the man convinced me that she would get even more of my money's worth. That membership was like American Express. Rayona could waltz out of there with any movie she wanted and not pay until she brought it back.

We had been awake all night, but the pills or the excitement or both gave me more energy than I had had in weeks. We loaded the car in the moist air of early morning, and, just as stores were opening, pulled into the parking lot of the Northgate mall where the Village Video Club had its headquarters. Ray was nervous, scared we'd get caught for exercising our rental privileges, but I answered her worries by asking the man what would happen if we were late in returning cassettes. He said it was no big deal, that it happened all the time.

What do you get for your daughter to remember you? There were tapes everywhere, on the walls, on shelves, stacked in rows on the tables, and I browsed like a rich woman at a buffet lunch. I considered *Flashdance*, which I liked a lot, *The Song of Bernadette*, for Ray's spiritual development, and *Beverly Hills Cop*, since the people at home went for anything funny. Then the clouds parted and I saw my first selection, because there it was, *Christine*, the car with a brain in its head. I had seen that movie I don't know how many times, some of them with Ray, and I even bought a bumper sticker of it for my car. I loved how my name looked, spelled out on the screen in big red letters, how that Christine took her revenge on anybody who messed with the guy she liked—even after she was gone—loved how tough she was. That was how I wanted Rayona to remember me.

My next choice took longer. Ray was worn out and wanted to get on the road, but to tell the truth there was a part of me that hung on to Seattle and I lingered, slow to make up my mind. It wasn't till I moved back to the golden oldies section that I remembered about *Little Big Man*. I had a connection to that show by going out a couple of times with one of the actors. Looking at the cassette box, I couldn't place his name, but I did remember that the old chief who took in the white boy had a sense of humor and a nice sad face.

When we drove out of the lot, Rayona looked at a map from the glove compartment and directed me to go south for Interstate 90 East, but instead I went north to Everett and took Route 2. I told her it was a road I was familiar with, one I had traveled before, and that was true enough. But more than that I figured there would be fewer state cops patrolling and less chance of me being stopped for my busted taillight. My license was expired.

We climbed toward Stevens Pass, stopped at the rest area for free coffee, and drove through the sage-covered rangelands east of Wenatchee. I got lost twice in Spokane—at one point I found myself pointed in the wrong direction—but before dark we had scaled the long hill through Bonners Ferry and were out of Idaho.

The stretch of Montana from Libby to Kalispell is all mountains and sharp curves, all national forest. Our headlights kept reflecting off small white crosses, some by themselves, some clustered in groups, that were placed along the side of the pavement. I couldn't decipher them until Ray learned from a sign that they marked the spots of traffic fatalities and were erected to warn drivers to be careful.

Some were looped by wreaths of plastic flowers, tended as carefully as gravesites. And every one spoke to me of what I didn't need to be reminded. They jumped from the night like rows of ghosts, faceless, waiting, lonesome, and I set my teeth to hold them still and played the radio for company after Rayona fell asleep.

I listened to a replay of "Country Countdown" and two of the new songs, especially, distracted me. The first one, lucky number thirteen and racing up the charts, was "Everything That Glitters Is Not Gold," about a man who was left all alone to raise his daughter, Casey, when his wife went out on the rodeo circuit. By the end of the lyrics he had resigned himself and was the wiser, even though his horse was getting old and Casey had questions he couldn't answer. I tapped my palms against the steering wheel to the rhythm.

The other song, "Until I Met You," at number twelve, was still prettier. I didn't even listen to the words, but Judy Rodman, who sang it, had such a sweet voice and the tune seemed so right for driving that when it was over I switched off the volume so I wouldn't lose the music. I hummed it over and over until the sun rose in Browning, just as I stopped to fill my tank at the Town Pump.

I never did hear what was number one.

The Volaré died a mile shy of Aunt Ida's, too close for me to change my mind. We hit a gully in the washed-out road, and the car sailed and broke like an old-time buffalo chased over a ridge. It was early afternoon and the sky was a pale yellow, a shade lighter than the dry grasses that shifted around us, stiff as the pages of a book. Even the air seemed to have the same tone, or maybe it was colored by blowing grains of pollen. It was so quiet that every sound we made was edged in black, stood out sharp as a rifle crack. You could have heard the car door slam a mile distant, and a Russian satellite could have picked up the shuffle of our feet on the gravel roadbed as we bent to inspect the damage.

What Rayona and I, put together, knew about auto mechanics wouldn't fill a bottlecap, but we prodded and listened like experts. She had unreasonable confidence in her ability to fix anything, and I knew if I didn't say something discouraging she would waste the day trying for a lucky guess, so I pronounced the worst thing I could imagine. I had heard that once the rods go, the car is shot, and though I wouldn't have known a rod if I tripped on it, I told her that's what had happened. She must have heard the same thing about rods, because she didn't argue, just looked at the car as if it was a broken-legged horse that had to be put out of its misery.

Our destination was just over the hill, easy enough to walk, even burdened with four trash bags. We reached the crest, out of breath and sweating with the effort, and came within sight of the house.

You know, it's strange, you live in a place half your life and yet the sight of it from an unfamiliar angle can still surprise you. It was as though I had never before seen that building, so small and hollowed out against the treeless land. Standing where I now stood, I thought of all the things that went on there over the years between Aunt Ida and Lee and Dayton and me. I thought of the windows lighted at night like beacons, and warm in the snowbound winter. I thought how glad I had been to walk away from it more than once, and how, no matter what, I kept coming back.

The earth by the front door was worn flat, smoothed by the dumping and drying of dishwater. Shingles were blown off the roof in an irregular pattern that reminded me of notes on a music sheet, and tan cardboard replaced glass in a pane of the attic window. The house and the land had been through so many seasons, shared so much rain and sun, so much expanding and shrinking with heat and cold, that the seams between them were all but gone. Now the walls rose from the ground like the sides of a short, square hill, dug out by the wind and exposed.

I heard a swishing sound like knives being sharpened on stones, and Aunt Ida appeared from where the building had concealed her. Her size amazed me, the breadth of her brown shoulders, the columns of her arms as they stretched before her, pushing a lawn mower, plowing through the grass. At first I thought she had dyed her hair, but then I saw it was a wig, the kind of thing advertised on the back pages of comic books, "$11.95 and natural-looking." She wore overalls and sunglasses and had false teeth. She sang like Stevie Wonder, tilting her neck as she moved, bellowing a Johnny Lee song in English to an invisible audience. I noted with satisfaction that she wore the Walkman set I sent her for Christmas, the one she never thanked me for.

She saw us but she pivoted the wheel of the mower in a ninety-degree turn and retreated. Then she stopped, pushed back her glasses, and let the earphones drop behind her head like a reversed necklace.

"What did the cat drag in?" she asked the sky.

"It's just me," I said. "I'm home." I tried to put my feelings behind my voice, to let the words carry my burden across the distance between us, to let her know it was important for her to be nice. At that minute she was my last hope, the one person who had no right to turn away from me. I wanted to find the soft pillow of her older age and rest against it. But more, I wanted to know she'd take care of Rayona, be a better mother to her than she was to me. All the drive from Seattle I had talked myself into believing that things would work out, and now there was no more time for guessing.

But she misunderstood. She thought that she had me where she wanted me at last, that her dream had come true and I had come crawling back, failed and without pride. She'd been waiting too long with that vision in her head to see that this was different.

"Give me three reasons I should be glad to see you," Aunt Ida crowed. She was proud to have thought of this line, I could tell, and she was ready to take her slow revenge.

The hate I had felt at the hospital for her coldness flooded into me, but I suppressed it for Rayona's sake. I played Aunt Ida's game and led off with my strong suit, her legal obligation.

"One, I'm your daughter, your only living child." I got Lee on the table from the first so she couldn't surprise me with him later, but I reminded her that it was me or nobody. I thought of saying she was my mother, but that would only turn her nasty, and the frown she gave my words was bad enough.

"Two, we need someplace to stay." I gave her satisfaction, the begging she wanted. If that's what it took, I could stand it. But Aunt Ida was a bad winner. Her face said a thousand things without making a sound. I had opened the door to all the memories stuck in her craw, to every time she didn't have the last word on me.

"Three..." I knew what she was waiting for, what she required to hear. If I said I had been wrong to defy her, that I was sorry for the grief I had caused, if I shamed myself there in front of Rayona, if I spent my last dime and ate shit, Aunt Ida would pay anything, even make a home for my daughter. It was the most expensive thing I ever considered buying and I had the exact cash and not a cent more. I ground the toe of my boot in the hard soil, dislodging a piece of flint.

I saw Rayona watching and it came to me that nothing, nothing was worth her witnessing me laid low. She could survive foster homes if she had to, she could make her own way, but what she couldn't do was erase the picture of her mother made a fool by an unforgiving old woman. That would never go away. Aunt Ida waited, greedy as a kid at McDonald's, but I turned the tables. I let her decide how mean she really was.

"Three, go fuck yourself anyway," I said, straight to Aunt Ida's face. My words were spit in her eye, caught her off-guard, gave me the minute I needed to shoot one more secret look at Ray, then grab the bags with my name on them and take off before Aunt Ida could outsmart me. This time I ran from that house as I never had before: I ran so nobody could catch me. All the way, stumbling down the slope of that steep, familiar hill, all the way, as the small rocks rolled under my boots and I thought I would die on the spot from the pain in my stomach, all the way to the flat ground where the road broke the grass, all the way, I said my good-byes.

15

My body jolted with every running step. My feet were heavy as stones, and the plastic of the bags I dragged stretched and spun. My ears throbbed with the beat of blood pumping through my veins. I yearned to fall down, to sprawl until I was rescued and comforted by strong hands. I wanted to hear someone say my problems weren't so bad, that I was upset over nothing. I needed a moment to feel sorry for myself, if nobody else would, but when I heard Ray barreling down the hill after me I went faster.

I saw a dust cloud, caught the race of a souped-up engine. I pulled sharp air into my lungs. The heels of my boots turned in on their worn edges, and the crotch of my jeans hung too low between my legs, hog-tying my stride. Sweat ran into my eyes and between my breasts and a stitch began in my side.

The truck stopped next to me. I looked to see if it was someone I knew, but the driver was just a kid with greased-down hair and a can of beer in his hand. He looked like every boy I went with in school, low-down and lying.

"Hey there," he called to me. I ignored him, struggled along. He threw the truck back into gear, trailed me in first, almost stalling out, I was going so slow.

"You drunk or what?" he called from his open window. "What's your name?"

"Get lost," I yelled, but that only made him laugh.

"I ain't seen you around before," he said. "You from here?"

"No more," I shot between short breaths.

"You at Ida's?" he asked. Then, "I know who you are. You're her girl. You're Christine."

My legs would hardly lift, and the truck was crowding me into the shallow ditch that ran along the embankment.

"So what?"

"Well, I'm your cousin," he said. "Foxy. Kennedy Cree, you knew me as. Pauline's my mom. Come on, get in. I'll give you a lift."

He reached over to flip the handle and the door swung open, almost knocking me down. The brakes squeaked and the motor roared. I smelled Wildroot, and saw a leather bridle on the floor of the cab. I remembered him as a fidgety kid, a pain in the butt. It was him or being caught. I used my last strength to swing the twisted and ripping bags over the rusted blue sides and into the bed, then stepped high with my toe, reached for his outstretched hand, and let myself be winched inside. Foxy gunned the engine, speed-clutched into second, and spun his back tires on the gravel so hard the odor of burning rubber rose around us.

And then, as if jerked from mud by a powerful tow, the truck shot forward, flying, faster than even a long-legged girl can run.

"Where to, then?" Foxy asked at last. I had shook my head in refusal to his offer of beer, had shut off his questions with the flat palm of my hand. I was too winded to speak, and had nothing to say. All I cared about was moving out of range, leaving Ray in the hands of Aunt Ida's duty, wondering had I done the right thing. Foxy expected a story out of me and was disappointed, but I knew he'd think of something. Boys like him always did.

"Which way are you headed?" I asked.

"I was just tooling. It don't matter. You want to go to Mom's? Just say the word."

The last person I wanted to see was Aunt Pauline. She'd make me kneel and pray for the forgiveness of my sins, and claim all my troubles came from skipping Mass on Sundays. She'd be over at Aunt Ida's before the day was over, going on about what a lost soul I was, and when she came home, kicked out as usual, she'd have Rayona with her. Foster homes were better than Pauline's.

Where do you go with no car, almost no cash, and two bags of old clothes? I raised my eyes and looked for landmarks, for a clue to my destination. We were heading north, back the way I had come this morning, and approaching the unpaved crossroad that led to the western end of the reservation. It was mostly leased grazing land out there, a lot of stock and not many people, but I knew one place, the place I used to go looking for Lee late at night or early in the morning.

"Does Dayton's mom still live at Pass Creek?"

"She's dead," Foxy said. "But Dayton's there. Boarded up her house and built new next door. His mom's wasn't good enough for him, none of the things either. He left them all inside. You want to go *there?*" He was surprised. "You *know* about Dayton?"

I nodded. I liked surprising Foxy. "I used to go with Dayton," I said, and ignored Foxy's double take. Let him think what he wanted. It was the second time today Dayton's name was mentioned. I had told Ray he'd fix our car. Over the years I had talked about him more than I thought about him, just to give her a name to recognize back where I was from. And what's more, I realized Dayton would take me in.

Foxy turned fast, tipping and hammering the truck. He tried to run down and crush every prairie dog on the road. I wondered what Pauline made of him, how she explained him to herself. We bounced hard on the road, swinging left and right to avoid the bigger holes. Wire fences, grounded to metal posts, lined either side, and cattle stood in small clusters, swinging their tails and raising their heads as the truck passed. The sky had turned whiter, a thin cream that blocked the sun and covered the land like a cup. Foxy pushed an eight-track tape into the deck below the dashboard. I didn't expect to recognize his music, but I did.

"Santana?" I asked.

"I got a whole box of this junk for five dollars," he said. "They can't give them away now that everybody's switched to cassettes."

"I used to listen to them," I said.

"Eight-tracks?"

"Santana. Who'd you buy it from?"

"I don't know. The Mission bazaar."

My mind was loose, unscrewed by my long drive and my run.

"Here we are," Foxy said. "You can still change your mind."

He stopped by a mailbox, painted silver with NICKLES stenciled in red. A gate padlocked across the driveway, and a slate walk led across a dirt yard to a prefab white ranch house with green shutters. There was a brown horse in a small corral in back, and, next to the barn, a monster TV satellite dish pointed at the sky. Everything looked well kept, not rundown the way it used to be, not the kind of place you'd think a bachelor would live in alone for long.

Off to the side was the old lease house, smaller than I remembered, two-by-fours nailed to block the doors and windows. Unreadable words had been written on the walls in white spray paint and Xed out with black.

"See that horse?" Foxy demanded, then continued, without waiting for my reply. "That's the wildest mare around here. They were going to shoot her, but Dayton bought her instead. And I'm going to bust her on the Fourth of July at the Havre rodeo. I asked for her special."

I listened to his boast and looked again at the horse. She was lean and muscled, with a thick black mane. She never paused in her circle of the fenced yard.

"Who else stays here?" I asked Foxy as I stepped from the truck.

He was impatient to get going, to find out more about me, and his hands drummed the steering wheel in time with the music.

"You shitting me? Nobody even visits."

I reached behind the cab for my bags and hoisted them over the side. One ripped and I held it close to my chest to keep the clothes from spilling out. The other I dropped over the gate, then turned.

"Thanks."

"You really going to stay here?"

I slammed the cab door and shouted through the open window. "Tell your mom I said hey."

Foxy was disappointed again, just as I knew he'd be. He assumed my presence was a secret that he could enjoy betraying. He studied me closely, deciding how well I read him, and Santana's electric guitar riffs curled and filled the air. Foxy took a slow pull on his beer, never breaking the contact between our eyes. Then he tossed the container out his window and drove off.

For a while the sounds competed, the loud but fast-fading music, the roar and pop of the muffler. But finally, as I stood trying to figure the best way to climb Dayton's fence without losing control of the split green bag in my arms, the only noise that remained was the clatter of the empty aluminum can as the wind turned it in gravel, over and over, over and over.

The house might be different, but Dayton still hid a spare key in a window ledge. I looked through the gray screen door, and, after the brightness of the yard, what I saw was as cool and shady as a forest. The walls and floor were polished wood, a round braid rug floated like a September pond before a green couch. On the coffee table, magazines were fanned like a winning hand of poker. Everything was so neat, so still, I hesitated before turning the lock and going inside.

I didn't know Dayton at all, not in the way one person knows another, and yet something about his living room spoke to me, made me notice things I otherwise wouldn't see, such as how my plastic sacks destroyed the balance and seemed out of place. I put them behind the counter that opened into the small modern kitchen, then I came back and turned a circle in the center of the rug. There was a smell I couldn't identify, not cigar smoke, not Air-Wick, but a ribbon of scent I felt high in my nose. I closed my eyes, tried to place it. I sniffed like a German shepherd, drawing the air into me, till I realized it was the smell of newness, of things just out of their boxes that haven't had time to blend with all that's ordinary around them. It was the smell of the first page of a school notebook in the fall, the inside of a car straight from Detroit, underwear fresh from its cellophane package.

I moved cautiously, touching Dayton's possessions: the arm of his chair, the dial of his TV, the reading glasses on the small, straightened desk against the far wall. I looked up and into my laughing brother's eyes. It was a photograph I had seen before, of Lee and Dayton, taken after one of Lee's rodeo victories. They stood grinning with their arms slung around each other's shoulders, their cowboy hats tilted back on their heads, a trophy in Lee's hands. But wait. I bent closer and saw it wasn't a photograph at all, but an oil painting, an exact duplicate, as though someone had traced the picture and then colored it in. And too, the more I looked, the more I was sure there was something not quite right. Finally I saw it. Lee was wearing his prize brass buckle, the one he kept guarded in its box, the one he had never even used.

There were other pictures on that wall, all snapshots that had been enlarged and set in frames that matched the paneling. There was Dayton's mom, looking as faded and exhausted as I remembered her. There was Dayton at his graduation from Holy Martyrs, dressed in a maroon cap and gown and carrying a diploma and some school prize book with a gold cross embossed on the cover. There was a color photo of Dayton's new house, viewed from the front, with him posed proud on the doorstep. I wondered who took it. And there—I couldn't believe it—there was me, slouched against a wall, holding Rayona when she was a baby. I examined the outfit I was wearing, and remembered. We were at the gym for Lee's honor ceremony, right after his funeral. I was staring off to the side, one leg crossed over the other. Ray's eyes were closed, her fat cheeks sagging in sleep.

My roadrunner ring shone from my finger where my hand supported her head.

I couldn't imagine what we were doing on that wall. I had always been nothing but trouble to Dayton, coming between him and Lee, wanting him for myself, and blaming him for not taking what I offered. I hadn't even given him the consolation of my pity when he bought my dinner the next-to-last time I saw him, the day Lee was buried.

I sat on the couch, swallowed a Percocet. The Ziploc bag was a quarter gone and I was counting on Charlene to mail me a new supply. If I went to one of the doctors at the Agency hospital they'd just want to keep me for more tests that I knew I'd fail. I didn't want to be pinned down where anybody could find me, could stand over my bed and feel lucky they weren't me.

I kicked off my boots and rubbed the blisters that had begun to form. These were boots made for dancing, not to run in. I positioned myself on the cushions so I could move the minute I heard Dayton, so that he'd never know I had disturbed his things. My mind was a record playing at the wrong speed, spinning back over events I wanted to forget. I tried to imagine what Rayona and Aunt Ida could be doing, but I drew a blank. I wondered if Elgin realized I was gone and decided he had no way of knowing, provided Charlene had kept her mouth shut. I thought of Dayton's old house, abandoned and boarded over with everything inside. I remembered the sadness of his mother's face, the white T-shirts she ironed for him to wear. It was so odd that I was here, such a surprise to end this day in a cool new room, on a couch by a pool, in the forest.

I woke at the first creak of the gate's opening and tensed my body to sit and greet Dayton in his own home. But then I reconsidered, adjusted my clothes, smoothed down my hair, and pretended to be asleep. I'd give him a few minutes in private to get used to my presence, to come to his position without the pressure of my need. And besides, the pill had not worn off and I didn't feel normal.

I looked through the slit of my closed eyes. It was like seeing the room through a dirty window or a thick sheet of plastic. Everything was in silhouette, hazy, shimmering. My field of vision was fixed, and after I heard the screen door open, stay open, then close softly, I had to wait until Dayton came in front of me to see his shape. He remained motionless for a long time, heavier, quiet not to wake me.

The floor shifted as he moved, tiptoe, over to the desk and out of my viewpoint. I heard a drawer slide. I stretched as if coming awake, rolled to my side, looked again. The light played on him now, and I saw his face. He was stiff as a porcupine in a hunter's sights, his hand frozen in some newspapers. He'd had enough time, and so had I. I fluttered my lids, yawned, and completely opened my eyes, then I drew back quickly, acting shocked to find him watching. I assumed an expression that said Where am I?, then got my bearings and relaxed. I gave him time to shut the drawer with the papers he was afraid I had found.

"Yes, it's me," I announced when he kept staring. "Surprised?"

"I don't get it." He moved away from the desk. "I didn't hear you were back."

"Nobody knows. I just blew in."

"Where's Rayona?"

"Oh, I left her over to Aunt Ida's. You'll see her."

I swung my feet to the floor, steadied myself with my hand. "Are you okay?" Dayton asked.

I thought about that for a minute. I stopped myself from saying Fine, since that wouldn't get us anywhere. Sooner or later I had to explain to Dayton what I was just beginning to believe myself. I had to ask him if he'd stick by me even though he had no reason in the world. I decided I might as well get it over with and see how he reacted.

"Well, no," I told him. "No, I'm not."

He waited for more, his head dipping forward, nodding to encourage me.

"You're not going to believe this." I laughed, and saw the

concern on his face. I must have looked pretty bad because I could tell he *would* believe it.

"The doctors..." I took a breath. I was going to make a joke about the Happy Hunting Ground or act as though I was in a soap and put the back of my hand to my forehead and say I only had one month to live. I was going to draw a line with my finger across my neck. But nothing would come. I sat there speechless above the words I had to say, afraid to hear them in my own voice. My throat got tight, refused to let me talk.

Dayton stared past me to his coffee table. His eyes widened, and I looked to see my transparent bag of white pills lying open. I turned my eyes back to Dayton, guilty as if we were still young and he had found me out, and he understood.

"Oh," is all he said. He waited for me to tell him he was wrong, but I gave him no help. It was his move to ask for details, now that I was out in the open. But he turned away from me, touched his hands on the surface of his desk, leaned back his head like a preacher. His shoulders lifted and fell once, two times. He swung to me.

"Who knows? What are you going to do?"

"Nobody. I've done it. Here I am." I brought my own shoulders up as if to answer his.

"What about Rayona?"

"She's okay. She'll get used to the idea."

"What about your husband?"

"What about him?" My intonation said it all, said that was finished. I waited for Dayton to work his way down to what it meant for him to find me lying on his couch.

"Where are you going?"

He made it.

I shrugged again.

"Oh," he said again. "Oh. . . . Oh."

For what started out as an impulse, my dying on his hands suddenly seemed an idea to be reasonably weighed. There was no easy way for him to refuse, but he could still do it. He walked over and sat next to me on his green couch. He stretched his legs before him and looked at his hands. I followed the direction of his eyes. His nails were in good shape, clipped and clean. He had a desk job.

"It's funny," he said. "Yesterday I decided to move, to get the hell off this reservation."

"Well," I said, "I could help you pack."

He glanced at me and I raised my eyebrows to make my face all innocent and comical. He laughed once in a way I recognized from when he was a kid, kind of like it escaped out of him.

"Come on," I said. "It'll be okay."

"I can't believe any of this." He shook his head.

"That's what I warned you."

Once Dayton had said he wanted to be like a brother to me, and now was his chance. His house had a guest room, new and neat as the rest of the place, with a double bed that looked as though it had never been slept in and a chest of drawers with not a thing inside it. I unpacked my plastic bags, took my time organizing. The shallow drawer for underwear, scarves, and hose, the second for tops, the third for pants, the fourth for my two sweaters and swimming suit. I set my photo albums on the shelf of the bedside table and put my cosmetics case and hair dryer in the bathroom. I made a row on the top of the bureau with my boxes and colognes. I plugged in my radio and tuned it for the station I used to like. I hung a dress and my parka in the empty closet and made the bed with the folded sheets and blanket Dayton provided. At the kitchen table I ate the Campbell's chunky meatball soup he had heated, and drank a tall glass of iron-tasting water. Then I went back to my room, closed the door, drew the curtains to, put on my nightgown, and slept for fourteen hours.

When I got up Dayton was gone, but he had left a fresh pot in his Mr. Coffee and a note propped against the toaster.

"Be home at four-thirty," it said.

When I read that, I finally cried.

• • •

It didn't take me long to go looking for the newspapers Dayton had tried to hide from me. I wasn't surprised that they were no longer in the desk drawer, but that fact only made me more curious. I spent my first afternoon alone in that house searching, behind books, among his neatly folded clothes, in the bins he stored on the high shelves of his pantry, until I finally put my hand on a brown mailing envelope tucked inside a reserve giant-size box of All-Temperature Cheer. I took it to the couch in the living room where I could spread out, and eased open the flap.

Inside was a bunch of white papers, each one with the date and the name of a newspaper at the top, and a clipping Scotch-taped below. The pages were in order, beginning with the earliest dates, starting over four years ago.

"Reservation Teacher Charged" read the first headline. The article was short, just a few inches long, and as I followed the lines I discovered that Dayton had become a teacher of science and a basketball coach at the public school just off the reservation. I had to give him credit. But then I understood why he was so secretive. The paper said a student had accused Dayton of "improper conduct" and that Dayton had been temporarily suspended from his duties while the allegation was under investigation. It ended with Dayton denying all wrongdoing, but you could tell that the writer didn't believe him. I turned to the next page.

There was Dayton, wearing a business suit, climbing a set of concrete steps along with a fancy-dressed woman, and holding a newspaper to shield his face. I was struck by how old he looked. According to the caption, he and his attorney were on their way to a trial in the county courthouse.

Then there were two pages of letters to the editor, printed in narrow columns. I skimmed over them quickly, stunned by the mean things total strangers wrote, about how somebody like Dayton should be jailed with the key thrown away, or executed in the electric chair. Not one said what he was supposed to have done, they just went on about how Dayton was a menace to society.

Finally I came to a piece that told more of the story, and

part of it from Dayton's side. A sixteen-year-old boy claimed that Dayton had kept him after school and touched him against his will, that Dayton had said things the boy didn't want to hear. The kid's lawyer held it against Dayton that he still lived alone with his mother, with no wife and no children, that he never served in the army. Everything about Dayton seemed suspicious. Dayton's lady lawyer defended him, and said the boy was failing Dayton's class and was mad at getting bad grades. She said the whole thing was a pack of lies, that Dayton was a respected member of the community, a churchgoer, and that his good name had been tarnished by an unfair public hearing. She said her client was just trying to be a friend to a disturbed teenager, and that his actions had been misinterpreted.

I put the stack of papers down and lit a cigarette. I inhaled, then set it to burn in the ashtray on the coffee table. I wished I could see a picture of the boy to help me think. All the jokes people used to make about Dayton and Lee came rushing back to me, all the things I never let myself wonder about because they couldn't be true. I could see how some people might believe the worst of Dayton in a case like this.

I turned the page to find he was convicted by a jury. An editorial in bold ink applauded the verdict and asked for the maximum sentence. The boy's mother said her son would never be right again, that Dayton was a fiend. She had some things to say about Indians in general too, and I wondered if her boy felt the same way and how he liked having an Indian teacher give him low marks.

There were only three pages left. The first one was arranged like all the others and had an article about how Dayton was sentenced to five years in the state penitentiary. He still claimed he was innocent but the judge came down hard.

The final two pages were different, on another kind of paper, with the articles Xeroxed and cut out instead of coming straight from the newspaper. The one was a notice, dated almost a year later, that Dayton's mom had died at age sixty-three. It said she was the widow of a man from Kansas City and survived by her son, the convicted juvenile sex offender.

The last clipping was recent, from just eight months ago. It was an interview with Dayton, released from jail early for good behavior. He was angry. He swore he had done nothing wrong and said the boy who accused him was disturbed. The reporter asked Dayton if he had any comment on the fact that the boy, whose name, Willson Delara, could finally be printed because he was eighteen, was currently on trial himself for manslaughter. Dayton said no, he had nothing to say about that. The reporter wanted to know what Dayton was going to do now that he was free. Dayton replied he intended to go on with his life and was building a new house on his late mother's land. No, he wasn't going back to teaching, but had studied accounting by correspondence when he was in prison and had a guaranteed job working on the tribe's books and helping them balance their budget and write proposals. He didn't believe in looking back.

I straightened the pages, slipped them into the envelope, closed and clasped the flap. I put it exactly where I found it, made sure the box was set just as it had been, then left Dayton's laundry room and shut the door. I went to the kitchen. I looked in the refrigerator, opened every Tupperware container of leftovers, checked for rot in the vegetable drawers, found a half-eaten carton of cherry vanilla ice cream and a porterhouse steak in the freezer. I browsed through the canned goods on the shelf and saw that Dayton had been raised to expect a blizzard: powdered milk, soups, chili, Jell-O, tea bags. A lot of food for a single man. I inspected his dishes, all matched, white with a stalk of wheat around the rim. Six plates, six cups, six bowls, six saucers, all the same pattern. I counted his silverware, each kind stacked in its own partition, six of everything. Four steak knives in a box, a heavy glass salad bowl with a pair of tongs, cooking knives stored in a square block of wood.

I went through Dayton's house like a detective, opening a drawer of pressed dish towels, a folder with his income-tax records, a broom closet with two mops. I turned the pages of his magazines, *Time, American West, National Geographic*. I found a roll of postage stamps, still sealed inside a clear case, and an envelope of discount coupons. I don't know what I was looking for but I didn't find it. I couldn't believe Dayton had a whole house with only one secret, but then I thought maybe the secret was that there wasn't anything to hide. It was as though he took himself at his word, he didn't look back. Except for those pictures on his wall and the envelope of clippings, there was nothing of Dayton in those rooms. He was cut loose, fresh as the things he owned, planning to move away, and here I arrived, a sad reminder of times that were behind him.

If I had somewhere else to go I would have gone, but because I didn't, I tried to make sense of where I was, searched for a reason to stay, and it wasn't long before I told myself that I was sent. I was the only photograph still breathing. Dayton needed some mess in his life, and I had plenty to spare.

So when Dayton returned that late afternoon, he was greeted by his half-thawed porterhouse steak, and me prepared to fry it for him. We sat down to the kitchen table together like a family that didn't need a lot of conversation. He took me, for better or worse. I never let on I had read his papers, never wasted another minute in wondering, and Dayton never mentioned to me Lee's Purple Heart, still in its original leather box, which he must have found the next time he looked on his desk.

On a Friday morning, a little more than two weeks later, I had to face the fact that my supply of pills was almost run out, and I called Charlene from Dayton's phone to see if she had mailed me more. I got her at the hospital, so she couldn't talk, much as she wanted to.

"Where are you calling from?" she asked in a whisper.

"I'm staying with a friend."

"Male or female?"

"Male."

"Uh-oh," she said. "You're down but you're not out."

"Listen, did you get me that refill?"

"Shhhh," she hushed me, as if the line was tapped.

"Well, did you?"

Her voice got formal.

"Yes, Mrs. Jones," she said, now too loudly, "I mailed your . . ." Charlene's voice trailed off, stumped.

"You forwarded my letter," I helped her out.

"I forwarded your letter to the address you gave me."

Damn, it went to Aunt Ida's. I was hoping she had put it off and could send it to Dayton's direct.

"How long ago?"

"Quite a while." Then Charlene answered my next question before I had a chance to ask it.

"And I won't be able to forward any more of your mail either," she said, underlining each word. *"My boss had to seek different employment."*

In other words, he got caught selling pills.

"Okay," I said. I made it sound like good-bye.

"Wait!" Charlene called into her receiver. "How is the . . . thing . . . that was . . . not working?"

"I'll be all right when I get the medicine."

Now she didn't want to get off the line. "I've been thinking about you, Mrs. Jones."

I tried to imagine someone sitting next to her listening in. They would probably figure she was pulling some drug deal, just as she was, only they'd have it all wrong.

"I appreciate that," I told her. "You say hello to everybody for me."

"Everybody?"

That meant for once she had kept her promise and hadn't run to Elgin. All those miles between us mellowed me, suddenly made me want him to know. I hadn't been all that easy for him to deal with myself. It took two to tango.

"Yeah," I said, "everybody."

"Even Mr. Jones?"

"Everybody."

I listened to the dial tone, trying to figure some way to get my pills from Aunt Ida without giving her the opportunity to give back Rayona.

It was eleven o'clock, and chances were if Ray was still on the reservation she was at school, so this was the best time to

go. I called Dayton at the tribal office and he answered the
phone on the first ring.

"It's me. Can you take off for a half hour?"

"What's the matter?" His voice was tight, ready for bad
news.

"Nothing," I said. "I just have to go over to Aunt Ida's.
There might be a package there for me."

"Did you hear from her?" Dayton was after me to talk to
Aunt Ida the way he now wished he'd spoken to his mother
before she died.

"She doesn't have a phone."

"That's right." He was disappointed.

"Well, can you?"

"This minute?"

"Well, not if it's too much trouble." I hated asking for
favors. I started thinking how I could damn well walk over
there.

"Don't start," Dayton said. "I'll come."

"I've got an idea," I said. "Why don't you go get the
package?" Aunt Ida had always liked Dayton. He wouldn't even
have to tell her I was staying with him.

"I can't do that."

"Why not? It's closer than here and back."

"I can't," he said. "I haven't seen her since . . . for years."

I caught on. Who knew what Aunt Ida would say after
him being in jail, after being accused like he was. I wouldn't
want to face her either, if I was Dayton.

"Well, then, give me a ride."

"I said I would, but I'll have to be quick. It's almost the
end of the fiscal year."

Whatever that was. I went to my room and picked an
outfit that I thought wouldn't annoy Aunt Ida. Just a plaid shirt
and jeans. I brushed my hair, put on some lipstick, real light.
There was nothing much I could do about being so pale without
looking painted, and my clothes fit poorly. My body had
changed, turning thick at the waist and thinning everywhere
else. I tried without success to plot what to say if Aunt Ida was

at home, and I prayed that if she wasn't, she had left my package where I could find it. Then I prayed she hadn't sent it back "addressee unknown." That would be like her.

When Dayton arrived, I was out the door before he switched off the motor, and all the way to the main road and all the way to Aunt Ida's turnoff, I twisted my abalone ring, getting looser by the day, round and round the index finger of my left hand.

I heard organ music from the television the minute Dayton cut his engine, which meant Aunt Ida was at home and watching her stories. She could not have missed our arrival, but she didn't appear. I looked at Dayton, gave the smile of a lunatic to show him how nervous I was, and got out. The front door was closed in spite of the noon heat, and hornets had built a nest under the slope of the porch roof. I hesitated, not knowing whether to knock or just walk in. I did both, since no footsteps approached, no voice called out, after I rapped my fingers on the peeling wood.

I blinked at the dimness. The huge, oddly colored face of a TV woman greeted me.

"Avery," she said. "We shouldn't."

Aunt Ida sat with her back to me, intent on the woman's problems. She leaned forward from her kitchen chair, bracing her hands on her knees. Without the black wig, her hair was the yellowy white of fresh milk. I stood in a square of sunlight, waiting for her to notice. I looked around the familiar room, and the very sameness of the place led me to the small package, wrapped in brown paper, on the table to my right, next to the wall. Besides me, it was the only thing in that room that didn't belong.

I thought of reaching over and snagging it, backing outside without a word, but I knew something Aunt Ida didn't. I knew we wouldn't get a second chance, so I took a step.

"Is Rayona all right?"

Her back stiffened. "What do you care?" The rough edges of the old language fell from her like crushed rock.

"I've got something to tell you," I said, switching from English to match her. "About why I came back. Why I left her here in the manner I did."

"Be quiet." Her voice boomed, drowning out the TV. "I can't hear."

"You don't know what I'm going to say. I'd rather I be the one."

"No!"

"Aunt Ida . . ."

"No!" she shouted, rose from her chair and turned. Her small eyes were shocking in their brightness. Lines of tears glistened on her cheeks. One hand was rounded into a fist, the other clutched a large flat book. She was a woman spoiling to fight but with no hope of winning. She licked her lips with the tip of her tongue, cornered.

"What . . . ?" I asked.

"You're not sick like she thinks. That isn't medicine." She jerked her head in the direction of the package. "It's lies."

"It's truth." My shoulders relaxed. My eyes kept returning to the book until I recognized it. It was my senior Annual.

"I never wanted you!" Aunt Ida shouted at me. "I had no choice."

A cry broke from me, halfway between outrage and hurt. "You made that clear," I yelled back. "You don't have to tell me."

"You don't know anything." With her free hand she gripped the back of the chair, squeezed it in her grasp, then flung it aside, smashing it into the wall.

She was more than I could take, more than I ever realized. I grabbed for the box, hugged it to me like a charm, retreated for the door.

"Tina!" That name, how she said it like a fierce question, sunk my legs in concrete. I couldn't look at her. I couldn't see her weak. I shut my eyes.

"Just take care of Rayona," I said, speaking each word separately.

There was a movement in the heavy air. I heard the rustle

of her clothing, felt the heat and size of her body as she pushed past me, looked to see the back of her as she ran, fast and straight, her arms and head held close to her body, past the truck where Dayton waited, past the clearing of walked-on grass, into the high thick scrub, into a place I couldn't see.

16

Dayton and I settled into the routine of an old married couple, watching TV after dinner, talking about the people he worked with or friends I knew in Seattle, and keeping our secrets to ourselves. I almost never went off his property because I didn't want to advertise my presence, and because as time passed I felt my strength ebb. It was the kind of change you notice only by the week, not by the day. One Sunday I was up ready to dice potatoes for hash browns; the next I cooked bacon and fried eggs; the next just scrambled and toast. There were periods when I didn't dress till afternoon, and others when I never changed out of my robe, but Dayton didn't comment, didn't ask, didn't make me explain.

He said no more about moving away, but there were two things I knew about that, without being told: one, I was what kept him on the reservation, and two, he didn't mind. So I didn't either.

Even on mornings when I sat alone with my coffee and looked out to the corral to watch Babe, the wild horse Dayton had saved from slaughter, had bought for a song and now planned to rodeo and breed, even then, there were topics I steered my thoughts away from. Elgin was one. He was like a letter that might come if I didn't expect it too hard, a letter I would be afraid to read when it arrived because its news could leave me better or worse but not the same. The state of my internal organs was another. And Rayona's future was the biggest of all. Instead, I reviewed the last go-round with Aunt Ida, tried to puzzle her out, tried to understand how it was that the cruelest words she could possibly say had somehow sounded to me like apology, like raw sympathy. I turned those minutes in my mind like pieces of bread dough, pulling and pushing, letting them rise and patting them down.

For the first time in my life, I sat still and let the world come to me, and I opened my eyes to what was in front of my face. I settled back into that land and the creatures that lived on it. If at some point in my day I went out to the yard and fed Babe alfalfa or wild clover, felt the soft, warm sweep of her lips on the palm of my hand, smiled into her skittish look, smelled the brown heat of her neck, I thought I had done something. When "Everything That Glitters" or "Until I Met You" moved up a notch on "Country Countdown" I took it as a good sign. If I read in Dayton's *National Geographic* about tropical fish or the mountains of Australia, I remembered it to repeat to him over supper.

One night I stood in the bathroom and studied my features in the lighted mirror of the medicine cabinet. Not my whole face put together, a face whose dark circles and jutting bones were strange and frightening to me, but bits and pieces. The color of my own eyes, wet bark surrounded by lashes people used to say were unusually long. The tiny, thin lines, seamed like water going over a falls, that ridged my lips. The needle-prick holes in my ear lobes, the way two of my lower front teeth bowed to each other, the deep straight wrinkle that ran from my eyebrow to the middle of my forehead. I was an amazement.

Toward the end of June, late on a Monday afternoon, a strange truck stopped in front of the house, and when I looked through the curtains I saw Father Hurlburt, his hair gone whiter, helping Aunt Ida down. I didn't have to wonder how she found me. There were no secrets on the reservation if you wanted to uncover them. But I couldn't imagine why she had come. That day I had put on my blue velour dress with short sleeves and buttons down the back, so I was at my best when I opened the door and Aunt Ida and I regarded each other with unusual calmness.

"Do you know where she went?" Aunt Ida demanded.

My whole body sagged. "She ran away?"

"She disappeared the day you came by. No note or nothing, then that young assistant priest said she's gone back to Seattle on her own and that it's for the best."

"Seattle?" I couldn't believe Rayona would do it.

"Could she be with the husband?" Aunt Ida said, meaning Elgin.

"No. I don't think so."

"Where then?"

"She didn't have any money," I offered, but that only made things worse.

Aunt Ida's eyes rested on me. They asked, "How are you?"

I let her look. She could see.

"You call for me . . . if you want to," she said.

"I will."

"You do it, sure."

"I will."

"Is he taking care of you?"

"Dayton's good to me. I couldn't ask for better."

She bit her lip, turned to go.

"Let me know if you hear from Rayona."

She nodded again without looking back, repeated, "You call for me."

"I will." I stood in the doorway, nodded to Father Hurlburt, watched him back his truck out carefully, then swing into a wide arc that almost overshot the road. Aunt Ida sat straight in her seat. We didn't wave because we didn't have to.

After that it was no longer possible to push Rayona from my thoughts. She spent each day at my side, silent, at every age: a baby in her hotel dresser-drawer crib; brave, going off to a new school; grown up, a mother herself; an old lady remembering me. It seemed to me that I had wasted all the time we had together, that I had told her nothing worth knowing, that I had given her no part of me to keep. I called Elgin in Seattle to see if she was there after all, but his line was disconnected. I called Charlene, but she was gone on vacation to God knows where. I even thought of the police, but I didn't want to make Ray a criminal. I told myself a mother would know it if something happened to her daughter, but when that feeling ambushed me, that sense of black dread, I told myself it was stupid to believe in it.

I couldn't escape that it was my fault. I put myself in Rayona's shoes: she was as good as an orphan, thrown into the lap of an odd old woman who didn't want her. I had to face it, she was the wrong color, had the wrong name, had the wrong family—all an accident, Elgin and me the same place at the same time. But somehow she turned out right. I could murder her for running away, because in running away she was killing me quicker than I had to go.

Worry made me talk, and I told Dayton everything I knew about Ray. Every detail of my life with him reminded me of some fact about her. She became our imaginary child, and it got to the point that he heard my tales so often he would sometimes tell them himself. "Rayona's favorite," he announced when spooning out Chun King Sweet and Sour Pork. Or, if we were watching a program on TV with a teenage girl in it, something like "Punky Brewster" or "Family Ties," Dayton might mention Ray. "She'd never do anything that dumb," he'd say, looking for me to agree with him. "She's got more on the ball." I thought at first he was just trying to cheer me up, but after a while he got into it for himself.

"Do you think me and Rayona will get along?" Dayton asked from his brown vinyl recliner one evening just before I was about to turn in. He was poker-faced, thinking. His hair was grown out, and curled over his collar. He wore red socks and the snaps of his shirt strained against the swell of his stomach.

I did.

Foxy came over early in the evening of July 3 to help Dayton load Babe into the back of the pickup for her ride to the rodeo.

Fencing had been fixed to the sides of the bed, which was pulled against the open gate of the corral. A runway made of thick boards covered with a piece of shag carpet was rigged to the tailgate. I watched from the open window while Dayton spread the flat bottom of the truck with fresh hay, then waited while Foxy rustled and spooked Babe. It took awhile. She raced by the ramp, flicking her tail and shaking her head, kicking dust into Foxy's new rodeo clothes. Her hooves struck the ground hard as hammers, and she shook the bit, flapping the rope out of Foxy's reach. Finally, as if she knew what she was doing, she charged into the truck so fast that Dayton backed against the cab and waved his arms to ward her off, but the next minute, she had lowered her head to chew some hay, her heaving sides the only sign she was excited.

Foxy slammed the tailgate closed and between the two of them, Dayton and Foxy crisscrossed new yellow rope until Babe was webbed, unable to strain more than a few inches in any direction. Her eyes rolled, keeping track of the men on either side, and from within her chest there rumbled a warning.

"Just keep mad for tomorrow and you'll win me my prize money." Foxy slapped Babe's flank with the flat of his hand. Her neck tensed and she unloaded a stream of shit onto his boot. "Goddamn fuck!" he said, and raised his fist to strike her again, but Dayton told him to get down and clean himself off at the outdoor spigot before the trip to town.

"Are you going to be all right?" Dayton asked when he came inside the house.

"I'm fine."

"What will you do?"

"You'll be back after the show tomorrow night. That's not long. I've got the TV, and I'll straighten the place a little." We looked around the room, which was clean and orderly the way Dayton always kept it, but my answer satisfied him.

"You know who to call if you need anything," he said. "I

hate to leave you, but I've got to make some sense out of buying that horse."

"Just seeing her crap on my lousy cousin should count for something."

Dayton's mouth struggled with a smile.

"If you want to come along I'll guarantee you'll see worse tomorrow. He's no match for her."

"You remember it to tell me," I said.

"You bet I will." He was ready to go, but we hadn't yet worked out between us how to say good-bye for more than a few hours. You couldn't just walk away, but in all the time I had been back, I don't think we had touched each other once.

"I'll call if I'm running late." He patted his back pocket to make sure he had his wallet.

"Go on now, and don't feel you have to put up with Foxy tonight." Then I continued without thinking how my words might sound. "You let him find his own place to sleep."

Dayton's eyes, alert and suspicious of my meaning, darted to challenge me.

"You need your rest with all this driving back and forth." My voice was as bare as the walls of the house, painted over without a chip. "He'll be going out drinking anyway, like as not."

Dayton brought a hand to his face and ran his thumbnail in between two teeth while he made up his mind.

"Well," he said, "okay."

He patted his back pocket again, then his side one for keys. Outside Foxy honked the truck's horn. I walked over to the kitchenette and ran water in the sink to wash the supper dishes. Behind me the door opened and shut, softly, as though Dayton had wanted to keep it from banging.

I never did switch on a light that night, just let the house collect shadows as the sun went down. I never turned on music or the TV. I sat leaned back in Dayton's La-Z-Boy, following the molding around the living room ceiling, sliding the tips of my fingers against the cool, smooth armrests. Before it got too dark to see, I pushed the chair in front of the screen door, hooked the latch, and fetched the blanket off my bed. I sat and raised the footrest, tucking the cover tight around my legs and feet, then pushed the lever and tilted, drawing the wool with me as I went. The evening wasn't cool yet, but it would be, and I didn't plan to move again. As the night deepened, the wire mesh became invisible, a passage opening into the lighter blackness, and before my eyes the stars lit. They were the windows of a faraway city. They were the points of silver nails pressing through tar paper. They were a field of glowbugs, motionless in time.

There'd be no stopping some people if they learned they had only so much time left. They would drink and smoke and party all night, they'd travel to Hawaii, they'd tell everybody off, spill every secret. But me, I took my Independence Day slow, got up with the sun, put away the dishes in the drainer, did a load of wash, made coffee. The hours passed quickly, and every time I saw a clock I wondered where the minutes went. I ate a poached egg for lunch because that was the only thing guaranteed to agree with me, and rested on the couch before I took my bath.

Later, I soaked in the tub until the water turned lukewarm and goosebumps rose on the loose skin of my thighs and upper arms. Then I dried off, put on my nightgown, wrapped myself in Dayton's red corduroy robe, and planned to eat a bowl of tomato soup while I watched for the headlights of Dayton's truck to swing and dip on the long, narrow road. There was about two weeks' worth of Percocet left, and I took each one as far apart as possible to stretch them out. Alone in the house, with no Dayton around to worry if I sighed or held on to furniture when I moved, I didn't plan to take any at all until just before he was due.

But he pulled up early and caught me unexpecting. I swallowed two pills, turned on the TV, and stepped through the door. I wanted to show him I was better, that I had an interest in things, that I was anxious to hear all his news.

• • •

I squinted into the red sun and Lee stepped toward me, young and tall, one braid slung over his shoulder. I shielded my eyes, and he turned into Rayona. I blamed the medicine and kept staring, kept waiting for her to become Dayton, but then I saw Dayton too, off to the side, and I confronted him in a panic he mistook for anger.

"Don't be mad," he said. "She was at the rodeo."

Before I could absorb this news, before I knew where I was, Rayona stepped closer, directly before me. I was weak from relief and confusion, so many questions answered. She was not lost in Seattle or forgetting me with Elgin, she wasn't run off on drugs.

"Don't you want to see me?" she said in a voice loaded with blame and no understanding. She opened in the middle of an argument I had forgotten for an instant that we were having. All the grief I had felt for her, all that I had not let myself think, crouched and sprang. I told her she had worried Aunt Ida to death, that I had been out of my mind, that she was no goddamn good.

That knocked her off her high horse.

"I meant to get in touch," she said, and the lameness of her answer only fired me more. I saw myself, Christine, abused and abandoned in my time of need while my own daughter was off, where?

"I had a job at Bearpaw Lake State Park," she said.

I imagined her at this park I'd never seen. Paddling canoes, roasting hotdogs on the end of sticks, laughing with her friends.

"You left first," she accused me, but I wouldn't hear. I turned to Dayton to take my side.

"It's *my* fault she walked out on Aunt Ida," I announced to him as if it was the stupidest idea in the world. I trusted him to shake his head in amazement, to chastise Ray himself, but all he did was tell me to keep calm.

"I thought you were dead!" I screamed at Rayona, then cut myself off. That was the word I never used.

"A lot you cared. You came for your precious box of pills from Charlene and didn't even wait around."

The pills, the pills.

"What do you know about pills?" I asked her, but she went on complaining. She had the upper hand.

"She has no heart," I said to Dayton. I felt as though I could faint, as though now that all these words were loose in the yard, I had no protection. Dayton moved toward me but Ray wouldn't quit.

"You tried that on Dad and it didn't work. You're not sick."

The thought of Elgin revived me.

"You're just like him," I told her.

Somehow Dayton got us inside. I was in a cloud storm and fought for a clear head. I hid my eyes. The TV news played too loud and filled the room. The announcer's voice battered at me without making any sense. Concentrating, I counted by twos to one hundred.

"Look at that, Christine," Dayton interrupted. Rayona was on TV, except she was back to Lee again, standing on a grandstand with Lee's special buckle, the one he never wore.

"You won't believe who rode Babe," Dayton said from somewhere. "Your kid is a star." His voice was proud, wanting a reaction from me, but I stared at the screen, trying to figure this out. Near me, Dayton and Ray were talking to each other, and I didn't understand their words. The story went off and I turned to Ray. She was still there.

"You rode?" I said. "You only had four lessons."

Dayton was full of his own excitement. He claimed Ray took Foxy's place, said Foxy was shamed good. His words made me think of what we had talked about as he left. Befores and afters mixed in my mind, pressed in on me.

"You're all right?" I asked Ray.

But now Dayton was saying that Lee taught Ray to ride. That was impossible. Nothing was real.

"I can't take this," I said to whoever was there. "I'm going to bed. We'll work this all out tomorrow."

Dayton came to me then, but even he wasn't himself. He put his arm around me, held me against his body like any man would, like I thought no man ever would again. He walked with me, matching steps, toward my room. I clung to him out of more than sickness, inhaled the smell of his sweat and breath, ready for anything.

Just before I reached my door I quick turned back, but Rayona had not vanished. She stood directly next to Lee.

Sometime in the night, the knob turned and Dayton came in. The pills were worn off enough that I was surprised to find him here, in my room, at night. He didn't put on a light, but sat on the bed beside me and reached out to touch my forehead.

"Better?" he whispered.

I moved to sit, but the gentle pressure of his palm held me down. I drew in a breath to ask questions, but he shushed me.

"Just rest. You're done in. She'll still be here in the morning. There's plenty of time."

Only the covers separated our legs. I nestled lower, curled to him in the dark. He was invisible except by feel.

"Stay awhile," I asked.

And it wasn't till I woke just as the sun lit the curtains that I knew he was gone.

In the living room I saw that the couch had been slept on, saw Rayona's clothes in an unfamiliar, open suitcase. The coffee was still on the machine from last night, and I poured myself a cup and then cut it with tap water. There was something I should notice about myself, something new. I drew my robe tight, ran a hand through my hair, then held it out in front of me. It was steady. The tremble I had fought every morning for weeks was gone, set free by events of the night before. Then I realized: the pain was different. It was there, but wrapped in a cotton quilt, stored in a closed room. I could put it out of my mind, take the receiver off the hook to its call. I moved a leg, stretched my upper body an inch at a time, but the ache stayed under control.

Like a woman walking light on her feet in a row just planted, I opened the door and stepped into the morning. I went toward Babe's corral as I usually did, but there before me, asleep on the ground just outside the split-wood fence, was Rayona. She lay stiff and tight the way Lee always looked the day after a rodeo, and I didn't care if she was real or not. I didn't care anything. She was my miracle, and I knelt beside her.

We set up housekeeping. I had my good days and my bad days, Ray was off for summer vacation, and Dayton's fiscal year was over. We did things together, the three of us, planting poplars for a windbreak and taking rides in the truck. On hot days we drove for coolness to the canyon and I was struck by how strong the natural bridge looked, not at all as flimsy as I had remembered. We visited the cemetery and laid wild roses on the markers of Lee and Dayton's mother. In the evenings we watched TV, though it was all reruns in the summer. It was too far to the drive-in even if I had felt good, so one day, as a surprise, Dayton came home with a VCR from Montgomery Ward. The reservation store had started to stock tapes for rent, and Dayton thought video would be the next best thing to going out. Rayona bowled him over when, from the bottom of her suitcase, she produced *Christine* and *Little Big Man*. That first night we had a double feature, starring my old date and the toughest car that ever was. Dayton and I watched from the couch, him sitting with my feet in his lap, and me stretched out with a bed pillow behind my head. Ray lay on her stomach on the floor and made popcorn while Dayton rewound the first movie.

On the Thursday night before my birthday, we invited Aunt Ida over for dinner, fixed by Dayton. He cooked one of those old-fashioned soups they used to make around here, with dried corn and pieces of boiled meat and fresh June berries. Rayona made a sheet of Betty Crocker spice cake and frosted it with instant vanilla pudding. I mixed iced tea and heated some dinner rolls Dayton had bought at the store.

We didn't know what to expect. Aunt Ida had cause to take on each of us, and, as I waited for Dayton to bring her in his truck, I thought it was just a question of which one of us would head the line. But she walked in the house with her natural hair pinned in a bun and a sweater I had sent her two years ago around her shoulders. She couldn't say enough nice about the house and the food, and she said most of it in English for Dayton's benefit. She told Ray to come visit her—that they had lots to talk over—and she brought me a present in a brown paper grocery bag. I couldn't guess what it was as I opened it on my lap. I reached inside and drew out my yearbook, Class of '63.

"I thought you might want it to remember," she said.

She had the page with my picture marked. I wore too much makeup and a ratted beehive hairdo. I had listed "Boys" as my hobby, and had been a member of the Daughters of Mary in my freshman year. To myself, I looked exactly the same.

Dayton angled over my shoulder to see. He flipped back from the seniors to the sophomores and there he was, burr haircut, skinny again, in one of his white T-shirts. They just gave his initial with his last name, "D. Nickles," and he had no activities listed for that year. I stared at his picture. Not long after it was made, I had got him out in an open field during a night powwow. Looking at the two of us, him and me as we were then, I could understand what scared him.

"Guess who?" Dayton said to Rayona, pointing at his picture.

"How come they didn't use your first name?" She seemed pissed off.

"A lot of people used to make fun of it."

I turned back another page.

"There's your Uncle Lee."

Rayona peered closer. "How old was he then?"

I thought about that, counted the years.

"About fifteen."

"My age," she said.

Dayton and I both turned to look at her. To us Ray was

still a kid and Lee, even then, was . . . something else. I tried to think about Rayona the way we did about Lee, and it was impossible.

Aunt Ida had been listening in. "You're taller," she said to Ray, "but he carried more weight. It amounts to the same thing."

Dayton went to the kitchen to make coffee and I lay on the couch. Rayona flicked back the recliner and snapped the remote control for the TV. She never tired of browsing through Dayton's sixty-six stations. Aunt Ida sat in a wooden chair that she insisted was better for her back.

It was nine o'clock, and "Knots Landing" was beginning. Aunt Ida said she never missed it. The rest of us usually watched "Hill Street Blues," so she explained the plot as it unfolded.

"Val and Gary really love each other," she said during the first commercial, "but he got to drinking and she divorced him. Then they had twin babies but nobody but Val knew he was the daddy. The babies got kidnapped and she lost her mind, but now they're back and Gary wants to claim them."

Gary was light blond and so were the babies. Anybody could see he was the father, and not the dark-haired Ben whom Val was married to now. It was all confused. Everybody loved everybody else and no one was happy.

"I like that Karen," Aunt Ida said during the next break. "She sees through them all, even Abby."

Abby was Gary's wife, but she cheated on him and rubbed smears of shadow around her eyes. She looked like me in my high school picture.

"What do you think's going to happen?" Ray asked when the program was over and Abby had gotten Gary to go to bed with her.

"Val ought to forget him," Aunt Ida said. She had lost her patience with their mistakes. "He's nothing but weak. That Ben's no good either. You can tell he's going to leave her when he finds out the truth. She's going to be stuck with those damn twins."

Dayton caught my eye and shook his head, but he didn't have to worry.

I limited myself to one activity a day, and I could handle that. Most of the time that thing was done with Rayona. Dayton had towed the Volaré to his house from where Aunt Ida had stored it, and he managed to get it running again. It turned out not to have such a serious problem, just a fuel line clogged for some reason with diesel gas. I decided to teach Rayona how to drive and she was a quick study. You have to have wheels, living in the country.

About that time, Dayton saw an announcement put in the paper by a man twenty miles west of Havre. "Top Quality Proven Appaloosa Brood Stallion," it said. "Stud Fee $175." He called the number that was listed, and the next day he and Ray lured Babe back into the converted pickup and carted her off for a week's stay. They wanted me to come along for the ride but I took a rain check. I had lost so much weight in my arms and legs, and had developed such a bloated stomach, that I was ashamed to be seen in public; plus, try as I might to hold down my dosage, I had to take more Percocets every day just to endure when people were around. At the rate I was going I would run out, and then I'd have no choice but to turn myself in at the Agency hospital.

At the start, Dayton was all for that idea. He was convinced that some medical breakthrough had occurred while I was holed up at his house, and that all my problems would be solved if I saw a doctor. I had no such faith. Too many people I knew checked into the hospital and never came out, and I was happy where I was, where no machines measured my decline and nobody told me when to go to bed or wake. At Dayton's there were times I could live as if I had forever.

On the day that Rayona and Dayton and Babe were gone, I had a visitor. When he came to the door I didn't know who he was, just a bald-headed, red-lipped man in a cheap green sports shirt and black pants, but I recognized the truck he drove as the same one Father Hurlburt used to bring Aunt Ida, after Ray ran away. I wasn't dressed, so I left the man outside while we talked.

"Christine?" he said, as if he had known me all his life. The "s" in my name hissed through his teeth, and no matter how much he spread his mouth in a smile, his eyes were hard. I nodded my head and wished somebody else was home.

"I hear you're a little under the weather," he went on.

I was afraid he was here to take me to the hospital.

"Who says?" I asked. "Who are you?"

"Where are my manners? I am Father Tom Novak, the assistant pastor at the Mission? Perhaps your daughter mentioned me to you?" His stare got even harder, like the eyes of an animal dead on the road, and he frightened me.

"No."

"Oh, I see. I thought she might have. Well, anyway, your—mother, is it?—dropped by the Mission the other day and persuaded me that you had need of my good services. She can be quite forceful."

I didn't know what he was talking about. Was he here, dressed in civilian clothes, to give me the Last Rites? Was I that bad off?

He searched in his pocket and brought out his hand, closed around something. I looked, expecting to see a crucifix or holy oils, but instead there was a big plastic bottle of white pills.

"I trust these are the right kind," he said. "Ida only had one sample with her, but my druggist friend was sure he recognized the type."

I was stunned. When he held out the bottle, I took it.

"And of course, after they're gone, you call the rectory and ask for Father Tom. No need to bother Father Hurlburt. Tell your mother that too. It will be our little secret."

"I thank you," I finally managed.

"Yes, well..." He looked behind me into the house. "Rayona is not here today?"

Then it came to me who he was. He must be the one who told Aunt Ida that Ray had gone to Seattle on her own.

"Aunt Ida *did* mention you," I said, embarrassed and ready to thank him again, but he closed his mouth in a pink line and turned back toward his truck. All his pretend friendliness was over.

"You've got what you wanted," he said. "So all of you just leave Father Hurlburt out of it."

For the flash of a second, as he climbed into the truck, the thin calf of his leg was exposed between his black sock and the cuff of his pants. After I closed the door, when I sat down at the kitchen table and opened my fingers to examine the beautiful bottle filled to the top, that was the only part of him I could clearly remember.

I thought about Babe often during that week, wondering what her proven brood stallion was like and if she was enjoying her honeymoon. I hoped for her sake that "top quality" was not just something to put in a newspaper ad. I wanted Dayton to call and see how she was getting along, but he said we'd find out soon enough. He meant we'd know whether or not she was pregnant, but I didn't. If the Appaloosa was that good, was the best, I knew Babe would have a colt.

Rayona had graduated to learning a stick, and I talked Dayton into driving the Volaré to work and leaving us the pickup to practice with. I was normal for a couple of hours in the mornings, and Ray and I went out on the empty roads together, though I felt every jerk and stall in my stomach. She sat high on the driver's seat, her back arched, her hands on either side of the wheel, her chin high. Sometimes she reminded me so much of Elgin when I first met him.

She wore a blue peaked cap and a red T-shirt from the park where she worked. She used her turn signals, even when you could see in all directions for three miles and no cars were in sight. She put on the emergency when she helped me down, and she cleaned the windshield inside and out with vinegar and wadded newspapers.

She was itching to take a long trip, to try out her wings, and when Babe's week was done I suggested to Dayton that Ray and I go alone to bring her home. I had called the man with the proven stallion, and he agreed to get Babe tied in the back of the truck for us.

"You're not up to it." Dayton sat across the kitchen table from me with his face worried in a new way, as though my idea made him wonder if I was fooling myself about the condition of my health.

"I'm as up to it as I'm going to get," I told him. "This is something I want to do."

"Let me come along, then. It's not that short a trip."

He was thinking of my brief span of grace, and concerned with what would happen when I ran out of steam. I reached across the woodgrain surface and nested my hand on top of his. Aging had changed us. My skin used to be so much darker and now we were almost the same color. He reached his other hand over and put it on mine, made a sandwich.

"Let me go alone with her this time." I closed my fingers on the tops of his knuckles, squeezed, and after a second, all around my bottom hand, he squeezed back, agreeing.

When I told Rayona, first thing on Friday morning, she looked immediately to Dayton to get his okay, and he didn't let on he had any objections.

"It would be a favor," he said. "I've got a desk full of proposals to submit for the tribe, and if I don't get that horse home today I'll have to pay another week's stud."

Ray didn't have to be asked twice. "You drive," I urged her. I lolled out my window, propping my chin on my fist, and yelled to Dayton in the doorway, "If we're not back by midnight, call out the marines!"

"I won't wait up," he said. "Don't you two pick up any cowboys now."

"Hey, can't a girl have some fun?"

Rayona started smooth and shifted into second without a hitch. It was the end of August and promised to be a hot day, over a hundred by afternoon. It was two hours to the ranch where we were headed, and two back. I figured an hour's stop for food and gas, an hour there, six altogether. Home by one o'clock. The truck had air conditioning but I worried about Babe, stuck in the open, if we were later than that.

"Sometime," Ray said, "I'll take you over to Bearpaw Lake and introduce you around to the people I stayed with."

"Maybe when it cools off."

"You met one of them," she went on. "Remember the hippie who tried to sell you the new tires when we drove out here."

I didn't but said I did.

"Sky," she said. "His wife Evelyn is the cook there."

"That reminds me. You want to eat?"

"You want to?"

"There's a Prairie Kitchen just this side of Havre," I said. "Breakfast twenty-four hours. All kinds of things."

"O-kay," Ray agreed.

Once we got off the reservation the road smoothed out and the going was easier. I turned on the radio, then regretted it. "Everything That Glitters" had slipped to number twenty-six. I rolled down the window to admit a blast of hot air with all the morning moisture already dried from it. I adjusted the side mirror till I could see myself, then I closed the glass and slouched down on the seat with my neck against the back. To Rayona it would appear that I was gazing at the scenery as it flew by, at the faded Burma Shave signs nailed to the fence posts, at the billboards advertising motels with HBO and waterbeds, at the elevators that rose from the land like towers without their castles. And I noticed those things, every one, but in the middle of them, riding high and steady as a lighted island, was my own reflection looking back at me.

The restaurant was cleared of the morning rush by the time we arrived, so we took a booth for four. The menu was printed on the placemats, and the waitress poured two coffees without being asked.

"You get anything you like," I told Ray. I still had most of the forty dollars I took with me from Seattle.

"What are you going to have?"

I wasn't hungry but I wanted to encourage her to think big.

"I think I'll order one of their Classic Breakfasts." I read the list and stopped at Cakes 'n' Eggs: Two country fresh eggs, two buttermilk pancakes, warm syrup, two strips of bacon and two sausage links for $2.99. I liked the idea of the warm syrup. "I'll get the number four, if you promise to finish what I can't."

Ray studied her placemat, choosing.

"Then I'll have the Skillet Number One," she said.

I read her choice aloud. "'Crispy hash-browned potatoes, topped with two farm fresh eggs and sausage, onion and green pepper, served with toast and jelly. Only $3.45.' If I ate that I wouldn't last another day."

My words hung between us until the waitress came for our order.

"Classic Four for me," I told her, "and Skillet One for my girlfriend here."

Rayona glanced up, woken out of her mood, and I winked. While she went to the rest room I took another pill, my third today, and by the time the food arrived I was buzzed, swimming along on top of it all. I even ate a little egg white and a bite of pancakes, then I pushed my plate in front of Rayona, and excused myself to the Ladies'.

The idea came to me while I was using the silky dispenser soap. With my hands slick and wet and my fingers now so thin, my rings fell into the porcelain sink like coins in a collection basket. I grabbed them up, started to put them back on, but then I stopped and examined them one at a time, looked at my empty fingers.

There was a paper towel dispenser, and I pulled out three sheets. The abalone I wrapped for Aunt Ida. The roadrunner for Dayton. The thin gold wedding ring, the one I had worn the longest, the one that still left a dent in my skin, I saved for Elgin. I put all three in the pocket of my jeans.

I buffed my prize, my solid silver turtle, on the soft material of my blouse, and it looked like new. I carried it in my fist.

"I've got something for you," I said when I slid back into my seat.

Rayona was chasing the last of her hash browns around the plate, anxious to start on my sausages, but I had her interest.

"This is to celebrate your license," I told her. "It's early but I know you'll pass when you take the test."

I set the ring on the table between us, in the place where it would catch the gleam of light from the window.

"It's real silver. Sandcast in the desert."

Ray didn't make a move, just sat frozen with her fork full of potatoes and ketchup.

"Try it on." The perfect little turtle, its pointy head raised, rode on the empty circle of the ring. "He always reminded me of me," I said. "Slow but gets there in the end."

Ray took it, pushed it as far as it would go on each of her fingers until it fit on the smallest. She turned her hand, showed me.

The waitress appeared with the tab and I reached for my purse, but Rayona was quicker.

"My treat. I earned good money at Bearpaw Lake." She opened her wallet and revealed a wad of cash, then, embarrassed, tried to stuff it back inside the pocket. A torn piece of notepaper dropped on the table and I retrieved it, afraid she hadn't seen. She took it from my hand, thought a minute, then crumpled it into the ashtray.

"I'm done," she said, and took the check to the cashier. I left the tip.

Babe was not happy to see us, which I took as a good sign. She braced her rear legs, and it took two men to push and pull her onto the bed of the pickup, and two more to hold her still while the ropes went around and under to restrain her. She gave them hell, whinnying back and forth with another horse, locked in the barn. I sat in the cool cab, listening to the radio, and watched through the window while Rayona got out to settle the fee with the rancher. The program was almost over. Just four songs left.

The sun was so glaring it gave me a headache. I groped in the glove compartment until I found a set of smudged amber-tinted glasses. When I put them on, they turned the world yellow as an old photograph. It was almost noon and we were behind my schedule. The truck shook with the stamp of Babe's hooves on the metal floor. I was more tired than I ever felt.

The driver's door opened and Rayona swung in, hot and pleased with herself. Sure as if she had been doing it for years, she wiggled the gearshift, and brought the engine from idle to life. She suddenly twisted her body toward me, and I leaned, ready to meet her, but she kept turning, a whole half-circle, to rest her elbow on the back of the seat and look out the rear before reversing the truck the length of the yard.

"You know what that guy said?" she asked me, her voice full of something to tell.

"What?"

"He said..." She swung forward and straightened her wheels. "He said that Babe and his horse fell in love. He said he never saw a thing like it. That's why it was so hard to get Babe into the truck. She wanted to stay."

Rayona accelerated down the long lane that led between fenced pastures. Babe's feet beat a constant rhythm. On "Country Countdown" Judy Rodman's song had reached number three and was still climbing. I let the music carry me as I resettled into my comfortable position and turned my head low to the window. It was a shock to see the dark glasses on my face. The light was so bright and gold I had forgotten I had them on.

Ida

17

I never grew up, but I got old.

I'm a woman who's lived for fifty-seven years and worn resentment like a medicine charm for forty. It hung heavier on my neck after each brief rest I took. I should have kept myself free of them all. If I were to live my life differently, I would start with the word No: first to him, my father; to Clara, then to Willard, before they left me; to Lee, to save his life. I was different with Christine, but it turned out no better.

I tell my story the way I remember, the way I want. And though I can speak their English better than they think, better than most of them, I prefer my own language. I use the words that shaped my construction of events as they happened, the words that followed my thought, the words that gave me power. My recollections are not tied to white paper. They have the depth of time.

I have to tell this story every day, add to it, revise, invent the parts I forget or never knew. No one but me carries it all and no one will—unless I tell Rayona, who might understand. She's heard her mother's side, and she's got eyes. But she doesn't guess what happened before. She doesn't know my true importance. She doesn't realize that I am the story, and that is my savings, to leave her or not.

My life is a ring of mountains, close together and separated by deep chasms. From any summit I look back and view, not an arm's length away, the ones before. The roads down and up are steep. They drop from view, and I stare into the places I've stood, across the log bridges of my memory.

I see the first peak clearly, as if only a minute came between then and now. I was fifteen, in the new rush of my awareness, too naïve to recognize a point of deciding, when Mama conceded her long fight to be well, and called for her baby sister, Clara.

When I opened our front door to Clara's knock, the laughter at some joke of Pauline's still falling from my mouth, my mind on the next retort I would make, she was so young and pretty, so prim and quiet, so unexpected an aunt, that I was instantly moved to protection. I reached for the handle of her carpet valise and closed my fingers around hers, drawing her into the room. Her hair was busy with curls and bobby pins, and her high-waisted dress was striped black and white. She wore sheer stockings, shiny patent high heels, and a spot of rose color on each cheek. For jewelry she had a sparkle ring and a gold cross hung around her neck. She stood uncertain in strange surroundings, wondering who I was, what her welcome would be, and the neatness of her took my breath.

I had never seen Clara before but I claimed her. The first words out of my mouth, even before introductions, were to tell her Pauline's joke, invite her to laugh too. She tried to join in, smiled her approval, measured the room with her eyes, and shook Pauline's shy hand.

"I should see Annie," she said, looking from one closed door to another, listening for signs of her sister, but I couldn't let her go yet.

"She's asleep, resting," I said.

I led her to my tiny room, sent Pauline across the fields for Papa. Clara sat on my bed and unpacked her clothes, described her brave ride on the train. I tried her leather shoes and found my own feet too long. I dabbed a drop of her perfume under my nose. She promised to someday arrange my hair in a wavy pompadour like hers.

The people where Clara lived had a way of speaking our

language just different enough to be interesting to me. The ends of her words hesitated and blurred, making her sentences run together. She sounded as though she had more⁺ to say than in fact she did.

I never relinquished the advantage of seeing Clara first, and it didn't take Pauline long to resent Clara for my fascination. I could see the beginning of jealousy in my sister's eyes when, winded and streaked with sweat, she burst through the door.

"Papa's coming," Pauline announced, quick to notice whose bed Clara used, whose room she inhabited. "What's that?"

Pauline had caught me with my arms and head lost in the soft white fabric of Clara's nightgown, bunched around my shoulders before I let it fall over my clothes and past my knees.

"Clara said I could," I told her after only a second's pause.

"It's too small for you, as any fool can see," Pauline sneered.

I blushed at my size, felt the material strain at the seams around the shoulders and across the back.

"No, no," Clara broke in. "It's just that she's still dressed."

I gave her a look of pure thanks, and the tips of her mouth curved in a private smile. An unworthy thought crossed my mind, too fast to catch: Mama's sickness brought me Clara.

I was shocked at my own greedy cruelty, but before I could feel shame, we heard Papa enter the next room. Clara leapt to her feet, clasped her hands together, wet her lips.

"We're in here, Papa," Pauline called and rushed out, leaving Clara and me alone. I paid her back.

"You look so nice," I said. "Not like someone who has had a long trip."

She touched her hair, shaped it in a mirror she had brought, licked the tips of her little fingers and ran them along her eyebrows, smoothing the dark hairs into straight lines.

"I haven't seen your father in years." She was talking to me because I was there, but it was more that she was thinking aloud to herself. "He used to be . . . I'll never forget when I met him for the first time, when he came to court Annie. So tall and forceful, big like you. He won't remember me, I was such a plump little thing."

Clara tugged at some hidden undergarment and plucked the material of her skirt away from the back of her legs, where it had stuck from sitting down. She cleared her throat, smiled at me again for courage. She carried her purse when she left the room, as if going to a store, and I followed in the scent of her perfume.

I ached for Clara, worried at what Papa would say to her. He hated to live under the watch of anyone, and had resisted bringing an outsider to our house. He had tried to manage alone during the weeks that Mama weakened, teetering between sickness and the hope of improvement. He went to the store for the food I cooked, he washed Mama's sheets for Pauline to hang in the sun, and he sat long into the night by Mama's side, stroking her arm and whispering words too soft for me to hear. But finally one morning Mama stayed in bed and was still there, her hair unbraided and snarled, her pale hand pressed to her chest, when we returned from our classes at the Mission.

With his spring day labor, Papa had to leave the house before the sun rose and often didn't get back until late at night. I volunteered to quit school, and argued that the nuns would be glad to see me go since I was their constant trial, an uncooperative girl who wouldn't obey the rules, who tormented her teachers by pretending to be stupid. They were not fooled, and that bothered them all the more. I was the one with potential, the one whose soul and grammar they had come to save, and I wouldn't let them.

But Papa was too proud, and refused my offer. He feared that others on the reservation would say he lived off the work of his daughter, that he had exhausted his wife. He was even ashamed of Mama's bad heart, as if that were his fault too, and made us promise to lie about her condition. Everyone must think us the perfect family.

Mama knew this, of course, and so from her bed she was able to devise a plan that Papa could not reject.

"Tell them," she said at last, "that my younger sister is homeless and has no place to go. Tell them we will shelter her until she finds direction. Then send for Clara."

I saw Papa think about this idea, weigh in his mind the comments that would follow such an announcement: remarks on his generosity, on his kindness to Mama's family in their need, on his ability to squeeze another person into a small space.

Mama waited, her face strained with worry that he would say no and leave her alone through the long hot hours of the lengthening days.

"Clara's quiet," Mama added to her argument. "You remember. She was called 'the fish.'"

Papa looked at her, his gaze bleak with intensity, willing her to be restored and remove this complication from his life, but Mama's head rested on her pillow as deep as if there were no muscles in her neck. The plea in her eyes absorbed all his questions, swallowed his objections, convinced him he had no choice.

"You get the new priest to send for her," he said. "Until you're well."

A priest was bound by his own vow of silence and could not reveal the incapacity admitted in Papa's house.

And now the letter had been answered. Papa sat at the kitchen table, staring into the tea Pauline had fixed for him, resisting the sounds of our approach. He held his privacy till the last second, then glanced at Clara. His lids widened. He held his breath, then expelled it. He lifted his head so he could look at her straight on, then he scraped back his chair and rose to his feet.

"You're Clara," he said, as if giving her news.

"Yes."

She stood nailed to the floor, the black stripes of her dress framing her body, the heels of her shoes pressed together, her lashes lowered.

Papa's eyes were set deep in the sun-darkened skin of his face. His hair was long and full, disappearing down his back behind his broad shoulders. He wore a green workshirt, stained with oil and white paint, tight around his waist. The sleeves were rolled over strong, hairless forearms that tapered to slim wrists before swelling again into thick square palms and blunt fingers. Above his mouth grew a few unplucked whiskers, and his brows were as black and rich as mink. The pale line of a healed cut passed over the arch of his nose before it dropped to furrow a cleft through the left side of his upper lip.

"I was sorry to hear about Annie," Clara whispered, nervous for his reaction, but silence rang in the room. Pauline and I were the audience, each standing behind her champion, caught in the spell of their confusion. A rattle drew our attention to the stove, to the kettle that had begun to boil afresh, and we spoke through it.

"Give her tea," Papa told Pauline.

"I'll do it." I moved around the table and into the drier, sharper heat of the wood fire.

"Don't trouble," Clara spoke. "If you have water, something cool." She raised her head to meet Papa's steady look. "You're very kind, but . . . the day seems hot for tea."

Papa gave Pauline a silent command, and she uncovered the barrel and dipped a cup into its darkness. She started to hand it over to Clara but then caught some further signal from Papa and stopped, found a clean glass on the shelf, and poured the water in. Papa took the glass from her, passed it himself, and Clara smiled her thanks through small sips.

"Do you think poor Annie's awake by now?" Clara inquired of us. "She's the one I came for, after all."

Mama told me later, before she died, that she and Clara had never been friendly. Too many years lay between their ages, and Clara was too much the baby of the family, the unanticipated late child, to behave like a true sister.

"Then why did you send for her?" I asked.

"Because she was the one who would come. I had no way to see what it would mean."

I shushed her, told her to rest. Still, she was to blame. She should have known, she might have predicted.

At first it seemed that Clara resisted everything I wanted to give her: my bed and my small room when I crowded in with Pauline, my drawers in the bureau, the organdy material I had saved for a new dress, the last slice of blackberry pie in the tin. It became a challenge to make her accept my presents, and I felt victorious when I overcame her objections. But Papa was worse than me. He insisted on buying her special hair soaps, and ordered new boots for her feet when summer rain turned our ground to mud. He wouldn't let Clara pack wood for the stove, much less chop it from the logs he kept behind the house, and he began to wash in the trough outdoors before coming inside at the end of the day.

At first it seemed that Clara's arrival had lightened the air we breathed. The bed rest brought color back to Mama's face, and while Pauline and I cleaned and cooked, Clara could spend a whole afternoon filing Mama's fingernails or picking flowers to decorate the rooms.

In the dusks of late summer, when a western breeze was strong enough to keep away the mosquitoes, I invited Clara to my special place, to the low overhang of roof, reached through the lone attic window, where no one could hear our conversations. Reclining full length on the shingles, still warm from the afternoon sun, I confided my secrets and sought her advice. I revealed my humiliation, my shame at being unloved by any boy in my class. Everyone else, it seemed to me, had paired into couples who would marry after graduation.

"Is there none that you want?" Clara asked one early evening.

I laughed in embarrassment but mentioned Willard Pretty Dog, the one all the girls wanted, the one whose golden life we dreamed to touch, the one whose rare smile was remarked about for days, the one who could have his choice, but kept to himself.

"Why not?" Clara asked.

I propped myself on my elbow and looked at her. All around us the moving clouds, flattened on the bottom and billowy on top, were streaked with the long red lines of sunset and the sky was a darkening pink. Clara's eyes were closed, and her arms stretched above her head. The wind had blown her skirt high on her legs and brushed the hair away from her face.

"He's shorter than I am," I said. "And anyway, he's heard of some all-Indian army regiment he wants to join. He's going to lie about his age so he can fight before the war is over."

"Just wait then," she told me. "Men come around in the end. If all the girls catch all the other boys, then you'll be the one left to get him."

I lay back, irrationally encouraged by her sureness. In my mind I molded myself into her shape, imagined that her features became my own, her delicate nose, her round face, her slanted eyes. I imagined greeting Willard on his return with this face, imagined the delight of his pleasure, the clasp of his hand.

Now that the task of Mama's care was lifted, Papa earned bonus money from his job. Exercise turned his body lean and young, and sometimes late at night I'd hear his laugh explode at something Mama or Clara had said, or at some joke of his own. To save Mama's comfort, he slept on the floor by the stove, on a pallet made of rugs and blankets, but he bragged he rested well, swore it was no hardship.

Only Pauline resisted the pull of Clara's presence. For a while I thought she had discovered a vocation, since every day after school she helped the nuns at the Mission with their labors. Her knees grew rough and red from kneeling in the scrub water she sloshed on the stone church tiles, and her prayerbook blossomed with holy cards the sisters gave her in payment. The rosary she won at the Labor Day bazaar was her pride. She let no one but Mama touch it, even when she first brought it home to show. Each set of its ten Hail Marys was a different pastel shade, pink and green and blue and violet and white, with the mysteries between them marked by silver metal balls. On its unusual cross, Christ stood clothed in a long-sleeved robe, His arms outstretched.

During the day Pauline displayed the beads around the post on her side of our bed, and at night she lay with them twined in her fingers, praying with such passion that any but the loudest sounds from elsewhere in the house were overwhelmed. It's no wonder the rosary attracted Clara's attention. One afternoon Pauline and I came home from school to find it on the kitchen table, spread like a lariat before Clara. She smiled at our surprised faces.

"Would you let me have this sometime, do you think, Pauline?" she asked. "I know my prayers would sing."

We stared into the loop of pale colors that seemed to float on the scrubbed wood like tangled fishline in water.

"They must have made this up with beads left over from regular rosaries," Clara continued in a pensive voice. "A sort of quilt, you know, scraps combined to good effect."

Described this way, it was impossible to think of the rosary otherwise. It turned into its own opposite, as secondhand as the contributed clothes we wore or the surplus foods we ate.

Clara's index finger nudged and lightly tapped the rosary while she talked, forming it rounder and rounder, with the string of five beads that ended in the cross jutting at an angle.

"Now it's the ball of the world in the Infant of Prague's hand." She rose and left the table, went into her room for something. All that she did was wonderful to me, so I followed, left Pauline to stand alone, to think what I had thought: that the two weren't at all alike. The Infant's globe was known to be solid gold, but the rosary was a hollow circle.

Those beads remained on the table, shoved in a heap to one side, through the weeks of surprises and troubles that followed. Pauline, whose job it was to clear, was blind to them. She collected the dirty dishes and mopped the spills of our meals, but left the rosary untouched. I grew so used to its presence that it became invisible, and by the next time I remembered to notice, it had been thrown out.

■ ■ ■

Another month passed, its time obscured by the late coming of winter. At night, grass turned brittle and gray, the ground crusty, but the sun by afternoon had restored color and moisture to the earth. My grades improved because if Clara helped me with my homework, I had her to myself for an hour after supper. She wrote a perfect Palmer hand, each letter of script shaped and sized, and I copied it. The sums and themes I submitted became suddenly the fulfillment of the nuns' wishes— on time, neat, humble. I took pride, as they had urged me to do, or, rather, Clara took it. She celebrated with me the receipt of a fine red A, exclaimed at every *Excellent,* cautioned Pauline to emulate my progress, praised my work to Mama and Papa.

I told Clara my every thought. Her compressed smile, surrendered only when I overcame all defenses of her composure, was my goal and my reward. I mimicked her speech, altered my clothes to match the drape of those she wore, traded Pauline's confidence without regret, and was wary for any sign of Mama's improvement lest it signal Clara's departure.

I need not have worried. Clara had not come to leave alone.

It was close on to Christmas, the beginning of vacation, when I arrived home to a dark house. All the way up the hill I wondered at the unlit lamps, the quiet, and quickened my steps. In my arms were the gifts I had made or earned under the supervision of the nuns—a baked clay ashtray for Papa, a Saint Joseph prayerbook for Pauline, a crocheted mat for Mama's tray—and a large package, wrapped in silver foil and tied with white satin ribbon, special for Clara. It was not until I stopped to set them inside the door, then stood, that I heard from two sources the sounds of crying. The louder noise, the wailing, came from Mama's room. But it was the soft sniffling from Clara's that attracted me, stumbling, clutched of heart, to the bed that had been mine.

My eyes fell first on the suitcase, belted and waiting by the door, and then on Clara, dressed in her striped travel clothes, sitting on the edge of the mattress, her face buried in the unfolded white handkerchief she held in her open palms. I knelt at her feet, wrapped my arms around her legs, rested my head against her knee, and wept also. Her grief was unexpected, overwhelming. I was beyond words, beyond questions.

"I had to wait for you," she said through the starched linen.

Tears poured from my eyes. I gripped her slim, silkened legs to my chest.

"She'll tell you to hate me now, I know it."

I pulled back. The thought of hating Clara was so incredible, so impossible, that I raised my head in shock.

"Who?" I demanded, ready to deny Clara's words, ready to defend her.

"Annie. Your mother. But it's not my fault. I never meant it to happen."

It occurred to me that Clara was prompting me to ask what she meant, to force the story from her, but I rejected this thought.

"Tell me," I begged.

"You'll hate me too."

"I'll never hate you."

"Promise?"

"Yes. Yes, I promise."

Clara straightened her back, lowered the handkerchief, blinked into the dim light. She squared herself on the mattress and brought her feet together. I leaned back against my heels and looked up at her, but she spoke to the door, to the persistent sounds of Mama's sorrow.

"I'm pregnant," Clara said.

My mind spun, searching for fathers.

"But you're not showing," I argued. "You've been here for months, and you'd show."

"I'm not that far along."

"Then..." You don't grow up on a reservation without knowing the time a baby takes.

Clara raised the cloth, a white curtain, a white flag, before her face. "Lecon" was all she said.

It took me more time than it should have, to recognize Papa's name.

For once Pauline stopped her night prayers. We lay side by side, not even pretending to sleep, listening to the argument in the room beyond. Mama charged Clara with sneaking into the house like an enemy, charged that she had always coveted Papa, berated her for taking advantage of illness to have her way. Clara offered no shield. She absorbed guilt like the bed of a dry pond sucks water. No name Mama hurled was as bad as those Clara called herself, no crime so evil as her own. In frustration Mama turned her anger on Papa, but was shouted down.

"Who invited her here? Who sent me from my own bed?"

When Mama was speechless, Papa railed at Clara.

"You swore it was safe. You knew the secrets. Now what will people say?"

"Nothing to me," Clara said. "I'm leaving. My bag is packed."

"But you told them at the store. When I went to buy tobacco they knew. 'A baby's due at your house,' they crowed."

"I never said mine. Ours. I just said 'a baby.' I had to tell someone."

There was a lull, a catching of breath. Mama coughed a long series, the raking sounds hard against the walls of the quiet room.

"Who will take care of *her*?" Clara's voice was calmer, under control.

There was no answer.

"It's your own shame you care about. Not mine, not Annie's. If you could think of a way to clear your name, you'd have me stay. To mind my sister."

"I don't want you here," Mama said. Her voice was painful, pitched high.

"There's no way." Papa was thinking, seeking a solution.

"It was an accident," Clara said. "Annie, I swear on the baby's life it won't happen again. I don't know why I let him."

"*Let* me?"

"I swear, Annie. You need me. The girls too. A 'little mother' till you're well."

"Little mother" was the name I called her, the old Indian word, rarely used, more than an aunt. Next to me, Pauline shifted. I could feel her muscles flex in protest, but I hung suspended, too confounded to know what I wanted or didn't want.

"If only we could think of a way." Clara's words had a tone I recognized. It was the same as when she helped me with an essay, when she'd ask, "Now *why* do you say that," trying to draw me out, leading me to what she planned for me to find.

"I only told them 'a baby,'" she repeated.

"They won't believe it's mine," Mama said. "They know I was barren after Pauline."

"If it wasn't me, they'd never suspect Lecon," Clara continued as if Mama had not spoken.

"Whose then?" Papa was impatient with this game. *"Pauline's? Ida's?"*

My name dropped in the air a beat too long. My skin went cold.

"If it *was* Ida's," Clara said, "no one would be surprised. Everyone's aware she's after Willard Pretty Dog. . . ."

I wanted to sink into the pillow at her betrayal, at her low opinion of me. She knew Willard was only a hope.

"And it's nothing for a young girl, inexperienced. People would forget, forgive her."

"No!" Mama was weak, tired. I listened for Papa's indignation, for his anger at Clara's suggestion, but instead he spoke, slow and careful.

"She would have to agree, even if we could hide the truth."

"I could go away with her, bring her back after." Clara was ready with ideas. "She would do it for me," she whispered. "Then I could stay here as long as I was needed. Raise the child. No one would know."

"Why don't *you* go away alone?" Mama said. "Go away and never come back."

The thought of missing Clara filled my mind. When this nightmare was over, she would be gone and I would be empty in her absence.

"Is that what you want, Lecon? Will you let me leave?" Clara shut Mama out, made it between herself and Papa. They weren't talking about a baby or about me, but about themselves.

There was another break, a waiting, a moment of choosing.

"She would never agree," Papa said, as if I were the only thing holding him back.

In my mind I imagined their eyes staring at our closed door, calling me to save them. I turned back the covers, shook off the hand Pauline grasped around my wrist. The boards were cold on my bare feet. I hugged a blanket around my shoulders and lifted the latch. They were placed where I pictured them from the distance of their voices: Mama seated at the table, Papa standing by the door, Clara on the floor by the stove, her back against the wall. They had known I would hear, but were surprised that I came so quickly.

"Yes," I said, when I should have said no.

That Christmas is a vacant place between those that came before and those that came after. I have no remembrance of the meal we ate, of the presents I received, the church service we must have attended. But I do recall one event, clear as a sharp photograph, apart and unconnected to anything else.

Clara wears the dress of my organdy, an artificial leaf of holly pinned in her hair just above her ear. She bends over the table, intent on her box from me. She loosens the bowknot with her fingernail, slowly winds and saves the satin ribbon into a thick tunnel around two fingers, then places it to the side. She rips the silver paper and raises the lid with both hands, prolonging the moment.

But then the picture stalls. All memory of my gift is gone.

The young priest at the Mission was named Hurlburt. He was dark-haired and thin, with eyes so blue people wouldn't look into them. In his first year on the reservation, he had gained a reputation for secrecy. He forgot the sins he heard in the box at the rear of the church. He never told his superior, Father Gephardt, if people came to Mass drunk or didn't come at all. He was a wall through which gossip didn't pass, and so was both feared and safe. People needed him for what he couldn't tell, and dreaded what he knew.

When he came in answer to Papa's message, when he listened to the story Clara repeated a third time for him—of her nighttime rape by a masked drifter, of our family's honor, of the scheme we now pressed on her in thanks for the help she had provided—his expression didn't change. Beneath his large nose, his thin lips touched and parted as he tried to follow her combination of Indian and English. His large black shoes protruded beneath his cassock, and his narrow hands with their tiny nails lay like dead pike in his lap.

The door to Mama's room was closed, for she refused to have a part in this plan. Since the midnight of the argument she had been cold and hostile, more to me than to anyone, but she offered no word of objection. Papa stood behind my chair where I couldn't see his face but felt his presence, heard the draw of his breath, sensed the shift of his weight from one foot to another. Pauline had not come home, but ate, as she had every night for a week, with her nuns, and returned late only to sleep, hunched into a tight lump on the far side of our bed.

Clara finished and Father Hurlburt turned his frightening eyes on me.

"Ida, my child," he said. "Do you know what is asked of you?"

I nodded, averting my look.

"Are you willing to endure this sacrifice, to suffer the scorn of others, to care for this child as if it were your own, to keep this secret forever?"

The words tumbled from him like one of the litanies they sang at Easter, words only used in church, recited like the vows at a wedding. I knew from his look that he would not override a refusal, that I could save myself with the single word I wouldn't say.

"Yes."

He directed his glance over my head, at Papa. "She is so young."

"It is our way." With this sentence Papa set the priest at a far distance, drew attention to the gulf that separated him from us, warned him from advice, put him at a disadvantage.

Father Hurlburt came back to me. There was a sadness about him, a lostness that made me wonder for the first time what he was doing here, an outsider, used but not wanted. I never thought of priests and nuns as living apart from the burdens they put on us. For a flash I saw the man within the priest and it startled me. I forgot to turn away and we looked at each other, curious as two animals who drink from the same stream.

"And her school?" he asked finally. "She is so near to completion."

"She can return later. My daughters finish what they start." Papa's impatience with the priest's reluctance threatened to boil over.

"I will be here for the baby," Clara broke in. "Only outside the house will it be hers."

Father Hurlburt looked around the room, from Papa and me to Clara. His eyes hesitated at Mama's door.

"In the illness, Annie needs her sister near. But people would wonder if the child was Clara's," Papa said. "Ida has said she is willing."

There seemed nothing more to ask.

"Do you know a place we can go?" Clara got to the point of the visit. "It must be soon, before I can be noticed."

Father Hurlburt touched his hand to the brown hair at his temple, then reached to massage the back of his neck while he considered the question.

"There may be. I can ask the nuns. I believe they have a motherhouse in Colorado that sometimes shelters unfortunate young girls." He stood, straightened the material of his robe, slipped a loose button into its hole. "I'll let you know."

"Where in Colorado?" Clara asked. "Denver?"

"Where in—" The priest turned to her sharply, as if misunderstanding her English. "Denver. Yes, I think it is Denver."

"I've never been there." Clara smiled to herself and rose to help Father Hurlburt with his coat. When the door closed on him, she turned to me where I remained in my chair.

"Don't look so gloomy," she said. "It's a city. We'll have a good time together, like best friends, and when we come home to your mama and papa, you'll be a mother the easy way."

She turned to light the stove, to heat soup she had made that afternoon, and Papa walked past me to chop more wood. I could almost feel a baby stir within my body, almost measure its weight in my arms. But when, in my imagination, I looked at its face, the eyes that accused me were dazzling blue.

18

The nuns in Denver were enraptured when they heard the story of Clara's attack. She was a victim, they said, an innocent lamb, abused like a martyr by a rampaging beast of a man. For them, Clara fit into the stories of their saints, the tales of virgins pursued by pagan Roman soldiers, the legends of women who preferred death to surrender.

They overlooked the fact that Clara had not died.

With the nuns as her audience, the recounting of Clara's experience became more vivid and complicated: she had fought until she fainted or, occasionally, until she had been knocked unconscious by a large stone; she had sacrificed herself to save me, her sister, who had cowered in terror in a closet or behind a bush; she had tracked down her assailant and brought him to justice, the savior of her tribe. But even in this last version, even at the trial in which Clara courageously testified, the man's mask never came off. He remained nameless, without identifying marks, any man, every man. Each nun was free to see him with her own eye, in her own memory, in her own appallment.

As the tagalong sister I had no rights, no reason except Clara's companionship to be at the convent, and so I had to work for my board. I did the jobs reserved for novices—scrubbed floors and polished brass candlesticks and, with broom handles, turned laundry in large tubs. The bleach ruined my hands, burned lines off my palms as I lifted the heavy, scalding sheets from the water and fed them to the wringer. I slept on a cot in a bare room, watched by a crucifix and a window too high to see out. I was permitted to borrow one book at a time from the convent's library, but all the titles seemed to me the same.

Some days I didn't even meet Clara in the dining room. She was the only wayward girl in residence and had made friends among the younger nuns. I heard them whisper the hope that she would give her baby in adoption to a childless Catholic couple and join their order. They brought her along whenever they went about the city, took her to museums and public buildings, bought her five lunches at restaurants, found her practically new maternity clothes to wear.

Sitting alone between my jobs, waiting for the baby to be born, I realized that Pauline would have been a better mother for this baby than either Clara or me. She would have enjoyed my life at the convent and, more than that, she might have discovered a vocation. Me, I just backslid. I began to act as if I could barely speak English. I became difficult to awaken in the mornings, refused to kneel erect in the chapel but instead dropped my behind on the pew and buried my head in my arms. I gained weight on a diet of white bread and butter, sent a day-old by a devout Catholic dairy. I was everything those nuns expected an Indian to be, and after a while they hardly noticed I was there. Clara was the object of their prayers.

Still, I thought that when the baby came—when we returned home, when I saved Clara's name, provided Mama's care, took the burden off Papa, had stories of convent life to tell Pauline— my life would be better than it had been. In our house I would once more be Clara's best company, and she, in my debt, would reopen her affections. I imagined a short vacation before returning for my last year of school, a flurry of scandal from which I would be saved in small ways by the truth Father Hurlburt guarded. I looked forward to the entertaining presence of a child, at once my brother or sister and my cousin, and to the resumption of my quest for Willard, who would return on leave from the army to see me in a new light.

I missed the smell of the reservation all that spring and early summer. Sometimes, in the breezes that blew through Denver from the north and west, I found the green scent of budding fields, the sharp catch of fresh dirt, the touch of air heated by the unshaded flow of sun. I missed the quiet, I missed easy talk. In my sleep, I dreamed conversations in which I made jokes and double meanings, in which I juggled words, weightless and fragile as abandoned mud dauber nests. In my dreams, I taught the baby to count.

I had one letter from Pauline, an assignment from her eighth-grade teacher, that was for the most part copied from a form in her schoolbook. On the front side of the page she said the winter had been mild, that everyone was well, that she had completed the nine First Fridays and received a large indulgence. She signed "Yours in Christ, your loving sister, Pauline George," and received a grade, recorded in thin red ink, of *B* +. On the back, far less carefully written, she added a note of her own creation.

> They fight all the time now. She is no better and he
> blames her for missing work. As soon as school is out
> he is going to hire on at a ranch and I have to take
> care of Mama. I hate this place. P.

I never answered.

I didn't hear that Clara had a girl until August 11, the day after the baby was born.

"Your brave sister bore a beautiful daughter," a young nun, Vivencia, told me when I came to breakfast.

I must have looked as if I didn't understand.

"An angel from heaven," she continued.

The child I had only vaguely imagined became female in my mind.

"Clara let us name her," Vivencia said. "We prayed over it and all agreed: Christine."

Like Christ, I thought. They had decided Clara was a virgin after all. Christine. I didn't mind it. I knew no Christines.

Vivencia was not satisfied that my English was sufficient to comprehend her news, so she spoke loud and slow, straight into my face.

"You are an *aunt*," she instructed. "You are Aunt Ida. That's you." She pointed her finger at my chest to make me see. "Say that, *Aunt Ida.*"

"Where is she?" I asked. "When can I see her?"

"Clara will rest in the infirmary for at least a week."

"No. The baby. Christine."

Vivencia pursed her lips. Her mouth was framed at each end with the wisps of a dark mustache. "Your sister has not yet decided what she will do. If she releases the child, it's best you not see it."

"She won't do that." I shook my head, stared her down. "Take me to Clara."

"She's resting now. She had a terrible time of it, she's so small. Perhaps tomorrow when she's stronger, when she has had more time to think clearly."

"Now," I insisted. "Now." I was bigger than Vivencia and frightened her. She stepped back from my determination, stroked the cross on her breast.

"Do not raise your voice to me," she hissed, but I could see she would do what I wanted. I was a mystery to her, a danger, a wild Indian not at all like her gentle Clara.

"I shall ask Mother. One of the sisters will accompany me to the hospital later. If you promise to behave, perhaps you may go too."

I promised nothing, but by afternoon I had ridden on a bus with a pair of nuns and followed them through brightly lit halls. I faced Clara in her white room. A picture of the Sacred Heart, framed in black wood, hung above her bed. I spoke to her in Indian so that only she could understand my words.

"Where is the baby?"

"Ida, don't be so loud. Why do you look at me like that?"

"You let them name her."

"You can always change it."

"They told me you might give her away." I expected her to laugh or be angry at the idea.

"They say it's for her own good, that someone else could take better care of her than a woman alone. Oh, my breasts hurt. You don't know the pain I suffered before I made them give me ether."

"You're not a woman alone."

"Well, *they* don't know that."

Her answers were so irrational that I wondered if her senses had been dulled by the gas the doctors had given her.

"Well, where is she, then," I said to change the subject. "Your breasts mean she's hungry."

"I'm not feeding her." Clara curled on her side, bunching the pillow under her head. "I'm too weak. They're giving her some other kind of milk."

I had never heard of such a thing, and Clara was not weak. I waited for her to go on. She took my hint.

"That way, if I should decide to let her go, there'd be no problem."

I raised my voice and shook the rungs at the foot of her bed. "What are you talking about? You can't give her away."

"I know, I know. That was our plan. But maybe not. I have to stay in the hospital for a while, then be near my doctor in Denver. What would I do with a baby?"

I realized that Clara had already decided that, for whatever reason, she would not keep Christine. Relief filled me like air. I had a vision of my life resumed intact, no gossip, no delays, no shame.

"So you understand?" Clara reposed in her white gown between clean white sheets. Sometime that day she had thought to draw lipstick on her mouth.

"No," I said. "I won't let you."

Clara's attention flew to my face.

"I can do what I want," she tried. "It's my baby."

"I'll tell them. They'll throw you out of here."

Her body froze in its spread position, flat as a centipede when you lift its rock. I saw her as I never wanted to see her, as what she was: moon-faced, whining, puny-limbed. My spine jerked as if awakened from a sound sleep. She was the other side of beautiful, and my love bore deep inside of me, leaving only a hole of passage to show it had ever existed.

"What do you want?" Clara's eyes, unaware, stared into the pillow beside her face.

"I'll take her home. You can come when you're well."

"She isn't even *pretty*," Clara whispered. "She's all nose."

"Where is she? Have them bring her here." I sat on the blue wood chair and looked at the cars parked along the street. I waited while Clara sighed, fussed, while she rang for the nurse and did as I had ordered. It was a hot day with almost no breeze. The leaves on the short trees looked heavy as tin. I wasn't pretty either. People would believe my story.

I did not turn my glance when the door opened or when I heard a nurse, moving softly in the room, say to Clara, "Here she is." I waited until we were alone again, and then I swiveled, rose, approached the bed. Only then, standing next to Clara's covered legs, did I extend my arms and see the child. One slanted eye was open, the other closed. Her lips were white from whatever she drank, her face was round as a yellow pear. On the very crown of her head was one thick patch of dark red hair, but otherwise she was bald. Her small hands pushed at her mother's uncomfortable grip. While I watched, her nostrils flared as if she smelled something alarming. I hesitated one last time, panicked to touch her, afraid to feel the bones beneath her skin, but Clara convinced me.

"Well, take her," she said. "Or let me do the sensible thing and give her up."

So I took her.

She weighed less than the candlesticks I polished, less than rinse water in a bucket. The skin of her face against my cheek was warm and clean. I moved to the window for better light and she squeezed her eyes against the glare, pressed her face to my sweater. I fed her when the nurse brought a bottle, and I let her sleep along the slope of my forearm, the back of her head supported by the palm of my hand. I waited like that, tense in all my muscles, until finally Vivencia and her Superior came back from their visits to the sick, until Clara disappointed them by announcing she would keep Christine, until I heard her say Aunt Ida would bring the baby home.

I steamed over Clara, how she didn't come to the depot for a last look at her own baby and how she refused to specify when she expected to return to the reservation. "There's so much I haven't seen in this city," she told me. "It would be a waste to miss it, because you never know when I'll be back this way."

During the two weeks since she had checked out of the hospital and returned to the convent, she had let me do everything for Christine—feed her, bathe her, rock her to sleep. Clara claimed to be still recovering, yet she had energy for herself. Those stupid nuns hadn't given up on her coming in with them. They treated her like glass, but to Clara their house was just a cheap place to sleep, the only rent that she say what they wanted to hear.

I wasn't afraid to travel alone. I was big and looked older than my years and had a baby to protect me. I took a Greyhound bus and transferred in Cheyenne for Billings. I arrived in early afternoon and sat on a bench in front of the station and waited for Father Hurlburt, my suitcase between my knees and Christine on my lap. By staying in Denver, Clara had made her design foolproof. In my dress and in the way I carried myself, in my sullenness and in my exhaustion, I was the picture of a girl who had borne a child in shame.

I had left six months ago with only promises in my pocket, and, except for Pauline's note, I had no idea what to expect. A part of me imagined everything remained the same, but another part knew better. I didn't calculate what my presence had added or subtracted to that house in the past, but in my absence, whatever poles I had held erect would have collapsed.

After an hour, Father Hurlburt arrived in old Father

Gephardt's green Ford. When he saw me, he parked in the lane and got out to help.

"I hope you haven't been waiting long," he said. "I was later than I planned in departing."

I lifted the blanket away from Christine's face, and he gave a long look.

"My, my. A little girl?"

"Christine."

"Christine. And where's her mother? Inside?"

"I'm her mother," I reminded him. "Clara stayed in Denver extra time. She'll be back when she's feeling better."

"She's not ill?" he asked, worried.

"No." With my foot, I pushed my suitcase toward the curb, but Father Hurlburt excused himself and put it into the backseat.

Inside the car he seemed smaller, almost thin. He drove two-handed, and slowed down long before he reached each red light. I watched his movements from the corner of my eye, followed the line of his profile from his brown hair to his white priest's collar. At one stop, something slid from under the seat and brushed my foot. I reached down and landed an empty pint of Old Crow.

A blush rose beneath Father Hurlburt's skin. His ear turned bright rose and his teeth clamped together. I set the bottle on the floor where I found it, and adjusted Christine's blanket. I was glad to have a secret back on him, even not a very surprising one.

Christine could never sleep when she was in motion, but she was content to consider my face. I wondered what she saw. In Denver I had grown taller and heavier. The muscles of my shoulders and back, already powerful from helping Papa in the fields, had thickened with my hard work at the convent. I wore one of Clara's maternity dresses to travel, since none of her regular clothes would fit me.

"When is she returning?" Father Hurlburt asked his question in Indian. I was impressed but didn't know how to show it, so I pretended it was as natural as day to hear a priest talk right.

"She doesn't know." I had to say something. "You've learned a lot."

He laughed, switched back to English. "I rehearsed that line for the last five miles. I'm not a good student."

It was not my place to contradict, so I looked out my window. Bales already dotted the fields.

"One reason I wanted to learn," Father Hurlburt said, "is that, well, you know I'm part Indian myself."

I turned to scrutinize him. I could see it.

"I don't know much about that branch of my family. My father's mother from New York State was a Seneca, but I only vaguely remember her."

"I've heard of them," I said, but I didn't know what.

"That's how I got interested in Indians, I guess. It must be in my blood." Father Hurlburt laughed at his own joke, and when I failed to join in, he didn't speak again for forty miles.

I closed my eyes and let my mind wander. I couldn't quite think of him as Indian, but knowing about that grandmother changed something. It made me less surprised about the night when he came to our house and listened to Clara's plan, when I noticed him as more than a priest. Now I had an explanation.

As we came closer to home, as I began to recognize the roll of the land, the familiar pattern of mountain ridges on the horizon, I could no longer avoid the anticipation of what awaited me. It occurred to me that with every mile we traveled, Christine was more my baby.

Father Hurlburt spoke again when we drove onto the reservation.

"Did you hear Pauline is no longer living with your parents?"

I tightened my hold on Christine, unwilling to admit my ignorance.

"She has not been happy there since... since your father has been out of work, so the good sisters found her a place with a family at the Agency."

"Mama?" I asked.

"I'm afraid her condition is no better. I, we, thought with the warm weather she would improve, but..." He raised his shoulders and his eyebrows and glanced at me in puzzlement. "Perhaps with your return."

"Is he drinking?" This was not something I would normally ask a priest, but I had no one else.

"That has been a problem," Father Hurlburt admitted, nodding as if the idea had not struck him before. "Yes, a problem."

A few miles later I saw the roof of the house, obscured by the low hills that built toward the canyon close to our land. No smoke rose from the chimney. Christine squirmed in restlessness. Even with the windows open, the car was musty and close, as if the air somehow blew past us without touching.

"Do they know I'm coming today?" The nuns in Denver had written directly to Father Hurlburt with my bus schedule.

"I did stop by on the way to Billings, to make sure," he said uncertainly. "I'm sure they are preparing for you."

However, it was Clara's return that had captured Papa.

When the car stopped, he burst from the house, his hair slicked back with water, the sleeves of his shirt rolled over his long johns. Papa's face was eager, his eyes scanned the front seat. He pulled open the door next to me, but looked beyond my shoulder at nothing but my suitcase.

"Where is Clara?" he demanded, as if I were hiding her for a mean joke. I crouched over Christine at his tone, and Father Hurlburt answered for me.

"She was not quite well enough to leave Denver yet, Lecon," he explained. "She'll be back soon. But look who *is* here."

Papa observed me, then the baby in my arms. I held her for him to see. I answered the only question in his eyes.

"Christine."

"It's in their family," he said, almost to himself. "Nothing but girls."

■ ■ ■

Those next two and a half years blur in my memory in chunks large as seasons. A winter of shoveling snow, a summer in which Christine learned to walk, a long damp fall in which Papa worked in town and came home only on weekends. On Friday nights he'd sit in the washtub filled with water I had heated on the stove, drinking the bottle he had bought before he crossed the reservation line. He'd sing at first, splash Christine, and ask after Pauline, but by midnight he would turn evil, yell for another bottle, curse Mama for her illness, cry for Clara who never came back, assail me for the shame he said I brought him. It was as if he forgot truth. He slept through Saturdays, all of us tiptoeing not to wake him, keeping Christine amused and quiet, and on Sundays he'd rise, purged and proper, to walk to church for a sight of Pauline, to show everyone they were still father and daughter. Sometimes he came home for an hour after that, other times he went immediately back to his job. By Sunday night our house of women could breathe easier.

Mama faded like a plant without sun. These days, they'd say it was a new stroke that stiffened her arm and slurred her speech, but, back then, it was as if she was breaking, a part at a time. She never forgave me either. In her weakness she said I had chosen Clara and all that followed was my doing. But she saved her greatest recriminations for herself. "What possessed me?" she demanded almost daily. "Why did I send for her?"

I had no answer.

I nursed her as best I could, yet there were nights I lay quiet until her calls for water or company, for a person or a moment in time to blame, had passed. I had Christine to think of, and if I missed too much sleep, she overwhelmed me the next morning with her questions and wants.

Christine had not been pretty at birth and she wasn't a pretty child, but there was a quality she had, a way of standing, that made you look at her twice. She had no fear. She would wake from a bad dream and want to tell it, hampered only by how few words she knew. She would stray from the house and sit content until I found her, watching ants build a nest or a cloud patch glide across the sky. She tried to climb anything she found in her path.

When the time came, I had Christine call me "Aunt Ida," both at home and when we went out among people who assumed I was ashamed to claim her. And every time she said it, the feelings for her I couldn't help, the feelings that came from being the one she came to when she was hurt and the one who heard her prayers, the feelings I fought against, got flaked away. That was as I intended. Someday Clara would arrive at the door and might steal Christine back.

In those years of Christine's early growth, I had few visitors. Mothers kept their daughters from my bad influence, and the few boys who hadn't enlisted and been shipped, like Willard, to fight in foreign countries, thought I must be too much for them. At least that was the excuse I made to myself. I had no leisure time anyway. For a while Pauline divorced herself from me in public, but occasionally, even during that period, she would find some special dress or coat in the nuns' rummage and bring it for Christine. In her whole life, she never asked me a word about Denver, never mentioned Clara's name, and forgot what she was too proud or too ashamed to know. To keep peace between us, I never disputed her ignorance. That was how we dealt with history.

The only honest one, tied to me by secrets, was Father Hurlburt. On Thursday nights, while Father Gephardt supervised Bingo in the Mission cafeteria, he came to lead me through my schoolbooks, to play with Christine, to practice our language, to ask if I had heard from Clara.

I didn't want to need those evenings—their regularity was irritating to me because I was sure that as soon as I expected Father Hurlburt, he would cease to come—so I remained aloof. I asked him no questions, and showed no interest in the things he said. I didn't offer him the third cup of tea or say thank you for the books he brought Christine. I showed him my indifference, and still he returned the next week, the next, the next.

One Wednesday he came unexpected and caught me off my guard. It had been a hot day in which the house had seemed too small, a day in which Mama cried in her sleep and the dread of Papa's return from a long absence closed over us both like the tight air that precedes a windstorm. After supper I carried Christine up the steps to the attic and out onto the coolness of the roof, belting a piece of clothesline around my waist and harnessing the other end around her shoulders so that she could not crawl to the edge. It was the place I came for quiet, for escape, and when Father Hurlburt's sedan, sun visors blocking the late sun, turned off the road and climbed the dirt path to the house, I resented the intrusion so much I did not retreat inside to greet him.

I watched the top of his head, the stoop of his shoulders, as he got out of his car and walked to call through the screen door. I waited to raise my voice until he had moved below the roof, then I spoke.

"I'm here."

His footsteps halted. I could imagine him looking side to side, then above, into the wooden underbeams from which two flowerpots hung. He reappeared from under the overhang and craned back his head. When he saw us, he moved to lean, hands in the pockets of his black pants, against the side of the car.

"You startled me."

I nodded, playing on the rope that confined Christine, snaking it with the flick of my wrist.

"I came to tell you I wouldn't be here tomorrow. Father Gephardt is in town till Friday, so it's my job to turn the Bingo wheel."

"It doesn't matter," I said, but it did. I was disappointed, and in my mind the week unfolded with nothing to break its monotony. I hated the need I had developed for his company. I let the rope out a few inches so that Christine, by extending it to its limit, could descend the roof low enough to sit with her feet dangling over the side. She was thrilled and terrified at this unusual liberty, afraid to refuse the opportunity but anxious that it be the last one offered.

Father Hurlburt pushed himself upright, then stooped to pry a small stone from the ground, examine it, and toss it side-armed into the high grass.

"It matters to me."

I met his eyes in surprise and we stared at each other, questioning, until he looked away, scratched his head, laughed. "Listen to me. But it's true. I look forward to these Thursday gabfests."

"Why?" I asked, without an answer in mind. That he liked to come, rather than that he came out of mercy or duty, was a new perception.

He glanced back in my direction, laughed again, and made an exaggerated shrug, hunching his shoulders and turning his palms to the sky. I cringed at his exposure, at his embarrassment.

"Are you in a hurry now?"

He shook his head. "No, I'm through for the evening. No funerals, no Daughters of Mary, no Canaan conferences. Not even any good programs on the radio."

I reeled in Christine and, without completely rising, inched up the slope of the roof toward the window.

"I'll make tea. I'll be down."

The second time I ushered Clara into our house, almost four years after her visit, there was no joke on my lips to greet her. I was boiling sheep ribs on the stove for soup, and had just put Christine to bed for her nap. I had rubbed liniment on Mama's back till my arms were sore. Papa was at a job, and the knock on our door, when it came, was so rare that at first I thought a bird had flown by accident into the chimney, and I opened the oven before realizing my mistake.

Clara shivered in a brown cloth coat and had her hair cut as short as a city man. She carried the same carpet valise in one hand, and in the other, a large white box. Round earrings matched her purple dress, and her nails were long and colored a dark red. I stood, holding a ladle in my hand, stunned. But no more than she.

"Ida?" she said, unbelieving. "*Ida?* I wouldn't have recognized you on the street."

I raised my chin, narrowed my eyes at her appraisal.

Clara was lost for words. Nothing that came to her mind was possible to say, but she didn't need to speak. I had not seen my face in the mirror for days, but I read it and more in her eyes. I was thick and big-boned. My hair, damp with sweat and dried by smoke, was pulled tight to my head. I wore no undergarments beneath my faded cotton dress, wore Papa's old shoes on my bare feet.

"You're blocking the gate," Clara said, and when I stepped back, she entered.

"Where's everybody? Where's Christine?"

I searched my mind for lies, but found none. I could only point to the closed door of my room.

Clara set down her bag and looked around. She sniffed the air, and at the smell of the cooking broth her mouth wrinkled in displeasure.

"Where's Lecon?"

I found my voice. "He's off at a job." If I gave her as little information as possible she might not be able to penetrate.

"And Annie?"

"Asleep."

"You probably thought I was dead."

I shook my head. That was one belief I never had. Clara always seemed to me just over the next hill, on her way.

"Ida, you stand with the posture of an old lady. You should see yourself. Isn't my mirror still in your room?"

She took my arm. Her fingers dug into my skin like small sticks as she pushed at me. I took one step, then stopped. I didn't want to look.

"Oh, all *right.* Who's going to see you anyway?" Her eyes fell on the package she had set on the floor.

"I brought Christine—do you still call her that?—a present. I can't wait another minute to see her."

I watched her go to the door, rap, open it a crack and peek in.

"She's asleep," she whispered over her shoulder. "But she'll want to wake for me."

I turned back to the stove, heard the hinges groan behind me. I put the metal ladle into the swarming water, knocked it against the bones, stared into the kettle as if some image would emerge.

"Christine!" Clara's voice was sharp and bright, loud. "Sleepyhead! See who's here."

I whirled, water dripping from the iron in my hand.

"It's your mother, come for you at last!"

I jerked to cover my ears, to block her words, but the torment only increased, searing, covering my body like poured paint. Unconsciously, I traced its source, discovered that I was pressing the scalding cup of the ladle against the side of my face, but my grip on the handle did not loosen. It tightened. I preferred the familiar pain of fire.

Christine was too young to understand anything. She saw no other children and so the word "mother" had no meaning for her. It was a name like any other, and she learned it for Clara as casually as if it had been "cousin." But she watched Clara in wonder, clung to her gift of a cloth doll as if it were her heart's desire, allowed Clara to examine her in every detail—the tender banks and valleys of her ear, the coarseness of her black hair, the length of her nose, the number of her white teeth, top and bottom.

I moved about, feeding them all, my cheek weighted by a plaster of dried mud. I watched every move Clara made, every reaction of Christine's. "This is just a visit," I told myself. "She will leave again, alone." The thing I feared above all else was that she would stay long enough to appreciate Christine, to see beyond her little girl plainness, and therefore want to reclaim her. I did my best to create situations in which temptation would overcome my training and Christine would misbehave, break things, show her willful side. I regretted Pauline's and my efforts to find for her only the nicest clothes, the best of the Mission's lot, and I distracted her whenever she threatened to reveal her musical voice in song. I encouraged Mama's complaints of Christine's noisiness—the way she let the door slam on her way in and out, the clatter she made in piling blocks of wood to make buildings and shelters for her imaginary playmates.

And I saw Clara watch, keep count, tally the goods and bads of Christine in her mind.

With Papa away, Mama was in no rush for Clara to leave. The women of the reservation visited less frequently than they had. The duration of Mama's illness, its stubbornness in denying any signs of improvement, eroded the optimism of all but a few. Father Hurlburt still came Thursday nights, and always brought her the Holy Sacrament and his sympathy, but she was starved for company. She had no choice but to settle for Clara, to forget what she needed to forget.

The days passed uneventfully. My burn healed over, leaving an ugly mark. Christine grew bored with the new freedom I gave her and fell back into her regular patterns of politeness. And still Clara waited, silent about why she had come, mum about when she would leave, becoming, I felt sure, used to the name "Mother."

Then Papa returned late on Friday night. He was a loud banging in the outer room, a voice that roused the house from the numbing slumber that comes before dawn. Lurching, looking for a match to light the lantern, he knocked an empty pot from the woodstove to the floor, cursed and kicked it, shouted my name to help him. I patted Christine, awake and listening in the crib set at the foot of my bed, and rushed to quiet him.

In the green and yellow light Papa's face was ravaged. Black shadowed his reddened eyes, his cheeks were sallow and drooping. He opened his mouth to bawl at my slowness, and I saw he had lost another tooth, that the blood from another fight darkened his lower lip. He wanted drink, needed it, he insisted, and pounded the table with his fist when I said there was none.

I dipped for water, spooned coffee into the pot with a hand unsure out of weariness more than fear or surprise, and endured his temper. If he continued, Christine would not fall back to sleep.

"Papa," I yelled into his din, astounding him into silence. I lowered my voice but held him with my gaze. "Who do you think is here? Who do you think is in Pauline's room?"

Papa's expression slackened. The lines in his brow softened, and his jaw gaped in concentration. His head remained fixed, but his eyes stole to the side, tried to see through the door and solve my riddle.

"Pauline!" he guessed, then looked scandalized that his holy daughter should catch him in such a condition. He tried to stand taller, clutched higher the waistband of his sagging jeans.

"No."

Mystery calmed him further. He cocked his head, pulled it back at some idea he couldn't accept, relaxed as he dismissed it. He was tied by a rope of confusion.

I let the ideas knock against his brain while I lit the stove and set the pot to boil, then I led him from my trap.

"Clara," I whispered loud enough for her to hear. "Clara has come back. She's here. We've been waiting for you."

He staggered, clumsy as if he had been pushed, then turned to me with a frown of denial. I answered with the blank face of honesty. He looked again to the door, shook his head like a wet dog.

"Clara?" He said her name clearly, careful not to slur.

The door opened. She stood small in its frame, her short white gown illuminated against the night. Her hair bristled from sleep and her eyes were cloudy mirrors.

Papa stretched out a hand, took breath as if to speak, and then found no words.

Clara crossed her arms beneath her breasts, hesitated, then stepped backward, disappeared. The door closed with the slightest of sounds.

Through the window I saw the first grayness of morning. I

poured two cups and carried them to the table where Papa slumped, his head in his hands. I set them down, and touched his heaving shoulder.

All through that weekend Papa and Clara avoided each other. I gave him my room and he slept until four on Saturday afternoon. Just as he rose, Clara decided it was such a lovely day she should take Christine for a walk through the fields, and it was the last moments of dusk before they returned, hungry and exhausted with opportunity really for little more than a nod in his direction before retiring themselves. On Sunday, Papa, Christine, and I went to Mass and visited afterward with the family who boarded Pauline. For the first time in years of invitations, we surprised them by accepting their offer of a meal.

Polly Cree rushed about her spotless kitchen, trying to expand the ingredients of their dinner for three more servings, while the rest of us waited uncomfortably in the living room of her government-built house. Buster Cree, a reformed mixed-blood from Wyoming who had joined the church when he married Polly, demonstrated electricity by switching on and off the ceiling light and twisting the knob of his radio in search of some Sunday religious program he said they never missed.

Pauline was not still for a moment, first assisting Polly, then sitting nervously in the room with us, trying to ease the guilt of the family who couldn't keep a daughter with the family who took her in. She centered her attentions on Dale, Buster and Polly's twenty-year-old son, who perched mute and tongue-tied, on the arm of his father's chair. Watching Dale and Pauline together, I realized the nuns had lost my sister forever.

Clara, who had stayed with Mama, said she had become agitated waiting for us. She paced the room, never staying in one spot. If you looked away, then looked back, she had moved on. She kept up a steady stream of talk about her life in Denver, the white husband she had married and divorced and lost track of, her series of fights with the nuns I had known, ending with them calling the police to remove her belongings and telling her never to return. They treated her like trash, she complained, made no exceptions for human frailty and were unforgiving in their righteousness. She talked about her jobs, the beauty parlors where she did nails, the restaurants where she waitressed, and the unfairness of the Indian Employment Office, whose jobs she had quit or lost one time too many. She just needed a new start, she said. Her trip to see us was her quick vacation, and afterward, soon, she would relocate to a city where she was unknown, where no one would speak behind her back.

Mama wore the expression of someone who had heard all this before, whether only this afternoon or previously during Clara's visit I didn't know. Papa asked no questions, and refused to laugh at the parts Clara tried to make funny. But he heard every word, understood Clara's requirements for amusement and gratitude, her dissatisfactions with second-best. He made no protest at the announcement of her impending departure, and refused her even the token of his handshake when he left the house to hitch to his job.

Christine could not have comprehended much of what Clara said, but she was amazed by the flow of words. She sat quiet, hoping I would forget her bedtime, her eyes following Clara's body as it traveled about the room. When Clara paused or ended some portion of her story, Christine would cry out, "More please, Mother. Another one!" and Clara would flash her a look of grim appreciation and continue.

I caught up on my sewing, repairing tears, letting out hems, sealing rips. I calculated the distance from our house to the nearest electrical wire and made lists of things I wanted to plug in. I plotted the changes I would someday make. Christine would have my room and I would take Mama's. Pauline's old room, the one Clara now used, I'd divide: turn one half into storage and put a bathroom in the other, once I had a well and a septic tank. I'd run a bannister along the attic stairs and fence a porch rail around the roof. This hill would be our refuge.

I was the last to bed. I dumped the wash water and

dropped the latch-bar into its catch. I put my ear to Mama's door and satisfied myself that she was asleep, then moved toward the peace of my own blanket.

But Clara waylaid me. She crept from her room with a finger to her lips and beckoned me back to the warmth of the stove. She sat on the bench, crossed her bare legs, and used a burning stick from the firebox to light the cigarette she carried between her fingers.

"What *happened* to him?" she asked me.

I knew what she meant but said nothing.

"He used to be so— I remember when I first saw him, tall and full of life. There never was such a man. He blinded me to every boy that came along. And then, when I came last time, he was much the way I remembered—older, but the same. And now..." She tapered off, tapped her ash into the cinder bucket, fluttered her foot, and closed her eyes.

"You came for him," I said, confirmed in my suspicions.

"No. No, just to *see*. But, I did come for something, Ida, as you must have guessed, and now that I will be going soon we must speak of it."

The blood stopped in my heart. I sat next to her so I wouldn't have to watch her face, so she could not see mine.

"It's Christine. You remember how I always thought she might be better off with a family that could provide for her? How I wanted what was best?"

At my silence, her pace quickened.

"Well, I never forgot. Never for a minute. And now that I see she's such a nice little girl, how she could be polished, and *polite* . . . and there's this family, you know. Very well-to-do, and they want a child so much, would give anything to get one of their own. I told them about Christine, how bad off you were, what a burden she was on you, and they *agreed*. They paid my way here, and will help out even more, provided I meet with this lawyer they have hired."

"Never."

"Now wait, be reasonable. Think of Christine for a change. It's not too late for you to have your own life."

I leaned forward, stood, walked from her.

"Well, it's not up to you," she called after me. "I'm her mother. I can do what I want, and I'm taking her. You have no say in it."

I put my door between us, blunted the sound of her voice. Christine slept with her cover thrown off and her knees pulled beneath her body. Her hair fanned across her face, and one hand dangled over the side of the cot. I knelt on the floor, rested my head on the rough sheet near her feet. I pictured Clara's invitation— "Would you like to take a trip with me to the city?"—and the joy that would blossom on Christine's face. Papa was gone out of my reach and Mama was so used to being powerless that she would merely add this to her tote of Clara's deceits. I thought of escape, just Christine and me hidden by the world, but I couldn't leave Mama, couldn't ruin Pauline's chances. I smelled the heavy earth scent of Christine's skin, a mix of leaves and moss, and opened the net of my thoughts to its widest extension.

I was back to the house before anyone woke. I was heavy with debt. I slipped into the room where Clara slept and shook her ankle to wake her.

"One thing, at least, you owe me," I whispered. "Let me tell her in my time, in my way. You say nothing until then."

Clara was groggy, but not so much that she didn't object.

"It must be soon," she warned. "I told them I'd be gone no more than two weeks."

"If I haven't told her by Wednesday you can do what you like," I said, and Clara was satisfied.

"All right." She pulled the pillow over her head to block out the light.

When Clara finally arose, I fed her. I washed clothes for her trip and hung them to dry. I judged the adoration Christine gave her with the cold eye of my own experience. I understood the capacity for betrayal better than anyone, and I felt a pang of regret for my estrangement from Pauline and Mama, for the barriers I let build between us. I moved with such stumbling fatigue that even Clara took pity on me.

"It's better in the long run." She tried to take my hand, to show me her sympathy, but I shrugged her off.

"When will you tell her?" she wanted to know.

"Before Wednesday."

That Monday night I slept like someone who leaps into deep water with stones tied to their legs. I had no dreams, and woke disoriented.

I pressed Clara's clothes, and Christine's too, heating the flatiron on the griddle, using my full weight to crush each wrinkle. I kept Christine from her nap, tired her with games and errands, and sent her to bed before the daylight had faded. Then I sat in my chair, listening to the stories Clara repeated to Mama, and watched the door.

He was on time. His eyes told me he had the paper.

"Clara," I called, standing from my chair and facing her. "Christine stays here. But you leave. Tonight."

She looked at me in shock, in humor, in shock again. Looked at Mama, who was as surprised as she, looked at him, who met her gaze and turned it.

"You've lost your mind," she said. "You can't tell me what to do with my own child."

Mama caught her breath, but I smiled.

"She's mine," I said softly.

"What do you mean? You can't..."

I reached out my hand. A paper filled it.

"You have no rights," I said.

"I carried her. I gave her birth."

"This paper says differently. This paper says what everyone on this reservation knows. That it was me, Ida, who had to leave in shame. That it was me, Ida, who came back here alone with a baby the image of my father. That it was me, Ida, who's raised her every day. Mama knows it was me who bore her."

I turned to Mama, fierce as the blow of a night storm. "Tell her."

She faltered, remembered her failed strength.

"Yes. Yes!" Her voice soared, released in hopeless revenge. "Liar!"

"And *he* knows. He signed the birth certificate as my witness. Father: unknown. Mother: . . . me."

Father Hurlburt stepped to my side. "I think the nuns in Denver will agree with me, if you ask them. No one would want to remove a child from her loving mother."

"It's *me* she calls Mother," Clara screamed.

"It's me on the paper."

Clara was bathed in her own rage, cut off at every escape, snared in her deceits.

"I think it's best you do leave." Father Hurlburt's voice was steady, less young. It carried a new tone of authority, of the unseen power of his secrets. "No point in further upsetting Christine."

"And never come back. I'll tell about Papa, I'll tell everyone you know."

I could feel her mind race, confined by the walls of the prison we had constructed. She tried for a foothold.

"Do you deny me the right to see my flesh and blood? Are you that cruel?"

But I remembered her triumph of two nights past, her plan to sell Christine, her false pity, her lying affection.

"You have no daughter," I said. "Except through me. If I call for you, you may come. Only then."

I walked past her into Pauline's room and returned with the suitcase I had packed with pressed clothes. "The priest will take you to Havre. You can catch a bus from there."

In my life, I saw Clara only twice more. The first time, in despair, I needed family and could not deny her, and the second, when I returned the favor, when years and illness had removed her threat and allowed that childish core of love I never altogether lost to surface for a last time. Those occasions, I let her see Christine. I gave her that, but nothing more.

19

With Mama a month dead and Papa run off somewhere in his shame, with Pauline out of school and married to Dale Cree, with the threat of Clara under control and Christine my child in the eyes of the law, I leased off land for annual cash. I improved the house with electrical wiring and plumbing. I cast around to choose my future, and heard Willard Pretty Dog was home.

He looked dreadful, Pauline said. He had tripped on a mine in Italy and was stitched together clumsy as a pieced blanket. He refused to be seen and had painted the backseat windows of his mother's car for when he rode from the reservation to his stays at the hospital. Willard had been more vain about his good looks than people realized, Pauline pronounced, and this was God's judgment.

She made me curious. When I was outdoors scything grass or hanging wash, I watched the road for Willard's passing. I asked for news from Father Hurlburt when he visited me on Bingo nights, while he entertained Christine with the card games you can play alone, and he was glad to keep me informed.

"He's a sorry soul." Father Hurlburt shook his head, ticked a six for Christine to play her five, and sighed. "Bitter."

"They say he has the face of a devil," I prompted, using Pauline's word.

"Of a hero, more like it. He's got a Silver Star and a letter

338

from Truman. An honorable discharge and veterans' benefits for life. And with the miracles of plastic surgery, someday his face will be less deformed."

"I can't think of him like that," I said.

"Neither can he, and that's his trouble. He needs some of your courage, Ida, some of your toughness."

I looked at him, pleased at this description but doubtful. Those were not words I would apply to myself. I knew my limits. On my own land I was confident, rooted, but once away, when I was in Denver or when I had to go to town, I was as nervous as an outdoor cat trapped in the house. It wasn't so much that I was afraid to leave, as that I was fearful to be gone.

Christine scrambled the cards into a pile, furious that they would not fall her way. She had no patience. Father Hurlburt gathered them, tapped the corners against the tabletop, and replaced them in their torn paper box.

"Perhaps you should visit Willard," he suggested. "He is so cut off from everyone since he returned."

"Will he see me?" I kept my face and voice calm, but I was excited at the prospect. Willard had once been far beyond any girl in our class, the type who would have left the reservation and then returned in a big car for visits. He was the type who would have married white.

"Not at his home, maybe, but he goes to the hospital on Thursday to have the bandages from the latest operation removed. I'm driving him. I'll suggest we drop in on the way back." Father Hurlburt reached for Christine but she shrieked with laughter and ran from his hands.

Thursday was a day away. I surveyed the room, imagining it through Willard's eyes. Rather than make things more attractive and modern, the harsh electric lights revealed every imperfection, every forgotten crack and stain. They betrayed me as well. My burned cheek had healed to an angry brand, the color of nails left in a rain bucket. My hair was dry black hay. I had the thick, strong body of a woman who fought the earth for every bite she ate. I was the one no one noticed until they needed something. Only Christine thought I was beautiful, and in time she'd learn her mistake.

Yet if Willard was as bad off as Pauline said, he could not be choosy. I told Father Hurlburt I might be home on Thursday. He could stop by with Willard to see.

On Wednesday night, when Christine had gone to sleep, I dragged out Papa's washtub and filled it with hot water. My first year's lease money had only stretched to install a toilet and two sinks, in addition to the wiring. I turned off the lights, draped my clothes on a chair, and, as a last thought before I stepped into the water, I turned on the radio. I liked the programs where they talked, where the politicians argued with each other or where they asked questions and gave prizes. I learned odd facts: the length of a wall in China, the value of the gold stored in Kentucky, the secret lives of movie stars.

The warmth enclosed me as I lowered my body. I thought of Papa yelling insults from this tub and I couldn't understand it. A bath brought me peace, made me float free. I raised one leg into the air and pointed my toes as I slid the soap along my skin. I washed myself beneath the water, slowly, and lifted my hips against my hand. When I sat, my breasts tightened with the jolt of coolness. They were my secret, round and firm, my glory. I leaned forward, spilled my hair over my forehead and showered water from my cupped hands till it was wet and sleek. Then, with the tips of my fingers, I massaged my scalp with Ivory soap. I had placed a fresh pitcher beside me on the floor, and I rinsed in its lukewarm flow.

I slept that night without a gown, fresh between sheets dried in the sun.

I was in the yard early with Christine and saw the Mission car head to town. I calculated the time it would take, there and back, the time for waiting at the hospital, the time for removing the bandages, the time for a doctor's words, and planned my day.

When Pauline came, she gave me a ride to the store and amused Christine in the front seat while I went inside. I nodded to those I knew. They were used to me and not surprised when I didn't stop to talk. I bought rice, meat for stew, flour and butter and new yeast, and expensive tea, packed in a fancy box, which I had never tried.

"You must be having a party," Pauline said when she saw my two sacks of groceries. "How much did you spend?"

"Just supplies," I told her, and let her look. The tea was hidden at the bottom of one bag and the heavy package of meat in the other. The only thing she found was the red candy stick for Christine, but even that displeased my sister.

"You're going to rot her teeth."

While the bread and canned-berry pie baked, I scrubbed the floors and washed down the walls. I gave Christine a bath and rewarded her with the licorice before putting her to bed. I cut the meat into small cubes, which I dropped off a spoon into a pot of boiling broth. I peeled potatoes and carrots and an onion, and let them simmer. I ironed the largest of Mama's dresses and put it on. I brushed my hair with rosewater and braided it loose while it was still damp, then I coiled its rope into a fat knot and pinned it low on my neck.

I dared a look in the mirror. The best face I had stared back. I bit my lips for color, and remained standing so my dress wouldn't wrinkle. Everything was ready.

I heard Father Hurlburt attempt to persuade Willard to get out of the car. He spoke our language better after all our conversations, and from just his voice, you might think he was one of us.

"She's expecting you, Willard," Father Hurlburt said. "She knows you were hurt. She's an old friend."

Willard replied with mumbled words I couldn't decipher.

"But it does look better, much better today," Father Hurlburt continued. "This last operation made more difference than you think. Once the swelling subsides and the bruises clear. It takes time, but there is progress."

Again I caught the sound of Willard's whisper. It was urgent, insistent.

"Just a short visit then." Father Hurlburt was pleading now, sure he was doing the right thing. "For Ida's sake."

I had had enough of this. I went outside, pushed past Father Hurlburt, and opened the car door, out-pulling the hand within that tried to keep it closed. Willard swung his face away from me, raised his shoulder as a shield, hunched against the seat.

"I cooked you stew," I said to him. "Come and eat it. There's nobody to see you but me and my girl, and she's asleep."

I recognized Willard's shape, the slim lines of his legs, the width of the chest within the checkered shirt, the back of his neck. My eyes fell to the hand he clutched in his lap and I saw that the two last fingers were gone and that white seams made a patchwork that disappeared under his cuff. He couldn't seem to move of his own will, but sat quivering like a cold child.

"Come on." I took his hand, urged him from the car. Without once looking at him, I led him to the house and went through the door first.

"The food is almost ready," I said, stirring the rice on the stove and adjusting the heat under the pot. "Sit down at the table."

Father Hurlburt stood, uncertain, in the doorway. I knew I should invite him to eat, but I also knew I shouldn't. I spoke to him with a tone of formality, the tone people ordinarily used with priests.

"Thank you, Father. Willard is fine now. I can get Pauline or one of the neighbors to take him home later." I tried to make my eyes gentle my words, and Father Hurlburt showed me he understood. He played the same game.

"I appreciate it, Mrs. George. I do have many duties to attend. So I will leave you then, Willard. If that's all right?"

We both waited for some signal, but none came.

"Good night, Father," I said.

When the sound of the car engine faded down the hill, I filled a plate to overflowing and carried it across the room.

In my imagination, Willard's face had been worse, but it was terrible enough. He bore little resemblance to the handsome, striking boy I had known in school. Ruts cut through his cheeks and the slope of his jaw was altered by a deep wedge. The space between his nose and his bottom lip was only partially covered with shiny skin, leaving exposed a row of white teeth too even to be real. A hole, only thinly veiled by the hair he had grown long, replaced one ear. But the worst thing about Willard was the flat, hate-filled surrender in his eyes.

His weakness made me bold.

"You're better than I expected," I said.

A sound like feeble laughter rose from his throat. "What would you know of anything?" His conceited self-pity splashed over me, irritating as spilled water.

So, without planning it or thinking, I told him. I laid my life on the table—Clara and Papa and Mama and Pauline; Christine, the lies, the loneliness—for Willard to examine and see if it was bad enough to suit him. As I listened to my own story, I lost the control of its interpretation. I heard it as a tale on the radio, so sad it deserved applause and a trip to Florida. Unhappiness was the only thing that Willard valued, and as I admitted mine, I put myself in his broken hands.

When I was done, when the tea had turned cold in its cup, when the stew broth had formed a crust on the side of the pot and the night had made us all but invisible for each other to see, I raised my palms to my face and breathed into them. My skin was cool and smelled of onion. The weight, where my elbows were propped on the table, was heavy and balanced.

The wood of Willard's chair crackled as he leaned toward me. His fingers tugged at mine, left my face exposed. I waited, hardly breathing, my eyes closed. Then I felt his touch, light as fog, upon my cheek.

Christine, still lonely for her grandma, was glad for Willard's presence. The novelty of his wounds wore off and when he realized Christine saw him without comparison to how he had once looked, he let down his defenses. He told her about the ship that took him across the ocean, and about the exotic animals he had seen in zoos. He let her ride him like a horse.

Pauline was distressed that I took Willard in.

"Think how it looks," she fussed. "My sister, alone in the house with a man not her husband. What will Papa say if he comes back? And your friend, Father Hurlburt?"

"It's not what you think," I told her, but of course it was. Willard had come to my bed that first night. He knew more than I—who only had schoolgirls' giggling stories to go by—but I soon took the lead. Any male body would have been unusual to me, so the wounds the war had carved in Willard made no difference. He was all I knew and all I wanted, and I was good for him, I could see that. When we were alone, he would sit in the sun with no shirt and let the warmth soak into his body.

When Father Hurlburt came as usual the next Thursday night, I knew he didn't condemn me, and little by little Willard participated in our talks, told his stories, made his jokes.

I used every jar of berries Mama had put aside in years of preserving, just to bake him a month's worth of pies. I didn't tire, as some might have done, at Willard's daily need for comfort, for reassurance, for sympathy. I made myself silly to hear him laugh, never corrected the errors he made in his grammar or in his bad memory of old-time stories. As he got more sure of himself and bragged about his soldiering, the battles he had won, the heroics he had performed, I listened with wide eyes and never put to him a question I didn't think he could answer.

Mrs. Pretty Dog asked half the reservation what she should do about me. She came from a respected family, was the widow of a good provider, and had looked to Willard for her future. When the war overseas started, she worked it into her design. The army was a way, she said, for Willard to expand his experience, to see foreign countries, and he would come back the better for it. When he returned the worse, beaten and unrecognizable to her, she despaired. Everyone was to blame: the Germans, the Americans, Willard's brave heart, and now finally me.

She didn't allow herself to visit us for almost three months, until just before Willard was set to return to the hospital for his next operation. Pauline had given me constant reports of Mrs. Pretty Dog's public humiliation, that her son, the famous veteran, should take up with such an odd woman, already with a bastard child and living alone and uncourted. I was not the one with whom she had expected her son to abuse her, not the one she had planned would lift from her the trial of Willard's medical care. But her hopes were nothing to me, so when she came to call, I was ignorant of her regrets and polite as a future daughter-in-law.

"You have electricity," she discerned first thing inside the house.

"Of course," I replied.

She peeked through the door I had left open.

"And a toilet!" She had heard the news of these things, but was still impressed to find them true.

Christine rushed from outdoors, her hair in disarray, the hem of her clean dress soaked from the slough behind the house. Without taking any notice of Mrs. Pretty Dog, she ran to the counter, reached for a cup, filled it with water from the faucet, drank, wiped her mouth with the back of her arm, and was gone. Her rudeness delighted and encouraged me.

Willard, brushed and ill at ease, sat at the table. He wore a loose blue shirt I had made for him, work pants, and Papa's soft deerskin moccasins. The sun had restored his color, and his shortened lip seemed almost to smile in nervousness.

"You have been a good nurse to my son," Mrs. Pretty Dog

began, settling herself on a chair. "Will he return here after the next trip to the hospital or will he come home?"

"Ask Willard," I said, and banged a bowl of jam on the table before her. "I'll get you a spoon and some fry bread."

The silence lengthened while both of us waited for Willard to speak, but he only stirred sugar into his tea.

"What will they do this time?" Mrs. Pretty Dog asked in exasperation.

"He gets an ear," I said. "Made from something that feels exactly like human skin. They'll work on his mouth and sew more skin to smooth his face."

Mrs. Pretty Dog recoiled at my bluntness, but I had learned that for Willard it was best to be direct, best to say the worst that hid in his mind.

"He'll be handsome," I added, out of fondness.

At the word, once so linked with her son, the corners of Mrs. Pretty Dog's mouth dove for her chin. Her forehead and eyebrows pulled up and together, ready for tears. But I interfered.

"The priest is taking me to the hospital after the operation. Do you want a ride?"

She was jarred by my presumption, by my control. Anger at me overcame the sympathy she felt for herself, and she pulled her lips into a taut pinch.

"Naturally I will be at my son's side when he needs me." Her eyes flashed a hundred messages to remind me of my place. I could understand why Willard was so afraid of her disapproval, but she had no influence over me.

"I'll tell Father Hurlburt to save you a seat, then," I said evenly and set a plate, heated in the electric oven and laden with rounds of golden bread, on the table. Then I moved behind where Willard sat, put my hands on each of his shoulders, and casually let them slide down his chest. I was no nurse. Mrs. Pretty Dog saw, had confirmed before her eyes the most extreme rumors she had spread. I felt a tremble in Willard's skin and thought perhaps I had gone too far. Then he relaxed his back, leaned his head for an instant against my breasts, and spoke.

"Eat, Mother, before it cools."

■ ■ ■

I got the news of Papa's death while Willard was recovering in the hospital from his operation. When Father Hurlburt came on a Monday, I knew he had something to tell, and when I saw his long face, I knew it was unpleasant.

"Willard or Papa?" I asked before he said a word.

"It's your father."

My body sagged, and Father Hurlburt put an arm around my shoulders. He didn't realize that my reaction was one of relief.

"I'm sorry," he said, as if he was guilty. "There was a phone call to the rectory."

"He's dead?"

Father Hurlburt nodded, tightened his embrace, but I pulled back.

"Where?" I asked. "How did he die?"

"I don't have all the details. He was in Minot. I think it was an accident of some kind."

I could imagine what kind. When Clara left the second time, when Mama had a stroke that took her speech, when Pauline asked none of us to witness her marriage and gave a poor excuse, the fear of scorn and disappointment lost its power over Papa. He existed without boundaries, and I never again met, even for an hour, the man who raised me.

"He lived too long," I said. Father Hurlburt thought he had misunderstood me.

"But Lecon's life was full."

I had missed my period, then another, but kept the news to myself. There was no one but Christine to see my morning sickness, and she was too occupied with her own concerns—the plugging of prairie dog holes with rocks, the endless parade of her dolls and toys—to notice.

The realization that my body was capable of bearing life came as an astonishment and a gift to me. Food tasted better, every sound was crisper, every light brought more clarity. The garden I had planted sprouted shoots of corn, bean vines, radish greens, and trailings of squash. Weeds grew even faster, and I let them be. I left the windows of the house open, day and night, and allowed the insects to fly freely beneath the shelter of my roof. I sometimes wore only my bra, sometimes not even that, when I worked outdoors.

Willard had to stay in the hospital in Billings this time until every cut was healed, until all danger of infection was past. Early in the morning on the day his new face was to be revealed, I waited beneath the porch roof. When Pauline had come earlier to take Christine for the day, I was tempted to confide in her, but I saved my news to add to Willard's celebration, or to comfort his disappointment. I carried it like flowers for the sick.

Mrs. Pretty Dog was already in the front seat of Father Hurlburt's car, and at first I barely minded. But reservation roads soon took their toll. My body rose and fell with every ditch and hole, I bit my tongue and drew blood, my head ached from the constant need to flex the muscles of my neck against the jerks and swings of the wheels. Nausea overwhelmed me, and the breeze from my window did little to settle my stomach. I thought of the baby, bouncing helplessly within me, and debated announcing my condition in order to gain the front seat. Mrs. Pretty Dog would have no choice but to trade her comfort for that of her grandchild. But I endured. No one would know before Willard.

My baby's father peered at us through openings in the spotless white bandages that covered his face and neck. His eyes were black as the water in a shallow well, timid and apprehensive. I smiled into their depth while Mrs. Pretty Dog petted his good hand and complained about her long trip, about the horrible dream that woke her in the night, the dream in which Willard's face was unveiled to be that of a lynx.

The doctor's arrival interrupted her story. He made Mrs. Pretty Dog, Father Hurlburt, and me move away, and we stood in a row against the wall, watching as the layers of gauze were unwound into snow mountains on the floor. The doctor's head blocked my view, so I did not know why Mrs. Pretty Dog gasped. I saw in my imagination the face of her dream and squeezed shut my eyes in alarm. But when I blinked, it was Willard who looked back—the blurred photograph of the boy I knew in school. He was as I had promised. He was the next thing to handsome.

Willard could not read our faces. He hesitated before lowering his gaze to the hand mirror the doctor offered, but once he saw he could not look away. He turned his head slowly, marveling, as did we all, at the perfect ear. He ran his tongue carefully along the length of his inflamed but longer upper lip. The line of his jaw was clean and unbroken once again.

"He was an excellent candidate," the doctor said. "You can see, when the healing is achieved his appearance will be dramatically improved."

Mrs. Pretty Dog was crying, wailing, still not satisfied at less than a total recovery, but praising God for His miracles, crediting the prayers and Masses she had offered for Willard's progress. Father Hurlburt was in conversation with the doctor, inquiring about the technique of the operation, the process of bone grafting, the lifelike quality of the material that formed the ear, the stability of the results. Willard continued lost in the glass, touching each part of his face, afraid to change his expression.

I was happy for him, of course, but the resurrection of his face frightened me too. There, in that foreign city hospital room, surrounded by other people, Willard and I were strangers, unlikely partners. His triumph threatened to overshadow mine.

After the doctors had left, after every nurse had come into the room to exclaim at the transformation, Mrs. Pretty Dog, Father Hurlburt, Willard, and I sat together in the solarium, surrounded by abandoned potted plants. The commotion of this morning was abating, and we were looking ahead.

"Your life is starting over," Mrs. Pretty Dog told Willard. "You have your second chance."

It was the ideal time to divulge my secret, but I wavered. Words in that open room seemed dangerous, betrayed hiding places, drew hostile attention.

"Are there more operations in store?" Father Hurlburt asked.

"In a year," Willard said. "But nothing like this one. I am the most changed I will be, they say."

"I don't believe that. They learn more all the time. Someday they'll fix it perfect." Mrs. Pretty Dog pulled the skirt of her dress over her wide knees. "When will they let you go home?"

I recognized her question and listened for Willard's reply.

"I'll be back at Ida's next week."

I caught the stir of a smile from Father Hurlburt, but I still said nothing, still waited, though I didn't know for what.

"Ida's?" Mrs. Pretty Dog sunk her teeth into the bait, sprung the trap, and made her stand. "Surely you don't need a nurse now!"

Willard spoke with a firmness I had not heard before.

"You know she's more to me than my nurse."

I prepared myself to reward him, to seal our bond.

"But you could have *anyone*. I could understand when you were so . . . sick, but you don't have to settle for her now. What does she have to offer you? A child without a father? A fat woman no one else wants?"

In her panic, she described me as if I weren't present, and I chose to let her. Willard must speak for me now, must make his position clear.

"Ida may not be beautiful," he said. "She may not be very smart. But when no one else cared for me, she was there. When I first went to her house, I . . . ."

His voice droned on, but I lost the sense of his meaning. I heard only the beginnings of his statement, again and again. The air in the little room was dry and unmoving. Yellow mums withered on stiff stalks, their pots wrapped in colored foil. I saw myself through his eyes, a person whose goodness overcame her drawbacks, a person Willard would love out of loyalty, out of spite toward his mother, out of his infirmity.

"...not the kind who'll turn his back just because..."

I watched his stiff new mouth open and close, saw the flash of teeth and tongue, the eyes that didn't see me, that couldn't, that never would.

He finished his proud declaration and looked to me for gratitude.

I heard my words as much as thought them.

"Your mother's right. It's better you go. Papa is coming home and I'll have to care for him. There won't be room for you." I turned to Father Hurlburt, cut off his objection. "We should go back before it gets late."

He read my glance and nodded.

Mrs. Pretty Dog was nervous at her success, afraid to spoil it.

"Well, of course we all appreciate what you've done for Willard, Ida. I know—"

"What do you mean?" Willard was dismayed and confused. He couldn't believe his real ear. My thanklessness angered him.

"I'm glad you're well," I said. Then in a softer voice, "It will be all right. This is the way it should be."

I didn't hate Willard, but I no longer wanted him. And I never let myself again.

When my pregnancy became public knowledge, I laughed when people suggested that Willard must be the father.

"*Willard?*" I'd say. "Willard *Pretty Dog?* And *me?*"

That didn't make them forsake their suspicions, but it made them not sure. Some speculated that Christine's father had visited me again. Men kept clear of me to distance themselves from incrimination.

"Who, then?" Pauline asked. She felt a married sister, even a disapproving one, had a right to know.

"Who do you think?" I invited her to guess, but would

never say yes or no to any of those she proposed. There was only one I ever absolutely denied.

"It couldn't be *Father Hurlburt?*" Pauline once whispered. His Thursday night visits, the puzzle of my friendship with him, troubled her.

He was the only man I didn't want to lose. I dropped the teasing from my voice.

"Not a priest. Never."

And she believed me.

Waiting was no hardship. There was no time that I wanted more than the present instant, no better day I could imagine.

Christine was all I needed. She was almost four and interested in everything around her. I taught her to read Father Hurlburt's books. With the next lease payment, I bought her a television—one of the first on the reservation—for company, and after the aerial was installed, we sat for hours in front of the tiny screen. It was unfamiliar to hear English in the house, but Christine had programs she would never fail to watch. She loved Miss Frances on "Ding Dong School," and I liked Kate Smith, especially her clothes. Willard stopped by now and again, and I neither discouraged nor encouraged him, but he found me different.

"I don't know what it is," he said as he was going home one afternoon. "But you've changed."

I knew what it was. I no longer pretended to be stupid. If Willard made a mistake in his speech or his telling of history, I pointed it out. Not in a mean way, not really, but clear enough so no doubt remained. I persuaded myself I was doing this for Christine's benefit—she remembered everything she heard so she might as well hear right—but it was more than that. I wanted her to see me smart, to know she could be that way herself in front of any man.

When I finally told Christine there was a baby coming, a brother or sister for her, she had many questions. She took my news as a serious matter.

"Where will I stay when you have to go away?" she demanded.

"If I have to leave, which I won't, you will go with Pauline and Dale."

"I don't like them. Can't Mother come back?"

That word in her mouth dug into me like a trowel. Christine's memory of Clara had faded with time but not disappeared.

"No," I said.

"What will the baby be called?"

That was the same question Pauline had asked, and then half answered: "If it's a girl it must be 'Ann' after Mama. And if it's a boy... would you name him for Papa?"

I raised my eyebrows, incredulous that she of all people had made such a suggestion.

"It's the custom." She was Papa's daughter all over: other people's thoughts mattered more to her than her own.

"Aunt Ida!" Christine's voice called me back to the present. She hated it when I didn't answer her immediately.

"I haven't decided on a name. It's bad luck to say too soon."

"Did you always know I was Christine?"

"No. Go outside now."

Everything she said made me think of Clara, not that I needed reminding. Pregnancy itself brought back those weeks in Denver, and left me even more unbelieving at Clara's coldness. It was beyond me how she could have cared so little about Christine, how she could have given her away with such a lack of regret. I was determined to make up for this with my baby, as if the balance of things had been thrown off by Clara and needed righting by me.

The baby grew so deeply within me that my pregnancy showed almost not at all. My body was large, satisfied in its fullness, and my waist merely filled into a curved line. Weight never hampered my movements, the way it does some women. I was due in April, but a month before, Pauline, whom the doctor in town said might never have children, started the practice of visiting every morning and every night. She read books that told what I should eat and drink, and she consulted old ladies, like her midwife mother-in-law, Polly, to discover the sex and disposition of my baby. I had sinned, not it, Pauline said. *It* was to be, she was sure, a nephew, and *he*, she had been told, would became a leader and a wise man. Pauline would be his godmother.

I joked about her predictions but I always listened. She had nothing bad to say, and over time I began to think of the baby as she described, only better. In my mind's eye, I had the advantage over all the soothsayers. I knew whose face he'd wear. Pauline's fascination and information gathering generated interest in the birth throughout the reservation and, I was later informed, people placed bets on the day and time of day I would deliver, as well as on which man the child would favor.

I don't know who won.

By late March, a thawing wind had blown away all traces of snow and left the land raw and stripped, the roll of the hills out my window bare against the low sky. One afternoon I put eggs on the stove to boil. I cleaned the house, changed sheets, washed the dishes left from breakfast. I gave Christine an early supper of beans and franks, her favorite food, and lay in bed to wait for Pauline to come. When I heard her car stop on the gravel in front of the house, I counted the seconds until my next contraction. I finished before she opened the door and called my name. I leveled my voice, so not to upset her.

"Go get Polly. I'm close."

Her footsteps sounded, running, on the polished floor. Christine appeared beside me and I took her hand. We made a game of it, counting, counting. She learned new high numbers, imitated the strain that shaped my words, laughed at her own cleverness, laughed at the faces I made.

Pauline returned in time and brought her husband and his mother. Polly had assisted many births and wasted no motion. She sent Christine into the other room with Dale, and gave Pauline and me abrupt instructions. At first I watched her eyes for signs and then, eventually, I depended upon her hands.

■ ■ ■

I don't know the hour of his birth, but I saw him first in lamplight. His head was long, his lips narrow. He was neither fat nor thin, neither big nor small for an eight months' pregnancy. In all his parts and all his measurements he was normal.

But even Polly, with all the babies she had seen, had to acknowledge it: my son was a beauty without mar.

"He is a picture," Pauline whispered, her arm supporting my shoulders as he drank the milk of my breast. I could see the wishing in her eyes, the yearning.

"If he were yours," I asked her, "what would his name be?"

She paused, regarded him closer. "I'd have to name him for Papa, after all. Lecon."

"But he'll go by Lee," I said. "To be different."

20

Every Advent I carried a religious calendar home from church and hung it from a nail on my wall. When I stuck a plaited palm behind it at the end of Lent I would realize the pages had not been turned and bring it up to date. Then I'd forget again. In my house, Christ was always being born or rising from the dead.

No two children living in the same house could have been more different, or more close. For two years after his birth, Lee awoke crying every night, banging his crib for attention, wanting to play. He was not content until he was rocked and lulled back to sleep, and usually it was Christine to his side ahead of me. Lee's first word was "Tina," and for a while that was his name for everything in the world: his food, his clothing, his toys, me. He was a fussy child, demanding that his surroundings be just right, and he wore the satin edge off two baby blankets with the constant friction of his fingers. There were foods he wouldn't touch, and others he ate only when mixed with applesauce. Until he started school, and even after that, he spent long stretches of the winter in bed, feverish from infections no one else caught. We bathed his head with cool milk, fed him from our fingers the breast meat of chicken, and watched the television programs he insisted upon.

Christine was happy to be the little mother, and resented me whenever I intruded between her and Lee, whenever I

356

performed a task for him that was beyond her ability or power. She was devastated the day she started school and had to surrender her brother to my exclusive care. She acted as though she would never see him again, as though I was incapable of tending my own child.

"He takes his nap in the morning," she reminded.

"If he's tired," I said. I was anxious for some time without Christine's scrutiny, for a few hours each day when I did not have to race her in answer to Lee's slightest whim, when I could teach him patience and self-control.

"He *has* to take it." Christine was appalled at my laxity. My remark met her worse suspicions of my capacity for neglect. She believed she held the house together by the force of her will.

"Worry for yourself. There will be other things for you to think about now."

She shot me a look of pure vexation. The impending confinement of school, its physical removal, infuriated her, but at seven she was hobbled in her ability to rebel. She had no option but to trust Lee to my supervision.

Pauline told me I was crazy, that any other woman would be glad for a child who welcomed so much responsibility, who couldn't get enough of baby-sitting, who was never jealous. Pauline, who took her godmother's role very seriously, didn't blame Christine for spoiling Lee. He was so sweet, she said, so gratifying. Not at all like other boys she could name. I had nothing to complain about.

And, though I found Christine's attitude toward my capabilities insulting some of the time, I agreed with Pauline. Our life on that hill was as peaceful and routine as anyone could want. Except for church and the events at the Mission Father Hurlburt refused to let me avoid, I stayed home surrounded by everything I needed. In the summers I planted a large garden and tended it like a third child. I dried the seeds of my best vegetables in the fall and sowed them in the spring, and over time I harvested beans and tomatoes and corn and squash of such beauty and size that it was a sin to eat them. We had little demand for cash, and so I spent my land-lease money on improving our house. One year I got a propane furnace, another year, new panes of glass for the downstairs and a storm window with a screen for the attic. I had a new wire run from the pole by the road, and bought a used water heater and refrigerator from the tribe. Except for Pauline, I had no family to speak of, but I rarely noticed.

Father Gephardt retired from the Mission when Lee was four, and Father Hurlburt took over his duties. He was sent no assistant by his order, and so had to manage alone. The continuing popularity of Bingo eliminated his Thursday evening visits to me, but I tried to keep those hours special all the same. I turned off the television and played card games, me against the team of Christine and Lee, or I told them stories in which they were the heroes, or I showed them the steps to Indian dances.

As the children got older, naturally they had questions. They could see that we lived differently from others, and they spent a short period of time obsessed by curiosities about themselves. They took it for granted they had the same father and wondered at his identity: Was he from around here? Would he come back? But that was a subject I declined to pursue. The truth could do them no good, and there were no clues to keep their game interesting. None of our few visitors were likely candidates. Willard had married one of the nurses who cared for him at the hospital, and now had a family of his own. When I saw him at church or at the store, I would nod to him the same as anyone else, and I suspected that even he began to doubt his memory that there had ever been more than that between us.

I never raised the subject of Clara with Christine. I didn't know what facts, if any, she retained, and I believed that the longer I let the past lie dormant, the less likely it was to come to life. Most of the time she acted as though she were born at the same moment as Lee, except that she had more consciousness. I didn't discourage this attitude. Yet, every once in a while, when she was angry at me or wanted to be a splinter in my skin, she'd call me "Mother"—her old name for Clara—instead of "Aunt Ida." I wasn't sure of her meaning. Was she taunting me with some concealed knowledge of Clara? Or was she merely innocent, envious of her friends and wanting to be like them? Whichever it was, I ignored the word and made her speak to me by my rightful name before I would reply.

I heard from Clara once a year, with a Christmas greeting. She always wrote a note on the bottom to tell me where she was, to brag of successes I didn't believe. Before I burned her cards, I'd tear the return address from the envelope and store the slip of paper in a box with all those that had come before, initially from Denver, and then all over: Oakland, Chicago, Phoenix, Los Angeles, Seattle. I had nothing to write back, but for some reason it seemed fair that I knew where she was. It seemed the least I had a right to. Now and then, when Christine looked pretty or when she had been especially good, I was tempted to have her picture taken, to mail it to Clara to show what she had missed, but I never actually came close to doing this. There remained in me the fear that Clara would knock on my door a third time, that I couldn't beat her twice.

Christine and Lee spoke two languages: Indian with me, and English with the television, secretly to each other, and proudly to their schoolteachers. I hadn't expected them to be so quick, and their public smartness made me shy. I took no credit and became the mute background against which they excelled. I observed them as if they were children from the moon, dropped into my care, and their complications entertained me, occupied my thoughts. Compared to Pauline and me, their actions swung in wide arcs, like the blades of scissors. Every excess was possible, every morning the beginning of new projects I could not foresee. I followed in their wake, responding to their passions, experiencing lives I might have lived. Lee was the easier of the two, for all he craved from me was adoration, and that was simple to give. Christine was more exhausting. For her I was the boulder to shove against, the obstacle in her path, the water through which she must swim. I looked for Papa in them, for Clara, for Willard, for me, but I never trusted those recognitions when I had them. Lee and Christine resembled nobody but themselves. They stood before the past and shaded it from my sight.

In my heart, I had no preferences—Lee was of my own body, but Christine was my first, and both were the result of foolish infatuations—but they required different things from me. When Lee was a baby I had to push him down from my lap in order to do my work, but Christine was never satisfied: When I held her she struggled for her freedom, but when free she fought to be held. Wherever he went, whomever he met, Lee conquered by his good looks and trusting eyes, but Christine had to make an effort. She was convinced she was fat—never true—and was forever dissatisfied wih her appearance. As she moved through school, she eventually won the approval of each successive nun—and the antagonism of other children—by working the hardest, by maintaining loyalty only to Lee and tattletaling on anyone else, and especially by making more of a demonstration of piety than was obliged or expected.

She plunged into the Catholic faith they fed her, clothed herself in its jewelry, and made it her own. She demanded its every extremity, and was satisfied only with its eternal promises and consequences. I was convinced for a while that she would become one of those nuns who wear hair shirts and whip themselves with strips of rawhide, but even they were too ordinary for Christine. She had no interest in the feast days of those who attained their sainthood by accumulated good deeds— Saint Francis and his gentle animals or Saint Helena and her search for the true cross meant little to her—but concentrated instead on supplicating the victims of bloody torture—Saint Martin roasted on a spit, Saint Joan burned at the stake, Saint Catherine pulled apart on a spiked wheel—all remembered not for a life of mercy but for a single brave endurance, and this appealed to Christine's impatience.

Her devotion followed her home. She decorated her bed-room with cutout pictures of Saint Sebastian punctured with arrows and Saint Agnes cowering before a lion, and sprinkled holy water within the case of her pillow. She draped a rough-backed scapular around her neck, and to the neckband of her undershirt she pinned the Saint Christopher medal she had been awarded for memorizing and reciting the ABCs backward.

From her Holy Communion through her eighth grade, she made the nine First Fridays repeatedly to ensure her happy death. During Lent she outdid herself, abstaining from desserts and TV, rising at dawn for daily Mass at the Mission, and keeping reign on her temper no matter what provocation she felt Lee or I gave her. We knew her fury through the press of her praying hands, by her loud choice of sorrowful mysteries on the rosary. When Holy Week arrived she lost all restraint. She covered her holy pictures with dyed handkerchiefs, made the Stations of the Cross on her knees, and kept silent from twelve to three o'clock on Friday to commemorate the Crucifixion. On Passion Sunday she stood without moving a finger during the reading of the long Gospel because the nuns guaranteed that this single act would liberate a suffering soul from Purgatory. I never discovered whom she designated for heaven, but I suspected it was the father she had convinced herself was dead and punished for abandoning her to me.

She was fascinated with the stories she heard in religion: the confrontation between the Pope and Attila the Hun, the martyrdom of the Jesuits who had come to save heart-eating Indians, the bravery of defiant mission priests in Red China. Christine prayed especially to candidates for beatification—Maria Goretti, stabbed twenty-three times, or Kateri Tekakwitha, potentially the first Indian saint—and was determined to experience the miracles that would certify they were with the angels. She kept close account of the indulgences she earned through the reciting of certain holy words or names, and she received Penance every Friday in the Mission church before she came home from school.

I was concerned at her fervor, but my sister applauded it. Pauline believed, though of course she never openly told me, that through some buried instinct, Christine was repaying the crime of her origination.

"She will be rewarded. Do not interfere. I understand her far better than you do."

I might have believed Pauline except for the other side of Christine's nature, the side that I knew she confessed weekly to the priests but never overcame, the side that was brash.

Lee brought it out in her. As a young boy, he was intimidated by his classmates when they failed to give him his way, and depended on Christine for status. He followed her, adoring and awestruck, wherever she went, and she defended him, protected him with the threat of her fists, impressed him with her daring. Some things I saw, some I only heard about.

I was watching out the window with my tea the night when she was eleven, the night when she danced in the air. I had heard children's voices on the hillside, taunts of "You wouldn't!" "Show us then!" and pulled the curtain to see. It was not late, and the sky was a violet blue, still red behind the western wall of mountains. The moon was so bright that the running figures tracked long shadows that merged with and separated from those of buildings and trees, so bright that I saw it reflect in their eyes. They assembled in a pack, and a little apart from the rest were Christine and Lee.

"I will," she said, and I heard the quaver in her voice.

"Do it, then."

As I stared, narrowing my lids to sharpen my vision, I saw the clothes fall from her body. Her skin was the grayish-white of rain clouds, the wax gleam of a snake's stomach. Lee stooped to locate the shoes she kicked off, then posed with the rest.

Like smoke up a flue, she was sucked down the hill, her moving feet silent, her hair a raven on the wing.

"All the way to the mailbox," someone called.

Christine vanished over a rise. A minute passed. I held my breath, too unnerved to move. What she did was beyond good or bad, outside my experience of knowing. I heard the clang of metal, loud as a bell, quieting the laughter.

When she appeared, she slowed, outlined against the sky on a contour of land. Her steps became unhurried. Stubborn nakedness cloaked her body and gave it strength. Lee ran to meet her and she let him walk by her side, her clothes in his hand. She returned to the place where she had started. Only then did she dress.

I waited the length of time it takes for water in a cup to lose heat, then I called.

"Lee! Christine!"

They entered, alert to see what I knew.

"Wash your faces," I said. "Go to sleep."

They hurried to be good, to avoid my suspicion.

Later, before I went to my own bed, I watched each of them in their slumber. Lee slept on a cot, enclosed within the main room by an alcove made of blankets strung on rope. He sprawled on his back, his lips parted, his eyelashes fluttering with the movement of his dream. I lowered my face to his, smelled the sweetness of his breath, drew the cover over his shoulder, touched the fan of his black hair. His limbs were fine as slender branches. He was better than Willard had ever been.

I pushed the door of Christine's room. She lay in her thin gown on a nest of blankets, her legs pressed together, her hands clenched across her chest. I caught a movement from her lips and saw them form fast, soundless words. Her eyes were squeezed shut, her body pulled into itself as if against a frost.

Lee confided to me the bold acts Christine committed, and some were quite dangerous. He swore she had frightened a snake with the sparkle of her eyes. He slyly showed me a coin she had given him, stolen from the collection basket at church. I could imagine the battles she fought with other children from the scratches and bruises on her arms and legs.

But still I did nothing to stop her. I only made Lee promise not to imitate, promise to protect himself.

Lee would make his mark in other ways. The summer before he entered third grade, he heard the applause and cheers during the dance contests at our powwow, and made up his mind to be a star. That year, Dale made three hoops and taught him to manipulate them in time with the drum, to slide them over his small-boned body and link them in a chain across his shoulders. Even as a very young boy, he danced with a natural balance. I sat for hours during that winter, beating the flat of my hand in time against the table, while he practiced steps in a cleared space in front of the stove. Lee was hard on himself, and twice deliberately broke a hoop after he accidentally dropped it. I mended them with tape until I could pay Dale to roll new ones.

Christine was as nervous about the execution of his routines as he, and made a Spring Novena to ensure his success. She and Pauline helped me make his costume. I beaded sky-blue medallions centered with gold stars onto dark maroon felt for his harness, and borrowed against my next payment to order a roach of the highest quality. When it came, I decorated it with long porcupine guard hairs and altered it to fit his head securely. Christine used the sewing machine in the girls' classroom at the Mission to stitch a flapped taffeta shirt from the material of a fine white dress Father Hurlburt's sister had sent to pass on. Pauline made wristlets of cowhide and tin bells, and a bustle of yellow-tipped turkey plumes, and I positioned one more matching medallion in its middle. Dale loaned a carved whistle and a small eagle fan that had been passed down from one Cree dancer to another. And Lee let his hair grow. By spring it was long enough to part and wrap thick with strips of cloth.

Yet the next summer, no matter what we said, no matter how much we praised his practice turns, he was unwilling to dance. He watched each powwow with a mix of fear and contempt, and laughed unkindly if a contestant faltered beyond the last drumbeat or if a feather dropped to the ground in the whirlwind of motion. Lee did not know his own power and feared to test it. He put away his outfit and, a little boy, hung on Christine's arm when he went back to school in the fall.

I believed it was her bravado that defeated him, her example that held him back.

On a Friday the following spring, though, something changed. Christine came home late for supper with no underwear and scrapes on her legs, and refused to leave her room.

Lee arrived a few moments later. He had a sureness about himself that brought Willard to my mind. And he had something to tell.

"What happened?" I asked. "Is Christine hurt?"

"She was *scared*, Aunt Ida," Lee said. "I saved her." He squeezed next to me where I stirred the potato soup I had simmering, and laid his head along the side of my body. My hand went automatically to his shoulder, down the length of his arm, then I stepped away and looked him over.

"You saved her? From what?"

There was conceit about the way he smiled that I didn't like, a cockiness, some male secret he didn't think I understood.

"Did someone try to hurt Christine?" I felt panic. I thought of all the things that could happen.

"She was scared," he repeated, still struck with the idea. "She climbed too high and couldn't get down until I helped her."

I went back to the potato slices, preventing them from burning to the bottom of the pot. I knew he wanted me to ask more questions, knew he wanted to hear himself praised, but I was chilled by his unfamiliar confidence and thought instead of Christine. Her defeat, whatever it was, impressed me more than Lee's victory. It made me tender toward her, made me lonely for the baby who strained against sleep all the way to Billings.

"Tell Christine to get washed for supper," I told Lee, frustrating him with my indifference. "We're late as it is."

When the first powwow of the summer was held, a few weeks later, Lee dressed in his finery and walked into the circle with no hesitation. He didn't win—he was never that good—but he took his performance seriously and made no mistakes. They gave him Best Newcomer.

Once Lee learned the value of surviving risks, he looked for situations where he could repeat his success. He became foolhardy and believed himself indestructible. I worried for his bad judgment.

Christine, on the other hand, gradually became afraid of everything around her. First she wouldn't swim in the pond near the canyon lest she catch her foot on some underwater root and drown. Then she stayed close to me at the store, and hid her face at the sight of any stranger. It came to a head the night she panicked in her bed, terror-struck by the idea of her own sinfulness and the certainty that if she died before she received absolution she would go to hell. I couldn't get her back to sleep for an hour.

At first Christine's behavior was so odd, so unlike the girl I knew, that I thought it must be some act, some new way for her to get attention.

"She's just discovered she's human," Pauline smiled. "It's part of growing up. She won't be with you long."

But I was not persuaded. I hated to hear Pauline's opinions because they were so predictable: everything to do with Christine was full of gloom, and everything about Lee was optimistic. That's why I never told her what I learned from Father Hurlburt when he visited in mid-December to leave Christmas gifts in bright packages.

"I'm worried about Christine," I said as he lingered over the tea I had offered him.

He raised his eyes, trying to imagine why.

"I was wondering: when she whispers her sins to you, does she ever tell anything really bad?"

He blew into his cup, and averted my inquiring stare. "You know I cannot reveal what she discloses under the seal of Confession."

I shook my head in impatience, irritated at his technicalities.

"She thinks she's going to hell," I said. "She's lost her nerve."

He rubbed his chin and considered my words. Then he nodded his head. "Of course. It must be the letter."

I drew air into my lungs and ran my tongue across the roof of my mouth. Had Clara written? "What letter?"

"It's Christine's teacher, Sister Alvina. She dwells far too heavily on a letter the Blessed Virgin reputedly gave to a young girl named Lucy, in Portugal."

I looked at him sharply. This made no sense to me. And even if it were true, what did it have to do with Christine's mood?

"The letter is to be opened this coming New Year's," he continued. "They say it will tell the future—the conversion of Russia through the intercession of the rosary, or the end of the world as we know it."

I tried to imagine such a letter. I seldom received mail, and then mostly from the tribe or from the man to whom I'd leased my land. I pictured Mary's letter as resting in a thick, pale gold envelope with a halo around it. It sat on a plate, addressed in a nun's fine script.

"Many children in Christine's class are distraught," Father Hurlburt said. "They take the message literally. I'll caution Sister Alvina."

The next morning, before she left for school, I confronted Christine.

"Do you believe in this Portugal letter?" I asked, and I could see, from the fright on her face, that she did.

"You know about it?" She was relieved, her eyes desperate for comfort.

"Father Hurlburt told me. He didn't seem so worried."

Christine jerked her head in exasperation. She had grown less fond of Father Hurlburt, and had complained to Pauline that the Our Fathers and Hail Marys he allotted for her sins were insultingly few, too lightly assigned. The only justice she took seriously was wrath.

"Sister Alvina knows all about it," she whispered. "She's heard that it's bad news. We pray every day, send money to the poor, but the Russian Bear does not believe."

My bewilderment was absolute, but I felt for Christine and was shaken by the depth of her worry as she continued.

"I didn't want to tell you. There's nothing we can do but follow the instructions of the prophecy."

"And what are they?"

"It will end in fire, and we must be ready. We have to wait on the roof for the Four Horsemen and be in a state of grace."

"What are you talking about?"

"It's all in the last book of the Bible. It says what to do."

"Does Lee know about this?" I had noticed no change in him.

"He doesn't believe. He says he won't go to Confession before." She was both angry and horrified.

I had the fleeting idea to embrace Christine, to ease her with the warmth of my body, to support her with the strength of my arms. But she did not expect this from me, and I did not give it.

When she left I sat at the table for a long time, staring out the window at the white blur of fine snow. This letter was a bad dream, a superstition the nuns concocted to control their students. Christine was snared by her innocence, by her belief in wonders of any kind, by her conviction that her life mattered. Lee's pride was a frail thing, easily jolted and undermined, but Christine took responsibility for the universe.

I could not deny her. At her insistence I gave her the money I had saved for Christmas gifts so that she could please her teacher by sending it to South America. I listened while she read the Apocalypse aloud, and planned with her how we would fulfill all the commands. On a day warmer than the others, I cleared stored boxes from the steps that opened to the attic and took out the screen from the storm window that led to the roof. I promised to make a list of all my sins to tell. I agreed that for this once we would not go to Pauline and Dale's, nor invite them to be with us, on New Year's Eve, but would be just the three of us. When Father Hurlburt offered to visit before his Midnight Mass, or to stop by and bring us all along, I declined.

"You could come here afterward, if you want," I said. "When Lee and Christine are asleep. If the world's still here, I'll tell you what happened."

• • •

The Last Day, which I gave to Christine, fell on a Thursday. To please her, I dressed in my newest clothes, though they were not meant for even the mild weather of this December, and wore around my neck a chain bearing the Sacred Heart medal she had given me for Christmas. We didn't talk about the fate she expected, but we behaved carefully, treated each other as politely as strangers in a car. I respected her pretense of normalcy, the attention she gave to every detail, the concern she showed for my salvation.

Lee resented my complicity. He was annoyed that I refused to commend his audacity in the face of Doomsday. He made a joke of Christine's fear, and so many times invited me to snicker with him that finally I had to take him aside.

"Leave your sister alone," I said.

"You always take her part." Lee and I looked at each other and both knew this was far from true. He changed his direction.

"She doesn't believe it anyway. She's just doing this because she didn't get invited to a party that a girl in her class is having."

"Christine is very devout," I insisted. I had stronger faith in her belief than I had in any religion.

Lee rolled his eyes. He thought I was foolish, taken in. I grabbed his arm as he made to leave.

"Be nice today." I rarely asked him for anything and he hesitated at my request. I didn't remind him of all he owed, of all that was done for him, but he understood. There was no good in explaining how I saw Christine, how much she needed mystery, how that was what gave her distinction. In exposing Christine's mortal fear, Lee had left her with nothing to look forward to but the prospect of paradise.

Though he shook off my hand, I trusted he would grant what I asked. But he persisted.

"This is my *last* bowl of chili," he sighed at lunch. Then later, "Sister Alvina says you get to know everybody's sins when they rise from the dead." He leered at Christine.

She ignored him. She gave me a permanent, poured a foul-smelling mixture on my head, and rolled my hair into tight knots. I lolled against the towel around my shoulders. I liked the touch of her hands on my scalp, the pull of her wet fingers. She was anxious to make her mark on me, to change my appearance. I sat on a hard kitchen chair facing the door and thought of Clara's wavy set that first day, and how I admired it.

"You'll be beautiful," Christine assured me.

She had a kind of authority, a woman's voice. In the hopelessness of her situation she had found strength, and in her strength there was irresistible pain. I believed whatever she needed. I would sacrifice the world to keep her faith in miracles.

As I dozed erect, I stroked the knitted scarf that Lee had bought me. I let its warmth spread over my bare arms, wrapping like a blanket around my summer dress.

When my hair was dry, Christine removed the clips and dragged narrow-toothed combs and brushes across my head while I made my neck stiff and immobile. She lifted each coil behind me and separated the curls to fall, light and airy, about my arms. I saw myself as I had always imagined I could be, and walked to Clara's mirror. I saw myself through Christine's wish, and touched the dark tangle that edged my face.

"You could have been a beauty operator," I said, wistful that she would have no chance. In the glass I found her eyes, spoke to them, was answered.

Lee's laugh tore my dream like stiff paper.

"Shut up!" Christine begged, but he went on, mocking her, ending the day, the year, with his ignorance. I wanted her to slap his face, to terrify him with prophecy. I wanted lightning and thunder, a rain of fire.

"Oh, I don't care!" Christine dropped on the floor the towel I had worn, kicked it into a corner. "It's all bullshit. Nothing's going to happen." She crossed the room to where Lee sat, pressed his cheeks between her hands and spoke directly into his face. "You win."

I fried hash for their dinner, listened to them bicker while they ate. Satisfied with himself, Lee was ready to make peace and wanted Christine to sing with her radio the way he liked. She resisted for a few minutes, but then went into her room, turned on the power, and returned, leaving the door ajar. Her voice, unnatural in its harmonizing, grated on my ears. She let Lee go and twist the dial to find a song he preferred, and she changed her pitch to match the new words, but it was no better.

I wound Lee's muffler around my head, crushing the wiry hair, and played the television to drown the sound of her racket.

Lee wanted to stay up till midnight.

"Just to make sure you were wrong," he teased Christine, and in reply she slammed into her room for good and increased the radio's volume. The program was full of horns and violins, not the kind of thing she usually listened to. It sounded like a celebration, a party. Alone with me, Lee was guilty and made no argument when I told him to go to bed.

I extinguished the lamps and sat in the blue glow thrown by the TV screen, switched to a show already under way on a station with no sound. It was stupid, the solemn, mute arguments those actors had with each other. I shut them off.

Christine had fallen asleep, forgetting her radio. The music poured into the dark house like water from a faucet. It rose about the walls, pressed me down, smothered me. I removed the scarf and shook out my hair, then spread my fingers against my brow and combed back, relieving the cramp of my frown.

Eventually, very late, the station left the air. First there was the dry hum of unconnected electricity and then, suddenly, nothing. No wind wore against the house, no cars passed on the road. I had remained so long without moving I had abandoned the feel of my body, and the boundary of my consciousness expanded endlessly, encountering no barrier. I disconnected, lost all track, opened my mouth without breathing.

A warm gust, summoned by the chill of the room, blew from the furnace and rustled the curtains that hung by the window. Lee sighed in his sleep and shifted his legs beneath the blankets. The sound of an engine approached in the distance. Headlamps swung into the lane that led up the hill to my house, then extinguished when the car stopped at the front door. I answered the knock.

"Were you sleeping?" Father Hurlburt spoke in a lowered voice. "I thought you'd be awake and I couldn't get Christine out of my mind tonight."

"Shhh," I warned.

I felt for his sleeve and led him inside, across the room, moving sightlessly through familiar paths. As I passed the couch I collected the purple blanket folded across its arm and carried it in a bundle. My knee grazed the stairs to the attic, and I tugged at Father Hurlburt to follow.

The window rose easily and we ducked and stepped, first me and then the priest, onto the eave. I shook out the blanket, wrapped it around me, and crouched onto the tar paper. Father Hurlburt shut the glass behind us and followed my lead. If he was surprised at my actions, he gave no sign.

"What time is it?" I wondered, and he looked at the luminous dial of his watch. The numbers glowed green, the only color in the sky.

"It's after two. Did she have a bad night?"

"Yes." I gazed into the distance and saw the land in my memory. The night was so black, it was impossible to know if my eyes were open or closed.

The cold was bearable because the air was so still. I let the blanket slip from my shoulders, lifted my arms about my head, and began.

"What are you doing?" Father Hurlburt asked.

As a man with cut hair, he did not identify the rhythm of three strands, the whispers of coming and going, of twisting and tying and blending, of catching and of letting go, of braiding.